Praise fo

'A p

'[A] ... provocative tale of and how the marginalised fight back'
Stylist Magazine

'It was refreshing to read a thriller that wasn't
full of twists, though I kept waiting for them,
as I've been conditioned to expect them. This
well-plotted story follows Michelle, who's recently
been released from prison. Does someone who's
committed an awful crime deserve to start again?'
Prima

'This intriguing procedural is above all a portrait of
two damaged women and a moving demonstration
of how race and class have affected their lives'
The Times and *The Sunday Times* Crime Club

'An absorbing, powerful slow-burn'
Lisa Howells, *Crime Monthly*

'A powerful look at institutionalised racism and the
after-effects of a childhood crime' *S Magazine*

C000157490

Jacqueline Roy was born and raised in London. Her father was Jamaican and her mother was English and she comes from a family of writers. She hated the pressure to conform at school and left early, so she did her degrees as a mature student before moving to Manchester to take up a full-time teaching post at Manchester Metropolitan University. She lectured in English for many years, specialising in postcolonial literatures. She also taught creative writing at MMU's Writing School. She is particularly interested in exploring racial identities and the ways in which those who are marginalised find strategies for fighting back. She is now a full-time writer and has produced fiction for adults and children. Her first novel, *The Fat Lady Sings*, was recently selected by Bernardine Evaristo for her Black Britain: Writing Back series.

Also by Jacqueline Roy:

The Fat Lady Sings

JACQUELINE ROY

THE GOSLING GIRL

**SIMON &
SCHUSTER**

London · New York · Sydney · Toronto · New Delhi

First published in Great Britain by Simon & Schuster UK Ltd, 2022

This paperback edition published in 2023

Copyright © Jacqueline Roy, 2022

The right of Jacqueline Roy to be identified as author of this work has been
asserted in accordance with the Copyright, Designs and Patents Act, 1988.

1 3 5 7 9 10 8 6 4 2

Simon & Schuster UK Ltd
1st Floor
222 Gray's Inn Road
London WC1X 8HB

Simon & Schuster Australia, Sydney
Simon & Schuster India, New Delhi

www.simonandschuster.co.uk
www.simonandschuster.com.au
www.simonandschuster.co.in

A CIP catalogue record for this book
is available from the British Library.

Paperback ISBN: 978-1-3985-0424-0
eBook ISBN: 978-1-3985-0423-3
Audio ISBN: 978-1-3985-1236-8

Typeset in the UK by M Rules
Printed and Bound in the UK using 100% Renewable
Electricity at CPI Group (UK) Ltd

MIX
Paper | Supporting
responsible forestry
FSC® C171272
FSC
www.fsc.org

For Pauline Edwards, with thanks for all the laughter and friendship.

PROLOGUE

The glass shatters and she runs, leaving spots of blood in the tangled weeds and dandelion puffs. She stops for breath; she doesn't feel the cut – she has long since learnt to block out pain – but the blood will lead them to her. What's DNA? she'll ask when questioned and they'll look at her baby face and they won't know how to answer.

She hides in some bushes, beds down for the night. She feels safer by herself, even though she fears the dark.

In the morning, the body is found. She watches the glass houses from her hiding place. Police cars pull up, blue lights flashing. She enjoys the sound the sirens make; it helps her feel alive.

What were you doing in the green house? the policeman will ask, and she'll laugh at his mistake until she has to stuff a tissue in her mouth to stop. The house wasn't green, it was grey and made of glass. It was the home she built for herself. There were teacups and saucers carefully removed from the pound shop on the high street. There was a blanket and

3

tealights secreted from the cardboard box in the front room. But glass tends to break.

They tell her Kerry's dead. She will be put away. She likes the words, they make her feel like a doll that no one wants to play with anymore, and she is so tired of playing now, those strange, grown-up games with grown-up men who act like twisted children. Being put away sounds good to her.

PART ONE

ONE

Everything is strange. She's been accustomed to rules, doing things when other people thought she should. Inside, there were rules about when to eat, who to eat with, when to get up, when the lights went out. Showers, not baths, and only a few minutes before they made you get out. You never thought about it, you did what you were told, it was just the way it was.

But she is outside now and there are endless choices to be made. She stays in bed for hours every morning, partly because she can and partly because she's afraid to get up; so many things she could do with her time that she's too scared to do anything. What if she makes the wrong choices? Has a bath when she should have had a shower? Wears shoes when she should have worn sandals? Goes out when she should have stayed indoors? She can walk or travel by Tube or get on a bus. She stands on the street beneath her block and watches the traffic, frantic drivers hooting their way past, cyclists hurtling through the smallest of gaps between pavement and car, death wish inscribed in the furious pedalling of their feet. Air thick with fumes, mothers with pushchairs ramming through crowds, children shouting and jostling their way to school. A cacophony of rage mingles with the smell of eggs and bacon from the café on the corner, dizzying her senses until she can't tell touch from taste or sight from sound. At first, outside, unaccompanied, she fears that if she goes too far she'll slide off the edges of the world.

There is a rug on the floor in her bedroom with dark, shiny patches of chewing gum embedded in the fibres. She stands barefoot feeling the softness, luxurious and alien. In the bathroom she stores rolls of cushioned toilet paper in fulfilment of a promise she made to herself that when she got out, she'd buy an endless supply. She still hasn't used it, not a single sheet. The cheap stuff, thin and coarse, creates the sense of the familiar she craves.

If freedom has a single sense, it's taste. Chocolate, any brand she wants. She buys Swiss bars, melting smooth. Popcorn, sweet and salty in a single bag; Tangfastics because their sharpness makes her tongue curl; the Aldi version of Ferrero Rocher, two big boxes at a time: suck the chocolate, crunch the nutty bits, ignore the churning of your stomach and the bloating when you've had enough but still can't seem to stop. These are choices she can deal with. Porridge or cornflakes, crisps or chips, she knows, without thinking, which to have.

Once a week she sees Dom, her new probation officer. He's old and dull and they have nothing in common so there's little conversation.

'How do you think you're coping with being out?' he asks,

the first time they meet, squinting at her through glasses that magnify the bags beneath his eyes. She doesn't answer the question, so he says, 'Most people find it harder than they expect and you were in Whytefields for ... how long?'

'Until I was seventeen,' she mutters.

'And then you were in a young offenders' institution,' he states.

'Yes. And then the halfway house.'

Her stubborn failure to talk about what she'd done had meant she was turned down for parole, so she'd remained inside until she was twenty-one. Young offenders' had been much stricter than Whytefields – as strict as an adult prison – but the worst place had been the halfway house. She hadn't understood what was expected of her, so she'd spent most of the time shut in her room, not daring to leave. She'd despised herself for the panic she'd felt when the hostel manager, or another resident, tried to persuade her to go outside. She should have been relishing her restricted freedom, but instead she'd been terrified of it. Perhaps it was understandable: at least, inside, you weren't expected to do much; most things were provided for you and she knew where she was with that.

They are sitting in a small, windowless room with the door closed so they can't be overheard. Other ex-cons are inter-viewed in the open-plan room next door.

'And you're coping all right with being out?' Dom repeats.

'I'm coping okay,' she answers. What else can she say? At Whytefields, and in young offenders', she'd longed for the chance to live alone, but now she longs to be put away again.

'It's a bit quiet,' she adds in a whisper, as if she's not allowed to say such things. She misses the shouting, the thing she'd most wanted to escape. In the silence of the night, she bangs her head against the wall, a combination of frustration and the need to feel. And she likes the sound, the steady thud. Sometimes she feels blood and knows she is alive.

'It does get easier.'

'It's different to how I thought it would be.'

'Different in what way?'

She can't explain.

'Have you been able to get out?'

'A few times.'

She is forbidden to go anywhere near the neighbourhood where she and Kerry used to live but she has returned, of course. Who would recognize her now? And what's the worst they could do to her? Put her back inside? Scared to take the bus, she walked for hours. The market was still there, with its bric-a-brac and mock-leather bags, and she'd stood outside the pie and mash shop she sometimes used to visit with her mum. They'd eaten off white china plates, watching the blurry outlines of passers-by through steamed-up windows, mopping up green liquor with dollops of bread. But not everything was the same. Someone else lived in the old terraced house. The front door wasn't brown anymore, it was burgundy. An up-and-coming area: pot plants everywhere, Golf GTIs parked half on the pavement. Blinds instead of curtains. Door knockers shaped like foxes. Ocado vans pulling up outside. Neatly trimmed hedges where no one threw up or had a piss. She'd felt out of place.

'Where did you go?'

'Nowhere in particular.'

'What are your neighbours like?'

She shrugs. She's seen them in the lift and glared at the pensioner who spies on her from the flat opposite, but she hasn't actually spoken to anyone.

'What do you do with yourself all day?'

She doesn't know how to answer so she remains silent.

Her phone rings. She gets it out of her pocket and stares at it. It's never rung before. No one has her number. No one even knows she has a phone: she only got it last week. As she'd sat in the café near the flat, where she sometimes goes to people-watch and pass the time, a bloke had come up to her, young and quite good looking. Okay, he was off his face, but beggars can't be choosers, so she didn't turn him away. She thought he was going to chat her up but instead he got out this phone and asked if she wanted it. She could have it dirt cheap. She knew it was nicked. She didn't care. She'd been desperate for a proper phone, one that could get the internet and would play music. She got it unlocked in one of those shops that doesn't ask any questions.

'Hello,' she says, her voice quivering.

'Have you had an accident?' someone asks. 'You could be owed thousands in compensation.'

'I haven't had an accident,' she answers in bewilderment. She ends the call and looks at Dom. 'Someone's got my number. How did they find me?' she asks.

'It's all right, it doesn't mean anything,' he says, 'they call people randomly.'

11

'They don't know me then?'

'No, it's just random. Cold calling.'

It's another example of the strangeness of the outside world. She continues to look at Dom closely, expecting him to know the phone was nicked. Receiving stolen goods. Now her licence will be revoked.

But he only says, 'Is there anything you'd like to talk about?'

Nothing she can name. Talking to Dom, she is aware of the strangeness of hearing her own voice saying things out loud.

Returning to the flat, she double-locks the door behind her and flings her bag on the sofa. She goes into the kitchen and opens the back door. The rain has stopped. She leans over the balcony and looks down on steepled churches. Railway lines criss-cross ahead and there are small silver trains. The dome of a mosque shines bright. The Thames glistens grey. Birds swoop past and on the top floor of the twelve-storey block opposite, a cat sits on a ledge, cleaning its paws, unaware that it only has nine lives. She doesn't know how much time goes by. An hour, perhaps. She sees the sun go down, orange and red, its vivid intensity seeming to signal the end of days.

Dom sees her each week for more than two months and each visit is much the same as the last. They sit in the windowless room and try to make conversation. 'What do you do during the day?' he asks, just as he usually does, and she replies: 'I don't do anything much. Sometimes I read. Watch TV. It's old though and the picture doesn't always come on. I sleep quite a lot during the day. I know I shouldn't.'

'What would you like to be doing?'

She thinks for a moment, half-closing her eyes. 'Normal things,' she answers.

'Normal is overrated,' he says.

Only someone who's normal thinks normal's overrated. She feels herself getting smaller.

'What sort of things would be normal?' he asks.

'A job. A boyfriend, maybe.' She bites her lip.

He nods and replies: 'I've spoken to someone who runs a factory. She's got a job going in the office. She's willing to try you out.'

'Does she know I've got a record?'

'Yes, she knows, but no actual details, just that you were a young offender.'

'What will I be doing?'

'General dogsbody. The pay isn't great but it's a step on the ladder. What do you think?'

'Maybe.' She taps the floor with her foot. What if they don't like her? What if she can't do it? She'll have to get up early, travel daily, get buses or the Tube. She'll have to be on time for things. She'll have to know what she is doing and she'll have to survive the boredom of a nine-to-five. Well, that last bit won't be so hard. Nothing is more boring than a prison cell or being alone in the flat. But she isn't used to doing ordinary things. She can't picture herself having a boss, being organized and learning the ropes, although she does permit herself to think of spending the money she earns on supersized boxes of chocolate.

'An interview's been arranged for Friday. I can give you a lift if you like.'

Dom is on time to pick her up. He says she'll be interviewed by Miss Ayres, who will seem stern but is fine once you get to know her. 'Make sure you tell her you've got a near-perfect memory.'

She frowns. It might be a lie, and she's not supposed to tell lies anymore.

Miss Ayres is old, at least sixty, but she can't abide idleness, she says. Unlikely then, that she has any plans for retirement. The interview goes well, even though it's full of questions and she has to think hard about the answers. Miss Ayres says she knows she has a record but she believes in second chances. She probably wouldn't believe in them quite so much if she knew what she'd been convicted of. She is asked where she is from. She is puzzled by the question. 'London?' she says.

'No, I mean where are you really from – your parents?'

It's implied that she doesn't belong, but she wants the job so she answers, 'My mum is white, from Bermondsey, and my dad is black, from Jamaica.'

Miss Ayres nods and says, 'Well, we run a tight ship here,' as if her parentage might somehow cause the ship to run aground.

She tries not to frown and she must have succeeded because she gets the job. She celebrates alone in the café with an all-day breakfast, and wonders if Miss Ayres could be Dom's girlfriend and that was how he knew about the vacancy. She pictures them together, Dom all proper and awkward, Miss Ayres flirtatious and always disappointed. Maybe she won't be able to do the job and she'll be sacked shortly after she starts. She spends the next few wakeful nights wondering how she'll cope. But it turns out she's an asset; even Cheryl Ayres says she isn't bad, her highest form of praise. She'll get to stay. She'll even get a permanent contract after a few months; her need to keep busy through a fear of being bored ensures she isn't prone to idleness.

The pay is shit, worse than she'd expected, barely as much as signing on. But that's a good thing. It tells her why Miss Ayres was willing to take her on: cheap labour, simple as that.

The travelling isn't as bad as she'd feared. She finds a routine and she's good at those. She catches the bus at eight every morning. She is never late. They think of her as a safe pair of hands, reliable but dull.

She knows that nobody has guessed who she really is but it's still a constant fear.

'I can't ever be Michelle again, can I?' she asks Dom one autumn afternoon, blinking nervously in the harsh light of the room.

'Is that still a problem?' he says.

'Yes,' she whispers.

Along with the change of name, they changed her date of birth. If she'd still been Michelle Cameron, it would have been her birthday today. She longs to be Michelle, if only for an hour or two, but Michelle is dead and buried and she can never come back.

Two

She doesn't like days off. She doesn't know what to do with herself. She gets breakfast at the café – egg, sausage, bacon and fried bread – and then goes to the shopping centre, not to buy anything – there's little she can afford – but to look. It still feels strange, being free to wander wherever she pleases; strange, and not quite right.

She goes into a store and tries on shoes. She's never worn heels and she hasn't got the knack of walking in them even in a shop, but she pretends to be sure of herself and tries not to wobble as she crosses the floor to stare at her feet in the mirror on the wall. Blue ones today, with pointy toes and shiny bows in patent leather. Well, not leather, probably, not in this kind of shop, where there are no assistants to assist and you have to rummage to find a pair that match. But they still look good, she thinks, and if her calves were a bit thinner, she might even look elegant.

She leaves the shop and puts on headphones, turning the music on her phone up loud. She's still thinking about the blue high heels. Alice, from the office, has invited her to a party next weekend; she could wear them then. She likes the name Alice, it makes her think of the book, *Alice in Wonderland*. She's been in wonderland most of her life, she suspects. She doesn't know if she'll go to the party, she's never been to an adult party before. She'll have to take something with her. Wine? Should it be red or white? That's the trouble: she'll have to make choices, get things right, even though she doesn't know how it's supposed to work. She can imagine the laughter round the office if she gets it wrong. *She didn't even know you shouldn't wear jeans. Did you see her shoes? Who wears shoes like that to a party? She brought lager – what was she thinking?* She'd better not go.

But she wants to join in. Every lunchtime, she sits in silence while people talk around her, tongue-tied, knowing that if she takes part in a conversation she might somehow be exposed. She doesn't really know anyone. This could be her chance to make some friends.

She goes back into the shop, the beat still loud in her ears. She buys the shoes, paying at the counter without turning off the music. She can't hear the assistant above the sound. It makes her seem rude, but she's just scared. She doesn't want to let herself know she's decided to go to the party, and silence might let the knowledge seep in.

She knows she shouldn't drink and she's scared of feeling out of control but it will be easier to remain at the party if alcohol reduces the ugly thoughts that fill her head to background noise.

It's awkward when her colleagues talk about themselves. That's why she shouldn't drink. What might she say when her lips are loosened and questions asked? She knows the story she's supposed to tell, but the real one might slip out unless she checks herself. There are long pauses before she speaks while she considers the answer she should give. It makes her seem slow – unintelligent. But maybe that's a good thing. No one expects slow people to tell elaborate lies.

She'd talked to Dom about this once – the risks involved in everyday conversation – and he'd replied, 'It's hard, reinventing yourself.' *Reinventing*, yes, that's what she's had to do. She'd wanted him to say there are no risks, no one will ever find out who you used to be, but he'd just sat nodding, as if agreeing risks were everywhere.

Alice hands her a glass of wine. She was right to bring a bottle, then, but it's awkward, being the first to arrive. She's never tasted wine before, she's only ever had cider. She wonders what Alice would think if she knew how many adult things she hasn't had the opportunity to do. She sips the drink, wrinkling her nose. She thought it would taste sweeter. It's warming, though. They make polite conversation.

'Where do your parents live?' asks Alice.

'It was just my mother. She died.'

Impossible to tell anyone the truth, that her mother is alive and well but doesn't want anything to do with her. She doesn't even know what she looks like anymore. Sometimes, when she says her mother is dead, people ask *when* she died, but mostly they don't, they just go quiet. Once, she was asked *how* she died. Or, more specifically, *Was it cancer?* She let her eyes fill with tears to block further questioning. *Oh, I'm sorry, I shouldn't have asked, I didn't mean to upset you.* If they feel crass enough, they leave you alone, so acting hurt when awkward questions arise has become second nature. She looks hurt now, so Alice changes the subject and asks, 'Do you like music?'

She nods.

'What kind?'

'Most things – R&B, hip hop.'

Alice docks her phone in a speaker and turns up the volume. She would like a speaker like that. Perhaps one day, if she saves enough from her wages, she'll be able to afford one.

It's hard to think of anything else to say.

Alice looks bored. 'I'm just going upstairs to get changed before the others arrive,' she says.

Left to herself, she wanders round the living room, taking in the orange cushions on the worn armchair and examining the framed portraits of gap-toothed children on the shelves. There's one of aged parents celebrating in a church hall that's full of creamy-white balloons and banners that say 30 YEARS. She imagines it as a homecoming party at the end of a thirty-year stretch and this makes her giggle. Aged miscreants. Arson, perhaps? Kidnapping? No, they're serial killers, the pair of them. Four bodies dug up from under the A40. Folie à deux. Look at them smiling at the camera; they seem so innocent.

There are no photos in *her* flat. Would people find it strange if they came round? Maybe not – a lot of people just keep photos in their phones. But her colleagues definitely find it strange that she's not on Facebook. She watches them in the office, updating their statuses surreptitiously and checking what everyone else is up to. Not being part of it makes it hard to join in with all the office gossip.

Alice returns in a dark green dress with freshly applied make-up. She's offered another drink that she doesn't mean to accept, but of course she does. She minds the lack of sweetness less this time. She can feel herself loosening up but she doesn't want to get any looser. She can't afford to, even if it does make being in Alice's flat seem almost normal.

The doorbell rings. Alice brings in a man and introduces him as Steve, one of her friends from school. He isn't tall and his red-brown hair is too short but he starts a conversation by telling her he's a hairdresser. One day, he'll have his very own salon. He can't do Afro hair, it's a bugger to get right, or he'd style hers for free. They sit side by side on a battered sofa that barely seats the two of them. Her replies are brief, measured, barely audible above the music. She can hear how her voice changes when she speaks to men. It is softer, and the vowels are more pronounced. Perhaps he can hear how desperate she is for his attention. He enjoys talking about himself and she likes to listen – it's safer. At work they say she's a good listener, that's why her colleagues like her – well, they don't *dis*like her anyway.

The room begins to fill. She says hi to her workmates as they arrive and they say hi back but they don't come and join her; they drift off to the kitchen or sit on the stairs. The smell of weed surrounds her, though she says no to the spliffs that start to circulate (she's finding it hard enough to focus as it is, the amount she's had to drink). Steve gets her another glass of wine and she swallows it quickly, even though she knows she shouldn't. But it does help. She starts to feel she doesn't have to find some excuse to leave. She gets up and fills her glass again, right to the brim, and she starts to feel like one of them, almost, as if she fits in and has the right to be there.

Steve is sitting close. He touches her arm every now and then as he makes a point. She nods in agreement. Safer to agree, she tends to find. The room is cosy. Their feet are resting on a blue, mock-sheepskin rug. She likes the silver lamp that stands in the corner, casting dappled shadows. It's warm; the central heating's on full blast. She takes off her cardigan but wishes she hadn't almost at once: her T-shirt is tight against her E-cup breasts. Steve is staring, obviously finding her repulsive. She pulls the cardigan back on and suddenly feels sick. She lurches to the bathroom, only it isn't a bathroom, it's a box room that's been turned into a single bedroom. Bile rises in her throat. She can't be sick on someone's bedroom floor. She finds the bathroom just in time but throws up on the toilet seat. She cleans it with toilet paper, feeling shame, and sprays the room with perfume from the windowsill. It's heavy and sweet and only marginally better than the smell of sick. She turns on the tap and cups cold water in her hand, splashing it on her skin to remove the yellow stain of vomit from her mouth.

By the time she comes out of the bathroom, Steve is chatting up someone else: a girl, sixteen, seventeen, blonde and skinny, who works on the factory floor. She'd thought he was interested in her, that he might ask her out on a date at the end of the evening. She stares at the two of them, chatting together, their lips curling into sneers that quickly turn to laughter. Are they laughing at her? She edges closer, trying to hear what they are saying, but the music is too loud. It's lucky she's been rehabilitated. If they only knew what she was capable of, used to be capable of, before she was reformed, they wouldn't look so pleased with themselves. She can feel the word forming in a speech bubble above her head as if she is a comic-book character. Re-formed, taken apart and put together again, made into something new, as if what was inside her before had to be excised. Exorcized, more like. In a different time, the devil would have been cast out of her. She knows she needs to leave. She thanks Alice for the invite and finds a mint in her bag that she sucks as she stumbles to the Tube. She can't walk in these stupid shoes. She yanks them off and goes barefoot, staring at the pavement to avoid the dog shit and the broken glass.

As the train hurtles in and out of the darkness, she looks at her reflection in the window and thinks about Steve. He didn't fancy her. Perhaps she just isn't attractive enough.

She doesn't like returning to the flat at night. Boys circle the tower blocks, doing deals in doorways. She pulls up the hood of her jacket and hurries towards her building, feeling the throb of the blisters forming on the soles of her feet. Something moves in the shadows, causing her to jump, and then she sees a dog, skinny like a rat, being chased by a mob on bikes. It's injured so it can't run fast and they're pursuing it as if they're playing polo: it's a ball for them to whack with sticks as they ride past. She grabs its collar, noticing its bloodied coat. One of its eyes is half closed. 'Leave it alone!' she shouts, scooping it into her arms.

A boy hits out at her, catching her on the forearm. A girl swings her stick across her back but she doesn't let go of the dog. She wants to drag every one of them to the ground and pulp them with her fists, make them pay for their cruelty, but she can't, she's totally outnumbered. She stumbles away to a chorus of laughter, thinking they will follow, but the group disperses and she's left alone.

The dog starts to whimper. It is in pain. Something flashes into her head, something not quite real, but something so terrible she can scarcely bear it: a hand round a throat; the strangled crying of a child. For a moment, she struggles to breathe. She enters the tower block, shaking uncontrollably. What will she do with the thing in her arms? She can barely look after herself. It doesn't have a name tag. Later she'll discover that it isn't chipped. She takes it up to her flat. It sleeps in her bed and covers the duvet with blood and piss. She'll call it Otis, she decides, after Otis Redding, her gran's favourite singer. Sober, she'd have left it to its own devices – that gang could have kicked her head in. She shouldn't drink, but sometimes she can't help herself.

THREE

Even though it's no longer warm, she sits on the bar stool she's placed on her balcony and looks out across the city, observing the point where the Thames fades into sky, a scarf wrapped round her neck to ward off the cold. She'd put a chair out there at first, but it wasn't high enough for her to see over the balcony wall. The stool, found in a charity shop, is perfectly positioned. She could move it to the very edge, stand on it and then dive off, merging gracefully into the landscape. She's considered it; she's considering it now. Days off are hard – there is nothing but unhappiness to focus on. She would far rather be at work than sitting on her own in the flat, even if she hasn't managed to make any real friends. It's cliquey, she thinks crossly. She's tried to fit in and she isn't disliked, but she remains on the fringes of it. She remembers reading once about a man who put rat poison in the tea of all his workmates; she can see his point and she has such tendencies, she's been told. It's getting colder. She kicks the stool into the corner, closes the door and goes inside.

The flat that had been her haven only a few months before feels confining now. It's drab and oppressive, hot when the weather is warm and freezing when it's cold. The walls are closing in.

She has to leave soon. She is due at the probation office to see Dom for her fortnightly appointment, boring and predictable.

How have you been?

Okay.

Is there anything you would like to discuss?

No.

You seem to be making good progress.

Yes.

Goodbye, then; see you in two weeks.

She doesn't know why she bothers. Or why Dom bothers, either. Or why the terms of her release force her to see him regularly.

Otis recognizes the signs that she is going out and starts to whine. He stands in front of her, obstructing her attempts to find her jacket. She shoves him aside with her foot. She took him out earlier, round the estate, so it's not like he hasn't had a walk today. She takes him out before and after work, however tired she is. He's not a neglected dog. If anything, he's pampered. She needs to be away from his constant presence. She likes to see him beside her, loves the way he follows her from room to room, but it irritates her, too. If she isn't going to throw herself off the balcony, she could be tempted to toss him to the cat who will still be on the window ledge outside the opposite block, twelve storeys up.

She's come to enjoy the Tube she used to fear: the rattle of the trains as they speed through the dark, and the dank and musty smell of the stops beneath the Thames that is a marker of the bustle of the city. It's early afternoon and the trains are relatively quiet; she is able to find a seat. She gazes at the window opposite, studying her reflection in the glass the way she often does, and is relieved to see that she's still there even as she flinches at the sight of her own ugliness. If only her skin was lighter. Her mum used to say she looked just like her dad, and that he was bad to the core.

Dom sits in the little room without windows just as he usually does. She sits opposite, a wobbly coffee table the barrier between them. But it isn't the predicted brief conversation. There's been an enquiry, he says, from someone who wants to be in touch with her. He passes her a letter, already opened and obviously read, even though it's meant to be for her. She glares at him. Being convicted of a crime means you lose all right to privacy.

She scans the letter rapidly. The sender is Zoe Laing and she wants to write a book, let people know what really happened with Kerry; that way there may be greater understanding about why such things occur. The Home Office has given permission, she says, so if she agrees, Zoe Laing believes that it will help. *Help who?* she thinks, but the letter says that people should hear her side of things – the story needs to be told from her point of view. Perhaps it does, she isn't sure. Everything will be stirred up again – the memories. How will she cope with that?

'What do you think?' asks Dom.

'I don't know,' she says warily.

'Do you think it's something you might like to do?'

'I'm not sure,' she says.

'Have a think about it and let me know what you decide. But my advice is, only do it if you want to. It won't be easy talking about things, so it's not something you should feel pressured into.'

She folds the letter up and puts it in her pocket.

She is still thinking about it as she steps into the sunlight, so she doesn't see the woman coming towards her until they have collided. Her phone falls from her hand and onto the pavement. She bends down to pick it up, relieved to find the screen is still intact.

'Can't you look where you're going?' the woman snaps.

The voice is familiar. She raises her head. 'Lucy?' she says, looking at her green eyes and small, pretty face. Her mid-length hair is still blonde.

The woman looks blank.

'Lucy? It's *me*. We were at Whytefields, remember?'

The blankness leaves Lucy's face. 'I didn't recognize you – you've put on weight.'

Tact was never Lucy's strong point. She nearly says, *Well, you're looking old and you're only in your mid-twenties*, but Lucy might just walk away and she doesn't want to lose the opportunity to talk and remember the good times they shared.

Perhaps Lucy sees she's been crass because she says, 'You were too thin back in the day, you're looking better now.'

'Where are you heading?' she asks, determined to be heading in the same direction.

'Probation office.'

'I've just come from there.'

They smile at one another, recognizing that their lives probably haven't altered all that much.

'What time's your appointment?'

'About ten minutes ago,' says Lucy.

'I could wait for you if you want,' she tells her, desperately hoping that Lucy will say yes.

'It could be a long wait, you know what they're like.'

She glances at the McDonald's opposite. 'I'll wait for you in there,' she says, pointing towards it.

The queue is short and she is served quickly. She gets a cup of coffee for herself and slides into a seat at a table by the window. She will need to watch carefully for Lucy, make sure she runs to catch up with her if she forgets to come over.

More time passes than expected. She starts to worry that she looked away at the wrong moment and Lucy managed to sneak off. But then she sees her approaching the door. She waves. Lucy comes in and slips into the seat beside her.

'Are you hungry? We could get something to eat – on me,' she says, hoping to give Lucy a reason to stay.

Lucy's blank face becomes animated. 'Yeah, why not?' she says.

It makes a change, having someone to be with on a day when she isn't at work. She can't believe her luck, bumping into Lucy after all this time.

They go up to the counter to order. She checks the prices. It's the end of the month and her wages aren't due for a day or two yet. Still, she should be able to afford it – just. But Lucy isn't content with a basic burger. She gets a Big Mac, sizes up her fries and adds a shake and onion rings. And an apple pie. And a chocolate muffin. 'You don't mind, do you?' she says. 'I'm starving. I haven't eaten since yesterday.'

She calculates that if she restricts herself to the cheapest thing on the menu it should be all right. She gets out her debit card and holds her breath in case the payment is rejected, sighing with relief when it goes through.

They carry their trays back to the table. Lucy eats greedily, shovelling fries into her mouth four or five at a time. She, on the other hand, has to eat at a fraction of her usual pace, picking at her burger (without fries) and claiming not to be hungry. It takes a massive effort. She looks at Lucy and says: 'I freaked a bit when you just left Whytefields one day and never came back. I didn't know where you'd gone. Then one of the staff said you'd been released, just like that. Is that what really happened?'

Lucy nods. 'My mother found a lawyer to do an appeal. He said the first brief I had was so crap he was incompetent. The new one pushed self-defence. Because I was underage it was rape, even though I'd solicited, and that should have been taken into account a lot more. After the appeal, when my sentence was reduced, they decided I'd served enough time and I was let out. Didn't anyone try to get you out? You were only a child then, too.'

29

She shakes her head and says, 'We were all just children.' Easier, though, if you'd been to private schools and had a mother who was willing to fight for you. Easier if you were pretty and fair-haired.

The unfairness of it makes her want to smash up everything in sight. She sees herself hauling up the chairs that are battened to the floor and heaving them through the window next to her. Glass shatters. She swings her arm through the gaping hole, grabs a long shard and sticks it in Lucy's neck. Blood spurts.

She sits on her hands. Shut it out, she tells herself, until the feelings subside.

She looks at Lucy, who is slurping strawberry milkshake through a straw like a bad-mannered eight-year-old. She doesn't want to be angry with her – furious with her – even if she has squandered every opportunity she had. She wants to be friends again. She changes the subject. 'What have you been doing since Whytefields?' she asks.

'This and that,' says Lucy.

Still on the game, then. Using, too, from the look of her, and the size of her taste for free food. There is a pause while she waits to be asked what *she* does, but Lucy says nothing, so she says, as if the question has been posed, 'I work in an office, organizing rotas, doing sales spreadsheets, that kind of stuff.'

Lucy looks as if she thinks this must be very dull.

'I like it,' she adds. She wants to say, *I'm good at it, I've made myself indispensable, and I've done really well for myself. I'm lucky to even have a job, all things considered*, but she doesn't because

30

this would make it plain that Lucy's opinion of her matters. 'How was it with probation?' she asks.

'Same old, same old. Dom is such a loser, hasn't got a fucking clue.'

She laughs. 'I know what you mean. He's my probation officer too.'

'Fucking clueless. Told me I'd end up back inside if I didn't make some fundamental changes to my lifestyle,' Lucy says, mimicking his voice. 'I nearly punched his teeth down his throat.'

She laughs again. 'I've often felt like giving him a punch as well. He's like Dr Rowe at Whytefields. Do you remember him? Always saying he just wanted us to grow up to be good citizens.'

'Yeah, I remember,' says Lucy. 'So much for that.'

'Carly Hughes probably did grow up to be a good citizen. Do you remember her?'

Lucy laughs. 'Always hanging round like a bad smell, just asking for it. She nicked my bag, the one with the sequins. And my silver top.' She strokes the ends of her hair.

She looks at Lucy, wondering if this is a test. Does she suspect it wasn't Carly Hughes at all? Is she trying to tease a confession out of her? 'You couldn't trust Carly, she'd nick anything. I always hated her,' she says, hoping she sounds convincing.

'She was tiny, wasn't she? It's not like my clothes would even have fitted her – she looked about six.'

'I think she just liked that top,' she says. 'I don't think she cared if it fitted or not.' No point in owning up now, it's not like it would make a difference one way or another to Carly.

Lucy examines her nails. The black varnish, which makes her fingertips look gangrenous, is chipped. 'There was that woman teacher, the one who set up pets' corner. Jake Billington got in there one day and wrung the necks of all the chickens and battered the rabbits. She cried for days. Her eyes were all red and swollen.' Lucy laughs.

She laughs too.

'Do you remember that time they had to restrain you for giving him a black eye?' asks Lucy, wiping ketchup from her mouth. 'About six of the staff waded in and sat on top of you. They hauled you off to the isolation room.' She laughs again.

She doesn't look at Lucy. She can't join in with her laughter. Jake had said that no one came to visit because no one cared – who would want to be around anyone as stupid and ugly as her? She'd had to shut him up. Her throat becomes tight at the memory. She can hardly breathe. She pushes it out of her mind, focusing on the box of fries on Lucy's side of the table, until she surfaces again in the over-bright light of the café. 'Not worth thinking about that, it was a long time ago, we're grown up now,' she says.

'Yeah, we're grown up now. Out of Whytefields. We can do what we like. No one can stop us.'

She thinks of all the ways it's possible for her to be stopped. Dom, for a start. Put a foot wrong with him and her licence will be revoked. Prison recall. The police. Maybe Lucy's life is different.

Lucy yawns. 'You wouldn't get me a coffee, would you?'

She checks the time. 'I've got to go now,' she says. 'Otis will be waiting for me.'

'Who's Otis? Is he your boyfriend?'

'No, he's my dog.' Perhaps she should have let her go on thinking Otis was her boyfriend. Maybe she would have been impressed. When they were young, they'd dated imaginary boys. Hers was called Byron, because she liked the name, and Lucy's was called Jack. After lights out, in the dark, they'd describe the clothes they would wear on a Saturday night, the food they would eat, the club where they would dance until 4 a.m. at least, and the way they'd be fucked after. She remembers the warm feeling she would get as they imagined tenderness and tongues between their thighs. It had made her think that sex, one day, could be something she might like.

'We could meet up again, couldn't we?' she asks as Lucy heads towards the door.

They exchange numbers.

'I'll call you,' says Lucy, hovering beside her, clearly wanting something more. 'I know I shouldn't ask, but you couldn't lend me some money, could you? I'll pay you back next time we meet, promise. This week's been a bit slow but I'll be doing a lot of business tomorrow.'

She hesitates and then gets out her purse. There is a single ten-pound note and a few coins. She hands the note to Lucy, suspecting that a tenner is the price of friendship.

On the Tube travelling home, she remembers the letter from

Zoe Laing. She gets it out and reads it again. She can't decide what to do.

Inside the flat, with Otis on her lap, she googles her. She's an author but she's also a psychologist. Perhaps she should be wary. There is a photo. She's thin with sleek, feather-cut hair and dangly gold earrings set with emeralds. A wide scarf in orange and lime is draped loosely round her shoulders. How old is she? Over forty, probably. She can't imagine speaking to anyone like her. But she is tired of the sound of her own voice inside her head, holding imaginary conversations because there are so few opportunities to talk to anybody real. And she does want to set the record straight, like Zoe Laing says. What happened wasn't fair. They talk about a justice system, but what was just about it? When she thinks of it, she wants to scream about the wrongness of the world. Nobody listened, and nobody believed her.

FOUR

Zoe is waiting impatiently for Michelle Cameron to arrive for her first appointment. She is hoping her anxiety won't show. It's not that she is afraid – she has worked with a number of men and women who have killed, and besides, it's very unlikely she is any sort of threat; extensive research has told her that child killers very rarely repeat offend. Her anxiety stems from a fear that she won't be able to persuade her to do the book, and it's become more important to her than anything else. She moves around the room, plumping up cushions and making sure that the lights are dimmed in a way that is calming yet still allows her a full view of the space where Michelle Cameron will sit. She has lit an expensive candle that has filled the room with the scent of roses and neroli and she has laid out plenty of sweet treats. If she feels welcomed – celebrated, even – she will be more likely to share her secrets.

Michelle Cameron arrives slightly late. She is breathless and a slight tremor shows as she stands in the hall.

'Can I take your coat?' Zoe asks.

She shakes her head.

She is wearing a cheap hooded jacket in a dull shade of blue. Her trainers are scuffed and a hole is appearing at the toe. Zoe continues to hold out her hand for the coat but Michelle Cameron shakes her head once more. 'No, it's okay, I'll keep it on,' she says.

'But you're wet.'

'It's okay,' she repeats.

Zoe nods. Michelle Cameron is tense; she is keeping the coat on, no doubt, so she can make a quick getaway if the need arises. She sighs, recognizing more fully than before that this meeting won't be easy.

She shows her into the consulting room and gestures to the large leather sofa. Michelle Cameron perches there inelegantly, failing to relax.

'Would you like something to drink?' asks Zoe, making her voice warm.

'Okay.'

'Tea? Coffee? I've just got a Nespresso machine. Would you like to try it?'

'What's a Nespresso machine?'

'It makes coffee in different flavours, like vanilla and caramel. It's very good. Come and choose a pod.'

The coffee machine rests on a mango-wood sideboard. She fingers the little cartons, squinting at each description. 'I'll have this one,' she says, putting the hazelnut aside.

'Help yourself to doughnuts.'

She takes a chocolate one eagerly.

'Have two if you like.'

She adds a toffee one to her plate.

Coffee sorted, Zoe settles into the armchair opposite, watching her, noting how keenly her gaze is returned. There is silence. It mustn't last too long, or she might become intimidated or tongue-tied, so Zoe breaks it carefully. 'I was really pleased you felt able to meet with me to discuss this project. As I said on the phone, you know you can't be paid?'

She nods.

'You are entitled to expenses, though. Meals for the day, return taxi fares and such.' Zoe wishes there could be a fee – a bigger incentive to do the interviews would have increased the chances of co-operation. 'Do you have any questions for me?' she asks, hoping to prompt Michelle Cameron to speak.

'How long have you lived in this flat?'

'In this apartment?' says Zoe, correcting her. 'About three years.'

She thinks for a moment, as if she is wondering what to say next, and then she asks: 'How does this work? I mean, what kind of things do you want me to say?'

'I am very interested in you, in learning about you as a person, and not just as a case that hit the headlines. I thought we could meet once or twice a week for an hour or two at a time. I know it's hard, talking to a stranger, so I don't expect you to jump straight in with anything difficult. We'll just chat and see where it leads.'

'How long for?'

'It depends on how much you feel able to say and how

quickly,' Zoe replies. 'But at least a few weeks. Does that sound okay to you?'

'And will I be able to see what you've written before it gets published?' Her tone is guarded – sullen, even. And she is rocking slightly as she speaks.

'If you'd like to,' Zoe answers, hoping this wish to see the manuscript will have subsided by the time the book is finished.

'And what if I don't like what you say about me?'

'I wouldn't want to go ahead with anything you weren't happy with.'

There is silence while she thinks about this. 'How do I know you're telling the truth?' she asks tentatively.

'That works both ways, doesn't it? How will I know that you're telling the truth when you tell me about yourself? To a large extent, it will be based on trust. We'll have to trust each other and build that trust up slowly.'

'I expect you think I did it.'

Zoe does, of course, think Michelle Cameron killed Kerry Gosling, but now is not the time to say so, not if she wants the sessions to continue. 'I don't know,' she replies, interested in the possibility that she is in a state of denial and wondering how she will penetrate this. 'That's something I hope to learn about through talking with you further.'

There is scratching at the door. Michelle Cameron looks at it anxiously.

'There's no one else here, it's just the cat,' says Zoe reassuringly.

'What's its name?'

'Her name is Midge.'

'You can let it in if you want.'

Zoe goes to the door. The cat comes running into the room. It stops and stares at the visitor, frozen for a moment, and then it jumps onto her lap, with a movement so sudden that she gasps.

'She likes you,' says Zoe, guessing she'll be flattered. 'She doesn't usually go near anyone she doesn't know.'

She smiles. It makes her look less at odds with the world. 'I've got a dog,' she says.

'What kind?'

'He was a stray. I think he's a cross between a poodle and a Yorkie.'

'What's he called?'

'Otis.'

'Good name.'

'Yes,' she says.

'Would you like another coffee?'

She says yes and sips it quietly, the cat still on her knee.

'When we spoke on the phone, you said you had a job,' says Zoe. 'What is it that you do?'

'I work in an office.'

'It's very hard for people to find work after a long period away. It's quite an achievement to have got a job for yourself. Do you enjoy it?'

'It's okay,' she replies.

'And what do you enjoy doing in your spare time?'

'I like being with Otis.'

'Your dog? He's obviously very important to you.'

'Yes,' she says.

Zoe nods encouragingly, hoping she will say more, but she remains silent. 'Is there anything else you enjoy?' she prompts after a moment or two.

'I suppose I like music.'

'What kind?'

'All kinds.'

'What's your favourite genre?'

'I don't really have one.'

'I like all kinds too,' says Zoe, 'everything from classical to hip hop. I sometimes listen to Jay-Z. Do you like him?'

'Jay-Z?' she says, with a smirk.

Zoe is uncomfortable. She shouldn't have pretended to know about youth culture – it's clear that Michelle Cameron sees through any obvious deception. She changes the subject. 'Is there anything you would like to talk about today?' she asks.

'I don't know what to talk about really,' Michelle Cameron replies, and Zoe suspects that there are lots of things she would love to share with somebody. She must be very isolated – lonely, in all likelihood. Perhaps that's the way to go with this; ensuring she feels liked will reduce her sense of isolation; she'll want to come to the sessions then.

Zoe offers her the plate of doughnuts. She takes two, one strawberry and one vanilla, even though she must be feeling uncomfortably full. 'I just want to check something with you,' Zoe says.

She takes her eyes off the doughnuts for a minute and looks at Zoe expectantly.

'As you know, the biggest part of my research for this book will be talking to you,' Zoe continues, 'but I'll be going to see your mother, too—'

'*No.*' She says it with such fierce emphasis that Zoe is taken aback. She feels the tension in her neck start to build as she thinks rapidly about how to negotiate this. Eventually, she says, 'What is it about me seeing your mother that bothers you so much?'

'You're not seeing her. If you do, I'm never coming back.'

'It would be really helpful to know why you're so opposed to it.'

There is a long silence. Then Michelle Cameron says breathlessly: 'She turns everyone against me. She'll turn you against me.'

'Can you give me an example of the way your mother turned people against you?'

'If I did something bad, she would phone my gran and tell her. She would say, "Lock up all your stuff because she steals things." It wasn't even true; she just wanted my gran not to like me anymore. It was to punish me.' She sits back in her seat and adds triumphantly, 'Anyway, it never worked, Gran never believed her.'

'What other things did your mother do that were meant to turn people against you?'

'She told the newspapers what a bad person I was after the trial.'

Zoe nods. In the process of her research, she had found a newspaper article in which Sandra Cameron had described her daughter as evil. 'What was it like for you when she did that?'

She doesn't answer. Instead, she says, 'You have got to promise you won't ever go to see her or I won't do the book.'

'I'm like your gran,' says Zoe. 'I wouldn't be influenced against you by anything your mother had to say, I can certainly promise you that.'

'No, I want you to promise you won't see her.' She thinks for a moment and then, as if suspecting Zoe might keep to the letter of a promise rather than the spirit of it, she adds: 'And you're not to phone her, either. Or write. You're not to get in touch with her in any way. I'll know if you do.' She folds her arms defiantly.

Zoe wants to confront her – this veiled threat, *I'll know if you do*, is ridiculous and deserves to be challenged. But she can't afford to lose her and she does believe that Michelle Cameron will decide not to work with her unless a promise is forthcoming. It's frustrating but there's no urgency here, it's something she can come back to once the work is sufficiently under way. Interesting that she is so adamant. Clearly her relationship with her mother has been a destructive one and it must have played some part in whatever led to the killing of Kerry Gosling.

'I promise you I won't see your mother,' Zoe says, 'not if you're so against it. I wouldn't want to do anything that is difficult or upsetting for you.' She is hoping that Michelle Cameron will see this promise as evidence of her trustworthiness. 'It must have been hard to come here today,' she says, moving the conversation forward.

Michelle Cameron nods rapidly.

'It was brave of you – it's not easy to talk to someone you don't know. But I can promise you that I will make this absolutely safe for you. I have a feeling we're going to work very well together and this is the start of something really worthwhile, something that will help you a lot in the long run.'

She nods again but she says nothing except, 'Can I go now?'

Zoe is disappointed but she knows that if she tries to persuade her to stay she is likely to lose her for good, so she says, 'Yes, of course, you'll always be free to go whenever you want,' and crosses the room to a desk piled with newspapers. The Apple logo on her laptop glints in the soft light of the room. She pulls an envelope from a drawer and hands it to her. 'The expenses I promised. Would you like me to phone for a taxi?'

'No, it's okay, thanks.'

'It's been lovely meeting you. I hope you've found this useful. Do you think you'll be coming back? As I said when we spoke on the phone, this is the chance for you to set the record straight. A lot has been written about you but you've never really been given the opportunity to have your say, have you? People need to hear about your life. I don't believe you've been treated fairly and this will help to redress the balance.'

Michelle Cameron hesitates for a moment, as if she might speak in response, but then she just shrugs.

In her work as a clinical psychologist, Zoe has become all too accustomed to awkward patients, but she still finds shrugs and muteness a source of irritation. She suppresses the feeling and tries to smile. 'I'll call you tomorrow and see if you want to set up another chat.'

She puts the cat on the floor and stands up to leave.

Zoe shows her out and returns to her consulting room, thinking about how the meeting went. She is disappointed that she couldn't get a real commitment to return from Michelle Cameron, but at the same time she knows that getting her to turn up at all was a pretty big achievement. She was bound to be resistant. She will have buried much of what happened on the day she choked and battered four-year-old Kerry Gosling to death. She will have had to deal with the impact of being incarcerated during her most formative years. Her defences will have been honed to the nth degree.

Zoe sighs. What if Michelle Cameron refuses to co-operate? She regrets investing so much in this book but it's too late now and she can't afford to lose this opportunity; her career really does depend on it. And she needs the money it will bring more desperately than anybody knows. Besides, she's told the people who matter most about it: senior colleagues, her father – even Oliver, her ex-husband. She is not prepared to face the humiliation of failure. For a moment, she feels uneasy; her clinical supervisor would say, no doubt, that a line is being crossed, therapeutically speaking, and that she needs to be wary of coercion. But, then again, it isn't a therapeutic relationship. Michelle Cameron isn't a patient, she is simply the subject of her research, so there is no need to take any of this to supervision.

She pictures the young woman who had sat opposite her on the sofa, unsure of herself, awkward, lacking communication skills. Traumatized, in all likelihood. She will take her under her wing, facilitate her in coming to terms with the terrible crime she committed and write about the process. Surely no one could object to that.

FIVE

She can't wait to see Lucy again. She waits for her to call, constantly checking her phone, but days pass and then a week. At the end of a fortnight, she makes the call herself and is elated when Lucy picks up, even though she sounds groggy and answers questions sullenly, irritation in her voice.

'Do you want to meet up?' she asks.

'I'm a bit busy at the moment,' Lucy replies.

She remembers the ten-pound note. Maybe that's why Lucy's been avoiding her – she can't afford to pay it back. 'You know the money I lent you? It's a present. You can keep it if you want.'

Lucy's tone changes. 'Thank you so much. I should have some time on Sunday. Do you want to go to McDonald's again?'

'Yes, let's do that,' she replies, wondering how much it will cost her.

But Lucy is less interested in the menu this time round. She orders half the amount of food she had before and most of her fries remain in the box getting cold.

'Do you want those?' she asks.

Lucy shakes her head, pushing them towards her, so she eats them herself and then gets coffee for them both. Returning to the table, she can see that Lucy doesn't look well. She is even paler than usual. There is the agitation of withdrawal in the gestures that she makes as she speaks about the flat she shares with her friend Amber, and tells her how this bloke, Ryan, turned up out of the blue, claiming to be Amber's brother. Now he's dossing on their couch.

'Don't you like him?' she asks.

'He's okay, but he doesn't have any money, he isn't paying rent, he's scrounging off us. He might not even be legit. He hasn't done DNA. We might be putting up with him for nothing.'

She doesn't really want to hear about Lucy's present life; she wants them to talk about the past, the months they spent together at Whytefields.

'Do you remember that time we tied up Carly Hughes and left her in the cupboard in the gym? She was there for hours.'

Lucy shakes her head. 'It can't have been me,' she says.

She stares at her in frustration. 'It was you, we did it together, it was your idea. Don't you remember?'

It's becoming obvious that she and Lucy don't remember the same things at all. It's as if they were never in Whytefields together. Lucy is the oldest friend she has. What's the point of friends if you can't share memories?

It's getting busy in McDonald's. They are having to share a

47

table with two women and a toddler, so private conversation is becoming hard. 'Do you want to go?' she asks.

Lucy nods.

They head towards Camberwell. Lucy's phone pings an alert. 'I have to see someone,' she says. 'It won't take long. You don't have anything I can borrow, do you? Earnings have been a bit short this week.'

She's anticipated this. She gets out her purse. There is a fiver in it and a twenty-pence piece. She gives this to Lucy as if it's all she has, knowing there is a twenty-pound note folded tightly in her trouser pocket.

'Wait here.' Lucy crosses the street and has a brief conversation with a man in a hooded top and jeans. The transaction is discreet; if she'd blinked, she would have missed it. Lucy was always quick, she thinks. Not quick mentally, quite slow in some respects. But her actions were always speedy.

On her return, Lucy says: 'There are some toilets in that pub over there. I just need to go in. Can you get me a vodka and tonic?'

She holds up the empty purse.

Lucy sighs. 'Okay, never mind, I'll go in on my own, then. I'll be back in a minute.'

There is a green space at the junction. She can see a children's playground. The grass is brown from days of unbroken sun. Up ahead, a middle-aged woman is eating a sandwich. Pigeons gather. She throws them the crusts.

Lucy returns and says, 'Do you want to come back to the flat? I won't be working till this evening.'

She seizes on the invitation; it's a sign of friendship. They walk through bleak estates where rubbish is piled in corners and the smells of roast lamb and curries mingle to create a single scent. It must be nice, she thinks, to have a proper dinner on a Sunday. She's always envied that: families sitting together at the dinner table, chatting about their week, Dad carving the joint, Mum serving roast potatoes. Everyone feeling part of something.

They stop outside a small, terraced house. 'Our flat's in the basement,' says Lucy as she lets them in.

The flat is cold despite the warm weather and it smells stale. She follows Lucy to the kitchen down the hall. There is a man, slumped across the table. 'That's Ryan,' Lucy says, pointing to him derisively. She gives him a shake. He murmurs something, half-opening his eyes. Then he loses consciousness again.

'Should we do something? Get him to hospital?' she asks.

Lucy shakes her head. 'He'll be all right, it'll wear off soon. He's just not used to it, that's all.'

'What's he taken?'

'I don't know. Amber will have given it to him. You'll have to ask her.'

Beside Ryan on the table, there are two dinner plates, greasy with the remains of egg and bacon. Dirty female underwear is strewn across the floor and a pair of worn shoes is resting on one of the chairs. Lucy picks them up impatiently and throws them into the wall. 'Amber's always leaving stuff around,' she says.

'Is she out?'

Lucy goes to the hall and listens for a moment. 'No, there's music coming from her room,' she says, returning to the kitchen. 'Do you want a cup of tea?'

She nods.

'Sit down,' says Lucy, 'make yourself comfortable.'

There isn't much that's comfortable in this flat. She sits on a chair with uneven legs that cause her to rock to one side. She thought she would envy Lucy, but her own place, depressing as it is, feels a lot brighter. She drinks builder's tea and starts to feel warmer. She peers at the brown ring at the bottom of her mug, wondering if she dares to speak the words that are popping into her head. Eventually she says, 'When you killed that bloke, that punter, what did it feel like?'

Lucy looks animated for the first time and says, 'Scary, I suppose, it was like someone else had done it. Easy in a way, but hard at the same time. There was blood coming out of his mouth, even though I didn't stab him there.'

'Did they arrest you straight away?'

Lucy nods. 'I didn't hide what I'd done, there wasn't any point. At the trial, they said I was brazen. I didn't know what it meant. I asked someone later. She said it meant hard, not caring. What about you? What did you feel when you did it?'

Lucy seldom shows an interest in anybody else so she rarely asks questions. She is thrown, unsure what to say. Stupid to have brought it up. The bad memories are surfacing: puffy, sweating faces; pitted, wrinkled skin; pain; an inability to breathe. She is choked by fear. She looks at Ryan; he is barely conscious. She focuses on him, making herself notice the hairs on his chin and the frayed ends of his sleeves. *Concentrate*, she tells herself, *it's going to be all right*. Yet she can feel the tremors building up inside her, the dizziness that always comes with having to remember. Lucy continues to gaze at her expectantly, so eventually she says in a low voice, 'It was different for me . . .' but she doesn't explain further.

Lucy returns to her own feelings and the tremors slowly subside. 'It was exciting, in a way, shanking that fat, old piece of shit. He wanted to . . . he wanted to do something that would hurt too much. And something so gross . . . I've done most things but I wasn't doing that. And when I said no, he kicked off, tried to make me. I always had a knife on me, just in case. His face, when he realized what I'd done . . .' She starts to laugh.

Ryan begins to come round. He stares at them both vacantly, then gets himself a glass of water, gulping it down and following it with another. Droplets splash his T-shirt; he is so thin she thinks she can see the outline of his ribs through the fabric. Perhaps he could be good-looking with more weight, but he hasn't shaved or showered for days, and his hair is matted. She thinks he would be smiling at her if he could just get control of his face. 'What's your name?' he asks.

'Samantha,' she says, 'most people call me Sam.'

He nods. 'I'm Ryan,' he tells her.

'She knows,' says Lucy, rolling her eyes.

They hear a bedroom door slam. Amber comes into the kitchen. She looks at her and says, 'Who the fuck are you?'

'She's someone I used to know,' Lucy tells her. 'We were kids together. I met her accidentally a few weeks back, I told you about it.'

Ryan shuffles out of the kitchen.

'Aww *bless*,' says Amber as he leaves. She finds half a packet of biscuits at the back of the cupboard and passes them round. 'So, were you in Whytefields with Lucy then?'

She nods.

'Why did they put you in there?'

She shakes her head.

'She doesn't really talk about it,' Lucy says.

'I was in Downview for more than a year. That was a head fuck,' says Amber.

The kettle boils. Amber's interest in her wanes. She asks Lucy if she's got any gear and is disappointed by the answer. 'What about you? Did you bring any?'

She shakes her head.

'She isn't using at the moment,' Lucy says.

She opens her mouth to say she's never been a user but a look from Lucy silences her. 'I'd better go,' she tells her.

Lucy shows her to the door.

'See you next week?' she says.

Lucy just nods.

She should have paid more attention to the route they took from Camberwell Green. She isn't sure where she is. She crosses the estates but quickly realizes they all look the same. In each street, she hopes to see a bus stop but there are none. It's even colder now. A pitted moon appears in a darkening sky. She's had dreams like this. She is in the centre of the city trying to find a way out, but each turning she takes leads back to the same place. She starts to run and then realizes how stupid she looks, darting up the street, manic and on the verge of tears. Ask someone, she tells herself. She sees an old man with a walking stick plodding up ahead. He starts as she reaches him, expecting her to mug him, no doubt. He points to a turning with a nod and a frown. She follows his directions. The streets widen. Red buses appear. She gets on the first one she sees.

On the front seat of the bus, on her way to Brixton, she thinks about the answer to the question Lucy asked, even though she tries to push it back. *What did you feel when you did it?* She has no answer, there is nothing there. She was numb when the accusations started all those years ago and the numbness lasted months. *Years.* Perhaps it's never left her.

SIX

The first time she saw Zoe Laing she took a taxi. Now she knows the location of the flat, she's no longer worried about getting lost, so she decides to save money and go by Tube.

She gets out at Notting Hill Gate and walks towards Ladbroke Grove. She is late for the appointment but she doesn't care; she isn't sure she wants to do the book anymore. She will have to think about long-buried things, put them into words. They will be written down, made permanent – real – in the writing of them. Coming back to see Zoe could be a big mistake.

Up ahead, there is a market that sells antiques and bric-a-brac. The street is lined with terraced houses and the brickwork is painted in purples and pinks that clash and blend simultaneously. It makes them seem unreal, like doll's houses. Further along, she looks in the window of a deli selling chocolate with chilli, fizzy rhubarb drinks and cheese called Stinking Bishop. There are little shops piled with quirky clothes, the kind that Mary Poppins might wear, and in the road, stalls that sell fruit and veg are packing up. She smells overripe bananas as her feet find discarded cabbage leaves dampened by the rain.

She reaches Zoe's flat, rings the bell and waits, shifting from one foot to the other. Zoe smiles as she opens the door. Perhaps she should smile back but she can't.

'I'm glad you came back,' Zoe tells her, pointing to her seat on the sofa. 'You're looking well. I like what you've done with your hair.'

She had extensions put in at the weekend in a proper salon that only did Afro hair. She felt proud, sitting there, able to pay with the money she'd earned, surrounded by other black women who didn't seem to think she looked out of place. Her hair is long now, and straight. She likes the way it swishes when she shakes her head. And she's bought a jacket, too, dark red, with an inside zipped pocket, brand new. It's the best thing she's ever worn so she keeps it on, even when Zoe tries to make her take it off the way she did the last time she was there.

'Help yourself to anything you want,' says Zoe, gesturing towards the sideboard.

There is more food, Krispy Kremes again, full of squishy filling and glazed on top – not cheap. She takes a chocolate one and worries that, like Homer Simpson, she's sold her soul for a doughnut.

Zoe doesn't eat the doughnuts. She is thin. So once again, she eats them on her own – three, maybe four. Her greed will probably make it into the book.

As she chews, she takes in her surroundings. The red rug on the floor is probably Persian. Zoe's walls are grey to set off monochrome prints of jazz musicians and colourful, hand-carved animal masks. Bespoke wooden bookshelves fill the alcoves. Everything looks expensive. 'You like books, don't you?' she says between doughnut bites.

'I've always enjoyed reading. Do you like it?'

'I suppose.' They let you read when you're banged up; keeps you out of mischief. It's one of the few pastimes that's actively encouraged. Boredom has made her an avid reader.

She asks to use the bathroom, more as a means of seeing the rest of Zoe's flat than because she actually needs to. It's at the top of a short flight of stairs and it's tiled in Aztec colours: gold and turquoise and earthy reds. There are bottles of perfume on the shelf and they're called things that Zoe probably thinks are naughty, like Guilty, and Opium, and there's one called Classique. It's in a bottle that's shaped like a curvy woman's body, but without a head, or arms or legs. It's a bit creepy, she thinks, but she would put it in her pocket if there wasn't any risk of getting caught. She makes do with spraying some on her wrist and sniffs it obsessively. Zoe will probably detect the scent when she returns but she won't say anything in case it dries up conversation.

It's her day off and she is tired. She would rather have spent it in bed, snuggled up with Otis, even though he snores. It's been extra busy at work. She's found ways of reducing wastage at the factory, so she's been given a promotion. It's meant a lot of overtime so it's been hard to fit in seeing Zoe, what with meeting up with Lucy and needing to spend time with Otis to make up for the days she leaves him by himself. She never imagined life would be so full that she'd struggle to fit things in. It makes her feel important. During the journey on the Tube, she'd studied the calendar on her phone, savouring the entries. On Friday, Lucy will be coming to the flat, her first ever visitor. She'll be able to show off all the things she's been buying with the extra money she's been earning.

She returns to Zoe's room with a new thought: she doesn't have to work to Zoe's agenda; she can grab the opportunity to talk about the things she's longed to say to somebody. Here, she has a captive audience, someone she can share her triumphs with. Her anxiety subsides. She comes alive.

She describes her work in detail, emphasizing the importance of it. She talks about the party at Alice's flat too, telling Zoe how welcomed she was and not mentioning Steve. In the version she gives, she shines, dancing with everybody, telling jokes and funny stories. She's thinking of moving off the estate, she says. She's earning so much money now she should be able to afford it.

Zoe doesn't want to hear how well things are going for her. That's not how it's supposed to work at all. She wants to know about the bad stuff so she can put it in the book. Every now and then, she brings up the past. *Did you get on with your mother when you were a child?* and *What was it like at Whytefields?*

Now she looks at her sharply and says, 'This may seem like a strange question, but can you describe your earliest memory?'

'Why do you want me to do that?' she asks warily.

'I'm just interested, that's all,' Zoe replies.

'I don't really have a memory from when I was young.'

'It could be your first day at school, or when you got your first pet,' Zoe persists.

57

'I don't really remember things,' she says. But something comes to her, even though she tries to shut it out. There is a little black doll dressed in frilly pink clothes. A man, old and fat, is talking gibberish: ickle baby coo coo, cuckoo, cock; bald head glistening in the glow of the teddy nightlight by the bed. He is rocking her to sleep. She puts her thumb inside her mouth. It comforts her. She'll keep it there no matter what he says or does to stop him thrusting anything else inside it. She becomes aware, with a start, that she is sucking her thumb now, even though it makes her look like a baby in front of Zoe.

Zoe leans forward. 'What's happening now?' she asks. 'Try to take some deep breaths. What was it you remembered?'

'Nothing,' she replies in a small voice. She fights to gain control of herself. She is aware that Zoe is staring at her again, trying to work her out, get inside her head. She wriggles in her seat. *Shut her out*, she says to herself. *You don't have to tell her anything unless you want to.*

But Zoe continues to gaze at her, so in the end, she removes her thumb from her mouth and says, to fill the silence: 'I bumped into Lucy the other day, someone I used to know at Whytefields. We've met up a few times since.'

'Why was she sent there?'

'She got involved with a drug dealer. They went on the run together. There was some kind of shoot-out.'

Zoe raises an eyebrow.

Perhaps that's an embellishment too far, but she can't help herself. Zoe asks for it.

'What's she doing now?'

'She's an actor. She's been on television.' She stifles a giggle, then makes her face look serious, hoping Zoe hasn't noticed.

'Will I know her? What's her surname?'

'She uses a stage name; I can't remember what it is. She's been in *Holby City*, though, and *Midsomer Murders*.' She shouldn't have added this. Now Zoe will think Lucy's done even better than she has.

'Would you like another coffee? Or another pastry?' Zoe asks.

Of course she would, even though she knows she's being bribed, paid for her memories in cake. She's told to help herself. She chooses a macaroon and a slice of Swiss roll, not the kind you buy at supermarkets, the kind that has real cream and homemade jam. Returning to her seat, she says: 'Lucy's coming round to my flat tomorrow. I said I'd cook.'

'Do you like cooking?'

'I've got a book by Heston Blumenthal. I thought I'd do one of his recipes.' (Or maybe beans on toast.)

'Did your mother do a lot of cooking when you lived at home?'

A not-at-all-subtle attempt to take her back into the past. 'Yes,' she says. 'Mum loved to cook. She studied cookery in Paris, cordon bleu. She used to do a lovely duck a l'orange with asparagus. And for pudding we'd have tarte Tatin. But only on Tuesdays.'

Zoe looks cross now but she speaks in a pretend-kind voice. 'I know it's difficult for you to talk truthfully about your past, but it seems to me that you've buried a lot of memories. I've worked with many people who have been through trauma and remembering is an important part of becoming whole again. I doubt if you will believe this, but telling me about the things that happened to you will help you greatly in the long run. It will only be possible for you to be truly happy in yourself when you face up to your past.'

Zoe is right. She doesn't believe it. She is running out of things to say. She looks beyond Zoe's head to the clock on the wall behind her. It is supersized and has Roman numerals. Maybe she'll get a clock like that for her own living room. It's almost 4.30 p.m. She's stayed longer than she meant to. She steps over the cat that's been sleeping at her feet and says, 'I'd better go home now, it's getting late.'

Zoe sighs. 'If you'd like to stay and talk for a while longer, I think it would be useful,' she tells her.

'No, it's okay,' she answers.

As Zoe gets up to show her out, she sees that she has lime-green pumps with ribbon ties that criss-cross round her ankles. She's wearing black cropped trousers and she looks even prettier today than she did on her last visit.

'When would you like to come back?' asks Zoe.

'I don't know,' she answers. 'I'm very busy at the moment. I might not have the time.'

Zoe pats her shoulder as she leaves. It's intrusive but she likes it; the confusion causes her to flee from the apartment towards the Tube.

SEVEN

She'd never been that bothered about cleaning beyond the basics but as soon as she moved into the flat, she could see that if she didn't keep on top of it, she'd end up playing host to the cockroaches that hid in the corners of the stairwells. Lucy's pending visit makes her even more determined to get everything clean. She's vacuumed every room and polished all the furniture. A new sofa had arrived the day before yesterday, grey, with orange flowers on. Well, it isn't new, but it's as good as – she got it from a charity shop. They'd even delivered it. She'd been afraid that the lifts would stop working and they wouldn't be able to get it up to her, so she'd gone onto the landing every few minutes to check. When the men had carried it in she could have hugged them with joy. It made the place a proper home.

Since meeting Lucy and seeing her place, grubby and run-down, she's become obsessed with making her own flat as nice as it can be. She's painted the walls, making them bright with a colour called sun yellow, and she's bought a few small items:

candle holders, a cushion and some china dogs. Next month, she plans to get a rug for the living room. In the evenings, she sits in candlelight, with Otis on her lap, absorbing the peace and quiet. She doesn't fear silence anymore – in fact, she relishes it. Sometimes, she reads. She's joined the local library. There are three books on the shelf she put up in her bedroom. It slopes very slightly but it's not bad at all for a first attempt at DIY. She even has a docking station now, just like the one Alice had. Rihanna is playing in the background as she cleans.

The floors have been scrubbed. Otis's bed has been washed and it's folded over the radiator in the living room to dry. He doesn't care, he'd rather be on the sofa. She's put a towel over it so he doesn't make it dirty. That will come off when Lucy arrives. He's lying there now, looking at her lazily, wondering what she's up to. Nothing of interest. He yawns and goes back to sleep.

It's probably pointless. Lucy won't care if the flat is clean, she'll only notice the valuables – not that she has that many, just her phone, the speaker and the new TV. It would be sensible, she decides, to keep her phone in her pocket while Lucy is there. She turns off the music, goes to her bedroom and slides the handbag containing her purse beneath the bed.

Returning to the living room, she puts the television on. A middle-aged couple are inspecting the house in the country they are thinking of buying with the £500,000 they've amassed. *It's a healthy budget,* their guide tells them, *but in this particular location, you will need to be prepared to compromise on some of the items on your wish list.*

Time to start doing the meal. Otis, ever hopeful that something might fall from the counter as she prepares the sausages, keeps getting under her feet. She drags him back to the living room by his collar. She can hear him whining even with the door shut.

She's never cooked for anyone before. No one visits the flat. She feels grown up as she peels potatoes and puts them in the pan. When she goes to Lucy's flat, there's only cups of tea or coffee and, if she's lucky, the occasional biscuit. She's been offered pills, which she's declined; it's not a habit she wants to get into. What she'd like most, she thinks, even more than a boyfriend and a better place to live, is to feel cared about. If you cook for someone, you're showing that they matter to you. She wishes somebody would cook for her.

Sometimes, when she's sitting at Lucy's table, fielding barbed comments from Amber (who thinks she should be Lucy's only friend) and prodding Ryan to make sure he's still on Planet Earth, she wonders why she bothers. Does Lucy even like her? She laughs when Amber makes fun of her for passing up the pills and she's never paid back any of the money that she's borrowed. How much is it now? More than she can afford to lose.

Lucy is late. Maybe she's not coming. She waits by the window in the living room hoping to catch sight of her, even though she's unable to see the pathway to the block. The sausages are congealed in fat and the mashed potatoes are cold. She knows how unreliable Lucy is. Why did she think today would be different?

The intercom sounds, causing her to jump. Otis starts to bark.

She buzzes Lucy into the block and goes to the door to meet her. 'You should have been here more than an hour ago,' she says crossly, as Lucy stands in the hall.

'Sorry, I lost track of time.' She strokes Otis absently.

'Go in the kitchen,' she says flatly, pointing the way, failing to be the gracious host.

Lucy sits at the table that only has space for two, still stroking Otis, while she scrapes the sausages from the frying pan and puts them on cold plates. The mash lands on them with a splat. They eat in silence. There is ice cream for pudding, with pineapple chunks. She puts a wafer on the top. Her gran used to give her that for a treat. Lucy picks at it without interest, eyes glazed.

'Do you want to see outside?' she asks, gathering up the plates and putting them in the sink.

Lucy nods.

She opens the door to the balcony and they lean over it. She talks Lucy through the landmarks ranged beneath them with excitement. She is so proud of the view, it's almost as if she's constructed it herself. Something about the air, the sense of space, brings Lucy back to life. They laugh at the cat on the opposite ledge. Lucy goes back in the kitchen and quickly returns with a banana from the fruit bowl that was resting on the table. It was there to impress, only acquired the day before yesterday. She expects Lucy to eat it, but instead she tosses it over the edge of the balcony and watches it fall. Laughing, she fetches some apples and does it again. There is a sack of potatoes under the sink. 'Try these, Lucy,' she says, joining in. They are young again. Friends. She is giddy with excitement. They laugh and shriek. Otis barks. The sounds are so shrill that they don't hear the rapping at the door until it gets even louder.

'Are you going to answer that?' says Lucy, still helpless with laughter.

She recovers herself. The urgent knocking continues. Who can it be? She never has visitors. She runs to open the door. A man, red with rage, is shouting. 'You could have killed somebody,' he roars, 'My kids are out there. What the fuck do you think you are playing at?'

She tries to close the door on him but he keeps advancing. Lucy appears. She tells him to leave, her face twisted with fury. She is almost as scary as he is. A child starts to cry. He turns to deal with it. She and Lucy push the door shut and put the deadbolt on.

They both start laughing again and are unable to stop. 'Did you see his face?' says Lucy. 'I thought he was going to kill you, stupid old prick.'

'Stupid old prick,' she repeats, and adds, '*What's his problem?*' Her laughter fades. She imagines the outcry there would have been if another child had died, even if it was by accident, not her fault at all, just the result of messing about with Lucy. They'd never let her out again, not ever.

'What's the matter?' Lucy asks.

'Nothing,' she says.

'Have you got anything to drink?'

She gets some cans of lager from the fridge. They take them into the living room and sprawl on the sofa. She switches on the television, selects a music channel and turns up the volume as loud as she dares.

'It's all right here,' says Lucy as she drains her third can. 'You've made it nice. You're lucky to have this place. I wish I had a place of my own.'

She's been wanting this response all afternoon; she'd almost given up hope. The cooking and cleaning were worth it. 'I'm writing a book,' she announces, keen to capitalize on the admiration. 'Well, *I'm* not writing it, exactly, someone else is doing that. But it will be about me.'

'About *you*? How come?'

'It's about what happened when I was young, why I was in Whytefields.'

'Will you get lots of money?'

She shakes her head. 'I won't get paid for it, just expenses for taxis and meals. It's to tell everyone the way kids are treated by the system. The woman writing it says people need to know.'

'I thought people made lots of money writing books. Look at that bloke, the one that wrote the Harry Potter books, he's rich now.'

'*She*.'

'She?'

'It wasn't a man, it was a woman that wrote Harry Potter.'

'Whatever. It still made shedloads of money.'

'I won't be making any money. Nothing, zero, zilch.'

'That's not fair. If it's about you, you should get money for it. Tell them you want to be paid.'

'They're not going to pay me, that's for definite,' she reiterates.

Lucy thinks for a moment and then she says, 'Maybe I should write a book about my life. I won't be doing it for free though, that's for sure. Then I could get a place of my own. I'm sick of living with Amber, the flat's always in a mess. One day, I'm going to get shot of it. I'm going to kick my habit, I swear to God I am. You're lucky you never used. I've tried to give up, no one knows how hard, but something always drags me back down again. You can't hold down a normal job when you're using. If I was clean, I'd have a dog and other nice things like you. You don't know how lucky you are.'

If anyone was lucky it was Lucy Fields. Maybe not anymore, but she was born lucky, she'd had everything: a big house to live in; a mum *and* a dad; shelves full of books; dolls and teddy bears; meals on the table three times a day; private schools – she'd had it all once. If *she'd* been that lucky, she wouldn't have wasted it, ending up on drugs and getting sent to Whytefields, she would have made something of her life. She can feel the anger simmering inside, threatening to burst out.

But Lucy's eyes are brimming with tears; as she sees this, her anger subsides.

'Did you know I've got a kid?' Lucy says, going to the side table and picking up another can.

She shakes her head. 'How old?'

'She's nearly three.'

'What's her name?'

'Poppy.'

'Is she in care?'

She shakes her head. 'I went to see her in Brighton at Easter.

67

My parents have got her. Poppy isn't happy, I could tell. She cried all the time, even seeing me didn't make her stop. You know what? I think my mum and dad have turned her against me, told Pops I'm not good for her, that I've let her down. She hardly even looked at me, and that's not right, is it? A kid needs to be with her mum. One day, I'm going to get my own place, somewhere nice, Sussex or Kent, with a garden she can play in. Then I'll get her back. She only got taken off me because I didn't have anywhere decent to live. The flat's a health hazard, it's a dump, you can't have a kid in a place like that. I miss her, you know?'

She nods, pleased to think that Lucy has shared something important.

Lucy gets up and starts pacing up and down the room. 'I can't do it anymore, all those sick arseholes treating me like I'm nothing, dealers battering the door. I kicked the habit for a while but they pushed a load of gear through the letter box. They know you can't hold out when they do that, they just want to keep you hooked. It isn't fair, it just isn't fair.' She stumbles back to the sofa, sobbing now, hiding her face with her hands.

She doesn't want the day to end like this. She'd wanted it to be happy. As she puts an arm round Lucy, tentatively and with fear, she recalls that it had been like this at Whytefields; children crying in corners, pulling out lumps of their hair by the roots. She'd only remembered the fun they'd had. She'd forgotten the sadness of the place.

EIGHT

Lucy knows exactly how to gain access to the house. She climbs the tree that rests against the wall and pushes open the bathroom window. She wriggles inside with ease. 'Are you coming?' she calls down.

'No,' she says, feeling anxious.

Lucy laughs. 'Okay, I'll open the door for you.'

There is a wait of a few minutes and she wonders why she's there. At first, she'd refused to do it, but there had been mockery in Lucy's laughter and she'd minded that. *What's the matter with you?* she'd said. *You never used to refuse a dare when we were at Whytefields*. But she isn't at Whytefields anymore and this is breaking and entering, with all the risks that carries. She starts to walk back down the path. If Lucy wants to break into the place she can do it on her own.

'Where are you going?' Lucy hisses, appearing at the back door. 'Come in quick, or you'll be seen.'

She hesitates and then she follows Lucy into a kitchen that has pots and pans suspended from a rack above an island.

There is a table to one side that seats fourteen and an Aga in the centre of the opposite wall. Lucy opens the fridge and takes out a beer. 'Catch,' she says, tossing one across. It lands at her feet with a bang, causing her to jump. One of the floor tiles cracks.

'You should have got that one, it was an easy catch.'

'You didn't throw straight.'

They are arguing as if they are fourteen again. Lucy drains her can and heads into the hall. 'Come on,' she says, sounding impatient, 'let's go upstairs.'

'I don't want to, this isn't right.'

'Oh for fuck's sake, stop whining! I wish I hadn't brought you.'

'Me too,' she mutters, but she follows Lucy to the master bedroom. It's huge with an en-suite bathroom the size of her living room. Lucy goes inside. There are crashes as bottles are dropped to the floor. The smell of Jo Malone is overpowering.

'Why did you do that?' she asks as Lucy comes out.

'They'll replace it on the insurance,' is all she says. She's holding a box, which she opens carefully, peeling back the tissue paper to reveal a scarf. 'Guess how much?'

She shrugs.

'Go on, guess.'

She goes high with the estimate, recognizing from Lucy's tone that it will be expensive. 'Fifty quid?' she suggests.

Lucy laughs. 'More like two hundred.'

'*Two hundred?*'

'It's cashmere.'

The name of the fabric means nothing to her but she nods as if she understands and touches the scarf lightly with her fingertips. It's soft, like Otis's fur. She imagines feeling cosy in it when the weather is cold.

Lucy pulls a big leather bag from the wardrobe and stashes the scarf inside.

'You can't *steal* it.'

Lucy rolls her eyes. 'We've broken into the house. What did you think we were here for? You take something. Here, have this necklace.' Lucy picks up some ethnic beads from the dressing table and presses them into her hands.

'I wouldn't wear it,' she says, returning it to its place.

'It'll suit you,' says Lucy, picking it up again and holding it near her face.

'I don't want it.'

'I'll have it then,' says Lucy, shoving it into the bag. 'What *would* you like to take?'

'Nothing.'

She picks up a little toy rabbit that's lying face down at the foot of the bed. 'Here, you can have this if you want.'

She hesitates. 'It'll belong to a kid,' she says. She'd noticed a trike lying on its side by a monkey puzzle tree in the garden.

'So? They'll just buy another one.'

She takes it hurriedly and conceals it underneath her jacket, in the pocket of her sweatshirt.

Lucy nods, satisfied.

She's a thief now. She'll be recalled to prison if anyone finds out.

There's a teddy bear too, in the corner of the room. Lucy picks it up and holds it. Then she stuffs it into the bag.

'We've been here ages, someone will be back if we don't leave soon.'

But Lucy isn't in a rush. Perhaps she wants to be caught. She goes to the walk-in wardrobe and tries on a top and a well-cut pair of trousers. They swamp her. Something to sell though – she adds them to the bag. Then she searches for cash but there's none to be found. She seems resigned to this. 'Okay, let's go then,' she says, sounding weary.

As they reach the bottom of the stairs, they hear the sound of keys in the lock. The front door begins to open. 'Run!' shouts Lucy and they hurtle towards the back of the house, across the garden and through a gap in the fence.

She catches up with Lucy on the common by the bandstand. The house is visible in the distance; the top of the monkey puzzle tree marks it out. She leans against a bench, mouth agape, fighting for breath.

'You need to get fit,' says Lucy, even though she is panting too.

They rest for a few minutes and then walk along the path in tense silence. Without warning, rain begins to fall. They make for the trees but even under the leaves there is no shelter. Lucy is wearing a sleeveless dress and her legs are bare. By contrast, she is dressed in layers for the vagaries of the British summer.

'Lend me your jacket,' says Lucy, her teeth chattering. She wraps her arms round her body as if this will keep her warm.

She shakes her head. Lucy has a habit of not returning things.

'Go on, you've got so much on and I'm fucking freezing.'

She should continue to say no but she doesn't dare; she still
needs Lucy too much. But she isn't having her new jacket.
Instead, she removes the sweatshirt she is wearing beneath it
and hands it over.

Lucy wrinkles her nose but she takes it anyway and puts it
on. It makes her look wide, like a toddler in a sibling's clothes
she has yet to grow into.

'I told you it would be okay,' says Lucy, referring to
the break-in.

She nods but her heart is still pounding. Why did she take
such a risk? She is full of rage. It's all right for Lucy, she's got
nothing to lose if they get pulled in, whereas she will lose her
home, Otis, everything.

'I have to go,' says Lucy. Her blonde hair has become mouse
in colour from the damp, and large wet patches have formed
around her neck and shoulders. She's still shivering; she looks
as if she needs to score.

They part company. She doesn't want to get involved with
dealers or the selling of stolen goods. She watches as Lucy
walks towards the Tube, still wearing the pink sweatshirt.
If she pulled up the hood, she'd be warmer but Lucy is too
pleased with her pretty, blonde looks for that, even though
she's drawn from years of heroin. As she watches her retreat,
she remembers the rabbit, stuffed inside the pocket. She
almost goes after her but she's aware of how ungainly she

looks when she runs. She is disappointed about the rabbit but tells herself it wasn't important and, anyway, it's safer not to be holding the evidence.

She walks in the opposite direction, avoiding the house with the monkey puzzle tree and the trike on its side in the garden. As she continues to think about Lucy and the break-in and the risk she's been exposed to, she shoves her hands deep into her pockets to stop herself tearing at the skin on her wrists the way she used to do at Whytefields when she couldn't contain the feelings she had. She is still angry, so furious with Lucy that she scarcely knows what to do with herself. And she is scared, too. What if Lucy tells someone about the break-in? She isn't exactly discreet when she's off her head on smack. If Lucy says anything about what they did, she'll end up back inside again, and she won't be able to bear it.

PART TWO

NINE

The body of a sex worker has been found at a flat in Southwark. The police arrive in the dark of evening prepared to work into daylight.

The lighting in the basement is poor; a low-watt bulb with a heavy shade throws shadows round the hall, limiting their power to observe. In a while, lights will be rigged up, but for now they work in semi-darkness.

The hall is narrow; the body, though gaunt, is an obstacle, limiting movement in and out. The DI crouches over the victim, trying to find a space to put his feet.

The woman is naked from the waist down but her upper body is clothed in a pale pink sweatshirt. Heart-shaped tattoos are etched on her thighs like the untidy scribbles of a toddler. Perhaps she scratched them on herself. Track marks on her arms have been flagged up; the cause of death appears to be an overdose but there are also signs of suffocation.

'She's probably in her thirties, but she's a user, so she could be a lot younger,' says Natalie Tyler, the detective constable.

77

She looks at the body again. If not for her gauntness and the signs of many years of drug abuse, she could have been seen as beautiful. 'Who called it in?' she asks.

'Her flatmate, Amber Johnson,' DI Henderson answers, without looking up. 'She's in the kitchen. She says she came home with some shopping and found her dead, here in the hall. She says she didn't touch the body.'

There is also a man on a sofa in a room off the hall, semi-conscious. He is so high that no one has been able to get him to speak. A young PC is standing guard, waiting for him to come round. He'll be taken to be interviewed shortly – whether as a witness or a suspect is impossible to determine yet.

The flat is littered with gear. There are used condoms in a bin, which the crime scene officers are bagging as evidence. The living room smells sweaty-sweet.

A dead, addicted prostitute. It is a cliché, common to the point of banality. There is a scene from Sherlock Holmes – whether film or book, Tyler can't recall. He lounges on a chaise longue, declaring he is bored with the mundane, like a spoilt adolescent. She feels more worn down than bored – tired of cycles repeating themselves.

A shrill voice penetrates the quiet, screaming obscenities.

Her boss looks up. 'Sounds like Amber's kicking off. See what she knows, Tyler, and if she can identify the man in the living room.'

Her boss calls some of her colleagues by their first name but never her, as if he is wary of the familiarity. She likes the use of the patronymic; it distances her from the job, emphasizes that at work she isn't really herself, it's just a role she plays. Her short hair and androgynous clothing – and her brown skin, of course – keep her workmates guessing, and she's seldom drawn into revealing herself.

Tyler finds Amber in the kitchen. She takes in her appearance: hair in need of a wash; the body of a boy, wasted and abused; tattoos, like the victim's, on the side of her neck. She reeks of knock-off perfume; heavy notes of musk and roses fill the air.

Amber glares at her. 'I don't want to talk to you, fucking leave me alone!'

She warns Amber to calm down or she'll be placed under arrest. The woman takes to muttering under her breath, the curses coming in whispers at regular intervals. She puts her head on the table and begins to cry, hoarse, bitter sobs. 'She can't be dead,' she says repeatedly, 'she can't be.'

'The man on the sofa,' says Tyler, 'any idea who he is?'

'My brother, Ryan.'

'Your brother?' There is no family resemblance. She has pale skin and red hair, while he has mid-brown skin and an unkempt Afro.

'Half-brother. I left him here while I went to get us some tea.' She points to a crumpled plastic bag that rests on the table. It's full of food she'll have nicked from the local supermarket.

'How long were you gone?'

'I don't know. An hour. Maybe two. I don't know. What's the time?'

Tyler looks at her watch. 'Quarter past nine.'

JACQUELINE ROY

Amber thinks for a moment, then spreads her hands in defeat. 'I don't know how long I was gone,' she repeats.

'And was Lucy in the flat when you left?'

'Yeah, she was with someone.'

'A punter?'

'Yeah, it must have been.'

'Did you see him?'

She shakes her head.

'Did you hear anything?'

She shakes her head again.

'And that was earlier this evening before you went out?'

She nods and starts crying once more.

Tyler reports back to her boss.

'Get someone to take her to the station. Get yourself down there too and find out more,' he replies. 'You'd better interview her under caution. We don't know what happened here yet.'

She nods, relieved to be leaving the grubby confines of the flat.

Amber is even more agitated at the station as Tyler escorts her into an interview room. 'Are you arresting me? You're not fucking arresting me!' she shouts.

'You need to help us with our enquiries.'

'I'm fucking not!'

'You fucking are, so get over it.'

Amber flings herself into a seat with a loud sigh. She raises her right leg and examines her thigh, seeming dissatisfied with what she sees. She makes rhythmic clicking noises with her tongue.

'Would you like a cup of tea?' asks Tyler, hoping this will get her on side.

'I have to go home. Let me go home, you cunt.' She is trembling, clearly in need of a fix. She is twenty-five years old, with eight convictions for soliciting. She also did time for aggravated burglary.

'The sooner you tell us what we need to know, the sooner you can go.'

'Will I be let back in the flat?'

'Not for a while.'

'Where am I supposed to sleep?'

'Do you have any friends who can put you up?'

'What do you fucking think?'

'I can try and get you a bed for the night at a hostel if you want.'

Amber shrugs. Once she leaves, she'll turn tricks until daylight in alleys round Camberwell Green.

The tea arrives, and a plate of biscuits. Amber eats rapidly. Aware that her next fix is contingent on co-operation, she begins to talk. Lucy's been a working girl for years. No, she can't think why anyone would want to kill her. She starts to cry again. Lucy has a daughter. Only two, maybe three. And now she won't have a mother anymore.

The tears are probably more for Amber's childhood self than Lucy's little girl; no doubt she's had a lifetime of abandonments.

'Where is the child?'

'How much longer do I have to stay here?'

'The sooner you answer the questions the sooner you can go.'

Amber takes a deep breath and starts to speak rapidly. She got taken away. Lives with Lucy's mum and dad in Clapham. Nice area. Good shops, lots of money. Lucy never saw her parents much. Tough love, that was all they gave her once the habit had kicked in. Chuck you out and forget you exist. For your own good. *This hurts us more than it hurts you.* The fuck it does. What choices do you have once you're on the streets? Lucy got reckless, didn't mind what she did, even liked it rough because it paid better. She was a sweet kid, good school, good home, could have gone to university. 'Can I go now? I'm not feeling very well. I've had some trouble with my kidneys.'

Her words are supported by the dark rings round her eyes; her pallor; a sweat that is becoming increasingly visible.

Tyler walks her down the staircase and lets her out through the yard. She walks unsteadily, turning her ankle on a paving stone that's come loose. It's mid-September and daytime temperatures have been higher than usual, but the night is chilly and her shoes are canvas pumps, the cold seeps in.

Tyler is dispatched to Clapham to break the news of their daughter's death to the Fields. They will be shocked, no doubt, but not surprised. A tiny, secret part of them will be relieved. No more lies to friends and neighbours. No more thefts. No more wondering when and where their daughter's body will be found.

The Fields live in a late Victorian villa on the south side of the common. There is a gravel driveway and a monkey puzzle tree to the side of the house. A child's tricycle in purples and pinks is parked beside the front door. She knocks and rings insistently but no one answers, the rooms are in darkness. Tyler sighs: she's psyched herself up for this and now she'll have to go through it all again tomorrow.

TEN

The Fields' house is even more attractive in daylight. The double-fronted building has recently been redecorated and the white paintwork glistens in the morning sun. A woman, who introduces herself as Freya, lets Tyler in wearily. A toddler in pyjamas clings to her leg, causing her to shuffle as she walks through to the living room. She gestures to Tyler to sit down and draws the child to her lap where she settles, half asleep, coughing fretfully. Freya is a striking woman: tall, with high cheekbones and long, blonde hair carelessly pinned to the top of her head. The resemblance to her daughter is clear despite the differences in stature.

'This is my granddaughter, Poppy,' she says. 'Yes, I know, Poppy Fields. What can you say? My daughter thought it was cute.'

Poppy, with her golden curls and big green eyes, has the looks that seem to run in the family. Tyler becomes as still as possible as a prelude to the words she is about to say, but too many visits from the police have dimmed Freya's instinct for alarm.

'Mrs Fields, is your husband home?'

'No, he's at work.'

'I'm afraid I have some very bad news.'

It is as if Freya hasn't heard. She removes Poppy's fingers from her jersey skirt and smooths the creases out. Tyler takes in its subtle shades of blue, a sign of her expensive taste.

'Oh my God,' she says, after a while. 'Lucy's dead, isn't she?'

'I'm very sorry, Mrs Fields.'

Freya draws Poppy closer. 'Was it an overdose?' she asks, her voice strained. Poppy struggles to break free from Freya's arms. She manages to escape and ambles across the floor, croaking that she wants a drink. Ignoring her, Freya speaks with bitterness. 'Once they start on the drugs, you know it's going to end like this.'

'We're still looking into the cause of death but it's possible it was suspicious. When did you last see Lucy?'

Freya draws a hand across her forehead. 'It would have been ... about four days ago? She wasn't answering her mobile so I went round to her flat to let her know that Poppy was in hospital with a chest infection.'

'Did Lucy still have contact with Poppy's father?'

Freya screws up her face as if she is about to cry, but no tears come. 'I can't cry!' she wails in panic. 'Why can't I cry? I used to be able to cry but I can't seem to do it anymore. It's the antidepressants.' She puts her hand to her mouth, aware of a disjunction between the expected response and the one she is able to give.

'Poppy's father?' Tyler says again. 'Did your daughter keep in contact?'

'Lucy never told us who the father was. I doubt if she actually knew.' Then she says in agitation: 'I have to tell Nick. Where's Nicholas? This will devastate him.' She runs to the corner and stands there, leaning against the wallpaper. The green floral shapes seem to dwarf her and then heaving sobs send her body into spasms. She looks relieved; in the presence of normal emotion, she can understand herself.

Tyler gets up and puts an arm round Freya, steering her back towards the sofa.

She becomes quiet again but remains standing. 'She was a good child once. I don't understand what happened. Was it me? Was it my fault she turned out the way she did?'

Tyler stays silent.

'She started doing drugs when she was thirteen and that was that, I lost control of her. She's been in trouble ever since even though we sent her to the best schools. None of them would put up with her, they all asked her to leave. She struggled at school, but with everything we gave her she could have been somebody. It doesn't seem to matter what you do, in the end, you can't hold on to them, and as for protecting them ... She's taken all my jewellery over the years, stolen it. She breaks into the house every now and then. Climbs in through the bathroom window. We thought about getting new locks fitted but we knew that if we did that she'd just do more damage. It was easier just to make sure there was never anything of value in the house. I'll phone Nick in a minute, I just need to think.' She becomes agitated again. 'Where's Poppy?'

'She's over there,' says Tyler, gesturing towards the window seat. 'Would you like *me* to ring your husband? Would that be easier?'

'No, it's better coming from me. Just give me a moment.' Freya sits down on the sofa, her arms wrapped tightly round the folds of her cardigan. Intermittent sobs become the only sound.

On a console table, there is a photo of Lucy holding Poppy. Tyler gets up to look at it more closely. A miniature Ferris wheel stands in the background. Poppy is smiling but Lucy looks sullen, as if she is there under sufferance.

'When did you take on looking after Poppy?' asks Tyler.

'When she was five months old,' answers Freya, blowing her nose. She suddenly seems dishevelled, her hair lank and her clothes faded, even though, apart from the tears, nothing about her outer appearance has changed. 'It was that or have her taken into care by social services. So we agreed, of course. We've never stopped Lucy seeing her but she didn't start coming until recently. What changed? I don't know. We thought she was starting to grow up at last. Before that she'd only come at Christmas, if she wasn't too out of it to know what day it was. Easter sometimes. That picture was taken a few weeks ago. We went to our apartment in Brighton, took Lucy along with us so that she could spend some time with Poppy. It was meant to be a happy, family time but, of course,

Lucy had to spoil it.' She looks up at Tyler fearfully, aware that she is speaking ill of the dead. 'She didn't really spoil things. She wasn't well, that was the trouble. She didn't know what she was doing a lot of the time.'

'How did she spoil things?'

'Arguments, constant arguments. Poppy cried most of the time, except when Lucy took her on that Ferris wheel. She enjoyed that.' Her tissue is starting to disintegrate so she wipes her nose with her sleeve.

'Do you want to phone your husband now?'

Freya picks up her mobile. The call is answered eventually. She gives Nicholas the news, struggling to find the words. Then she turns to Tyler and she says, 'He'll be here as soon as he can.'

Tyler tries to keep her talking, aiming to distance herself from the intensity of grief. 'You have a beautiful home,' she says, gauging that taste is important to Freya.

'Thank you. We have a chain of shops. *Nouveau*. We specialize in *decor*.'

It explains the sophistication of Freya's living space with its Cappellini furniture and quirky, coloured accents.

Poppy runs over to Freya who scoops her on to her lap. 'I put her to bed earlier,' she says. 'The hospital said to make sure she has plenty of rest but she won't sleep, she's up and down the stairs every five minutes so in the end I let her stay with me on the sofa. Takes after her mother. I never could get Lucy to stay in bed for long, she always wanted entertaining. I suppose I gave in to her too much. It's better to be firm. I don't think I've ever been firm enough.' She begins to cry again, half-forced, choking sobs. 'I need some water,' she says.

Tyler goes to fetch some from the kitchen. The space is huge, with designer pots and pans suspended from the ceiling on a rack the size of a dining table. She takes in the mosaic tiles in shiny cream and gold and the rounded fireclay sinks.

Freya is standing again when she returns. She seems calmer. Tyler asks if Lucy had a boyfriend.

'No,' says Freya, 'not for a while. I think her line of work precluded that.'

They fall silent until they hear the front door open. '*Nick!*' Freya runs towards him. She clutches his shirt, crying, 'She's dead,' over and over.

He takes hold of her hands tightly and removes them without looking at her. He walks towards Tyler. He is tall, greying and good-looking, with deep blue eyes. 'Who are you?' he says.

'I'm DC Natalie Tyler. I'm very sorry for your loss.'

He waves the condolences aside; he has no time for platitudes. 'Was it drugs?'

'We don't know yet.'

'I expect you'll need me to come and identify the body.'

'Yes, thank you, we will need formal identification.'

'I'll just be a moment, I need to put on a lighter jacket. It's warm for the time of year.'

Freya watches from an upstairs window as they leave the house. Poppy is standing beside her. Nicholas looks up at them and says, 'She can be very emotional, my wife. I'm sorry.'

'No apologies necessary, Mr Fields,' replies Tyler.

At the mortuary, Nicholas Fields stands behind the glass screen and identifies the body of his daughter. 'Yes, that's her.' He turns away, unable to look at Tyler, but he isn't quick enough; she sees his formidable need to conceal emotion in the set of his jaw and features so impassive they seem to have been Botoxed.

ELEVEN

Ryan has been declared fit for interview but Tyler is starting to think they shouldn't proceed; as the interview progresses it becomes evident that he's still addled from whatever pills he's been taking, and has an inability to string sentences together.

She and her DI sit opposite, making their postures neutral. He has been cautioned; Lucy's death has been confirmed as suspicious and they need to find out what he knows. In the silences, Tyler is more aware than usual of the shabbiness of the room, the crack across the ceiling and the rickety chairs that are never comfortable. Ryan's restlessness is making her restless too, as if it is contagious. The slowness of his speech is frustrating. Every time Tyler thinks they've found a way to penetrate his resistance, he shuts down again. He stinks of urine (even though his clothes have been taken to be analysed and he is wearing scrubs). That and skunk.

'Toilet,' he says.

They walk him down the corridor.

'I don't think he did it,' the DI mutters once they are alone. 'I doubt if he could punch his way out of a paper bag. He barely knows what day it is.'

Tyler also thinks it's unlikely that Ryan killed Lucy, but he's a potential witness. It's hard to tell if he knows something and is too scared to say it or if he was in a stupor throughout the attack and has no memory of it. Or perhaps he's buried it somewhere in the back of his mind because he doesn't want to face it.

Ryan comes out of the toilet. The stench causes Tyler to catch her breath.

'Gut rot,' he says.

He smells as if it is happening more literally than the phrase usually implies.

'Can I have a drink?'

Tyler gets him a cup of tea. Like his sister, he gulps it noisily and with enthusiasm. It's the first time he's shown any animation.

More questions and no answers. Tyler wonders if he's cleverer than they thought and is only playing at idiocy. Then she asks if Lucy had been with anyone that night.

A smile slowly spreads across his face. 'With me,' he says, as if he's only just remembered it.

'With you?'

'Yes.'

'What do you mean by *with you*? Are you saying you were in the house together?'

No answer.

'With *you*, Ryan?'

'With *me*.'

'Was she your girlfriend?'

He starts to cry, gut-wrenching sobs.

The DI rolls his eyes. 'Come on, Ryan, stop arsing about. How long was she with you? What was she doing while she was with you?'

He begins to sing. He is out of tune and rhythm but Tyler recognizes the hook of the song. 'That's Rick Ross, isn't it?' 'Hustlin''. Perhaps he's playing with them.

'Did Lucy like Rick Ross too?' asks the DI.

Tyler can't see where the answer to this question will get them, even if Ryan provides one.

The DI says: 'When you say Lucy was with you, do you mean you were having sex? Is that what you mean?'

There is a pause, then Ryan lets up a howl that seems to fill the building. He holds his head in his hands and then lets it go, smacking it on the desk. Blood seeps from the corner of his forehead. He tries to pull his paper trousers down. The DI hits the panic button. Six officers steam in. He's returned to his cell, kicking and screaming, all passivity abated.

'I take back what I said,' the DI tells Tyler in a low voice. 'He definitely could have done it.'

Twelve

She sees the two men enter the office and she knows, without being told, that they are detectives. They have come for her. She becomes motionless, holding her breath, as if her stillness will stop them seeing her. They stride past the photocopier and tell her she must go with them.

'Why?' she whispers, aware that her colleagues are starting to take an interest. 'What have I done?'

'We need you to assist us with our enquiries,' the taller man says.

She stands between them. Alice looks at her questioningly. Miss Ayres is watching her with her mouth wide open.

She thinks rapidly, going over possibilities. Maybe she was spotted near her old house, recognized by a former neighbour. That would be enough to get her pulled. Or perhaps it was breaking into the house with the monkey puzzle tree. They would have dusted for fingerprints and she'd been careless that day.

She walks quickly, matching the pace of the officers,

struggling to breathe. She feels the humiliation of being marched past colleagues; she can hear them whispering. Somebody starts to giggle. She glances at the people round her. They are staring at her. Their curiosity is palpable.

She knows it's over. Even if no one finds out who she really is, the shame of this moment will never leave her – she'll never be able to go back.

She doesn't speak in the car. There isn't any point. She looks at the officers in the mirror, trying to work out what they're thinking but their faces are blank. She would shed tears, but she won't let them see how frightened she feels. When the car stops, and she is made to get out, her legs barely carry her.

They bundle her into the building surreptitiously, via the back entrance, as if she isn't worthy of being at the front. They go up a dark staircase and into an office. They caution her: the words are the same as the ones they used when she was a child. She repeats them back to herself under her breath as if doing so will make all this seem real.

She refuses a solicitor. Lawyers didn't help the last time she was there. Why would it be different now? Before she can shut down the memory, she is sucked back into a small room with pictures of flowers on the walls. There is a can of Coke in her hand and a chocolate biscuit. She's enjoying herself, all the attention she is getting. The police are being kind, not suspecting what she's done, not able to believe it, perhaps. She is gorging on their kindness, savouring each smile, every warm word. She remembers the way it had been afterwards, when they'd decided it was her; the looks of disgust on their faces, their shock. The withdrawal of all the softness.

She'd thought her mum would come. She'd been sure she would. But she hadn't. Some woman she didn't even know had been brought in to be her responsible adult, as they'd called it. They kept asking about Kerry. 'I didn't do it,' she'd said, over and over. It wasn't even her, how could it have been? Children don't die. She *couldn't* have done it.

She is feeling that same disbelief now. Why is she here? Why won't they believe her? What will she do if she gets put away again?

Her hands are busy all the time, tapping, stroking her hair, working their way down to the top of her mouth. She barely knows that she is doing it. They keep on questioning her, saying things that seem impossible. 'Lucy's *dead*?' she keeps repeating.

'Are you saying you knew her, Samantha?'

They are using her other name but she can tell they know who she really is. The room is full of tension. The officers are fascinated by her and repelled, both at once.

'I can't believe she's dead,' she says flatly. 'How did it happen?'

'You tell us,' says the senior officer. 'Your DNA's all over the body.'

'It wasn't me, I didn't kill her.'

'We haven't said she was killed by anyone.'

'But it's what you mean. Or else why would you be questioning me like this? I didn't kill her,' she repeats.

'That's what you said when you murdered little Kerry.'

'That was different.'

'Different?'

She doesn't answer.

'How did your DNA come to be on Lucy if you didn't touch her?'

'I don't know.' She spreads her fingers across her forehead and stares at the table. Then she starts tapping again.

'Can you tell us where you were on the night of the murder?'

'Which night?'

'The fourteenth.'

'What day was that?'

'Tuesday.'

'I'm not sure.'

'You're not sure?'

'Just a minute, I have to think.' She covers her forehead with her hands again. 'I was at work. Then I went home.' It's barely more than a whisper.

'What time was this?'

'I stayed late at work, until about seven. I got home just before eight.'

'Was anyone else there?'

'Cheryl Ayres, my boss was with me at work. No one was at home, I live on my own.'

'So no one can confirm you were at home?'

She says nothing.

The second officer says, 'How did you know Lucy Fields?'

She looks up for the first time. 'We were in the same unit

when we were young – Whytefields Lodge, in Surrey. I think it's been closed down now.'

The interviewers look interested. 'And you kept in contact?'

'No, not really, I mean, not for a long time. We met again by accident after my release.'

'Where did you meet?'

'Near the probation office.'

'And did you ever go to her flat?'

'Once or twice, and we went to McDonald's a few times.'

'Why?'

'*Why?* Because we knew each other.'

'The terms of your licence prevent you from having contact with former inmates from any of the institutions you've been in,' the senior officer says.

She shrugs expressively, conveying how little she cares about this.

'So what happened? Did she threaten to go to the press, tell everyone she knew Michelle Cameron? Sell her story? Was she out to expose you? Did you decide to stop her?'

'No, nothing like that. She hardly even remembered ...' She begins to cry slow, silent tears. 'I didn't kill her. I wouldn't have.'

'Your DNA is on the body.'

'She was round at mine a couple of weeks ago. She was upset. I put my arm round her. Could that be it?' she asks hopefully. 'I mean, can DNA be left from touching someone? Is that possible? I mean if she didn't shower or something?'

There is no response. More tears fall. 'I don't understand,' she says.

'Look, you're not stupid,' the senior officer says. 'We have the evidence. Soon the press will get hold of the story. And once that happens, you'll be better off in here than outside. You know what kind of frenzy this will create. The public will be lining up to have a piece of you. Whatever you've done, we can protect you, but only if you start telling us the truth.'

She listens silently. She isn't sure what to believe. Would people really line up to have a piece of her or is he making it up, just to get her to admit that she harmed Lucy?

'Just tell the truth, that's all we're asking.'

'I am telling the truth,' she says sullenly. '*I am telling the truth*. I don't want to speak to you anymore.' She sits back in her chair, arms folded. She feels like a stubborn child.

'Okay,' says the senior officer, stating the time and turning off the recorder, 'we're done for now.'

'I've got a dog,' she says. 'Can someone sort him out? He'll starve to death if I'm kept in here. He'll be really thirsty.' She imagines Otis, dying in the flat, thinking she has abandoned him.

'The sooner you co-operate, the sooner you can leave.'

'But I haven't done anything. How can I co-operate if it wasn't me?' She gets up slowly, stumbling towards the door. She doesn't want to be returned to the cell and its walls; it reminds her too much of the past.

She sits on a hard, narrow bed, shivering, a blanket wrapped round her shoulders. She remembers the expression on Alice's face as she was marched past the photocopier, and Miss Ayres's open mouth. They talk about open-mouthed astonishment, but she'd never actually seen it in action.

They will be laughing at her, in the office, telling each other they knew there was something evil about her. She was always such a liar, they will say. The detectives don't believe her, they think she's a liar, too. She'll be sent back to prison, it doesn't matter that she hasn't done anything wrong. What will she do now? Stay calm, she tells herself. *Think of nice things.* An image of Otis pops into her head. His tail is wagging. She feels the warmth of his fur as he nestles into her lap. She remembers the view from her balcony, the way that London stretches out before her, its towers and domes and the coil of the river. She thinks of bus rides, and the Tube. She sits in her flat, tea lights flickering, a plate of biscuits beside her on the table. She is reading or watching TV. The flat is clean. The cushions are plump. The new sofa creaks reassuringly as she picks up the remote to change the channel. It's quiet but it isn't lonely.

But she isn't at home, she's in a prison cell, as if all the time since her release has never been. But she was released – she'd had a taste of freedom; how much harder would it be to have that freedom taken from her for a second time? She would never see Otis again or feel his fur against her skin. No walks with him tugging on the lead. No sunlight. No rain. No sound of the wind in the trees. No music playing through her head-phones, soothing her, exciting her, telling her who she is. No sweet biscuits to savour as they melt upon her tongue.

She'll be taken to trial again. She thinks about how solemn

it all was, how much trouble she knew she was in, everything feeling heavy and dark, unreal like a bad dream. Everyone was angry with her, really angry, not shouting, but angry in that cold, hard way that's a lot more frightening. There was a man in court, Adam Kenyon he was called, the worst of the angry people. He kept staring at her, telling everyone how bad she was, all the naughty things she'd done. He said she'd killed Kerry. He kept on repeating it in his firm, posh voice, adding long words she didn't understand, and she wasn't allowed to argue or tell them that she hadn't done it. She remembers the judge saying she'd shown no remorse. What's remorse? she'd said, but no one had heard her. No one is hearing her now.

In the cell, cold and trembling, she tries to take a breath but she's forgotten how. A sob becomes a cry as she sees the end of everything; she won't be going home again.

THIRTEEN

Lucy's death has been confirmed as murder. She was smothered: fur fabric fibres have been found round her nose and mouth.

Tyler is called into DI Henderson's office. She is told, in the strictest confidence, that Michelle Cameron's DNA has been found on Lucy Fields' body so she has been brought in and interviewed under caution. Tyler is considered reliable and not given to idle talk (by which Henderson means she keeps herself to herself and has no real friends at the station). He is sure he can count on her discretion.

A search warrant has been obtained for her flat in the hope of finding the item that could have been used to kill Lucy Fields – a brown fur cushion, or a throw. Her colleagues are not to be told of Michelle Cameron's involvement, nor are they to know that it's her flat they will be searching. As far as they are concerned, they are dealing with Samantha Robinson.

Tyler knows who Michelle Cameron is, of course. She remembers the case from when she was young. The Gosling

Girl, the press had called her; a child killer, who had excited endless media attention. She wonders what she's like. Hard to envisage a child with the capacity to end a life.

She drives to the flat in south-west London slightly behind the rest of the team, her usual position, not in terms of ability to do the job but in terms of the way she is perceived: as someone who isn't one of the gang. She remembers what the sergeant had said to her at training college: that she was bright – though nowhere near as bright as you think you are, he'd added with a sneer – but way too mouthy and prone to insubordination. Any other recruit would have been kicked off the course as unsuitable, but they had to keep her, he'd told her, because she was a woman, and because of the colour of her skin. And it looked like she batted for the other side as well. 'All you need to do now is lose a leg and become a vegan and then the world's your oyster,' he'd muttered as he'd walked away from her. She'd stayed in the job, largely out of defiance, refusing to let him win, but he had won, in a way, because after that she'd become a lot more circumspect, more careful about the battles she picked. She smiles ruefully to herself. If she'd decked him there and then the way she'd wanted to, she wouldn't be here now, outside Michelle Cameron's flat. Perhaps she should have done it.

The block is an ugly high-rise building, stark and grey. She wonders what she will find there.

As she goes through the front door, she is greeted by a small white dog who is desperately pleased to see them. It's been on its own for well over twenty-four hours and has left a mess in the hall. The smell makes Tyler feel queasy as she steps over it. She takes the dog into the kitchen and gives it some water. It's thirsty; it drinks without pausing for breath. She finds a canister of dried food and puts some in a bowl. It's devoured in a matter of seconds. She gives it more. It licks the bowl clean. She makes a call and arranges to have the animal taken to a kennel. She's told it will be at least a couple of hours before anyone will be free to collect it.

She isn't sure what she had expected to see in the flat but she is surprised by the normality of the place, and its neat-ness. There is a sofa in the living room. The fabric is loud: there are orange and pink flowers with thick green stems on a grey background; not her taste at all, but it gives even more colour to the yellow walls and the pale blue skirting boards. It's homely, with candle holders and a mock-sheepskin rug on the floor. The woody scent of a reed diffuser, that had been masked by the dog shit on the floor, now starts to come through. An old copy of *Glamour* magazine rests on an orange-pine side table. There is a pottery vase beside it with some red artificial flowers that are more convincing than most. Some postcards are pinned to the door of a small built-in cupboard, carefully arranged. She looks at them more closely. They are images of the city's landmarks: the Tower of London; St Paul's Cathedral; Covent Garden Piazza; the Imperial War Museum. China dog ornaments, that resemble the real version in the kitchen, are resting on the windowsill.

There is one bedroom with a double bed. There are books: an ex-library copy of *I Know Why the Caged Bird Sings* sits on a rickety shelf that's been attached amateurishly to the wall. The trilogy, *His Dark Materials*, leans beside it. The spine is broken. A battered copy of *Catch-22* is also visible. The bedside cabinet contains paracetamol, some hairbands, a box of tampons and several bars of chocolate. She closes the drawer quickly. She has never liked rummaging through other people's things; it always seemed sordid. An old suitcase at the foot of the bed functions as a blanket box; there is a spare sheet, a duvet cover and a couple of towels. This is a teenage room with posters of boy bands on the walls and a clutter of old make-up arranged in rows on a small table. There is no wardrobe, just a silver rail on castors with a few clothes: a dark red jacket; jeans; two grey hooded tops; an orange dress and a couple of short skirts, one pink, one purple. The shoes are lined up beneath it: trainers, black sandals and a pair of blue high heels with bows on the front.

The dog barks. It's been tied to a door handle by a lead that was found in the hall while Tyler's colleagues complete the search of the kitchen. There is no sign of anything that could have been used to smother Lucy Fields they conclude, with disappointment.

It's obvious to Tyler that this will be a high-profile case. Now she understands the tension that filled the office earlier, and the scurrying back and forth that her boss has been doing for most of the day. He'd been making more phone calls than usual, too, holed up in his office, waving away their attempts to speak to him with impatience. Management had arrived and there was speculation about that – redundancies, perhaps. But it was Michelle Cameron.

She'd seen a number of people who had killed in the course of her career as a detective. They'd usually been men, dull and belligerent, their actions spurred by drink and the need to control a girlfriend or wife. Sometimes it was some small slight in a pub that had led to a drunken killer punch they barely even remembered. And then there were those in their teens or early twenties, who had knifed someone in a fight or a gang dispute: quietly sullen, muttering *no comment*, resigned to the fact that it all had got out of hand. But a child? She'd never come across anything like that. Tyler doesn't believe in evil, but something must have been deeply wrong with Michelle Cameron. Yet there are no indicators in the flat of the pathology that must have fuelled her actions.

There is a knock. A woman has arrived to take charge of the dog. Tyler frees it from the kitchen and hands it over. The last of her colleagues departs from the flat. Tyler checks that everything has been left as they found it and carefully locks the front door.

FOURTEEN

So much for secrecy. It seems that everyone now knows that Michelle Cameron is being held in custody. Tyler goes, along with the rest of her colleagues, to catch a glimpse of her as she is escorted from the cells, even though she promised herself she wouldn't be part of the circus all this has become. Cameron bears no resemblance to the skinny child from the photograph of more than fourteen years before; she has put on weight and her hair is now long. She looks surprisingly ordinary and flinches as she catches sight of the officers roaming around on the pretext of having something to do in her vicinity. She looks down again, covering her eyes with her fingers, and ducks towards the interview room. Unable to see, she misjudges the distance and bangs her head on the edge of the door. The sound of laughter follows her.

Tyler is embarrassed by the childish spite of her colleagues. Her own curiosity embarrasses her. She sits in the canteen looking out of the window, wanting to distance herself but seeing the impossibility of that. She's realized that the DI sees her as a resource. He will continue to involve her now, to mitigate any potential suggestion that the handling of the situation has been influenced by racial factors.

She gets a message; the DI wants to see her urgently. And now it all starts, she thinks.

She stands in his office, feeling uncomfortable. He speaks quickly, anger in his tone. In spite of their best efforts to keep it under wraps, the news that Michelle Cameron has been helping police with their enquiries is about to break. There must be a leak, he tells her. 'Did you have anything to do with this?'

'No, of course I didn't,' she answers angrily.

He nods, but she can't tell if he believes her. He continues wearily: 'We don't want the Gosling family hearing that Michelle Cameron is in custody again when they switch on the news. Go and break it to them and make sure they know we're in no way to blame.'

It's early Saturday morning so there is little traffic. Tyler drives slowly, trying to give herself time to think; she's had little space to prepare herself mentally for the visit. She stops at a zebra crossing and watches a family of three small boys straggle across the road, resolutely avoiding their mother's hands. She pops some gum in her mouth and wonders how the Goslings will react to the news. With anger, most probably. Their daughter is dead but Michelle Cameron is all too alive. They're divorced now – nothing has the potential to divide a family more than the murder of a child, she thinks – but they were happy once. She remembers the photos that still appear in the papers at regular intervals. At the time of Kerry's death, they lived in a pretty, new-build cul-de-sac with a neat front lawn and a cherry tree that blossomed in the spring. Now Julie Gosling's home is a tower block in Lewisham. She'll go there first, get it over with.

She parks the car and walks across the yard. Mrs Gosling doesn't respond to her attempts to get into the building so she slips in after a group of teenage boys and enters the lift. It stops at the third floor and refuses to move any further, so she follows the boys up the remaining flights of stairs, ignoring their lewd mutterings.

She knocks on Mrs Gosling's door. She opens it a little, leaving on the chain, and says, 'Who is it?'

'I'm DC Natalie Tyler. Can I come in please, Mrs Gosling? I just want a word if that's okay.'

'What's it about?' she asks.

'Can I come in? It won't take long.'

As Julie Gosling opens the door, Tyler recognizes her from pictures she's seen, even though she's older now. Her face is pinched and pale, and her eyes won't alight on anything for more than a moment. They go into the living room and Tyler sits on a sofa that's too big for the space. Julie sits opposite, scraping her forearm with her fingernails. She has scars from the times she's dug so deep she's split the skin.

She talks rapidly, barely drawing breath, as if she'll never be able to summon the energy to speak again if she stops. 'It's about Kerry, isn't it?' she says. She lights a cigarette and it hangs from her fingers, its tip slowly turning to ash that drops unnoticed on the carpet. The room is dark and the air is stale and dishes of half-eaten food are piled up on the coffee table. There was a small TV that is probably on all the time but seldom watched; it flickers in the background.

My little girl, she keeps saying, like a mantra. And each time she says it, she holds out a photo of Kerry, the one that was in all the papers, making Tyler look, as if she hasn't shown her several times already.

Tyler delivers the news. She can't be sure that Julie has absorbed it so she says it again: 'Michelle Cameron has been helping us with our investigation of a case, nothing to do with Kerry. The press have got on to it and there will be reports in tomorrow's papers.'

'My little girl,' Julie repeats. 'Where is she, Michelle Cameron?'

'She's in custody.'

'Where?'

'I can't tell you that,' says Tyler.

She expects Julie to argue that she has a right to know, but instead she sighs and looks out of the window. 'We used to have her round to tea, Shelley Cameron,' she says, her words slower than before.

'Is there anyone I can call for you?'

She shakes her head.

'A friend?'

She shakes her head again. 'They never knew what to say.' She wanders over to the window and peers out, speaking with her back to Tyler. 'I only took my eye off her for a moment. The baby was crying and needed changing; he'd been sick, too, so I took him upstairs. I should have taken

Kerry but she would have wanted to help the way they do at that age, she would have been in everything and I didn't want her catching what the baby had. Shannon, my oldest, was keeping an eye on her while she was in the garden, so I thought it would be all right.'

'It wasn't your fault, it really wasn't,' Tyler says, but she isn't listening.

'I sorted out the baby and brought him downstairs again, but I couldn't see Kerry. I said to Shannon, what have you done with her, thinking they were playing a game, but Shannon thought she was still in the garden. I even looked in the shed, but there was no sign of her. I didn't panic, I thought, she'll have gone back in the house. I went in every room, calling her, thinking she was hiding, just being naughty like little ones are, but she didn't come out.

'I still get letters. Every time it's in the news again, the letters come. Condolences, most of them, but then there are the ones that say I shouldn't have left her, my little girl, shouldn't have let her out of my sight. Of course I shouldn't have, I know that, you take your eyes off them for a second and they're gone.'

She turns round, her face expressionless. Tyler wants her to stop talking – there is something deeply unsettling about the way she is – but she doesn't. 'Shelley used to like fish cakes, same as Kerry,' she says. 'I used to make them from scratch, with proper fish and potatoes. They say fish is good for the brain. Maybe I should eat some.' She laughs and holds the cigarette to her forearm, letting it rest.

Tyler snatches it from her fingers and stubs it out in the full ashtray on the coffee table. 'What's the name of your doctor's surgery? I'll give them a ring, get someone to come out.'

Julie shakes her head, using her fingernails to score her skin once more. 'I should have been someone different. Nobody gave me a new identity. I'm the woman whose child was killed by Michelle Cameron, that's all I am.'

'I'll make some tea,' says Tyler.

There is no electric kettle in the kitchen, just an old-fashioned metal one with a whistle in the spout. She has to remove some of the dirty dishes from the sink in order to fill it. Julie follows her there. She looks embarrassed. 'No one comes,' she says. 'I know I should keep it nicer than this, I just can't seem to get round to it.' Then she asks, 'Did she take another child?'

'She's just giving us information at the moment, but you know what the media's like, they've got on to it and we just wanted you to know so that it wouldn't come as too much of a shock to see her name in the news again.'

'*Shelley*. I used to feel sorry for her, have her round to tea, try to feed her up a bit. Where is she now?'

'I'm sorry, I can't say.'

'Does she know why she did it?'

'I don't know,' says Tyler.

'She was only a tot herself. Why would she do a thing like that? I try to understand, but I can't.'

The kettle starts to whistle. Julie jumps. 'Sorry, I'm all over the place,' she says. She laughs; as before, the sound is vacant.

Tyler wonders if she would be more amenable to a visit from her doctor now she's talking more rationally, so she asks again but Julie doesn't answer. Instead, she squats on the floor and places her head on her knees so Tyler can no longer see her face.

She passes her the mug of tea awkwardly, touching her shoulder to let her know it's there but Julie is so deep inside herself that the contact seems intrusive.

She takes the mug blindly, still resting her head on her knees. She places it on the floor beside her. 'Please go now,' she says.

'Are you sure you want me to leave?' asks Tyler.

She nods.

Tyler hesitates and then presses a card into her hand. 'Ring me on this number if there's anything I can do,' she says.

Tyler lets herself out and walks down to the car. She realizes she's been holding her breath since leaving the house, keeping herself reined in. She leans against the side of the vehicle, trying to stay calm. She pictures Julie gouging pieces out of herself because the physical pain is so much easier to bear than the loneliness of grief. She imagines the press camping on her doorstep, making her relive the moments when she first heard the news of her daughter's death.

She drives extra carefully to Martin Gosling's house, aware of how distracted she is. The concrete decay of Lewisham morphs into suburban greenery: chrysanthemums appear in neat, well-tended gardens. The Goslings live in a semi on a quiet road. Martin was a builder, it said that in the papers. The house has recently had a loft conversion and double-glazed windows have been installed.

A slight woman with dark hair in a ponytail lets her in. Tyler introduces herself. 'Tina Gosling,' she replies. She looks wound up, unaccustomed to police visits, but she leads Tyler into the lounge where Martin and two identical prepubescent boys are sprawled on the sofa in pyjamas, watching television. Every now and then a toddler, who is lining bears up against the wall, taps Martin's knee, wanting him to look. He resembles the pictures Tyler has seen of Kerry.

Martin gets up and greets her. 'Sorry about the PJs. It's my day off.'

The twin boys glance at each other anxiously, as if they are expecting to be accused of something.

'Can I speak to you alone, please, Mr Gosling?' asks Tyler.

'What's this about? Is it the boys? Has our neighbour complained again? They're not bad kids, they just get out of hand sometimes.'

'It's nothing to do with the boys, but I need a word with you *alone.*'

Tina picks up the toddler and says, 'Come on guys, upstairs now, you need to get ready for football practice.' They follow her reluctantly, stopping off in the kitchen for cereal bars to take with them.

A woman who is probably in her mid-twenties and a boy in his mid-teens come bounding down the stairs. 'What's going on?' the woman asks.

'This is Shannon,' says Martin, 'and that's Aaron.'

'What's going on?' repeats Shannon, arms folded. 'What's this about?'

'Mr Gosling,' says Tyler, 'this is private, I'd really like to speak to you alone.'

Martin turns off the television and says: 'It's her, isn't it? Michelle Cameron.' He puts an arm round each of his older children. 'Aaron was just a baby when Kerry died. Shannon was two years older than Michelle Cameron. They've lived most of their lives in the shadow of what happened. They need to hear this – I don't want to keep any secrets from them.'

Aaron stands stiff and angry. Shannon stares at Tyler, her face bleak with confusion and fear. She hoists up the baggy jeans that are starting to slip down her hips. The gesture is childlike in its awkwardness.

'I just need to tell you, Mr Gosling, that Michelle Cameron has been assisting us with some enquiries,' says Tyler. 'The story's breaking this morning. We just want you to be prepared.'

'What's happened? Has she hurt another child?'

'It's all right, Dad,' says Shannon.

'No, it's not all right,' says Aaron. 'They let that bitch Cameron out and now she's killed again.'

'Aaron, don't swear,' his father says.

'We didn't have a say in her release,' Tyler told them. 'The decision was made by the Home Office.' She is quoting her boss, something she'd promised herself she would never do.

Martin Gosling suddenly looks tired.

'Dad,' says Shannon, clutching at the sleeve of his shirt.

He pulls her to him and gives her a quick hug. 'Best go upstairs now, Shannon, give Tina a hand with the boys.'

She doesn't move. Instead, she sits down on the sofa defiantly. Aaron joins her there. 'Have you told Mum?' he asks.

'Yes, she knows,' says Tyler.

'How did she take it?' asks Shannon. 'I'd better go round, Dad, she'll be distraught.'

'No, leave it, Shannon. You can't handle her when she's upset. Tina will go later.'

'But Dad—'

'I said Tina will go.'

'Tina will go where?' asks Tina, appearing in the doorway with the youngest child.

'Michelle Cameron's in the news again. Shannon's worried about Julie. I said you'd go and take care of her.'

Tina nods. Aaron makes space and Tina joins them on the sofa, placing the youngest on her knee. She takes Shannon's hand. 'So what is it the papers will be saying about Cameron?' she asks.

'We can't give you any details, I'm afraid,' says Tyler.

'So what's the point of coming round here then?' asks Aaron.

'Let's switch on the news,' says Shannon, in support of her brother. She grabs the remote control and flicks through the channels. A man is solemnly pronouncing on the weather. Upstairs, the boys begin to roar, sounds of temper and frustration. Tina hurries to their bedroom.

'Will the papers be writing about Kerry again?' asks Shannon in a low voice.

'It's very likely,' answers Tyler. She pictures the angelic, blonde-haired child whose face is now synonymous with innocence destroyed. The papers only seemed to have one photograph between them and it circulates endlessly, freezing her forever in a single, violent moment, as if that was all her life had ever been.

'And will she be put away for good, this time?' asks Aaron.

'I really don't know.'

Aaron stands up. He looks as if he wants to hit her. Shannon pulls him back to the sofa.

'I'm sorry, he gets angry,' says Martin.

'Don't you apologize for me, Dad,' says Aaron. 'What's wrong with you all? Doesn't anyone care except me?'

Kerry's face flashes on the television screen. They all fall silent. Michelle Cameron's face follows, not the one she has now, but her young, thin face. A newsreader says, 'Michelle Cameron, often referred to as the Gosling Girl, is currently being held in custody ...'

Aaron jumps to his feet. Shannon pulls him down on the sofa again. 'What right does she have to be called Gosling? It's our name, *Kerry's* name,' he says.

'I'm sorry this has happened,' Tyler answers quietly.

'Just go,' Aaron tells her.

'Aaron, stop this,' says Martin, 'it's not her fault.'

'It's okay, Mr Gosling. If you have any questions or concerns, don't hesitate to phone.' Tyler produces her card, just as she had done for Julie.

Martin puts it in his pocket. He starts to walk her to the door.

'It's okay, I'll see myself out,' says Tyler.

She leaves to the dispassionate tone of the newsreader recounting the events of fourteen years before, when little Kerry Gosling, aged four, was killed by Michelle Cameron, aged ten.

FIFTEEN

DI Henderson tells Tyler that she will be with him for Cameron's second interview. She knows her presence as a black officer will be designed to encourage Cameron to speak. She is briefed about the way the interview will be conducted. She is told to remain silent until Henderson gives her the nod.

As she listens, Tyler considers Michelle Cameron. If she knew they were talking about her, weighing her up, would she mind? If she could see Tyler sitting with her DI, fingers wound tightly around her mug of coffee, sipping tentatively, speaking her name in a low voice, wondering what makes her tick, how she could have done the thing she'd done, would she smile, gratified by the attention, or would she wish that people could see the real her and not recoil from it?

Tyler and her boss continue to talk conspiratorially. Henderson seems pleased to be part of the drama. If Michelle Cameron could see them, perhaps she would want to ask why it is so hard to understand. Or perhaps she knows why: *evil*. That's the word Henderson is using, a word that would make Cameron stare at them, bemused, unable to recognize herself. They are coming to conclusions, or the DI is; Tyler is slower to decide. She walks to the door, picturing Kerry the way people always do, no longer seeing the skinny girl with the flattened Afro hair and the crooked smile, but seeing instead the toddler with the blonde curly hair and the rosy red cheeks.

The custody period has been extended in the light of Cameron's past. She is sitting in the same place as before, but whereas she'd been moving constantly throughout the last interview, she is perfectly still now, like an animal straining to hear predators. She still hasn't asked for a solicitor.

'I didn't kill her,' she states, for the umpteenth time. 'I would never have hurt Lucy. You do believe me, don't you?'

'I want to believe you. What can you tell me to help me to do that?' asks the DI.

Michelle Cameron's face is pale and the skin beneath her eyes looks bruised, as if she has been crying. Yet at the same time, she seems composed, almost too much so, except for the gestures she starts to make with her hands, surreptitiously under the table.

'I didn't do it,' she repeats. 'Please, just tell me you know that.' She is gazing at Tyler now, as if they have something in common, willing her to say that she believes her.

Tyler says nothing so Cameron falls silent.

'Did you like Lucy?' asks Tyler after a while, picking up her cue from her boss.

'We were friends,' Cameron replies, though she had to think about it.

'What was it that you liked about her?'

Cameron's head drops. She begins to twist her fingers again beneath the desk. 'She made me laugh,' she replies.

'What kinds of things did you laugh about?'

She smiles at the memories. It transforms her face; she looks pretty. 'Lots of stuff. People. Things.'

'And did she like you?'

Cameron considers this for a moment. Tyler thinks how measured her communications are. Covering herself? Unsure who to trust?

'I think she liked me,' she replies.

'But you're not sure?' says the DI.

'How do you know if somebody likes you?'

The DI doesn't seem sure how to respond to this, so he says, 'Where did the two of you meet?'

'At Whytefields Lodge. I've already told you that.'

'How old were you?'

'I was thirteen, I think. About that. She was a bit older, maybe fourteen and a half?'

'Why was she there?'

'I think she knifed some bloke. We didn't really talk about that. We just had a laugh together. She could tell me things about what it was like outside. We could do girl stuff, you know? Make-up, things like that. The other kids were much older or they were boys, except for Carly Hughes, she was younger and ... sort of different, so no one bothered with her. There wasn't a girl anywhere near my age until Lucy came.'

'You said earlier that you last saw her about a week ago. Where was that? At her house?'

'No, not that time.'

'Where then?' asks Tyler softly. She has been told to sound friendly, to encourage Cameron to talk.

She hesitates for a moment or two. Then she says, 'We were on Clapham Common. There's a café near there and they have good doughnuts. And tablecloths, proper ones in Wedgwood blue. I like colours. The world would be very dark if there was no colour in it. You don't like colours, do you? Your clothes are all grey.'

Tyler ignores this and says, 'Do you remember what you and Lucy talked about that day, Samantha?' She hopes that Cameron will see that by using her current name she is making reference to her new identity, appearing to see her as the person she has become, rather than the person she was then. She wants Cameron to believe her guilt is not assumed.

She becomes lively as she recalls the conversation she'd had with Lucy. 'She talked about Ryan, this bloke she knew. She said he fancied her, followed her around like a little lost puppy.' She laughs suddenly, a loud, exaggerated laugh; it stands at odds with the earlier softness of her voice and the air of gentleness she'd been at pains to cultivate. 'She said he was boring and he had no money so she definitely wasn't going to end up getting off with him.' She is speaking more confidently now that the focus has moved away from her. The DI decides to bring it back. 'Why do you think we found your DNA on Lucy's body?'

She folds her arms and turns away a little. 'I've told you, I don't know.'

'Lucy talked to you about Ryan, you said. What did *you* talk about?'

She takes a strand of her hair and wraps it round her finger.

'Nothing, really. I mainly listened. I'm good at listening. I wouldn't have killed Lucy. She was the only friend I had.'

'That must be lonely,' says Tyler.

'I'm not *lonely*,' she replies hurriedly.

'No, but being alone isn't easy, is it? Did Lucy know who you really were, did she know you as Michelle Cameron? You see, I'm imagining that it must be very isolating, having to be somebody else, scared all the time that someone will work out who you really are. And having a friend, just one person who knows the truth about you, that's a really important bond.'

'That's why I couldn't have hurt her. She was the only person who knew, the only person I could talk to without worrying I'd give myself away, apart from probation officers ... and psychologists, but they're people who are assessing me all of the time. It wasn't like that with Lucy. I could be free with her. And now she isn't here anymore. Don't you see? I couldn't lose that. How could I deliberately lose that?'

The babyish tone has gone and has been replaced by a harsher, more abrasive one. The calm is evaporating, too.

The DI says: 'And yet, it must also have been scary, having

someone know you, someone like Lucy, who was off her face half the time. How could you be sure she wouldn't sell the story to someone? She must have needed the money. She was a prostitute, she'd have sold anything to anyone.'

'She didn't know who I was.'

'Come on,' says the DI, 'which is it? A moment ago you said she was the only person who knew who you really were. Did she know or didn't she?'

She spreads her hands as if despairing of their denseness. 'She didn't remember. She knew, but she didn't remember. Don't you see? It wasn't that important to her. Who I used to be didn't even register with Lucy. I didn't kill her,' she says again. 'I know you think I must have done because of Kerry, but that was such a long time ago. I'm not who I was then. I don't just mean my name is different, I mean I'm not the same. I'm not that person anymore.'

Her tone is flat as she says this. It's as if she is repeating something she believes they want to hear.

The DI tries to get her back to thinking about Lucy. 'You said last time you met it was on Clapham Common. That's a trek from where you both live. What were you doing there?'

'Lucy liked it there. I had a day off so I went with her. We talked.'

'When you and Lucy finished talking, what did you do next?'

'Nothing. We just went home.'

'You took her back to your flat?'

'No. She went home and I went home. We were going to

stay on the common for a bit longer but then it started rain-ing.' The expression on her face changes. She looks excited. 'I think I know what happened,' she says. 'I've remembered. It was pouring down, really heavy rain, and Lucy had on this sleeveless dress and I had a jacket and a sweatshirt, you know, a sweatshirt with a zip, and I gave it to her to wear and I said give it back next time we see each other. She was wearing a sweatshirt, wasn't she, a pink sweatshirt with a hood and a zip?'

Tyler recalls Lucy's body. She remembers the low-cut green top she'd been wearing and the pale pink hooded sweatshirt that had partially covered it, the one that had been the same colour as the threadbare carpet. It had been too big for her, of course, and if it had been hers she would have chosen some-thing more fitted, more on trend. 'Interview suspended at 11.05 a.m.' the DI says, as he switches off the recorder.

Tyler escorts Cameron back to the cells. As the door is being locked, she hears the words 'black bitch' muttered after her.

A spike of anger surges through her. She hears racist slurs so often from the people she brings into custody that she barely even notices anymore but this is the first time she's encountered it in anyone who isn't white. It puzzles her. Why would Michelle Cameron, with her light-brown face and Afro hair (straightened though it is) have said such a thing? She feels hurt too – disproportionately so, she thinks – but then she reminds herself that Michelle Cameron is of no significance to her. She's just another con.

Cameron's story is confirmed by forensics. The DNA could

have come from a borrowed sweatshirt. She is innocent then, most likely – of Lucy's murder at least.

Tyler needs a cigarette even though she seldom smokes. As she stands in the yard, she becomes aware that a crowd is gathering opposite the station. A chant begins, building slowly to a crescendo: *Michelle Cameron* on constant repeat. The picture of her, taken when she was ten, is on placards that demand permanent imprisonment: LIFE FOR A LIFE, they state.

Tyler hurries back inside. It seems that Cameron's details are all over the internet – her new name, where she's living now, the fact that she's there at the station. There's even a photo of her as she is now.

Henderson is in his office. 'She won't be our concern for too much longer. We should be able to release her shortly,' he tells Tyler. 'At least then we'll be rid of that mob outside as well.'

'We can't send her back home, not if her details are known,' Tyler tells him incredulously. She thinks she is stating the obvious.

'She murdered a child,' he replies. 'When you commit that kind of crime, there are consequences.'

She is silent, trying not to show how uneasy she feels about what he is saying. 'You've seen them outside, their anger. Anything could happen to her.'

The DI's phone rings. He gestures that she should wait outside his office. She goes to sit at her desk while he takes the call. After a few minutes, she is called into his office again. There is tension in Henderson's face. 'As far as upstairs are concerned, we're to pull out all the stops to keep her safe,' he tells her. 'You're to be her liaison officer. They're organizing a place of safety for her but it can't be done tonight. She's to remain here, voluntarily, of course, until it's sorted. They're blaming us, saying we acted prematurely bringing her in. And then there's the leak. It definitely came from this department, they're investigating it already.'

The DI starts talking about how much all this will cost. Tyler screens him out, angry at his crassness. The cost to management could be huge, literally and metaphorically, so Michelle Cameron won't be the focus of their efforts to protect. Their reputations will be all they'll want to salvage.

Sixteen

In the cell, she hears her name, *Michelle Cameron*, called out endlessly. Who are they? Why are they repeating her name, her old name, not the one she has now? There is rage in the way they are chanting it.

And then she understands. They know she has been arrested again. They know where she is, and like the police, the mob outside thinks she murdered Lucy Fields. In her mind's eye, she sees them storming through the station, breaking down doors, dragging her from the cell, putting their boots to her head. She curls up on the narrow bed. She doesn't know what to do with herself. She scrapes the skin on her arms with her fingernails until they bleed. She can't absorb what's happening.

She doesn't sleep. She doesn't dare. She dozes momentarily, thumb in her mouth, and then jerks upright with a start. There is a man squatting on the bed, his breath, warm and stale, upon her face. His hands close around her throat. She leaps up and runs to the door, crying out in fear. The custody sergeant arrives and speaks to her calmly, insisting that there's no one there, no one could have got inside the cell. She doesn't believe him. She is sick, once, in the dirty toilet bowl. She drinks thirstily from the water they've provided.

In the morning, in the light, she is calmer, though she can't get warm. She pulls the scratchy blanket round her. She misses Otis. She wants to feel him beside her, to bury her face in his fur. She wants to feel his warm body. She raises her head as Tyler enters the cell, hoping it's time to go home.

Tyler sits on the bed beside her. 'You can't return to your flat, I'm afraid,' she tells her. 'Your details were leaked, so it isn't safe for you anymore. We've found somewhere else for you to be.'

She becomes agitated, close to tears. 'I have to go back to the flat,' she says, 'it's where I live, and what about Otis? He won't want to be away.'

'Who's Otis?'

She observes the expression on Tyler's face: studied neutrality, the look people often wear when they are trying to conceal their dislike of her. 'He's my dog,' she tells her sullenly.

'I've seen your dog, he's safe, he was taken to a kennel,' Tyler tells her. 'He'll be brought to the new place.'

'But I'll be able to go back home in a few days, won't I? You don't mean I have to move out for ever, do you?'

'I'm really sorry.'

'But I can't move, I like it where I am.'

'It's not safe for you to be there anymore, you really do have to move away from there,' Tyler tells her firmly.

'You don't like me, do you?' she states. She looks at her suspiciously, recalling the formality of the interview, the sense of injustice she'd felt. But she doesn't want to think about that, she just wants to go home. She swallows hard and says, 'I have to get our things, Otis's bowl and his basket.'

'It's been taken care of.'

'Are you sure it's not safe for me to go back home?'

Tyler looks down as if she is about to deliver bad news but isn't sure how to do it.

She steels herself in preparation, scared of what she is about to hear.

'I'm really sorry to tell you this but, as you know, when you were helping us with our enquiries, it got out and the papers printed the story. Your change of name was circulated on the internet so people found out where you've been living. They did some damage to your flat.'

She takes a deep breath. 'What did they do?'

'A lot of things were smashed, I'm sorry. We need to get you out of here and moved into the new place as soon as possible.'

'What was smashed?'

'I don't know the details,' Tyler replies. 'I'm sorry,' she repeats.

She thinks of the flat and the things she'd put in it, things that had given her joy and a sense of herself. They were there to remind her of all she had achieved. Each ornament was a sign that she was moving forward, succeeding with her life, even though everyone had said she'd always fail.

'I don't want anyone to go with me to the new place,'

she says. 'Just give me the address and I'll go on my own.' Accompanied, she won't be able to show her fear, how much she minds what's happened to her. She is holding it back – just – but the ability to suppress it won't last for long. Tyler mustn't see it.

'You can't go unaccompanied. I've been assigned to you, so I'll be taking you, getting you settled.'

She blinks back the tears that are threatening to fall, holding her stomach tight, as if this is where her fear is lodged. 'Did they break much?' she asks.

'We salvaged as much as we could,' Tyler replies.

In the dark of evening, as they drive to the new flat, Tyler says her name will need to be changed.

'Why?'

'You were named as Samantha Robinson on the internet.'

'There must be a few Samantha Robinsons, it's not an especially unusual name.'

'People will put two and two together. You are very visible.'

'What do you mean, visible?'

Tyler doesn't answer.

'You mean I'm not white.'

Tyler doesn't respond; she only says: 'It really is necessary. What would you like your first name to be? Once you've decided, the Home Office will sort out the paperwork.'

She shrugs. 'I don't mind. What's in a name?' she says wryly. Pretending that it doesn't matter is helping her to manage the fear. She puts her hands to her stomach again. Then she adds,

'Do you think I'll feel different when I'm called something else? I did, for a while, when I first became Samantha.'

'It must be strange, having different names,' says Tyler, but the observation isn't directed at her, it's more as if she's thinking aloud.

She looks out of the window and says: 'Before I went to Whytefields ... before the trial and everything ... I had this hot-water bottle cover. It was knitted for me by my gran, she said to cuddle it whenever I wasn't feeling well. It was red and green and gold and it had my old name on it, MICHELLE, in big black letters. They took it off me when my name got changed. I don't know what happened to it. I expect it got put in the incinerator.' There is silence for a while. Then she says, 'I don't know what I should call myself.'

'Have a think,' answers Tyler.

They drive through dreary A-roads: bland suburbia flanked by concrete housing estates and business parks. She wants to ask where they are going but she doesn't dare. If she ends up outside London she doesn't think she'll be able to cope; London is all she knows and the city is part of her. She tries to read the signs. They are in the north and west of the capital, she thinks. She hasn't been here before and she doesn't expect to like it. She sits very, very still because the fear, the sadness, are building up and up inside of her and almost breaking out; the stillness of her body holds them back.

Tyler pulls up outside a block of 1960s flats, even starker than her last accommodation.

'Is this it? Where are we?' she asks.

'Neasden.'

'Is it still London?'

'Yes, it's still London,' Tyler replies.

'Which floor am I on?' she asks, getting out of the car, hand across her stomach, her body stiff.

'You're on the top floor. It's not high-rise like your last place and it should be a lot quieter.'

'I had a good view. I could see all over London. I don't like this, it's too built up, there won't be any privacy. And it's got a flat roof. Flat roofs leak. If I'm on the top floor, I'll be leaked on. Can't I go back to the other flat?'

Tyler looks impatient. 'No, I'm sorry, it's not safe,' she reiterates.

Her possessions are unloaded from a van that is already waiting outside and taken upstairs.

As soon as she's inside, she starts opening the boxes, checking each item, relieved to see the things she finds. The large TV that was in her living room was smashed but, surprisingly, the smaller, portable one that used to be in her bedroom is still intact. She places it on a wooden box in the living room and switches it on.

'Do you have home insurance?' Tyler asks. 'If you do, I'm sure you could make a claim to get your things replaced.'

She gives Tyler a look that is intended to convey the stupidity of the question. She isn't sure what you have to do to get insurance but it's expensive and almost certainly would have involved filling in forms, dealing with officialdom, something she avoids at all costs – too many questions, the need to demonstrate who you are. Opening a bank account had been bad enough with little identification (she's never had a passport, never needed one, and all her other papers are Home Office fakes) but at least Dom had helped with that. She wonders how long it will take to replace the things she's lost now she doesn't have a job. Years, probably, if she ever manages it. She remembers showing off to Lucy. Nothing to show off now. She won't be able to go back to work, not now that she's been outed. No money. No role to play. She'd had purpose when she was working. No purpose anymore. She wonders what Cheryl Ayres and Alice will think. It's probably the most exciting thing that's ever happened to them.

Otis arrives from the kennels where he's been kept in her absence. He runs into her arms and she holds him close. She fills a bowl with water and watches him drink and then lays out his basket. 'Can I see the bedroom?' she asks.

'This is your flat now, you can go wherever you want.'

The room is bare apart from a bed that's been stripped. She looks at the stained mattress with abhorrence. 'There are clean sheets in a carrier bag by the door,' Tyler says. 'I'm going to have to leave you soon, but I'll be back first thing tomorrow to talk to you about security. And I'll also help you alter your appearance. It's just a precaution, we need to make sure you won't be recognized.'

She is wary. 'I don't think I want to look different.'

'It will keep you safe,' says Tyler.

She is tired of hearing the phrase. What's the point of being safe if everything has been taken from you?

'Have you thought of a name yet?'

She nods. 'I'd like to be Carly.'

She's always liked the name. She remembers the first time she heard it, when Carly Hughes, smaller than the rest of them and a lot less tough, had appeared one day during lunch at Whytefields. As far as the other children were concerned, Carly was there solely to be mocked and despised. She had joined in. Perhaps she'd even been one of the instigators. She remembers telling Lucy how much she hated her. She recalls laughing over shared memories of Carly's uselessness.

But the reality was different. Carly was clever. She was pretty and slim with thick hair that fell to her waist and a pale pink complexion. All the staff liked her, she never seemed to get told off. She had a mother and father who visited practically every week. They provided her with clothes from Topshop and Miss Selfridge in paper carrier bags. They brought her sweets and cakes.

She will be married now, and living in a semi-detached house in Richmond, opposite the park, with a baby son and her own BMW in the garage. She will have a beautiful garden with a tree that has fruit that will be made into apple pies in the autumn. She will be working, three days a week, as an air hostess, travelling all over the world. Her husband will love her completely – she is the most wonderful person he has ever met and he will do anything to prove that to her. She will be totally happy; no one will remember whatever crime she once committed.

Her taunting of Carly Hughes hadn't occurred because

she'd disliked her, it had happened because deep down she had wanted not to be *like* Carly, but to actually *be* her.

'Carly,' Tyler repeats with a nod. 'Right then, leave it with me, I'll sort it out.'

Tyler gets up to leave. Otis follows her to the door. He seems to like her. She pats him before she departs.

Alone in the flat, the anguish leaves her body in a long, low cry. She bangs her head against the wall. She finds a bottle under the sink, empties it and cracks it against the tabletop. She picks one of the shards of glass and presses it into her skin. The release of blood is a relief. She doesn't make the bed, she sleeps on top of it, fully clothed, blood trickling unchecked on to the mattress.

She is too exhausted from the interrogations and her time in the cells not to sleep that night, but she wakes every couple of hours, full of confusion, unable to work out where she is. Perhaps the crowd is outside, no longer chanting, just waiting silently for her in the dark. The bedside light she used to have wasn't among the possessions that were brought from the flat, so she shines the torch in her phone round the room, aware of its starkness and the harsh light from the street lamp that glows beneath the window. She listens to the sound of the traffic from the street below. She takes Otis from his basket and places him in bed with her. It eases the anxiety for a while. What will happen now? How will she bear the fear, and the weight of starting over?

SEVENTEEN

At home that evening, Tyler watches the ten o'clock news. The sole childhood picture of Michelle Cameron fills the screen, side by side with a photo of Kerry, whose hair is tied in a pony-tail with a wide red ribbon. Her milk teeth show as she smiles.

The next shot is of the commander, who says that Cameron has indeed been helping with enquiries but has now been released without charge.

'I understand that the Gosling Girl was being held on suspi-cion of the murder of Lucy Fields,' says a male journalist from one of the tabloids.

The commander looks into the camera. 'She knew Lucy Fields and was therefore interviewed as a possible witness, as indeed were all Lucy's friends and associates.'

'So you're saying she was never a suspect in the murder?'

'No, she was never a suspect.'

'But you can confirm that Michelle Cameron was an asso-ciate of Lucy Fields, a known prostitute? Is Michelle Cameron a prostitute?'

'I would like to make it clear that Michelle Cameron is not and has never been involved in any kind of prostitution.'

'Then how did they know each other?'

'I can't comment on that.'

'She's out on licence. Will she be recalled to prison?'

'Michelle Cameron has not committed any offence so her licence is not being revoked.'

'What about her anonymity?' asks another journalist. 'If she's a prostitute and dangerous, shouldn't she forfeit the right to a false identity? Doesn't the public have the right to know who and where she is?'

'Michelle Cameron isn't a sex worker, nor is she a danger to the public. That's it, ladies and gentlemen. Thank you for your time.' The commander walks briskly from the platform.

The following morning, Tyler arrives at Cameron's flat. She seems to have come round to the idea that she will be given a makeover. She sits on a folding chair in the middle of the kitchen. The space is small but it's a lot bigger than the bathroom and the sink is deeper. Tyler sighs and starts on the hair. Cameron has relaxed hair that has been made much longer with extensions. She has to take them out. It's time-consuming and irritating. She'd told her boss she had trouble enough getting her own hair to look good, let alone someone else's, but he'd just said that only a handful of people could know of Cameron's whereabouts, and she was one of them, so it was down to her. She had purchased Afro hair products from her local market with petty cash before driving to the flat in Neasden.

As her hair is washed, Cameron talks non-stop, evidently pleased to have a captive audience.

'Keep still,' Tyler tells her repeatedly. She keeps turning round to look at her, trying to gauge her response to the things she's being told. It's about her job, mostly. She talks about how good she was at it and how angry she is that she can't go back there again, even though she didn't do anything wrong.

The chemicals in Cameron's hair take longer than expected to rinse out. 'Can you keep still?' says Tyler again.

'Couldn't they have got someone to fix this who knows what they're doing?' she asks.

Tyler has been wondering this herself, so she doesn't reply.

The dog is sleeping by Cameron's chair. It starts to snore. 'Do you like animals?' she asks.

'Yes, I like them, but my hours are too irregular. It wouldn't be fair to have one.

'Dogs or cats?'

'I prefer cats. Dogs are too clingy.'

'They're better company.'

'I suppose it depends on what you're after.'

'Maybe as you're police, you could have a sniffer dog. Or a police horse. Do you know how to ride?' She sounds like a child. She yawns, saying how tired she feels from the nights she slept in the cell, and then changes the subject. 'Now that I'm Carly, I'll be slower because it is a slower name than Samantha. I'm trying to pause my thoughts because that's what Carly would do. Carly doesn't hurry, but she knows things. She's clever. She likes cauliflower cheese and the colour yellow, which is a

139

shame because it doesn't really go with my complexion. You like brown, don't you?' she asks, pointing to Tyler's trousers. 'What kind of music do you like? Carly will probably like indie music – not sure I'll be able to get used to that. Samantha liked hip hop but she didn't like cauliflower, she preferred burgers, definitely a carnivore, and her favourite colour was red. I can't remember what Michelle liked anymore.'

'Keep still,' says Tyler again.

Otis is obviously dreaming about something good because his tail is wagging and he's making little murmurs of excitement.

Cameron notices this and says: 'I get scared to sleep. I don't get good dreams, do you?'

Tyler doesn't answer. She doesn't get good dreams, only nightmares. A young black man with a gun. Shots fired. Shadows that are impossible to name but which haunt even her waking hours. She puts down the comb she is using for a moment and steadies herself. Cameron doesn't notice. She is still talking.

'. . . Otis doesn't know I'm not Samantha now. To him, I'm just the same.'

Tyler starts to see why she needs the dog.

'Can you pull the blinds?' asks Cameron. 'I don't want to be looked at.'

There is no one to see her from the back window, the flat isn't overlooked. Tyler says this, but Cameron repeats the request so she pulls the metal blinds.

'I don't think I like it here,' says Cameron, her voice quivering.

'In the old flat, there were these blue curtains I made; I had to do them by hand, it took ages. Curtains are nicer than blinds, more homely. It's funny, the cooker here comes on straight away. My old cooker didn't, it was like you had to persuade it to work. I like the old cooker best. I wish I could go back home.' There is a pause and then she adds, in a much brighter voice, 'Still, nothing is permanent, is it?'

'No, nothing is permanent,' Tyler says.

'Did you notice, there is a small garden with some rose bushes across the way? I saw it when I took Otis for a wee this morning. I like roses, I like the smell. Do you?'

The chirpiness of her tone is unconvincing. Whistling in the dark, Tyler thinks. She can almost smell the panic Cameron is exuding yet trying to conceal.

She begins to cut her hair. There's too much intimacy in styling near her forehead so Tyler makes her lean back. She is no expert; the result is a jagged mess. 'You usually wear make-up so try not to use any for a while, it will make you look different.' She steps back to look at her handiwork. 'I really don't think anyone's going to know you. I've brought some glasses, as well. The lenses are clear.'

'Disguise,' says Cameron. 'Why not attach a funny nose as well?' and she starts to laugh in an artificial way that puts Tyler on edge.

'Come on,' she says as she finishes the cut, 'I'll talk you through the security stuff. Have you got a pen? You'll need to write it down.'

'I won't, I'll remember,' she replies.

She listens with a look of scepticism as Tyler talks her through the security measures, as if she suspects that feelings towards her are such that no one will be rushing to her aid, however much she presses on the panic button.

She takes the glasses and puts them on. She wants to see what she looks like now.

In the living room, there is a mirror over the space where a fireplace would be in an older flat. It's speckled with black spots but Cameron stands on tiptoe and peers into it.

'I look so different,' she says, 'not like myself at all.'

'That's the idea,' Tyler answers.

She is subdued again. She obviously doesn't like the look – and why would she? – or maybe it's one change too many. Tyler doesn't ask, she just gathers up her things and leaves.

It's not that she actively dislikes Michelle Cameron, it's more that she doesn't know how to handle her: the nakedness of her need for attention, her desire for acceptance and the nature of the crime she committed all those years ago cause Tyler to shy away from her. When she'd suggested their actions had probably led to the trashing of Cameron's flat, DI Henderson had said, 'What goes around comes around,' as if the punishing of her should never come to an end. She thinks of Julie Gosling: perhaps it shouldn't. But Cameron was only ten when she killed Kerry. Should she really have to suffer for the rest of her life? She still isn't safe. They haven't yet found the source of the leak. It could happen again. Perhaps next time, Michelle Cameron will be alone in her flat when they come for her. Will anybody care? She doubts it very much.

EIGHTEEN

She barges her way into the apartment. The heat of anger is causing her to sweat; the perspiration on her forehead trickles down her nose. 'I don't want anything I say to be recorded,' she tells Zoe before she even sits down.

'If the things you say are recorded, I'll be able to keep them accurate,' Zoe replies. 'It's in your interest as much as mine for the recorder to be on.'

'No,' she says, 'turn it off.'

Zoe complies, judging she's too angry to respond to reason.

She flings herself into the chair and launches into a diatribe about the way she's been treated. 'It's in the news, you'll have seen it, I hadn't even done anything and they pulled me in, treated me like I'm nothing.' She puts her hand to her head, feeling her hair. 'It isn't fair. I didn't even do anything and they wrecked my flat, it's all been stirred up again even though it was years and years ago. I hate everyone, I hate them! They're never going to let me forget it are they? One stupid mistake and it follows you around for ever.' She pauses to draw breath.

'That mistake you're referring to – do you mean Kerry?' asks Zoe.

She gives her a glare that says back off.

'The "mistake" you mentioned. You mean when Kerry was killed?' Zoe repeats, speaking calmly in the hope that this will alleviate some of the rage. The use of the passive form of speech is designed not to alienate her further.

She isn't going to name it. She evades the question and says: 'They sent this cop round to change the way I look. Look what she's fucking done to me.' Her voice has risen to a shriek. She looks at Zoe, seeming embarrassed, momentarily, by the ferocity of her outburst. 'Can I have one of those biscuits?' she asks in a much quieter voice. She gets up and takes a couple of Florentines. 'Most people only have these at Christmas,' she says, returning to her seat.

Zoe wants to return the conversation to the phrase she just used. 'The "mistake" you mentioned, what did you—'

She cuts in, quickly. 'What do you think of how I look now? I want to go back to the way I looked before, I don't care if I get recognized or not. I hate my hair, all short and frizzy. I want my old hair back. I like long hair. I don't like this kind of hair. If Lucy had given back that sweatshirt none of this would have happened. She could have brought it round to the flat, she knew it wasn't a keep. She never gave back anything, not money, not clothes, nothing.'

'I'm not sure what you mean about the sweatshirt. Did Lucy

borrow one from you? Why wouldn't all this have happened if Lucy had given it back?' Zoe takes in her agitation: her legs are moving up and down and her hands are trembling so much that drops of coffee are spilling out of the cup onto the blue T-shirt she is wearing.

'I'm not Samantha now,' she says. 'They made me change my name again as well. So my flat's gone, my job, my best friend, and I can't even be the second version anymore I'm on to the third.'

'The third version? What do you mean by that?'

She doesn't answer.

'Do you mean the third version of you? What's your new name, can you tell me?'

Again, she ignores the question. 'It probably won't even stop with that. There will be five versions, six versions maybe. What am I supposed to do?' She stares at Zoe, challenging her to find an answer for her.

'I'm sorry all this has happened,' says Zoe. 'I heard a rumour about it even before it was in the news. I tried to contact you but the police refused to say what was happening or even to confirm you were in custody. I wasn't allowed to see you.'

'They interrogated me for hours and stuck me in a cell. Even when they knew for sure it wasn't me, they kept me in there, just rotting.'

'My understanding was that they couldn't release you because of the things on social media – it wasn't safe for you to leave – and that you were there voluntarily.'

'What's voluntary about having to stay in a place because people have threatened to kill you? They could have found somewhere nice for me to be. They just didn't want to.'

'It was only for that one night, though, wasn't it? While they tried to find somewhere safe for you?'

She kicks out at the footstool beside her, sending it sliding across the floor. 'How could they think I would have killed Lucy? She was my best friend. "We have to keep you here to keep you safe," they kept saying to me. All this crap about keeping me safe, like they give a shit. I'm not safe. It doesn't matter where I am, someone will find me. All these people stood outside the police station, shouting my name. I thought they were going to come and get me. I thought they'd do something terrible to me. What if they find me again? Why does it matter after all this time? Why can't they just leave me alone, forget about it, let me live my life? I've done my time, that should mean it's over, shouldn't it?'

'Why do you think people aren't able to leave you alone?
She shrugs.

Zoe makes her tone as friendly as she can. 'How would you say people see you?'

She looks at the floor. 'They think I'm bad. Very bad,' she whispers.

'Why do they think that, do you suppose?'

'I don't know.'

'Do you think it has something to do with Kerry?'

'I don't know.'

'Perhaps people were shocked by what you did.'

She folds her arms and gazes into the distance. 'I don't know,' she repeats. 'Anyway, I couldn't have done the things they said I did, you know that. But all anyone thinks is that I'm bad. Evil. That's what they say. Everybody says it.' She is flushed with anger and sadness.

'What's it like, being thought of as so bad?'

'What do you think it's like?'

Zoe knows it's a rhetorical question, but she says: 'I think it's probably scary. Lonely. Hard to get your head round. And it's unfair too, that's what I think. You had a friend with you when Kerry was killed, didn't you? She was never thought of as bad or evil.'

She looks startled. 'No, she wasn't,' she says.

'You were named and taken to court, but nothing happened to her, she remained anonymous. What was her name?'

'Her name was Jessie.'

'Have you thought about why she got let off and you were made to take the blame by yourself?'

'I don't know why Jessie got let off,' she says flatly. She wriggles in her seat, squirming, literally, at the memory.

'What was Jessie like?'

'She was pretty. She had long fair hair and green eyes, a bit like Lucy. What I don't understand is why she didn't own up, tell people she was there as well. I had to tell them and no one even believed me. I never saw her again after. She just disappeared. I thought she was my friend.' Her eyes are starting to fill with tears.

'That must have hurt an awful lot.'

She is crying now, as if in acknowledgement of just how much it hurt.

Zoe pushes harder. 'What happened when you both took Kerry out of the garden that day?'

'*Stop!*' she shouts. 'I don't want to talk about this anymore. I hate you, I really hate you! I hate everyone!'

She launches herself at Zoe, attacking with her fists. The force of the blows leaves Zoe breathless, but she is taller and stronger than Michelle Cameron and she holds her off until the rage subsides and she collapses, sobbing, into her arms.

They are both shaken by the depth of the emotion that has been unleashed. Zoe continues to hold her until the crying stops. Then she eases her away and returns her to her seat, wondering if she's done too much too soon; if she has, Michelle Cameron won't be coming back.

She buries her face in her hands. 'It was just me in the prison cell,' she says in a muffled voice, 'me, on my own.'

'After Kerry?'

'Yes, then too,' she says shakily, 'but I meant at the police station the day before yesterday. It's the exact same thing, don't you see? I didn't do anything to Lucy but I'm being blamed all over again. People are saying they want to kill me. If I died, no one in the whole world would be sorry, not one single person.'

'I would be sorry. I mean that.'

She stares at Zoe, weighing up, most probably, whether she's telling the truth.

'I want you to know that I believe you when you say you

didn't kill Lucy. But I think you need to face up to what happened with Kerry.'

'I can't do this, I can't, I just want to go home, let me go home,' she says. She gets up but then she freezes. 'Except home's gone, hasn't it? I can't go home, I don't live there anymore.' She looks at Zoe, her eyes red, a hunted expression on her face. Then she runs through the door.

Zoe follows but it's too late, she's already out of sight.

Nineteen

The leaks regarding Michelle Cameron have been traced to Dave Donaldson, ex-cop; Tyler remembers that over the years he had given press interviews and statements, often speaking for the Gosling family. The serving officer who passed him the information will face internal disciplinary proceedings but no charges will be brought against either of them, despite the injunction: it's not in the public interest. She knows what this means; it's expedient to forget about the leaks and their consequences – too many questions would be asked about the role the police played in the unnecessary exposure of Michelle Cameron. Her boss dispatches Tyler to 'have a word' with Donaldson.

'Shouldn't we bring him in, make this formal?' she asks.

Henderson shakes his head. 'We can't risk stirring up interest in Michelle Cameron again. I used to work with him, he'll feed on that kind of attention, lap it up. Best to keep it as low-key as possible. He's a bit of a dinosaur, so make sure you keep it professional.'

Donaldson lives in a small terraced house off the Old Kent Road that he probably bought in the 1970s. As she approaches, Tyler thinks it will be worth a fortune now, even though it's in need of renovation – or modernization, as an estate agent would put it.

Donaldson shows her into the front room. There are traces of dust on the blinds and sunlight has faded the carpet. A dull seascape, depicting a lighthouse and a ship being battered by the waves, has been placed above the empty fireplace. She sits on a beige chintz sofa, declines the tea and cake he offers, and delivers the news that he will not face prosecution, adding warnings (as instructed) about any further activities in this vein in the future. She is angry that he is getting away with it, so she makes her tone as formal as she can; difficult when she is sitting in his front room rather than in an interview room at the station. She expects him to be relieved, but he seems dejected; she concedes that her boss might have had a point when he'd told her to adopt a low-key approach.

The walls are lined with shelves containing files and folders. Donaldson insists on bringing some of these to the coffee table, opening each at a carefully selected page.

'The newspapers contact me whenever they want to brush up on Cameron. I know all the details,' he tells her. 'I've been on the BBC, a programme that looked at child killers. I was asked to explain to the viewers why people like Cameron should be locked up for life. I was on Channel 4 too, and I'm often on the radio.'

If he'd been prosecuted, Tyler thinks, it would have meant

more media exposure and further opportunities to demonstrate his expertise regarding Michelle Cameron. No wonder
he'd been disappointed by a visit from one female detective
and nothing more than a slap on the wrist.

He sits beside Tyler on the sofa and continues to show her
pages from his folders. 'What's your involvement with the
Gosling Girl?' he asks.

'None, really,' she says, refusing to be drawn.

'I was the family liaison officer for the Goslings, got to
know them very well by the end of it all. And I saw the pictures of that child's body. I was used to bodies, had to be, I
was in the murder squad, all you get is bodies, but nothing
prepares you for what was done to that child. She'd been tortured, I mean, *tortured*, and she was only a baby. I had to look
members of that family in the eye and tell them it was done by
another kid. I'll never forget the looks on their faces, I'll never
forget any of it. You don't forget that kind of case, not ever. I
couldn't get the picture of that child's body out of my head, it
wasn't natural, none of it. When the trial finished I couldn't
do the job anymore, couldn't see the point of it. I'm in security
now. Less complicated.'

The jacket of his uniform, complete with company logo, is
hanging on the newel post at the foot of the stairs. She'd seen
it on her way in.

'Do you want a cuppa? A slice of cake?' he asks once more.

'No, I'm fine thanks.'

'I've got everything that's ever been written on Cameron.
Look, here's the stuff on the trial. Cool as a cucumber all the

way through it, not a word of remorse, didn't shed a tear. They had to build up the dock because she wasn't tall enough to be seen. And here, this is when they were deciding whether she could be released.' He stabs at the front page of the *Guardian*. 'Do you know there are still people who say it was wrong to name her because she was only a child? What everyone forgets is that only someone with the mind of an adult could have done what she did. The judge was right to waive her anonymity. Why should she have been allowed to hide? She shouldn't be allowed to hide now and she should still be inside. They want the prison doors thrown open. Let them all out, that's what they say. I never thought the Home Office would allow her to go free but I should have known better. What must the Goslings be thinking? You see, these days, nobody cares about the victims. I email them, sometimes, the Goslings. Well, not Julie, I don't want to stir things up for her, she can't take it. But Aaron, little Aaron, he's a young man now. Martin Gosling said I did wonders, helped his boy through it. We've kept in touch, still meet up from time to time. He likes fishing, I like fishing. Aaron's a bright lad and his life's been blighted. He's come through it, though, and Martin says it's mainly thanks to me.'

He walks over to a shelf and takes down a photo of Kerry. She is crouching by a paddling pool in the garden, playing with a doll. Her parents are in the background, smiling at her fondly. He passes it to Tyler. 'Martin Gosling gave me that, in a frame, because he knew how much I cared about his little girl. It matters to people that you care.'

He picks up another folder, opens it and says: 'And this

is where they put Cameron. It was meant to be a secret but everybody knew the location, of course they did. I had to go there to get this photo, but they wouldn't let me inside.'

It is a picture of a three-storey building with barbed wire around the perimeter. Tyler assumes it is Whytefields Lodge.

'I would have liked to have seen what her room was like but it doesn't really matter, I've got a DVD. It's not about Cameron, it's a documentary about some other little thug that was there a while after, but it shows you what it's like inside. I got some stills from it and scanned them in, look. I expect all the rooms are much the same. They've got TV, video games, you name it. And they call it punishment.'

The picture shows a small study bedroom, not unlike the one she used to have in halls at university. Donaldson shows her images of other places he hasn't actually seen in person and lays down further articles for her to look at.

'It's an archive, that's what I've been working on. All properly ordered, all accurate for the book I'm doing. It's been years in the making. Well, you can't rush something like this, it needs proper consideration. You know, people think that if someone kills a child when they're a child themselves, it's not a proper crime.'

'I'm not sure people do think that—'

'Everyone comes up with reasons, makes excuses for her: *oh she was from a broken home, she was smacked when she was little, she was sexually abused*. Excuses. But I saw the consequences, to the Goslings, to myself and to others who came across Michelle Cameron.'

'Which others?'

'Colleagues of mine. It takes something away from you to be involved with a case like that, and you don't get it back. We were all harmed by Cameron, one way or another.'

Donaldson is leaning over her. He smells of tobacco and old wool. 'What made you become one of us?' he asks.

'One of us?'

'What made you join the force?'

It's none of his business, but she says, 'I don't know, it just seemed right.'

'I expect people like you are the future.'

She feels her body grow tense. 'People like me?'

'Graduates – attractive, young, energetic. Don't get all defensive on me.'

She knows what he really meant, but she says nothing: there isn't any point.

He stands up and snaps his folder shut. 'I expect you think she got some kind of raw deal because she was black, that the trial was racist or some such thing. I know how you all stick together.'

She is determined not to lose her temper. She knows how he will construe it if she does; it will be typical of her kind. 'I can assure you—'

'Well, I'm telling you there was nothing racist about that trial, whatever you might think. I'm no racist, there's good and bad in every race, of course there is, but you tell me why so many immigrants end up behind bars. You can't ignore the statistics, can you? We should be sending them back, this country's falling apart, it's full of scroungers. I don't mean you, of course, you're one of us, but not everyone's like you. That was the thing about Michelle Cameron. She was bad by nature. You could see it in her face.'

As she leaves, Tyler wonders why she said nothing in the face of Dave Donaldson's racism. *Professionalism*: don't be drawn, you must remain professional. But sometimes, she concludes, professional is just another word for silent.

TWENTY

Zoe is disappointed that her last session with Michelle Cameron ended so abruptly. She shouldn't have let her bolt before she'd committed to a further meeting. She had been too exhausted to make any notes yesterday evening, once Cameron had fled, but she needs to do it now, before she loses hold of the discussion in all its complexity. It's a pity the recorder had been off. Next time, she will have to ensure it stays on, whether she likes it or not. Typically, Michelle Cameron had tried to control the session, with her insistence that it should not be recorded, with her aggression, and by fleeing when the discussion had moved into areas that were threatening.

She opens her laptop and thinks about the anger she had shown; most people would have been angry in such circumstances, but the childlike rawness of her rage had been bleakly comical – in the first half of the session, at least. After that, it had become something else, something much darker. Michelle Cameron's violence hadn't been so out of control that Zoe had been frightened by it – she had often dealt with far worse in her work – and she had managed to contain it with relative ease. It had taken her off guard, though, and that had been unsettling. They'd been close to a breakthrough and it was regrettable that this had been lost. If Michelle Cameron hadn't responded to the questions so defensively, they might have been able to make the progress that was needed.

She sighs and closes the laptop again. She is still unfocused. Yesterday's session has thrown her more than she realized. Right now, she could do with a drink. She goes into the kitchen and opens a bottle of wine. Then she thinks better of it and pours some whisky instead, adding a splash of ginger. She'd been hoping to have enough material by early spring but that seems much less likely now that the arrest and relocation of Michelle Cameron has set everything on another course. Still, she thinks, it's important to keep in mind that the murder accusation isn't necessarily a problem as far as their work together is concerned. It has reignited curiosity in the Gosling Girl. Of course, she would never have wanted such an awful thing to happen, but the killing of Lucy Fields really wouldn't do any harm to the commercial prospects of the book.

TWENTY-ONE

Michelle Cameron has failed to turn up for her weekly appointment with her probation officer. Tyler is instructed to go to her flat; she is in breach of her licence. 'Am I supposed to be arresting her?' asks Tyler.

'Christ, no,' says DI Henderson. 'The last thing we want is to have to bring her in again. As long as she doesn't look like she's doing anything unlawful, leave her exactly where she is. We just have to check, that's all. We don't want anyone saying we haven't been on top of this if something goes wrong.'

Tyler would have preferred not to have further dealings with Michelle Cameron. She hasn't forgotten the words that were spoken to her as she was closing the door to the cell. Hoping to avoid face-to-face contact, she tries phoning repeatedly but she is unable to get through, so eventually she arrives at Cameron's flat unannounced. She presses the intercom to the entry system several times but no one responds, so she tries the other flats. Eventually, somebody answers. She says she's police and gets buzzed in.

All is quiet on the landing where Cameron lives. She bangs on the front door and calls through the letter box. Eventually, Michelle Cameron opens the door.

She looks unwell. Her hair is dishevelled and her eyes are swollen. She looks at Tyler but she doesn't speak. 'Can I come in?' Tyler asks.

She stands aside to allow Tyler into the hall. Otis runs towards them and paws at Tyler's trouser legs. She pats him dutifully. She and Cameron go into the living room and perch opposite one another on hard folding chairs, the only seating in the flat.

'You didn't keep your appointment with Dom, your probation officer,' Tyler says, aware that there is hostility in her tone.

'Am I being sent back to prison?' she asks.

'You could be, you're in breach of the terms of your licence.'

She is silent for a while. Then she says, 'What does it matter anyhow?'

'You want to return to prison?'

She gestures round the room. 'What do you think this is, if it isn't a prison? At least if I was properly inside, I'd have people to talk to.'

'You will get used to being here.'

'Maybe I don't want to get used to it. Anyway, I could get used to it, settle in and it all kicks off again and I'm on the internet and have to move. What's the point?'

She has such a forlorn look about her that Tyler reins in her annoyance and speaks more gently. 'Look, I know it's difficult but no one wants to send you back to prison. You just need to make sure you keep your appointments with Dom. They're thinking of tagging you. You don't want that.'

She stands up, looking even more defeated. 'What's the point?' she says once more.

'Why didn't you go to your appointment?'

'I don't know where I am. I don't know how to get to south London from here. I didn't know how much it would be to get a taxi – a lot, I expect. I probably don't have enough money.'

'Couldn't you have phoned Dom to let him know that? It would have saved a lot of trouble.'

'I don't have any charge on my phone and this flat doesn't have a landline!' she yells in frustration.

'All right,' says Tyler, 'I can see it's difficult. I'll phone Dom now and let him know, okay?'

Once this is dealt with, Cameron seems to calm down. They go into the kitchen. 'Have you eaten today?' asks Tyler.

She shakes her head.

Tyler goes to the fridge thinking she can make sandwiches. There's nothing in it and the light fails to come on.

'It's okay,' Cameron says, 'I'm not hungry.'

'Are you out of electricity, is that what the problem is?'

'It stopped working. I don't know how to get it back on again.'

'There will be a meter somewhere.' Tyler searches the flat and locates it. There is a key on a shelf below. 'You have to add credit using this,' Tyler tells her. There are instructions and numbers on a piece of cardboard pinned beside it. 'We'll top it up in a bit,' she adds.

It's clear to Tyler she'll need to stay a while longer. They sit together at the kitchen table, struggling to find things to say. Otis perches on his own chair and stares dolefully at the empty food bowl on the floor by the sink.

'What have you been doing with yourself these past few days?' asks Tyler.

'Nothing much. There's a convenience store on the corner. I've been there a few times with Otis. I haven't been able to walk him like I used to. I don't like going far. It's too weird, being here, and people might know who I am. They might be watching me.'

'No one's watching you.'

'You don't know that.'

'I do, honestly. No one knows where you are. What other things have you been doing?'

'I played music from the TV and watched stuff before the electricity went off. You can get cable channels in this flat. Someone who lived here before must have signed up for it.' There is another long pause. Then she says to Tyler, 'What sort of things do you like to do when you're not at work?'

Recognizing that it will be easier to manage the situation if she tries to engage with Cameron, Tyler makes a tentative response: 'I run a lot.' She would find running even more enjoyable if she could just give up smoking. She doesn't do it often, but she shouldn't do it at all if she really wants to stay fit. Trouble is, it does take the edge off any stress. 'I used to play ice hockey but I don't have time for that anymore,' she adds. 'Sometimes I watch TV but I've got to be in the mood.'

'I like films,' she says, 'fantasy, mainly.' Then, changing the subject, she asks, 'Why did you join the police?'

It ought to be a simple question, but it isn't. Tyler remembers university, her plan to do a doctorate and lecture in sociology. It was a difficult field to get into, but she was academic and she loved to study. You have to excel, and she did, for the first two years, and then life intervened: in her final year, she fell for somebody – hopelessly, completely and in a way she has vowed she never will repeat. Her first intimate relationship, even though she was in her twenties: Maddie – funny, and clever. Beautiful, with violet eyes. Clear pale skin. A talented artist, too. They'd visited art galleries together. She remembers how happy she had been as they'd walked round, laughing and talking. Maddie had known so much about the exhibits and taking her cues from her, she had come to appreciate twisting sculptures suspended from ceilings thirty or forty feet high.

They'd popped Es in gay bars, eaten French food she couldn't afford in Shoreditch and gone to Stonehenge on a whim to mark the winter solstice. She had lost herself in Maddie and then Maddie had lost interest in her. Remote, Maddie had said, with a tendency to overthink; an inability just to be free. Why all the talk of commitment? Why can't we just *be*?

And when it had ended, as it was always destined to do, she hadn't been able to handle it. While she hadn't failed her degree, she had been far from her predicted first, graduating with a 2:2. The career she had set her heart on was now out of her reach. She remembers how angry she'd felt, mainly with herself; all that work for nothing. What would she do? Careers weren't easy to come by for mediocre graduates and she was deep in debt, with a student loan around her neck. She applied for every decent job she thought she had a shot at but didn't get a single interview. Then, at a graduate careers fair, she was handed a leaflet and persuaded to go to a stand manned by the police. They wanted diversity, they said. The service needed to change. She could be part of that, they told her. She could make a difference. At first, she couldn't see it, but then she thought at least it wasn't nine-to-five – she definitely wasn't suited to routine – and being active was another aspect of the job. And it seemed that a degree in sociology, even a 2:2, meant an accelerated career path. She convinced herself that it could work.

'I suppose,' Tyler says aloud, in answer to the question, 'I thought I could make a difference.' She is aware of the naivety of that even as the words escape her mouth.

In the silence that follows, she looks around the room, observing the mould round the small window and the polystyrene ceiling tiles from another era. There are patches of damp on the floor round the kitchen sink. There is nothing comfortable here. Cameron is right. It is like a prison. There is something callous about the way she's been rehoused in such a place, with nothing that's familiar. The remaining possessions from her old life are few and most are broken. She can't go back to work. Even the name Samantha Robinson (which was never really hers to begin with) has been taken from her and replaced with another. She is disquieted by the part she played in delivering Cameron here.

The door rattles as the post arrives. Cameron jumps and goes to retrieve it. When she returns, she says, 'It's quiet in here, isn't it?' She picks up the letters and examines the envelopes. 'It's just junk,' she says, putting them aside. Then she adds: 'When I was inside, there was always sound. You could hear noisy calls from payphones on the landing. There was the sound of clattering when plates were loaded on trolleys in the canteen. There were radios and the TV in the recreation room. Lots of the time you could hear people laughing. This flat is so quiet and empty.'

Tyler recalls that Cameron was released months ago and spent time after that in a hostel, but she still uses detention as the benchmark for gauging her surroundings.

A dull banging sound causes Cameron to jump.

'It's all right,' says Tyler, 'it was just your neighbour's front door slamming.'

'I thought it was ... I thought they were coming for me ...' She falters, twisting her hands. Then she says, 'I'm never going to be left alone, am I?'

Tyler remains silent, aware of her suppressed agitation but unable to see how to keep her calm.

Otis jumps off the chair and returns to his basket. It's as if there is now no buffer between her and Cameron. Tyler wants to pick him up and put him back where he was but he's already asleep so she lets him be.

'I didn't mean to do it,' she says.

'Didn't mean to do what?' asks Tyler. She thinks she knows what Cameron is referring to, but she wants her to name it.

Cameron doesn't reply. She picks up a catalogue that had landed on the mat and thumbs the pages. 'This isn't addressed to me. Does it matter that I opened it? I think I read somewhere it's illegal to open other people's mail.'

Tyler doesn't respond.

'That's nice,' she says, pushing the catalogue towards her. There is a glossy picture of a fair-haired model wearing a teddy fur coat.

Tyler pushes it back across the table with barely a glance. She gazes at Cameron, who pretends to be absorbed in the knee-high boots the next model is wearing. She's in denial, then, Tyler concludes in the silence that follows; she's obviously not willing to take responsibility for what she did to Kerry.

'Most of the time, I can't talk about Michelle with actual words,' Cameron says after a while.

'What do you mean?' Tyler asks.

She thinks for a moment. Then she says, 'I can't explain. Do you think the news people really believe the things they say about me or do they just make them up and not care?'

'I don't know,' Tyler answers.

She falls silent. Tyler can hear her breathing deeply, as if every intake of air is a struggle that can't be taken for granted. Then she begins to laugh and the sound is so strange – strangled, yet loud – that Tyler doesn't know how to deal with it. She fetches her some water and decides she needs to get out of there. She rings her boss to check it's okay to leave the flat for a while and tells Cameron they're going out.

She drives, just under the speed limit, barely noticing where they are heading. Cameron keeps peering at herself in the rear-view mirror. 'I can't get used to the way I look now,' she says. 'I feel like an alien.' Tyler pictures her on her knees each night appealing to the mother ship to return and whisk her away from earth. 'You look fine,' is all she says.

An out-of-town supermarket comes into view. Cameron slips further down in her seat, clearly wanting to hide. Tyler parks but Cameron won't get out of the car; she seems over-whelmed by the size of the place. Tyler starts to worry that she might run off – she seems poised for flight – but eventually she decides to give the store a try and reluctantly goes inside.

It's a mistake. Too much has happened in the past couple of weeks and Cameron hasn't absorbed it all yet; the artifice of the store is only serving to heighten her sense of the unreal.

Tyler decides to keep things ordinary, matter-of-fact. 'Do you have enough money for a few groceries?' she asks.

Cameron nods.

'You need to stock up on some basics, get a few days' supply.' She escorts Cameron through the aisles, encouraging her to pick up cans of soup and beans.

'What if someone realizes who I am?' Cameron keeps whispering but the shopping does seem to calm her down and Tyler is relieved.

There is an in-store café so Tyler buys a sandwich for each of them. Cameron eats rapidly, watching the passers-by, but if they try to meet her gaze her head goes down and she pretends to be absorbed in the food on her plate.

'Can we go now?' she asks, picking at a slice of cucumber that has fallen from her sub.

'If you want to,' Tyler answers. She feels like a parent dealing with a child.

As they pay for the groceries, Cameron seems to relax a little, meeting the gaze of the girl on the till at the checkout. She tops up the key to the meter. On the return journey to the flat, Tyler shows her where the bus stops are and maps out the way to the Tube.

Cameron seems tired. Her eyes are closed. And then she says, without opening them, 'I expect you're wanting to know what happened with Kerry.'

'No, not really,' Tyler answers, shutting down the conversation, but it isn't true. She tells herself she objects to being sent to Michelle Cameron's flat but really, she wants to be there. She wants to know more. She wants to know why. She wants to figure out if Michelle Cameron really is the monster she's made out to be.

TWENTY-TWO

Now that she has charged her phone, she sees there are several missed calls from Zoe. She doesn't know what to do. She remembers the questions Zoe had asked and the fear she'd felt. She remembers wanting to hurt Zoe. Perhaps she did hurt her when she lashed out. But most of all, she remembers being held. She wonders how long it's been since she really felt the warmth of human touch. She can't remember when it last happened, the last time she was sad and someone tried to comfort her – years ago, she thinks. She didn't run away because she didn't like it; she fled, in part, because she liked it too much.

She holds the phone tightly, wondering what she should do. Zoe must be angry with her. Maybe she's phoning to say don't ever think of coming back.

She goes into the kitchen and puts the kettle on, still holding the phone. And then it starts to ring, shrill and insistent. Zoe's name pops up.

She answers but doesn't speak.

'Hello?' says Zoe, 'are you there?'

'Yes,' she says softly.

'I was just phoning to check when you wanted to come and see me. You left in such a rush we didn't get the chance to make another appointment.'

She remains silent.

'I could see you this afternoon if you like. I know it's short notice but someone's cancelled. Would you like to come?'

She remembers the warmth of being comforted again. 'Yes,' she says softly, 'but I don't have any money left for a taxi.'

'I'll pay for it when you get here,' says Zoe.

In the back of a black cab, she gazes out of the window, trying to orientate herself. They pass a church, two pubs and a park. She is getting used to the flat, she thinks, as they head towards west London, but she still doesn't like it; the view from her old place had given her moments of joy, keeping her grounded. There is nothing like that where she lives now. Each day she sits on one of the folding chairs and spends her time watching TV or listening to music through the headphones that the wreckers of her home only partially destroyed; the right ear cup functions but the left is dead so the sound is tinny and distorted. She can't read; too much concentration is required. She remembers to feed Otis (and herself, of course; she wishes she could forget to do that) but everything else is too much effort.

The taxi driver wants to talk; he is asking what she does for a living. She tells him she's a writer, working on a book, and she is travelling to do some research. He asks what the book is about. She is still angry about all Zoe's questions so she says it's a novel about psychologists and the damage they do to their clients.

As they pull up outside Zoe's apartment, she nearly gets the driver to take her straight back. She doesn't want to talk. There is nothing to say. Zoe didn't sound cross with her on the phone, but that could just mean she's hiding it. She can't face anymore anger from people. But she doesn't have enough money to pay the driver unless she knocks on Zoe's door, and besides, being with someone is better than being alone.

She enters the apartment slowly, head down, not making eye contact. Once she has settled on the sofa, Zoe points out that she still seems distressed. 'I was worried about you after you ran off,' she adds.

Usually, she helps herself to the snacks provided, but she can't be bothered today. Zoe seems to notice because she gets up, pours coffee for them both and presents her with a plateful of mini fruit tarts – fresh fruit, of course, with cream on the top. She eats slowly and feels slightly sick.

'What's going on for you right now?' asks Zoe.

'Nothing much,' she replies, licking sticky fruit sauce from her fingers.

'You look tired.'

She doesn't look at Zoe but she says: 'I can't sleep. I keep thinking the crowd outside the police station are coming to get me. They could find out where I live.'

'It's very unlikely,' Zoe replies. 'There's an injunction. That's a legal document and it means that anyone who exposes you in any way will be prosecuted.'

'I know what an injunction is,' she answers flatly, 'and an injunction didn't stop them naming me when I was in custody.'

There is a long silence. She can hear the ticking of the big clock on the wall. She would leave, if she could summon the energy.

Zoe says, 'We don't seem to be making much progress in these meetings; we're not really moving forward.'

Like Alice in Lewis Carroll's book, she thinks, *it takes all the running I can do to stay in the same place.*

Zoe continues, 'We really need to talk about what happened last time we met, when you started attacking me.'

She gets up to take another tart. She doesn't really want one, she just needs to have her back to Zoe so the scared expression on her face can't be read.

'Do you remember what you were feeling just before it happened?'

'I don't know,' she says, almost inaudibly.

'I think you do know,' Zoe replies. 'Come and sit down again and try to tell me.'

She perches on the sofa, nibbling at the edges of her tart. 'I don't remember, I'm not making it up,' she says in agitation. 'I can't tell you what I don't know. And I'm sorry I did it, I didn't mean to hurt you.'

'We were talking about Jessie. We were talking about how you felt when you were brought to trial and Jessie wasn't.'

'Were we? I don't remember that.'

'I think you were feeling angry and hurt, and I'm wondering if the feelings you had before you lashed out at me were the same as the feelings you had just before you and Jessie hurt Kerry.'

She holds her breath and goes very still. '*No*,' she says, barely daring to exhale. 'I don't want to do this, I want to go now, I don't want to do the book anymore.' She stands up to leave.

'Sit back down, please,' Zoe tells her, 'we need to look at this.'

As before, the authority of Zoe's tone causes her to comply. She feels cold inside.

'You see, I'm in a really difficult position,' Zoe continues. 'When you lashed out, you showed me you aren't always in control of your feelings. You are out on licence and although I believe you when you say you didn't mean to hurt me, what happened was assault.'

She tries to absorb this. 'Are you going to report me? To probation or to the police?'

'I really don't want to, but if I have a sense that you are a danger, to yourself or to other people, I don't have a choice.'

'I won't do it again, I promise,' she says, desperately hoping this will be enough.

'How do you know that? If you can't or won't tell me what's going on for you, if you're not willing to do the work involved to get to the bottom of what happened with Kerry, how can either of us be sure you won't reoffend, especially in the light of all the anger you're storing?'

'I'm sorry,' she says again. 'I really am sorry.'

'I accept that you're sorry but what I really need from you

is a commitment to see me regularly and do the very best that you can so we can really move on with this book.'

She feels trapped. She can't talk about what happened, she can't even remember most of it, but now Zoe is saying that if she doesn't, she'll end up back in prison. She begins to cry silently and then, realizing she has little choice, she says, 'All right then, yes, I'll still do the book.'

'All I want is to help you, you do know that, don't you?' says Zoe. Kindness has returned to her voice.

She doesn't want to hear kindness, it's too hard – painful – like sandpaper being rubbed across a raw wound. It confuses her, too. Is Zoe angry or does she still like her? Is she trying to help her or does she want to put her back inside?

'Do you know what's upsetting you so much right now?'

Everything's upsetting her. She doesn't understand anything anymore. She is overwhelmed by days and days of loss and confusion. She is being hunted by the world; newspapers, TV, people on the street; a life for a life, that's what they say. If they catch up with her, she will be dead. There is no safe place for her to be, not now. She misses her old flat and the things she used to have that made it seem like home. They'd given her a sense of who she was. She'd chosen them so carefully: the cushions, the candle holders, the china dogs that looked like Otis, wanting them to be an extension of her. And they'd given her the sense that she was safe because she was worth something. Now they were gone, destroyed, all the things that had brought her happiness.

And she misses Lucy. She'd thought having someone to

share things with was a luxury she could manage without. But being out and about with Lucy, texting her, laughing about silly things, looking forward to her next visit to the flat, these things had been necessities, she's come to realize, and now they're also gone. 'I wish Lucy was here.' She's said it aloud. She didn't mean to. She expects Zoe to recoil from her sadness, but instead she comes over and crouches beside her, stroking her arm as if her feelings are important. She is being comforted again. She can't stop the tears. She wishes she could, they make her feel stupid and exposed, but they keep on flowing.

Zoe goes over to one of the bookcases in the alcove. She picks something off a shelf and presses it into her hand. It's a little elephant, carved out of wood. She clutches it so hard that the trunk cuts into her palm, drawing blood. When she leaves, she takes it with her. 'It's a gift,' Zoe says. She isn't sure she wants it. She will be beholden now, she'll have to be grateful. But she needs it, and as she holds it tight in her hand it starts to ease the pain.

Twenty-three

Zoe warned her about the documentary – told her not to watch. So of course, she watches, mesmerized, as someone plays the part of Michelle Cameron, child killer, on a channel called ID. What had she expected? To see herself just as she had been at ten years old, reproduced in every detail: small, slight, more like eight than ten, with light-brown skin, hair that frizzed and didn't stay flat however much she tried to squash it into place? Is she disappointed to see the dark brown figure with cropped curls, tall and adult, frowning at the camera, breasts fully formed beneath the jumper stretched across her chest? Disappointed, no. Puzzled, yes. There is no reflection here, no sense of herself mirrored back, no reaching back into the past and seeing events unfold exactly as they had occurred. Instead, she sees a narrative that tells someone else's story. She takes another chocolate from the box. She never watches TV without something in her mouth. Even when she cries because something moves or frightens her, there's something in her mouth, sweet and satisfying.

A woman appears on the screen. She doesn't know her at first and then there is a caption: Shannon Gosling. *Shannon.* Is it really her? She leans forward in her seat, scanning the screen. Shannon Gosling is grown up now, twenty-six at least. She's wearing a V-neck top in a muted shade of green, not like the old Shannon, who used to like bright colours. Pink was her favourite; she used to wear a deep pink scarf with a matching pom-pom hat. It suited her straight fair hair. She is darker now. Mouse-brown. *Dull.* Stupid not to have known that everyone would be different. People grow old, it's a fact of life. Except that Kerry doesn't, and in a way, she doesn't either because there are no pictures of Michelle Cameron as she is now. There are only pictures of Michelle aged ten.

Shannon speaks slowly, staring dully into the lens of the camera. A single tear trickles down the left side of her face. Everything changed when Kerry died, she says. An old family photo appears on the screen. Parents Martin and Julie Gosling are standing behind a bench in the garden, while Shannon is seated, holding Kerry by the waist as she stands on her lap, leaning perilously to one side. Where's Aaron? Not born yet. The sisters are each wearing jeans and hooded sweatshirts. Ten-year-old Shannon and two-year-old Kerry have the same deep pink canvas shoes – in different sizes, of course. She always copied me, says Shannon. For a moment, she looks proud.

Michelle Cameron was evil, she says. She almost destroyed our family.

More chocolate goes into her mouth as she contemplates

the nature of evil. What does it mean, this word that describes her constantly? Someone who doesn't tell the truth? Someone who does bad things? Someone who doesn't care? Is she evil? Perhaps.

Only she does care. She minds that Shannon is so sad, the Shannon who, at twelve years old, laughed helplessly at silly jokes and was her friend. And she minds that Shannon doesn't like her anymore and never will again. The pain of loss is like a punch in her side.

There is an aerial view of a stark modern building several storeys high. The caption says this is the hospital where Julie Gosling has been treated following her nervous breakdowns. 'At the time of making this programme, she was too ill to be interviewed.' *Michelle Cameron destroyed our family.*

Well, families do get destroyed, all the time. You have to learn not to care. Caring is stupid. Caring makes you shed a single tear that trickles down the left side of your face.

The pretend version of Michelle is back on the screen, paired with a smaller, blue-eyed child. Who is that? They are play fighting but it's starting to get serious. 'Michelle' hits the little one who screams, falling to the ground. A few minutes later, they are shown escorting a pretend Kerry from the house. The little blue-eyed child, the voiceover says, is the second child involved in the abduction, the one who was never charged.

Jessie Wallis. The fake Jessie is even less real than the fake Michelle. She was much taller than Michelle and her eyes were green, not blue. And why would they have had a fight before they left the house with Kerry? It doesn't make sense.

The real, old Shannon is walking down the street where she used to live. It's deserted. She stops outside their former home. The door is still green and the orange azalea still flowers in the front garden. The house looks uninhabited. Is the swing still in the back? Shannon used to push the younger ones, never losing patience, never getting bored and saying it was time to stop. She sees herself flying high on that swing, yelling *higher, higher*, squealing with delight.

The camera points up at the windows. They are grimy. One of the panes is cracked. There was a mobile once; purple butterflies swung against fake leaded glass, tapping spookily in the breeze. It's not there anymore. What else has gone?

She eats another chocolate. Raspberry cream. Too sharp: it disappoints. Pictures of the house as it was on the day that Kerry's body was found are put up on the screen. Journalists surround it, baying for the story.

We had to move, Shannon says.

Have you had an accident that wasn't your fault? You could be owed thousands in compensation.

A welcome break. She balances the chocolates on the arm of the chair and gets up to go to the toilet.

When she takes her seat again, Shannon is at a different house. She opens the front door. Martin greets her with a sad smile. Is that Aaron perched on the arm of the chair, all grown up? He was a baby last time she saw him. A woman in a faded pair of jeans that are too tight sits beside him, deep in thought. *Tina Gosling*, the caption says, *Martin Gosling's second wife*. The marriage broke down, Martin tells the camera. Julie became a different person. The loss of little Kerry ate her up.

The footage of the hospital is shown again. It's not one of those old asylums. They don't exist anymore. It's a general hospital that has a psychiatric wing. She caresses the chocolate box and wishes she was also somewhere safe, cared for and looked after.

She's on the screen again, the real Michelle Cameron, that same old photograph. They're asking if she should ever have been released. *No. If you commit murder, you should be behind bars for life, and life should mean life.*

She can barely taste the chocolate. She sucks and sucks, pushing it round her teeth with her tongue. Why can't they leave her alone? Years have gone by, yet still it all continues, on and on.

A middle-aged professor from a university is asked if it was nature or nurture that caused Michelle Cameron to kill. He talks about psychopaths.

The chocolates slide off the arm of the sofa. Otis springs into action, gobbling them up before she can stop him. Chocolate is bad for dogs. He could die. She tries to force her hand into his mouth and pull them out, eyes still fixed on the TV screen, as the professor says that psychopaths have no genuine feelings.

Otis bites her hand and breaks the skin. He's never done that before. She looks at him now, stunned by his betrayal, and lashes out before she can stop herself, giving him a hefty slap. As he runs into the kitchen with a yelp, she wonders if he'll ever want to come near her again. Dogs aren't like humans, though – they're far more ready to forgive and she was only trying to save him from himself. *Please don't let him die from eating chocolate*, she says.

She focuses on the TV once more. The professor has disappeared. They are showing an old video of Kerry now. She is playing in the garden, trying to dance. She covers her eyes, wishing she could stop watching, turn off the TV. She needs to shut it out. *Make it stop*, she whispers to herself. The professor comes back on screen. 'Psychopaths don't feel things in the way the rest of us do and they can't be cured,' he says. 'That's what makes them so dangerous.'

She nurses her hand as she stares at the television, wondering about infection. Otis returns and settles on her lap as if nothing has happened. She strokes him with her good hand.

They are back at the Goslings' house again, the new one that has a swing at the front rather than the back. Aaron speaks to the camera. 'Evil,' he says, repeating his sister's phrase. That word again. She doesn't know what it means.

Kerry Gosling's picture is on the screen once more. She looks away. By the time she looks again, the credits are rolling.

PART THREE

TWENTY-FOUR

It's easier to be alone when you have to pretend to be someone else, but hard to fill the time. She still misses the views she used to have from her old flat. When she'd looked across London, she'd felt that she was part of things.

Bored, and desperate for something to break the monotony, she decides it's no good sitting indoors all the time, scared to go anywhere. She needs to do something, not get trapped inside herself. She decides to find the places she used to gaze at from her balcony. It means getting used to public transport again and she eases herself in, going just a few stops at a time and venturing further each day. Soon she wonders why it had ever been a problem for her and she discovers, to her surprise, that visiting the places she used to be able to see is even better than looking. She starts to venture further afield, taking in scenes that are unfamiliar. Each day she leaves the flat, even though the nagging feeling that it isn't safe remains and walks to the Tube. She starts to relish the freedom travelling round London brings; a short time ago, she only had four walls, but now she has a city.

Some of the money Zoe gives her goes on topping up her Oyster card. She catches the first train that comes and goes to the stops that take her fancy on the Jubilee, Northern and Central lines: London Bridge because in the song it's falling down; Holland Park, because there should be fields of tulips; Chancery Lane because she's read *Bleak House*.

On a dull Monday morning she takes the Tube, changing at Bank for the Northern Line. As the train heads south, she thinks of the day she last saw Lucy. If she hadn't lent her the sweatshirt, she would still be anonymous, she supposes. Samantha Robinson. Ordinary. Dull but reliable. Who is she now? Carly Wilson. The surname was chosen for her. She's been Carly for almost eight weeks. She thought she would like her but she doesn't. She's even duller than Samantha and much less reliable. She doesn't have a job. Doesn't have a hope of getting a job. She's less attractive, too: short hair does nothing for her and it's frizzy, her least favourite look. Glasses: big mistake. Her skin looks darker, somehow, as if she's constantly in shadow, and it's rebelling against the amount of fat and sugar she's consuming; she's got spots on her nose and chin. Not even her own mother would recognize her now – the only plus she can think of.

She gets off at Elephant and Castle and catches a bus. As she looks out of the window she sees her reflection in the glass. Devil-child, a paper called her once. She stares at her face and wonders if evil is etched in the light brown layers of her skin.

The street where Lucy used to live is full of tall, terraced houses on short-term lets, multi-occupancy, mostly. Why is she here? Perhaps she is lonely with only Otis for company. Lucy's flat looks just the same, though of course it isn't. It's stupid to have come, it only underscores the fact that Lucy has gone and isn't coming back. She misses the laughter.

'Hi?' says someone, a question in his tone, as if he isn't sure if he should speak to her.

She turns. It's a man, slim with loose Afro curls that frame his face. She remembers him but keeps her expression blank.

'Weren't you Lucy's friend? Sorry, I've forgotten your name.'

She hesitates. 'It's Carly,' she tells him eventually. 'Yes, I was Lucy's friend.'

'I thought so. I'm Ryan. I used to see you at Amber's flat. How come you're back?'

'Just come from seeing a friend in the next street.' She hopes he will believe her. She's trying not to stare. He is looking better now; his face isn't drawn and his clothes are clean.

'I nearly didn't recognize you,' he says. 'You look a lot different.'

'So do you,' she replies. She's worried that he knew her even with all the changes that have been made to her appearance. Maybe other people will recognize her too.

He falls into step with her and they head towards the high street. 'Do you want to go for a drink?' he asks.

'Sure,' she replies, surprised and flattered to be asked.

They see a pub on the corner, so they go inside. It's still only November but there's a Christmas tree with twinkling lights and a real log fire. She settles into an armchair in an alcove, positioning herself so she can see the yellow-orange flames, and

Ryan gets her a glass of wine. She watches as he leans over the bar. He is taller than she remembers him.

'How have you been?' asks Ryan as he reaches her table, putting the wine down in front of her.

She takes a sip. 'Okay, thanks.' She's aware of how awkward they are.

He stares into his beer before taking a swig. 'It was terrible, what happened to Lucy. I expect you miss her. You two were tight.'

She nods.

'So what do you think happened that night?'

'I don't know.'

He changes the subject. 'Do you work?'

'I'm between jobs at the moment.'

'Me too,' he says. He hesitates, as if he isn't sure whether to say more, and then he adds, 'I've been ill, I was in hospital for a bit, but I'm a lot better now.'

'That's good,' she replies, observing that he doesn't seem out of it anymore.

They slip into silence. She looks into the fire. It spits and crackles and casts shadows on the opposite wall. A song plays faintly in the background.

'I love the lyrics to this,' says Ryan, with a smile. The woman is singing about loneliness to an R&B beat. 'Do you like music?'

'Yes.' She wants to say more, but she is tongue-tied by a need to impress and the awareness that she's unlikely to manage it.

'Me too.' He takes a sip of his drink. 'Music tells me who I am,' he adds.

188

She wants to ask why he doesn't know who he is without it, but she stays silent.

His phone vibrates. 'It's Amber,' he says, glancing at the screen.

'Take it if you want,' she tells him, even though she would rather he focused solely on her.

He shakes his head. 'I've only just left her, it can't be anything important. I'll call her later.' He rests the phone on the table. 'Did you know Amber's my half-sister?'

'Yes, I remember. Same mum?'

He nods. 'My birth father was black, hers was white.'

'My dad was black too,' she says. A link between them.

'Me and Amber, we didn't grow up together. I only met her a few months back.'

'How come?'

'Amber's older than me. She got taken off our birth mother when she was five and put into care. She was in a children's home not far from here. I didn't even know she existed until a couple of months ago.'

'Did you stay with your mum?' He starts to look sad (genuine, she wonders, or the trick she uses to deflect awkward questions?) so she says, 'You don't have to talk about this if you don't want to.'

In his silence, she wonders if the people laughing and drinking around them are assuming they're a couple. It would be good if they did think that.

Ryan starts to speak again. 'My birth mother moved to Kent and I was taken off her when I was a year old. I was adopted. I was only in care for a few months but Amber wasn't so lucky. She got fostered a few times, but she always ended up being sent back.'

'Are your adoptive parents okay?'

'Yeah, more than okay. But my dad died when I was ten, so it's just been me and my mum since then. How about you? What are your mum and dad like?'

'I never really knew my dad. My mum died.' Lying again, but she doesn't have a choice.

'I'm sorry. I know how bad it was for me and Mum when we lost my dad.'

'We didn't really get on.'

She shouldn't have said that. She can feel his disapproval. Blood ties are important to him. He tracked down Amber and he stuck around, even though she's a smackhead and on the game. So she adds hastily, 'I was brought up more by my gran. She was great.'

He smiles at her. She smiles back, relieved to have turned it round. The music changes. A band are wishing it could be Christmas every day.

'Do you and Amber get on?' she asks.

'It's early days.'

She waits, but he doesn't add anything to this.

'When you looked for Amber, did you also look for your birth mum?'

'Yeah, I looked. She died years ago. Drug overdose.'

'That's a shame.'

He nods. 'I found an uncle, though, my birth mum's brother.

He lives in Willesden. I've been staying with him since I got out of hospital.'

'What about your birth dad? Did you find him?' she asks, draining her glass.

'Impossible to trace. There's no name on the birth certificate or with social services. I wish I'd known him. I've always felt like the odd one out, not knowing my birth parents. It's like there's a hole I can't fill. I thought Amber would help straighten it out for me but that's not really happening.'

He looks sad again. Best to keep the conversation light. So she forces herself to chat, and he seems interested when she talks about her bus trips and the Tube and the street markets she visits.

When she arrived, she told herself she would only stay for as long as she could see the flames of the fire. It's starting to go out. 'I'd better go, I have a dog,' she says, putting on her jacket.

'Okay.'

'It's just that he's been left by himself for ages and I've got to feed him.'

'Do you want to meet up again, then?'

'If you want,' she says, wondering if he means it, and if he'll bother turning up.

They sort out a time and place. 'Next week, then,' says Ryan.

'Next week, then,' she replies. She would like to flirt but she isn't sure how, so she just smiles at him. She doesn't want to see if he smiles back, it will be too disappointing if he doesn't, so she turns abruptly, bumping into somebody behind her. She feels stupid; who could be interested in anyone so awkward? By the time she does look back, Ryan has gone.

TWENTY-FIVE

An occupational hazard, Tyler thinks, but she does as she is told and goes to A&E to get her hand examined. The bite mark sits deep between her thumb and forefinger and there is blood and bruising.

'What happened?' asks the triage nurse, checking to see that all her fingers are still working.

'An arrest. He didn't come quietly,' Tyler answers. It had been a routine call but the man had described her as a fucking black cunt before sinking his teeth into her hand.

The wound is cleaned and dressed. She is told to wait for a tetanus jab. There will be blood tests too, for hepatitis and HIV. The anxiety this generates is hard to shut out. She sits in the cubicle, listening to the sounds around her. A man shouts, a baby starts to cry. She takes out her phone and tries to get online but nothing's working. Must be the hospital equipment, interfering with the signal.

She's been here before as a patient, rushed into Resus. She'd drunk vodka and taken a large quantity of pills. She'd been

found by her flatmate, who'd come home early from a conference. She recalls her sense of dread when she'd come round;
she'd made things worse, not better, and now she'd be studied
and assessed – and still alive. Her colleagues would find out
and she'd be transferred from the Firearms Unit, unable to
hack it, feeble and female, unfit for the job.

Why? everyone had asked. She'd been evasive, uncommu-
nicative. None of their business, even if she could have put it
into words.

She should have known that joining the Firearms Unit
was the last thing she should have done, but she'd been head-
hunted and she was flattered. Cool in a crisis, her bosses had
called her; the new face of a unit long overdue for change – far
too masculine. And the not-said: far too white. It was much
the same inducement that had led her to join the police in the
first place. She really shouldn't have fallen for it a second time.

She hadn't found the training difficult. She was certainly
good at the negotiation side and she was a crack shot with
deadly accurate hand-eye co-ordination. But she hadn't been
welcomed with open arms. Snide remarks, just audible, as
she passed. Laughter that ended abruptly when she entered
a room. References to our immigrant friends and jokes with
punchlines that pointed to the stupidity of anyone who wasn't
white. She should have reported it, but who to? The unit was
riddled with it from top to bottom. And then there were things
that were harder to ignore: missing equipment that had been
there ten minutes earlier, causing her to be reprimanded, and
dirt smeared over her spare uniform, even though it had been

hanging, spotlessly clean, in her locker. She'd been too stubborn to demand a transfer – she wouldn't let them win. And more than that, she wouldn't fail.

So there she remained until she'd had to use a gun for its intended purpose. She hadn't done it alone, she'd been a member of a team, but she had fired the fatal shot. Her actions had been justified, the investigation had concluded: the man had taken aim, and there had been no way of knowing his gun was a replica. Yet she couldn't get his face out of her head – another black man killed by the police, another with a history of mental illness. Mandatory counselling hadn't helped. She'd been ashamed of what she'd done, and ashamed she couldn't cope with having done it.

The harsh lights of the A&E department highlight the shabbiness of the cubicle curtains. She thinks she can see spots of blood. The chair beside the trolley has a deep rip in the seat; it looks as if it was done on purpose, with a long-bladed kitchen knife.

Even when she joined the Firearms Unit, she had assumed she would only act in accordance with the prevention of violence. She'd never believed that she would be its instigator. Hard to see now how she could have been so stupid.

The nurse returns to administer the jab and to take samples of blood. They exchange a few words about workplace injuries and joke about compensation.

It's the end of the day. She's not expected back at work. She goes to the hospital canteen and gets coffee and a sandwich – that's dinner sorted, now there'll be no need to shop.

As she walks down the long, ground-floor corridor, she thinks she recognizes someone coming towards her – a woman, pushing an empty buggy, with a small child following behind. As they grow nearer, she tries to think who it is. *Freya Fields*, of course. She looks different – thinner, and plodding, as if she can barely be bothered. Her arm is in a sling and a cast is visible beneath it. The child – Lucy's daughter, she can't remember her name – is trailing a teddy bear across the floor. Tyler hopes to pass unrecognized, but Freya sees her and says: 'DC Tyler, isn't it? You came to the house that day . . .'

She nods and says, 'How are you?' looking at Freya's arm.

'I've had a fall,' she answers. 'Silly, really. We're having some work done on the house and I tripped over the workmen's tools.' She points to the sling with her good hand. 'Broken in two places. I've been here for hours, you know what it's like.'

The child is slamming the bear's head into the wall repeatedly.

'Don't do that, Pops,' Freya says. 'Look, have you got a minute? There was quite a lot of information in the beginning but now it's all died down and I really need to know how the investigation's going.'

'You need to contact your family liaison officer.'

'I've tried. He's on sick leave, apparently. They're meant to be assigning someone new but they haven't got round to it yet.'

'I'm sorry, I've just had some treatment . . .' Tyler says.

'Please, I won't keep you long, I just need to know what's happening.'

Her voice is rising. Tyler gauges that it will be easier to say a few words to her than to try to make an escape.

They sit on a bench in the corridor. There is a long window behind them that looks out on to a small piece of garden with a few dwarf shrubs.

Freya turns to Tyler and says, 'You've stopped looking now, for the person who ... haven't you?'

'We haven't stopped looking, Mrs Fields. We put everything we can into solving a suspicious death.' She is trying not to use the word murder. It sounds too brutal when said to the mother of a victim.

'They say that if the police don't solve a crime in the first forty-eight hours it's unlikely that it's going to happen,' Freya tells her.

'I'll be honest with you, we haven't progressed as well as we'd have liked, but we haven't stopped trying, I promise you, and we may well still catch whoever did it. I'm sorry I can't offer you more.'

Freya nods, but she still seems anxious.

'Ice cream,' says Poppy.

'In a minute,' Freya replies. 'Lucy had a flatmate, Amber, I think her name was. Does she know anything about what happened?'

'She gave us a statement,' Tyler says.

'But did she know anything?'

'I can't really comment, Mrs Fields. All I can say is that we're still pursuing all avenues of enquiry.' As far as she knows, Ryan Morris is still at the top of the list, but they have nothing concrete. She is tired now, and wanting to get home. 'I'm sorry, I can't tell you what you want to hear. We're doing our best and we'll continue to do so. I'm sorry we haven't apprehended anyone yet, but it's not been an easy case.' Too many people in and out of the flat. Too much DNA. Too little evidence.

'What about that girl, Michelle Cameron, the one who murdered Kerry Gosling? Is it definite that she didn't have anything to do with it? She knew Lucy, the media said. You arrested her, had her in custody for a while.'

'She was completely cleared. It wasn't her, Mrs Fields.'

'You *say* that but—'

'It really wasn't her. It's all been checked out; we wouldn't have let her go otherwise.'

Freya nods again.

'Ice cream *now*,' insists Poppy, taking Freya's good hand and trying to pull her from the bench.

'In a minute!' Freya snaps.

Poppy looks startled.

'Sorry, Pops,' says Freya, 'but it's really irritating when you keep on like that.'

Poppy holds the teddy bear to her chest.

'That's nice,' says Tyler, pointing to it. 'What's its name?'

'Bear,' says Poppy, slamming the toy's head into the wall again.

'I'm sorry, Mrs Fields, I really do need to go now,' Tyler says, rising from her seat.

'If there's any news at all . . .'

'We'll let you know, I promise,' Tyler replies. She hurries towards the double doors that lead on to the street, desperate to get away. She thinks of Julie Gosling, losing her child, and Freya Fields losing hers. She can't imagine what it must be like; the worst thing it's possible to endure, most probably. She is tired of absorbing other people's pain. When she goes home, she will take more pills, even though they rarely bring her sleep.

At home, alone in bed, dreaming of black men wielding guns that are not real, mothers losing daughters and children beating children, Tyler awakens in the small hours, knowing what it means to take a life, to end the existence of another, the only thing a person really has. The hugeness of it overtakes her and she freezes in the bed, desperate to close down the bleakness of this recognition. It won't leave her. She is haunted, not by ghosts or spirits, but by her own capacity for destruction. It won't allow her to exist. It grips her by the throat, choking the life out of her. She takes pills to block it out, but always it returns, this unbearable awareness.

It's plain to her why Michelle Cameron has had to shut out the thing she did, is unable to name it. You can't survive in the full knowledge of it.

TWENTY-SIX

'I've got a boyfriend,' she announces. There's a real Christmas tree in Zoe's apartment. The decorations are co-ordinated; red and gold glass baubles in various shapes and sizes glow in the warmth of static lights. Perhaps one day, she will have a tree like this.

Zoe looks interested. 'What's his name?' she asks.

'Ryan. We've known each other for a while but we've only just started being together.' Is being together the right phrase? She isn't sure. She would like to tell someone that they haven't shagged yet because being touched by Ryan causes such a complex tangle of feelings, but she doesn't say things like that to Zoe. Besides, it's a word that just means sex, and when it happens with Ryan she wants it to be more than that.

'We've been out a few times, to some really interesting places,' she tells Zoe. 'The food at the café we went to on our first date was amazing. You wouldn't have known to look at it from the outside. Ryan knew it was special, though.'

Zoe says: 'I've been thinking you've seemed different lately. Happier.'

She nods. 'I am happier. When I'm with Ryan, everything is normal.'

'Normal?'

'I'm like everyone else.'

'And that's what you want? To be like everyone else?'

She rolls her eyes.

Zoe notices and says, 'Was that a stupid question?'

'Doesn't everyone want to be the same as other people?'

'Not everyone. Some people long to be different, less ordinary.'

'Only when they have a choice.'

'Perhaps that's true,' says Zoe. 'I'll have to think about that.'

She goes quiet and looks at the pictures of jazz musicians on the wall, all African-American. Zoe probably thinks they make her look cool.

'Do you know what you will be doing for Christmas?' asks Zoe, clearly bored with the silence.

'Ryan's coming over after he's had dinner with his uncle. We'll have the evening together.'

'Are you looking forward to it?'

'I suppose.' *She's counting the minutes.*

'What was Christmas like for you when you were growing up?' asks Zoe.

She doesn't want to talk about that, she wants to talk about Ryan. 'Ryan and me went shopping last week, to buy

Christmas presents he could send to his mum, and something for his uncle. I helped him choose.'

'And you enjoyed it?' Zoe asks.

She doesn't reply; she is remembering how happy she'd been that day with Ryan – the happiest, perhaps, she'd ever felt. They'd gone to a market and then they'd eaten the home-made sandwiches he'd brought side by side on a park bench. She hadn't even felt the cold. She'll be seeing him again the day after tomorrow but that's too long. She wants to message him all the time, find out what he's doing, tell him she misses him and can't wait to see him. But she knows she has to stop herself. If she chases him, he might get scared, think she's too full on and back away from her. But it's hard. If she knew how, she would write songs for Ryan, beautiful, soulful songs about love.

She doesn't say this to Zoe, who is impatient to hear about Christmases past. 'What was Christmas like when you were growing up?' she repeats.

'When I was living with my mother?'

Zoe nods.

'I spent it with my gran, mostly. Fred and my mum usually stayed in a hotel at Christmas.'

'Who's Fred?'

'He was my mum's boyfriend.'

'How did you get on with him?' asks Zoe, looking at her as if she can see right through her, the way she always does when she's hoping to hear something important.

'Okay,' she replies, trying to contain the sick feeling that is starting to overwhelm her. *Don't think about it*, she tells herself. *Think about Ryan*. But no good thoughts come. She'd gone there all happy, wanting to talk about having a boyfriend, but somehow, sharing it with Zoe has trashed it, just as she had feared it would. And now she's remembering Fred. She starts to shiver. She can't stop herself.

'You're shaking. What's happening?' asks Zoe.

'I'm just a bit cold,' she replies, hoping Zoe will believe her.

'It is rather cold in here,' says Zoe, adjusting the little scarf she is wearing so it covers her neck more closely. She goes to turn up the heating. When she returns she says, 'Can you tell me what you remember about Christmas when you were a child?'

'Gran made mince pies, she didn't buy them from the shop. And we had turkey dinner with all the trimmings. One year, the one before I got sent away, she got me a Gameboy, with three games. It was the best present ever. I gave her a calendar I made at school. She said it was beautiful.'

'What kind of presents did your mother buy for you?'

'Clothes, sometimes.' Not the kind of clothes she would have chosen for herself. Girly stuff, pink and frilly, nothing practical. Pretty underwear that she despised. She was made to put it on during the weekends she spent away. *Little black slag*. The words pop into her head. She puts her thumb into her mouth.

'What just happened?' Zoe asks. 'What did you remember?'

She doesn't answer.

There is the usual long silence that follows when she fails to respond to one of Zoe's questions. And as usual, Zoe is the first to break it. 'What was Christmas like at Whytefields Lodge?'

She removes her thumb from her mouth to speak. 'It was all right.' They'd got a present each, usually educational, meant to improve the mind. She remembers Lucy ripping the pages from the book she received and stuffing them into Carly Hughes's mouth. That was how grateful she was for Christmas crap from Whytefields. 'What did you used to do for Christmas when you were young?' she asks Zoe, tired of the questions being one way.

'The usual, I suppose,' Zoe replies. 'Our family Christmases were always quite traditional.'

Our family. She belonged somewhere, fitted in, did things the usual way. She minds Zoe's normality.

Zoe seems to sense she's losing ground, so she changes the subject. 'How's the new flat?'

'It's okay.'

'It's in Neasden, I think you said?'

'Yes.' Drab. Colourless. Suburbia: 1930s semis vie with sprawling estates and high-rise tower blocks. Scrubland. Scrubby. Desolate. Alien. But Ryan lives with his uncle in Willesden. They are within walking distance. Maybe the move isn't so bad after all.

'Are you starting to like it there?'

'It's all right,' she says.

Zoe sighs once more, clearly wishing, as she so often seems to do, that conversation was easier. She returns to Ryan, asking what he's like.

She smiles. She could talk about Ryan all day long. 'Just ordinary.' *Except he isn't.*

'How old is he?'

'A bit younger than me.' She's embarrassed to admit it. There's more than four years between them and it's awkward. Zoe might think she can't act her age and, of course, she can't, she doesn't know how, that's why she likes to be around people who are younger than she is. They used to say she was childish when she was inside – prison officers, and the psychologist at Whytefields – and it never sounded complimentary. It meant you lacked something you should have, something others have mastered: *grown-upness*. But it's not something you can just acquire. She knows this; she's tried hard enough.

'What does he do?'

'He's a chef, but he's between jobs at the moment.' A *chef*. He knew all about food. He was making it his life's work. It was as if he was made for her.

'How did you meet?'

'He was at Lucy's flat sometimes. I bumped into him again about three weeks ago in a chicken shop.' She isn't going to say she met him when she was standing outside Lucy's flat, just looking at it. That might sound weird.

'Why did he have to go away?'

'He had a few problems; I think it was to do with Lucy dying.'

'What kind of problems?'

She should have phrased it differently. She doesn't want

Zoe knowing about the drugs, or his breakdown or the time he spent in hospital. She'll think he's only interested in her because there's something wrong with him, or she'll write him off as a waste of space. 'I don't really know what kind of problems,' she says. 'Will you be putting Ryan in the book?'

'Would you like me to?'

She thinks about it. She would like the world to know that somebody wants her and cares about her and that she is normal, capable of having a relationship. But Ryan might not like it. 'I don't know,' she answers.

'Does Ryan know your identity?'

'No.'

'Do you think you'll tell him?'

'I don't know.' She can't imagine telling him, the shock he would feel, the contempt for her. The risk of exposure. But she can't imagine keeping the secret from him, either. It's too big a part of herself.

TWENTY-SEVEN

She's standing outside Dollis Hill station waiting for Ryan, bored, wishing her headphones still worked. The remaining ear cup died the day before yesterday. He should have been there ten minutes ago. Perhaps he isn't coming. She can feel her agitation growing but then he texts to say he's running late and won't be with her for another twenty minutes. It's cold and she's tired of standing there. She was early, the way she usually is, scared she might miss him. She's cross that he can't be bothered to get there on time. She'd wait in a café but you can't just sit, you have to buy something and even a cup of tea would take money away from the savings she's putting together for treats at Christmas. She starts to pace, stamping her feet every now and then to warm them up. A man comes out of the station and puts a rolled-up copy of the *Daily Mail* in the bin beside her. She fishes it out, checks that it's clean and glances at the front page. She feels the colour leave her face. It's there, headline news:

MICHELLE CAMERON TO WRITE A BOOK.
SHE WILL BE RECEIVING £200,000! GOSLING
FAMILY DEVASTATED

She scurries into a corner, scared that someone will see her reading the article and realize who she is. How could they have found out? It was meant to be a secret. *£200,000?* What the fuck? She continues to scan the page, her heart beating too fast.

Michelle Cameron, who murdered four-year-old Kerry Gosling when she was just a child herself, is to write a book. She intends to sell her story to Jamieson's Press for £200,000.

'The idea that a monster like Michelle Cameron is making money out of killing little Kerry beggars belief,' said Dave Donaldson, a former police officer and Gosling family friend. 'What kind of world are we living in when someone like her can make a fortune out of murder? The Goslings don't want her blood money, but what about them? They're the victims in all of this and they won't see a penny. It's disgusting, they're having to relive the nightmare all over again. They're in a state of shock.'

Corinne Bexford from Jamieson's Press said that Michelle Cameron would not be receiving any money for the book beyond expenses. She believes that the book is in the public interest: 'While we have no wish to cause the Gosling family any further distress, Michelle Cameron's story needs to be told. We need to have a better understanding of the reasons why children kill. The book will help the justice system and social services to find more effective ways of dealing with such crimes. It could even help to prevent them.'

Sources from within Jamieson's have said that Cameron will be working with Zoe Laing, who has produced several other books about killers, including the notorious *Bayside Murderers*. Her father, Adam Kenyon, who was the prosecution barrister at Michelle Cameron's trial (and is now a leading judge), had no comment to make about his daughter's involvement in the book.

We understand that it will reveal hitherto unknown details about the crime and the events leading to the arrest of Michelle Cameron (and the other anonymous child who was never charged). It will divulge the shocking details of Cameron's early life of abuse and shed new light on the killing. Whytefields Lodge, the lax secure unit that housed both Michelle Cameron and Lucy Fields (the prostitute Cameron was accused of murdering in September) will also come under scrutiny.

We live in a society where the victims of crime are ignored and the perpetrators are allowed to get away with murder. Should this book be published? Let us know what you think.

She folds the paper in half and then she keeps on folding, struggling to make the pages smaller. She'd put it back in the bin, but maybe someone will pick it out again, the way she just did. Ryan might even see it. She starts to walk away from the station. She can't see him, not like this, he'll know something's wrong and what will she say to him? A bus is coming. She gets on it, relieved as the traffic lights turn green and it speeds up the street. A loud sob escapes from her mouth before she can stop it. The other passengers turn to look. She forces her expression into neutral and studies her phone. She'll have to text Ryan, say she's ill, felt faint while she was waiting, had to go home. Will he believe her? She can't lose him now. What if he reads the papers and puts two and two together, works out who she is?

He texts her back. *Sorry u ill. friday same place if u well? sorry*

Two sorrys. What's he sorry for? She's the one who should be sorry.

Inside the flat, she eats half a packet of biscuits and starts to feel better. Okay, people know she's writing a book. But she's Carly Wilson now, not Samantha Robinson and certainly not Michelle Cameron. Why would anyone know it's her? Except that they found her when Lucy died. They could easily find her again. She unfolds the paper and reads it once more. It's obvious that people are angry about the book. Angry about her, and that she still exists. They definitely could come for her, angry, angry, *angry*. What will they do to her? She can't even think about it. She puts the paper down on the kitchen table. She shouldn't have agreed to do it. She could be exposed again, and for what? Because Zoe wants to write about her? It wasn't even her idea; she'd never have thought of doing it for herself, never have supposed anyone would be interested in what she had to say. *Zoe bloody Laing*, it's all her fault. Was she the one who told? But why would she tell people about the book before it's even written? Nothing makes sense anymore.

She gets up and goes to the window in the living room, just in case she's being watched. She peers through the semi-closed blinds. Down on the pavement, people are going about their business as if nothing's happening at all. She checks the door again, makes sure it's double locked. She secures the chain. Would anyone come if she pressed the panic button? Maybe Tyler would, but out of duty, not because she cared.

She runs into the living room and lies on the cold lino floor, not moving. She used to do this when she was little, play dead, in the hope she'd be left alone. She remains there until long after dark.

She gets up, feeling slightly dizzy, listening for chanting voices from the street. There is no sound. Relieved, she goes to make a cup of tea, stepping over Otis who has fallen asleep. No sugar left. She sips her tea without it, struggling to calm herself. What will she do if Ryan finds out who she was because of the book? She hadn't really thought it through, she'd only got as far as thinking about the process of working on the book with Zoe, not what might happen once it was finished.

One day, in the not-too-distant future, it will be published. Anyone will be able to read it. They will see who she is – or who she is according to Zoe. How long does it take for a book to come out? She has no idea. In a few weeks, or a year, or however long it takes, there will be more articles expressing outrage that she has been allowed to have her say. Perhaps she'll be settled once more, happy, building a life with Ryan, and then the book will come out, and it will all be taken away again. She should never have agreed to do it. She turns the pages of the paper and sees a picture of Zoe Laing wearing a chunky necklace and more earrings that dangle almost to her chin. She never said her father was the prosecution barrister – obvious why not. She remembers Adam Kenyon, how fiercely he'd looked at her, some of the horrible things he'd said. Zoe's dad. What else has she hidden from her?

She is angry. She's been taken in.

Recently, she'd started to like Zoe a bit. She feels so stupid. How could she have thought that Zoe might ever really like her? She doesn't want to see her anymore. She turns on the charm and tries to pretend she's on your side. She keeps digging around, stirring things up that are best forgotten. Right now, she thinks she actually hates her.

She looks up at the carved elephant that sits on a shelf. She remembers Zoe's kindness and how much she likes the way that Zoe listens. She's the only person left who really knows anything about her. Perhaps she can't afford to lose that yet.

TWENTY-EIGHT

Zoe is waiting for her to arrive. She's late. No doubt she's heard the outcry about the book; all over the media questions are being asked about whether or not it should be published. Her editor has given assurances that everything will go ahead as planned, which is something at least, but no doubt the leak will make it difficult for her to turn up, especially with the revelation of her father's role in the case. Perhaps she should have been up front about that.

It's hard to settle to anything just in case she decides to keep the appointment. Zoe is anxious. She needs Michelle Cameron to stay the course. And she minds that her time is being wasted. She turns on Radio 4 but the conversation is dull and doesn't engage her. She feels restless and her mouth is dry but coffee doesn't seem to help. She needs to learn far more about Kerry Gosling's murder, and if the article has scared Michelle Cameron off, that possibility will end, as will the prospect of producing a credible book – just as they were getting somewhere.

There is a knock. The way Michelle Cameron raps on the door tells Zoe what mood she is in even before she enters the apartment. She is battering at it angrily. Last time she was there, the knock was tentative, barely audible.

She doesn't apologize for being late, she merely pushes past her and sinks into the sofa in the consulting room without removing her coat, a sign of her resistance. 'You didn't tell me Adam Kenyon is your dad,' she says, placing a foot on the stool in front of her.

Zoe picks up the recorder on the coffee table and checks that it's working. She adjusts it and says: 'I'm sorry about that. I should have told you. I meant to.'

'No you didn't,' she replies.

'You're angry.'

'No shit, Sherlock.'

There is silence for a moment. Then Zoe says: 'You have every right to be angry with me. I don't know if it helps but my father and I clashed quite strongly about your case. I didn't think he should have taken it. I wrote some articles about it.'

'Why didn't you think he should have taken it?'

'You were a child being tried in an adult court. That shouldn't have happened. And the judge should never have ended your anonymity. That was completely wrong in my view.'

The cat pushes its way through the door and sits in the middle of the floor licking its paws. She gets up to stroke her and she says, 'Why did you say the book will make allegations of abuse? When did I tell you *that*?'

Zoe sighs. 'Someone leaked the information about the book. I don't know where it came from. I can promise you, I didn't say that at all. Someone, and I don't know who, has made an assumption.'

Zoe has decided not to say she has her suspicions. Her marriage had ended acrimoniously so she made sure Oliver knew about the book. They are in the same field; he is a consultant psychiatrist at a major hospital. She shouldn't have told him. She'd wanted him to see how successful she had continued to be, in spite of all his efforts to undermine her. It seemed she had played into his hands by giving him something else to try to take away from her.

Michelle Cameron interrupts her thoughts. 'Why would anyone assume there was abuse?'

Zoe knows she needs to tread very carefully. She thinks for a moment and then she says, 'I suppose they assumed something like that had happened because when a child kills another child, there is nearly always a history of some kind of abuse, whether it's sexual, physical or emotional.' She waits, hoping this will trigger a disclosure of some sort, but none is forthcoming.

She stops stroking the cat and returns to the sofa. 'You said I couldn't have any money because it wasn't allowed.'

'It's a bit of a grey area, legally speaking, because it's so complex. But whatever the legality, there would be a public outcry if you were to receive any money, and we wouldn't want to generate that kind of hostility.'

'Will you be getting the two hundred thousand pounds, then?'

Zoe laughs. 'I don't know where on earth they got that figure from. Trust me, it's nonsense.' Money is continuing to be an issue. She will need to take on more hours at the clinic soon, and then there will be less time to write.

She gets up and makes another coffee, using the Nespresso machine without asking. She seems to like the caramel flavour. She takes a doughnut and sits down again. 'You must be married because your surname isn't Kenyon,' she states.

Zoe sighs. She would have reverted to her maiden name when Oliver left, but all her publications were in the name of Laing so she'd had to keep it. She would rather focus on Michelle Cameron's life but she says: 'I was married. I'm divorced now.'

'Did you divorce because of a betrayal?'

'Is that how you're feeling at the moment? Betrayed?'

She doesn't answer. Instead, she repeats the question: 'Did you divorce because of a betrayal?'

Zoe thinks for a while, weighing up whether to respond or not, and then she says, 'I suppose so, in a way.'

'He cheated on you.'

'Why do you say that?'

She shrugs. 'Well, did he?'

'It's not something I really want to discuss.'

'Why not?'

Zoe picks up the pen on the coffee table and twirls it between her fingers. Too late to deny it, which is what she should have done. Not quick enough off the mark. She minds the way the tables are being turned. She knows where this line of questioning is going; Michelle Cameron will be angry, say that she's required to answer questions but it's all one-way – everything she asks remains unanswered. The only way to head her off would be to talk about her marriage and she isn't prepared to do that. She remains silent, thinking of her divorce in all its bitterness, and the child she'd hoped to have but had been denied. Then she says: 'Our meetings need to focus on you, not me. The book is about you.'

'Do you get on with your dad – Adam Kenyon?' she asks, as if Zoe hadn't spoken.

She thinks of her father, his relationships with women other than her mother and his denial of these. She considers the conflict it caused within the family; her brother no longer speaks to him and refuses to attend family gatherings, while her sister has sided with their father against their mother, deciding her lack of warmth pushed him to adultery. She isn't sure if her decision to do the book came from a desire to be closer to her father or to alienate him further. She sighs once more. A psychoanalyst would have a field day, but she's never set much store by the Freudian school of thought.

'You expect me to tell you loads of personal stuff, even though you didn't tell me the truth about who you are, but you won't answer any of my questions,' she says truculently.

There it is, exactly as predicted. Zoe doesn't take the bait but replies: 'I really am sorry I didn't tell you about my father. I suppose I thought if I did, you wouldn't want to do the book and that would have been disappointing. I've been wanting to work with you for a long time.'

'Why?'

Zoe calculates that flattery is the most effective way of getting things back on track. 'Because I'm interested in you. You really interest me,' she says. 'And I want people to know *you*, the kind of person you are, because if they did, they wouldn't be so quick to judge you.'

Michelle Cameron sinks lower into the leather sofa and studies the ceiling. 'I'm sick of it, the way people treat me. Everyone betrays me in the end – my mum, my dad, you ...'

'How did your father betray you?'

She kicks the coffee table. 'He promised he'd come for me and have me live with him but he never did.'

'And your mum?'

'You're trying to change the subject to stop me talking about the things the newspaper said. How am I supposed to trust you? The book could turn out just like the TV documentary they did on me, full of untrue things that are made out to be real. You could put anything about me in it, couldn't you? No one would know if you made stuff up. You could say I was the most evil person you ever met if you wanted. You don't have to say any of the things I tell you, and if you do say them, you can say them in a way that makes me sound really, really bad.'

'I suppose, in theory, I could say untrue things about you,' Zoe replies, 'but for me the most important thing is to present you and what really happened as accurately as possible. Like I said, I want people to know the real you, the likeable, interesting you, not the sensationalized Michelle Cameron of the headlines. And if that happens, people might start to have a better understanding of why children end up in prison and what can be done to prevent it.'

'You're very careful about how you say things, aren't you?'

It sounds like a criticism so she keeps her tone neutral, not wanting to seem defensive. 'Words are my stock in trade,' she replies.

'In the newspaper article, the publisher said that, too, about people needing to understand, but I don't think that's why they'll read the book.'

'Why do you think they'll read it?'

'They'll find it sort of exciting.' She thinks for a while. 'I don't know if that's the right word; it's something like that, though. When I got arrested because of Lucy, in the police station they were all looking at me like I was some kind of wild beast they'd never seen before. It was like I could set them all on fire with one big breath.'

Zoe smiles and says, 'What's it like, having people think of you like that?'

'Scary.'

'What's scary about it?'

'It's like I'm too big. I don't mean too fat, I mean ... I don't know ... I mean it's like I'm much more than I am. Does that make sense?'

'I think so. Magnified.'

'Yes, *magnified*. And people see something that isn't real. But I don't know what the real me is.'

'When you said you'd do the book, do you know why you agreed to it?'

'I think the biggest reason was . . . I don't know. I don't really want to talk about it.'

'I may be putting words into your mouth, but did you agree to do it because it seemed like a chance to say what happened, and to be real?'

'Sort of. I think what I wanted most of all was to be Michelle again, just for a little while, and not have to hide. Does that make sense?'

Zoe says it does.

'It's not that I liked being Michelle or I think it was good to be her, I just want to stop having to pretend. I'm tired of pretending, you know? I'm just so tired of having to pretend.'

She gets up to go. Zoe is careful to set up the next meeting before she leaves. She presents her with the usual envelope.

Once she's out of the apartment, the tension leaves Zoe's body – she hadn't even realized she was feeling it. She thinks about her reasons for finding Michelle Cameron so difficult. Lots of demands. They are there implicitly; everything she says requires a particular response, with the tacit threat of withdrawal unless the reaction she craves is received. Each question has to be posed delicately, in case she sees evidence of hostility and takes flight. It's like fighting a verbal duel; she's having to think several steps ahead. 'You're very careful about how you say things,' she'd said. She's perceptive, too, which doesn't help. It's hard to conceal yourself from her.

And yet she's also vulnerable. It's become clear in the course of their conversations that she did most of her living before she was ten. Shut off from the world since then, her knowledge of it has been largely second-hand, gleaned from TV screens and filtered access to the internet. The teenage bluster of the residents of Whytefields had often been mistaken for reality; her view of other people's lives is skewed. She hasn't been to clubs or got drunk underage (or not since she was nine) and, being better staffed than children's homes, Whytefields had kept illegal highs outside its walls. In some respects, Michelle Cameron has led a sheltered life since she was ten; even when she'd been in the young offenders' institution, her comparative naivety had invited some of the other inmates to keep her out of harm's way.

All this will go into Zoe's book, but there is still so much to be done; she is more relieved than she can say that she managed to get Michelle Cameron back on side. She needs a drink but that will have to wait until later. She wants to be clear-headed when she phones Oliver. She is angry with him but there is elation, too; his desperate attempt to stop the book tells her how much he fears the promise of its success. Towards the end of their marriage, as her career had really taken off, he had become increasingly threatened by her work – she wasn't even medically qualified, he would tell her, trying to emphasize that whatever she achieved, she would never match his dizzy heights. Her work was populist, he would say, not to be taken seriously. He would deconstruct each article or conference paper word by word, telling her how facile her arguments were, how ill-informed. When he'd had the affair, he'd said it was because she'd failed to support him in his career and he needed someone younger, with fresh, exciting ideas and energy enough to inspire him. His bit on the side, now his new wife, has a run-of-the-mill career as a psychiatric nurse, but she probably won't be allowed to keep it. She has already been forced to go part-time. No competition there, nothing that can undermine him. She glances at the clock on the wall. She'll ring him at 8 p.m. just as he and his wife are sitting down to dinner. She will tell him that his pathetic attempts to derail the book haven't worked. She will do it calmly and coldly. She will emphasize that no publicity is bad publicity, and tell him that all he has accomplished with his malice has been to provide her with the prospect of even greater success.

She goes to the laptop to write up her notes while they are still fresh. She wants the book to be accurate but, more than that, she needs it to be important.

TWENTY-NINE

Tyler receives a phone call. Michelle Cameron says there's been a disturbance at her flat. She can't see anyone but eggs have been thrown and there's been some shouting. She thinks it's the mob from the time she was questioned at the station; they've found her again because of the book.

Tyler drives as quickly as she can, fearing she is under attack. There's no answer when she knocks and calls to Cameron through the letter box so she lets herself in with the key she holds. It takes her a while to find Cameron. She has locked herself in the bathroom and won't come out. She can't, she says. Tyler can't see why not but she lets it go for the time being and checks the flat for signs of intrusion. Smears of egg yolk and shell are evident on the outside of the window but there's no sign of anything more sinister.

She makes some tea and waits for Cameron to calm down, checking emails on her phone to ward off the boredom. Several retirements are announced, and her boss has sent a message warning colleagues against using work computers for online Christmas shopping. Eventually Cameron appears, as if hiding in a bathroom for an hour and a half is a perfectly normal thing to do.

The dog seems to have taken a shine to Tyler. He jumps on her lap, expecting her to stroke his stomach. As she obliges, he moans with pleasure, wagging his tail. She doesn't usually like dogs but he is convert material.

The tea has gone cold so she brews more. They sit in the kitchen making strained conversation. She's been told to stay for a few hours, keep an eye on Cameron just in case – whatever that means. The liberal broadsheets have taken senior management to task for exposing her after Lucy's death, pointing, as was feared, to leaks and cover-ups. They have implied that racism played a part. Tyler is there to demonstrate an absence of culpability and she minds her role in this. She is tired of feeling angry. Since the Cameron situation, with all its complexity, she has felt little else.

It's making her more terse with Michelle Cameron than she means to be. As they continue to talk about nothing very much, she becomes conscious of her body language, her folded arms and the way she is leaning away from her. She's been trained to read people, but she's been failing to recognize her own responses. She forces her body into a more neutral posture.

'I haven't really got used to living here,' Cameron says. 'I wish I hadn't had to move.'

'I expect you'll get used to it in time,' Tyler says mildly, trying to combat the irrational irritation she feels when faced with her vulnerability.

'When Lucy was alive, she used to visit me. She liked the views from my old balcony. You could see all over London.'

There has been no progress with the Lucy Fields enquiry. Nothing has been found to justify charging Ryan Morris, so although he is still the most likely suspect, they are looking further afield, at dealers and at Lucy's clients – the ones they've been able to trace. DI Henderson doesn't think they'll get a result. He believes that loss of life is the inevitable outcome if you lead Lucy's kind of existence. It's as if her life had no importance.

Tyler looks at Michelle Cameron as she sits across the table seeming tired and distracted. She was surprised to hear about the book. Not the best move if you want to conceal your identity.

'Do you think the people who threw the eggs will come back?' asks Cameron anxiously.

'I doubt it. I honestly don't think you were being targeted. The eggs are coincidence, just empty vandalism. The windows of the flat below were spattered, too.'

The hunted expression on Cameron's face suggests that she doesn't believe her. 'When my old flat was wrecked, it happened through people remembering about me again because of Lucy's death. They started looking for me, didn't they? The stuff about the book will remind them, too. There was a photo in the paper, the one they always print. Do you think anyone will recognize me? Maybe I haven't changed enough? It never goes away, that picture. I look so ugly in it,' she says, touching the skin beneath the collar of her shirt.

Tyler looks at her. Ugly isn't the word she would have used. Even at ten, although she was stick-thin, she was attractive, with large eyes and an oval face. She remembers what Cameron had called her on the day she'd been detained in the cell: *black bitch*. The words still make her flinch but she's starting to make sense of them. The media had traded on Michelle Cameron's 'blackness' for years (whether consciously or not she isn't sure): bad blood; a savage attack; devil child – always placing her photo side by side with that of fair-haired Kerry Gosling. In recent times, it had become less overt, but it was encoded between the lines of most of the articles about her. No wonder she had internalized the idea that to be black was something to be ashamed of. She thinks of Dave Donaldson again. *She was bad by nature. You could see it in her face.* He was less subtle than most of the professional journalists, but they came from much the same perspective.

Tyler is aware that Cameron is still looking shaky. 'Do you have anyone you can spend some time with?' she says.

'I've got a boyfriend now,' she answers with a half-smile.

'Right,' Tyler replies.

'His name's Ryan. He's a chef. I knew him through Lucy. He brought some brownies round the other night. His cakes are legend.'

'Right,' says Tyler again, aware of a dilemma. Perhaps she should she tell Michelle Cameron that her boyfriend is the chief suspect in Lucy Fields' murder and that she could also be at risk. But there is no concrete evidence as yet, so she doesn't see how she can.

'Ryan doesn't know who I really am. Do you think he could find out because of the book?'

'I don't see how.'

'I should tell him, shouldn't I?'

Tyler sighs. 'I don't know. It's a big thing to talk about.'

'You think I *shouldn't* tell him?'

'I don't know,' Tyler repeats.

She turns away, disappointed, most probably, in Tyler's failure to offer guidance. 'If I tell him, he'll probably hate me,' she says quietly. 'Everybody hates me, don't they? I didn't know I was hated, really *hated*, until I was arrested when you thought I killed Lucy. It's such a strange feeling.'

Tyler thinks it's the kind of thing a bullied child might say: *Everybody hates me*. Except in Michelle Cameron's case, it's barely an exaggeration, and she's being bullied by a nation.

On the drive back to the station, she thinks about the way a single act can change a life. When she was young, she didn't have friends. The other kids found her odd – they mistook her aloofness for a sense of superiority and saw her as bookish and dull. As a result of her isolation, she'd withdrawn further into herself and hadn't troubled to hide her eccentricity. Her classmates dressed in street clothes, with hoodies and jeans, but she'd found a cloak in a charity shop and she'd worn it constantly, fostering childish rumours that she was a vampire or a witch. She'd liked their wariness of her; it had stemmed from her sharp tongue and the fact that she wasn't one of them. She didn't date, either, so she was an enigma to those around her, just as she is now an enigma to her colleagues. She got a bike. It was large and second-hand, with rusty mudguards and high handlebars that forced her to sit upright. She must have looked strange but she'd wanted that back then; she'd wanted to assert her difference.

One day, in a deserted street, they cornered her. They dragged her from her bike and started to kick and punch, venting their outrage at her refusal to conform. She'd been feeling angry for months. She didn't know why, or not exactly. It was something to do with her sense that the world was an unjust place, where you were second class if you weren't straight, white and able-bodied. That anger had overwhelmed her as she was attacked that night, and she'd fought back, taking them all on. She'd punched one of them and he had cracked his head on the pavement. She can see him now, bloodied and bewildered, not quite knowing how his defeat had come about. He'd got up and staggered home along with the rest of them, leaving her alone.

It should have been a victory, but it wasn't. Scared of herself, she'd got rid of the bike and the cloak. She had started to conform. What if the boy she had knocked to the ground hadn't got up again? What if he'd hit the pavement so hard that something in his skull had cracked for good? She hadn't thought about consequences, in her fury. Perhaps Michelle Cameron hadn't thought about consequences in hers.

THIRTY

She's usually at her most desperate after Christmas. Most years there had been few cards, no presents and no one who actually cared about her to spend the time with. But this time, she'd had Ryan.

She wants to tell Zoe about it as she settles on the sofa in Zoe's spacious apartment, but before she can say anything, Zoe says: 'I didn't know if you'd come today. You didn't turn up to the session we arranged for the week before Christmas. What was going on there?' She can hear hostility in Zoe's voice.

'I don't know,' she answers, though she knows full well.

'I thought perhaps you were still angry with me because of the newspaper article.'

'Why would I be angry with you?' she says. But she is still angry. And it is about the article. She hadn't turned up just before Christmas because she'd wanted to teach Zoe a lesson, pay her back for deceiving her. She'd known it might mean that Zoe would threaten to tell probation about the time she'd hit her but she'd also worked out that Zoe wanted the book too much to risk sending her back inside and not being able to finish it.

Zoe sighs the way she so often does during their meetings, a sign of suppressed irritation. 'Perhaps you could let me know you're not coming if it happens again in future? It's the polite thing to do and it saves me wasting time.'

She doesn't respond. She doesn't owe Zoe anything; she shouldn't have to account for herself. But at the same time, she fears her anger, so when Zoe asks about Christmas, she is quick to say it was good and tries not to sound too hostile. 'Ryan made a Christmas pudding from scratch. We had that. It was just *amazing*. He put fresh orange peel in, and he poured real alcohol on it. He turned out the lights and set it on fire, it looked beautiful.'

He'd brought beer and a bottle of wine. Chocolates too, explaining that his mum had sent him money for Christmas. And he'd spent it on her. He'd handed her a gift, neatly wrapped in paper that had sausage dogs with angel wings and halos. She'd laughed as she'd ripped off the paper, eager to see what he'd given her. It was a necklace, with polished brown and green beads: tasteful, the kind of thing Zoe might wear.

She touches it with her fingertips. 'Ryan gave me this,' she tells Zoe.

'It's lovely,' Zoe replies.

Her present to him was only second-hand, a backpack from a charity shop, but he really liked it. He filled it with his wallet and the cushion from one of the chairs and walked round the living room with it on his back. He took hold of her and kissed her lightly on the lips. Even though she'd been afraid, she hadn't pulled away.

'How did you spend the day?' asks Zoe.

'We watched television,' she replies.

They'd put two of the folding wooden chairs together and placed them in front of the TV in her living room. They'd watch the queen's speech side by side.

'I don't get this,' Ryan had said.

'What don't you get?' she'd asked.

'The queen. Royalty. Why it still matters. I used to feel like I belonged here but I don't know if I do anymore. It's all changing. There was someone from the EDL on TV the other day going on about getting our country back, taking back control, making it like the good old days. They don't want the likes of us.'

She'd leaned into him, basking in the solidarity implicit in his use of the word 'us'. They certainly didn't want the likes of *her*. It was disconcerting to think there were other kinds of people Britain didn't want. Perhaps she was doubly not wanted.

She remembered the job interview with Cheryl Ayres and being asked where she was from. She told Ryan about it.

'That's what I mean, we're not seen as British. The exact same thing keeps happening to me and it was even worse when I was growing up,' he said.

It's one of the reasons she is so drawn to him – the things they have in common, the similarities in the way they look.

She never looked like her mother, however hard Sandra tried to change her. She didn't look like her dad, either. She never even looked like Gran.

She doesn't say any of this to Zoe. She doesn't think she'll understand. Instead she asks about Zoe's Christmas, like the polite little reformed person she's supposed to be.

'It was quiet, but good. I feel rested, ready to be back at work.'

'Did you spend it with your family?'

'Yes, I did.'

The Kenyons, all happy together, drinking expensive wine with their three-bird roast. And they'll have picked at a Christmas pudding from Harrods and exchanged luxurious gifts wrapped in gold paper. She would be envious if not for Ryan. She fingers the necklace again. She will always wear it.

She resents being in Zoe's apartment today. She resents having to be polite. She crosses her legs tightly. She doesn't want to talk. What's the point? The book will be written whether she speaks or not.

It's only two o'clock, but it's a dull day so everything looks dark. Zoe switches her tree lights on. 'That's better,' she says, pleased with the effect.

Only it isn't better. Once Christmas is over, it's over. Decorations after Christmas are just depressing, however classy they may be.

Zoe watches her for a minute, as if she is calculating what to ask next. Then she says: 'Last time you were here, you mentioned your mother's boyfriend, Fred. What was he like?'

She freezes; a child is crying again. Fingers are squeezing its throat. She starts to cough. Zoe fetches her some water.

'I was asking about Fred,' she continues. 'Did you get on with him?'

'He was all right. What are you doing for New Year?'

Zoe says, 'I've noticed that often, when you're asked something that feels uncomfortable, you ask me a question and try to change the subject.'

'It isn't uncomfortable, I just don't want to talk to you today.'

'Do you know why not?'

'Not really.'

'And yet you kept the appointment, so you must want something out of being here.'

Well, that was a mistake, she thinks to herself. *Why did she come?* To talk about Ryan. She's feeling things she's never felt before, not towards anyone, not even Gran. She would like to check it out with Zoe, see if Ryan really cares about her the way she thinks he does. She'd like to check out if she's behaving the way she should with him.

She doesn't really know how to behave, that's the trouble. She might make a mistake, say or do stuff that marks her out as different. She could lose him if she doesn't get it right. They still haven't slept together. She'd thought they would on Christmas Day. As the evening had gone on she'd got more and more scared. Would he want to stay the night? She couldn't let him, not yet. She'd tensed up, wondering what she would do if he tried to stay. Saying no never worked, it only made them angry, and once that happened it hurt even more. But she needn't have worried. At about half past ten, he'd said it was time for him to go. He'd kissed her again, but that was all.

As he'd left the flat, she'd felt desolate. Maybe he didn't fancy her. How could anyone want to be with her? Even though she'd had the happiest Christmas ever, she'd cried herself to sleep; she'd wanted two opposing things with the exact same intensity: to sleep with him and to make sure it didn't happen.

She wishes she could say some of this to Zoe. But what if speaking just confirms how weird she is? It's safer to be silent.

As she is leaving, Zoe hands her a package wrapped in embossed silver paper. 'I would have given you this before Christmas but you didn't turn up.'

'I didn't get you anything,' she says, awkwardly.

Zoe just pats her shoulder.

On the journey home, she sits upstairs on the back seat of a bus as it weaves round Piccadilly, past the statue of Eros and the tourists who are clustered round it taking photographs. On-screen advertisements brighten the bus with their light. It's almost dusk and the journey is slow; rush hour traffic, even though it's still the Christmas holidays. Buzzing with curiosity, she opens the present Zoe has given her. There's a box under the silver paper, wrapped in cellophane – the perfume she's been using when she goes to Zoe's bathroom, the one in the bottle like a carved-up female corpse. She feels the blood rush to her face; her longing for things she can't have has been exposed, and her wish to be like Zoe. When the bus reaches Neasden, she gets off, leaving the package behind her.

THIRTY-ONE

New Year's Day. A fresh start. She lets him in. Perhaps she shouldn't, perhaps it isn't safe, but they go to bed together. It's fun. She wasn't expecting that. He laughs at the silliness of it all, the fumbling in the dark, the awkwardness. He finds it entertaining but he isn't laughing at her, he's laughing at himself. And she laughs too as he tries to get inside her and can't at first because he doesn't really seem to know what he is doing even though he's not a virgin and she's never been one, at least that's the way it seems. And when he is inside her and it hurts the way it always does, he stops, pulls out and comforts her, saying it's okay and they don't have to do anything that gives her pain.

The tenderness is frightening. She wants him. It's new to want somebody. Why is he being kind to her? Is he only pretending? Has he guessed who she is? Is he fucking her just so he can sell the story to the tabloids? She freezes then. She'd cry if she could. She turns away and faces the wall, refusing to look at him.

'What have I done?' Ryan says, sounding curious and pained at the same time.

She doesn't answer. There are only clichés: *It isn't you, it's me.*

He repeats the question. There's irritation in his voice, she can hear it.

'Nothing,' she whispers.

'What's wrong then?'

'Nothing,' she replies.

He sits up and looks at her quizzically. 'I'm sorry I hurt you,' he says, 'I honestly didn't do it on purpose.'

'I know,' she answers.

He scratches his neck. There are pimples on it. It's a turn off. What turns *him* off? What does she do that makes him squirm? She'd ask if she dared but he might tell her and it might be something she can't change: her ugly face. The rolls of fat spread across her thighs.

She doesn't sleep until dawn, so when she awakens she's heavy with exhaustion. Ryan has left her bed but she can hear him whistling in the bathroom next door. Why is he happy? He didn't come, so why hasn't happiness turned to rage? She feels it too, the pulling in her groin, the longing for release. Her nipples are hard and wanting to be touched.

He returns to bed with a grin on his face. She doesn't know what to make of it. He runs his fingers along her fat thighs and sucks lightly on her breasts as if they are attractive to him. She strokes his hair. This time, when he presses gently into her, she doesn't whimper or cry in pain and it pleases her to feel him there even though it hurts. She's surprised at how ordinary it all is. Is this what it's like to feel love? she wonders.

It won't last, she tells herself as he pulls his T-shirt over his head and zips up his jeans. He is skinnier than she would have liked but then she's fatter than she should be, far fatter than is attractive. He says that she is beautiful, and she wonders why he lies to her.

'What do you want for breakfast?' she asks. It's the polite thing to say.

'I'll get it,' he replies, kissing her on the cheek.

He poaches eggs that they eat on toast. He'll be going soon, she sighs to herself as yoke trickles down her chin. Perhaps she wants him to leave, the pain between her legs is sharp and in the shadowy space by the kitchen door, a man appears; he is grinning, his face contorted with pleasure. She shuts him out.

'Are you all right?' Ryan asks.

'I'm fine,' she says, though she isn't, not really. She is afraid of nameless, painful things, and the shadows won't leave her. Perhaps they never will, she thinks. Perhaps it's impossible for her to be happy. She stares at the wall. Above the boiler, the paper, damp, with small black patches, has started a slow descent. She doesn't even know who her landlord is. How are safe houses obtained? Rented from private landlords? Too many questions for that, most probably. Bought by the state? Much more likely. Can she complain? She isn't sure. Anyway, it's temporary, the way things always are.

The table rocks precariously as she picks up her coffee.

'I could fix that,' says Ryan.

'Yes,' she replies quickly. Fixing things will mean he'll stay for longer.

*

It's a pity Amber doesn't like her. They visit her flat that afternoon. 'Hi Sam,' she says, glaring at her.

The use of her previous name is unexpected. It scares her. She tells Amber that her name is Carly but people who knew her when she was young, like Lucy, called her Sam because that was her birth name; as she got older she started calling herself by her middle name – Carly – because she liked it better. The explanation is rather convoluted. She looks at Amber to see if she's convinced. Her expression is one of slight puzzlement that quickly fades. She has little interest in other people and has no reason not to believe her so she lets it go. Ryan has forgotten she was ever called Samantha and is smiling the way he so often does now he's not off his face, so that's okay, thank God. But Amber's antagonism is still clear. 'What did you bring her for?' she whispers in Ryan's ear, loud enough for her to hear.

'She's all right,' Ryan replies.

It's faint praise, far fainter than she'd hoped for.

'If you want tea, I haven't got any milk,' says Amber, as if this will persuade her to leave.

'I don't need anything,' she answers.

Amber turns her back on them and busies herself with the washing up.

They sit at the kitchen table, viewing Amber's back apprehensively. She moves briskly, bristling with irritation. She sighs. Amber was like this when she visited with Lucy – envious of their apparent closeness. It'll be even worse with Ryan. 'I could go,' she whispers to him.

'No, don't go,' he says. She is surprised by his defiance. Up until now, he's seemed like someone who'd cave in at the least sign of resistance.

Amber, sensing she is there to stay, discovers a fresh carton of milk at the back of the fridge.

She'd start a conversation if she could find the words. It used to be like this at work. In prison, it was easier – she was quite chatty most of the time, so perhaps her ineptness is to do with the need to make sure that outside, no one ever knows too much about her.

Or maybe she is simply out of practice. Where do you start? *How's work?* Not the right question for Amber – she might actually answer it and, to be fair, it's better not to know. *Have you been to see any good films?* With what? Amber is on the breadline, barely money for essentials, and, besides, she has nothing to add to that conversation herself; it's ages since she's seen anything, too busy with Zoe – and Ryan, of course. *The weather isn't bad for the time of year.* Seriously? Is that the best she can offer? The kind of things elderly strangers say to one another?

'What time's your next client?' There. She's said something. Not bad: it mentions Amber's work without sounding judgemental; makes it seem normal. And it gives the visit an implicit time limit – *definitely* necessary. The boredom round the table is palpable.

'Not seeing anyone until this evening. Things are slow,' Amber answers.

Ryan pours himself another cup of tea.

Amber rests her feet on the empty chair beside her. 'Do you ever wonder who killed Lucy?' she says.

'It wasn't me,' says Ryan.

'It wasn't me neither,' says Amber.

'Nor me,' she adds.

The laughter that follows this is full of tension. 'They really did think it was me, though,' says Ryan. 'Still do, I reckon, it's just they can't prove it. I think they're keeping tabs on me, still hoping to find something. I swear I got followed the other day.'

She doesn't say they really thought she'd killed Lucy too. Perhaps she's also being followed and the police are outside now, just waiting for them.

'No one's following you, Ryan, you're still paranoid like you were in hospital,' says Amber.

He looks uncomfortable. 'I'm not paranoid anymore, I swear I'm not. But I'm worried I could still end up inside.'

'You didn't do it so no one's going to put you inside,' Amber tells him.

She frowns, remembering her time in the cells. If Amber thinks not having done something keeps you safe from ending up in jail, she's thicker than she thought.

'Now Lucy's gone, I'll have to get another girl to move in here soon,' Amber tells them. 'Can't afford the rent on my own and the landlord's on my back. Have you got anything I can borrow off you, Ryan? It'll just be till Thursday.'

'Sorry, I'm skint,' he says. Then he adds, 'Who do you think killed Lucy?'

Amber shrugs. 'No one cares who did it. I keep thinking, what if whoever it was comes back for me as well? I'd move out of here if I could. I don't even sleep anymore but no one gives a shit. The police have given up investigating. What's another dead druggie whore?'

As they are leaving, Amber takes Ryan aside. They talk for a few moments. She tries to give him a small packet. He hesitates but doesn't take it. There is a brief argument that she strains to hear but their voices are too low. She looks round her. The streets are empty. There is no sign of the police and no one seems to follow as they wander down the road.

They walk hand in hand. She is flattered that Ryan doesn't mind being seen with her.

'Do you think Amber will be all right?' he asks. 'What if whoever did it does come back? I've been thinking I should move in with her just in case.'

'If they were going to come back they would have done it by now. You don't want to live with her, it might set you back, put you in hospital again. And you could end up with a record as well, she could drag you into all kinds of crap.'

'I suppose,' he says, still sounding worried.

'What was all that with the packet she was wanting you to take?'

'Nothing,' he says.

'Was she trying to get you to buy some gear off her?'

'She said it would help, keep me calm.'

She snorts her disbelief. 'Seriously? And you believed her?'

'I did when I first met her.' He is sounding defensive.

'She'd never give me class As, she wouldn't. Just Es, and a bit of skunk.'

And amphetamines. And nameless pills in see-through packets that caused him to see devils in hell.

When she was inside, they'd spiked people sometimes, just for entertainment, to break up the boredom. A laugh. See them make idiots of themselves, off their heads, literally climbing the walls. Perhaps Ryan was Amber's side show. Or perhaps it was about Amber needing to punish him for the luck he'd had in being taken out of care. Maybe she wanted to make his life as shitty as her own. His innocence is part of his appeal, but it scares her too. She wants to warn him about Amber but she can't. She doesn't want him to think she is trying to turn him against his sister.

It's almost dark. She wonders if he'll want to go home with her again. Two nights in a row. Does she want that? She isn't sure. She's still remembering the pain between her thighs and the shadow in the corner of the kitchen. But a part of her does wonder what it would be like to have him with her, needing her, loving her. Better not to feel the hope.

THIRTY-TWO

Tyler had worked all through Christmas. She preferred it that way. When she was young, she'd enjoyed the festive season, but since joining the service, time spent with her family was strained, something to be avoided. Easier to tell them she was working. Easier to tell herself that not seeing them didn't matter to her.

A call comes in. It's Freya Fields. She takes it reluctantly. They still haven't been able to arrest anyone for the killing of her daughter. Most of her colleagues have lost interest. A sex worker, who would in all probability have had her life cut short by drugs or STIs if she hadn't been murdered. There were more worthy victims.

'Please,' says Freya, 'you have to help me. It's Poppy, she's been taken.'

'What do you mean, *taken*?'

'She was playing on her trike in the garden and now she's gone. My mobile phone was upstairs, I heard it ring, I only left her for a few minutes.'

It's the story Julie Gosling related when Kerry was abducted. For a moment Tyler wonders if history is repeating itself and Michelle Cameron has taken another child, a twenty-first century bogyman who snatches small children from the safety of their back gardens.

'I think my husband has her,' Freya continues. 'We've been separated since Lucy, more or less. We spoke last night and I said I wanted a divorce.'

Tyler points out that if this is the case, there's nothing they can do. Nicholas has as much right to spend time with Poppy as Freya does.

'But he's taken her without letting me know. I'm scared of what he'll do. I think he's going to hurt her, just to get at me for saying I was leaving him for good. Please, you have to help me, he's violent. I should have reported him, but I couldn't, he told me I'd lose everything. He wants Poppy, he doesn't want me to have her anymore.'

Tyler remembers meeting Freya at the hospital; the broken arm, the story about tripping over workmen's tools and falling down the stairs. Perhaps, if she hadn't been a patient there herself, she would have seen the signs.

An alert is put out. Nicholas Fields' car is stopped en route to Brighton, just before Haywards Heath. He is shocked to be pulled over; he is simply taking his granddaughter on a day trip to the seaside.

In an interview room, Nicholas Fields states that his wife is a hysteric who hasn't been able to cope for some time. The death of their daughter Lucy has pushed her over the edge.

The idea that he abducted Poppy is absurd. Freya handed his grandchild over as usual; weekly visits had been agreed between them. It suits her to claim he took the child; it's a scheme to get a better settlement in the divorce he is seeking.

Freya's accusations of violence mean he is now suspected of Lucy's murder. He looks incredulous at the idea that he could have killed his own daughter. 'I know I said I was with my wife when our daughter was killed, but I was actually with a friend that night. She will confirm that,' he says.

Tyler sits opposite, taking in his defiant posture and his measured denial that he has ever done anything wrong. He is the victim, smeared by Freya's vile accusations. He would never have harmed Lucy nor his wife; no complaint of violence has ever been made. Surely it would have been? They were together for more than thirty years. When, in that time, had the police ever been called? Where is the evidence? If he was such a bad husband and father, why would Freya have stayed with him for all these years? He asks for his solicitor.

Poppy has been taken to hospital and examined. The report comes back: there are no signs of abuse.

'Do you seriously think I'd ever contemplate such a thing?' Nicholas says to Tyler, when she tells him of Freya's fears.

Social services have no reason to keep Poppy from the family home so she is returned to Freya. Tyler drives there in the early morning, hoping that Freya will provide something solid that will help them to charge her husband with killing his daughter. She parks outside the house in Clapham, preparing the

244

words she will say to trigger Freya into remembering. There will be something she knows without awareness of it: a half-buried memory that will prove Nicholas had been with Lucy on the night she died.

Tyler is greeted warmly by Freya. She sits with her at the kitchen table. Janine, a social worker, is there, taking steps to ensure that Nicholas will not be allowed to see his granddaughter unless and until all charges of violence are disproved or dropped.

Freya clutches Poppy to her with her good arm. 'He didn't hurt her, did he? Promise me he didn't hurt her.'

Janine has already told her that no harm came to Poppy, but Tyler confirms it too. Janine offers to take her to the sitting room to play so Tyler and Freya can talk.

As Janine closes the kitchen door, Freya says, 'You're sure he didn't hurt her?'

'Quite sure. When did it start – with you and Lucy, I mean?' asks Tyler.

'The violence started not long after we were married. He needed things to be perfect. He didn't like mess. I'm not the tidiest of people and I'm not very organized. He needed things to be organized in order to succeed. We were building a business. You can't have chaos when you're starting that kind of project. I wasn't really the right woman for him, I can see that now.'

'And Lucy?' says Tyler.

'I don't know when that started. She wasn't an easy child. I think she reacted to the way Nicholas was with me. She was very difficult at school, she was excluded from every place we sent her to. The more Nicholas punished her, the worse she became. There wasn't anything we could do with her. When she ran away from home, in many respects it seemed for the best.'

Lucy was thirteen when she first became a runaway and she started using drugs even earlier. Tyler recalls that the post-mortem had flagged up old injuries, but these were consistent with her lifestyle, so they hadn't raised suspicion with regard to the family – nice, middle-class people.

Freya gets up and takes a bottled mineral water from the American-style fridge. 'Would you like one?' she asks.

'I'm good, thank you.'

Her arm is still in a cast so Freya struggles to open the two-litre bottle.

'Here, let me,' says Tyler, standing beside her. The bottle opens with a loud fizz and some of the water erupts over the top of it. Freya wipes it with a cloth and pours some into a glass. They both return to the table.

'I need to rehydrate as much as possible,' Freya says, 'I have to stay fit and well for Poppy.'

'That day I saw you at the hospital, it wasn't the first time you'd ended up there, was it?'

'No, not the first time.'

'Would you be willing to press charges?'

'I don't know. I'll have to think about it.' Freya leans back in her chair. She seems deep in thought. 'Nicholas must have lost his temper with Lucy on the night of her death. He wasn't with me, you know. Will I get into trouble for lying? Only he said I had to stick to the story, tell your colleagues we were together, here in the house.'

Tyler doesn't let her know he's claiming he was with another woman on that particular night.

'Have you charged him yet?' asks Freya.

Tyler doesn't answer. They hear Poppy crying in the other room.

'I have to go to her,' says Freya, 'excuse me for a moment.'

Tyler looks out of the kitchen window on to the spacious back garden. She pictures summer barbecues eaten at the wooden table in the middle of the lawn. There is an apple tree, and a swing is tethered from a silver birch. Happy families, a familiar lie.

Freya comes in and sits down again. She says of Poppy: 'She's all right again now. The medical check upset her. She hates being away from me. She'll need lots of looking after for a while.' After a pause, she says: 'I am going to press charges with regard to Nicholas breaking my arm. If he goes to prison, he won't be able to see Poppy anymore, or do anything to her. I've been so afraid we'd lose her. You can't imagine what it's been like.'

'You said "we". Do you mean you and Nicholas? Why would you have lost Poppy?'

'Because of Lucy.'

'No one would have wanted to take Poppy away from you because of Lucy's death,' says Tyler, aware that Freya seems fragile, muddled.

'No, Lucy wanted to take her away from us. Because of Nicholas.'

'Because of his violence?'

'Yes.'

'I went to see her, you know, that's when she told me. I didn't want to go to that house, it was a squalid little place and I knew we'd end up arguing, we always did. But she'd broken in and stolen from us again. She took Bear.' Freya points to the teddy that is sitting on a chair in the corner of the kitchen. 'Nicholas gave it to Lucy when she was little. She carried it around with her everywhere. She broke into the house shortly before she died; she came in through the bathroom window and she stole it, that and a rabbit. She stole toys from her own child.'

'But didn't you say just now that it *belonged* to Lucy?'

'She was a grown-up, what did she need with toys anymore? We gave it to Poppy, it was Poppy's, she needed it, she couldn't sleep without it, I had to get it back.'

'So you went to Lucy's flat to fetch it?'

Freya nods. 'I left Poppy with a friend – only for an hour or so – and I took a taxi. I tried to talk some sense into her but she wouldn't give Bear back. She said it was hers. Poppy couldn't settle without it, she was crying and crying. She loved that bear, she missed it and she wasn't well. Lucy could be so childish, taking a toy from her own daughter, refusing to let her have it anymore.'

'What happened when you saw Lucy?' Tyler asks.

Freya takes another sip of water from the bottle. She wipes

her nose with her sleeve and then looks up, straining to hear what's going on in the living room. 'Was that Poppy?' she asks. 'Is she all right?' She listens for a moment or two, then satisfied that Poppy isn't making any further sounds of distress, she says: 'Lucy came to the door. She hardly had anything on. She'd always been like that, careless about herself. She told me a friend of hers was writing this book, it was going to reveal things that had happened in her life and Lucy wanted to do the same, get it published. That didn't worry me, I knew it was nonsense. She could hardly read, she played truant right through her school days. How was she going to write a book? She could tell I wasn't taking her seriously so she said she was going to the police. She said she was going to make sure her father got arrested for cruelty, the things he did to her when she was young. Then she'd get Poppy back.'

The landline rings. Freya jumps, then gets up to answer it. 'Leave it, it's okay,' says Tyler. 'If it's anything important they'll leave a message or phone back.' She takes Freya by her sleeve and eases her into her seat. The phone stops.

'Freya, listen, I'm going to have to caution you, do you understand?' Tyler says the words, but Freya doesn't seem to be listening; she just nods vacantly as the caution comes to an end. 'You probably shouldn't say any more. I think you need a solicitor,' Tyler adds.

But Freya doesn't seem to hear. 'I offered her money,' she continues, 'but she just ignored me, she was high on something, even I knew that. Then she took off her skirt, and her knickers. Told me that was what usually happened when somebody offered her cash. She spun round and round, naked from the waist, saying all these things, telling me she had to get Poppy away from us before she was damaged beyond saving too. And then she collapsed, started convulsing, I knew it was an overdose and I thought, this is the best thing that could happen for all of us. I don't mean I wanted her to die, of course I didn't, I just wanted it all to stop and to know we had Poppy for good, that Lucy couldn't take her away from us whenever she felt like it. I stood beside her and I thought, okay, I'll be here until you go, I won't leave you. And then after a few minutes, she started to come round and all the hope I had was disappearing and I could see Poppy being taken from us by some woman from social services and put into care. So I picked up the bear and put it over her face and then I brought it home again for Poppy.' Freya stands up. 'Is that Poppy crying? I don't think she likes that social worker. I need to take her upstairs, she should have a nap, she'll have been awake all last night. I'll just go and see to her. Would you excuse me for a moment, please?'

The Fields will have the best lawyers. No evidence will be found to support the accusations made against Nicholas, so his granddaughter will be returned to him. His violence will be masked by affluence and respectability. Poppy will become her mother, turning to drugs to suppress unbearable memories of childhood.

Michelle Cameron will be shocked when she hears, full of disbelief. They exposed her to all the hatred of the public and the press, forcing her to move and change her name again and all the time it was Lucy's own mother. It will lead to tears and self-harm. Then she will batten down the anger that she feels and try not to think of it again, aware, perhaps, that rage has never served her well.

The jury will be sympathetic to Freya. They will see frailty, an inability to cope. She will be thin and drawn and her clothes will be discreetly elegant, markers of taste and class. Her daughter was given the best of everything but squandered her opportunities, falling into addiction and prostitution. No wonder Freya had snapped. They will note her losses and feel she's been punished enough. In time, she will sell her story, telling of the destruction of her family: 'Michelle Cameron was my daughter's closest friend,' she will say. 'Once the Gosling Girl came into our lives, there was no return for us.'

THIRTY-THREE

She thought the fair would stand on grass beneath the trees but it's been pitched on concrete by the road. It's not yet dusk: the flashing reds and greens of childhood memory are dulled by daylight and the music barely sounds above the traffic, constantly missing the beat. The worn rides circle sluggishly.

'We shouldn't have come,' she says to Ryan, but he's gone to buy the wristbands and he doesn't hear.

It's a treat he has been planning for her. He's got a job now, working in an all-night café, so it's a celebration, though she isn't as pleased about it as Ryan – she won't be able to see him so often.

She's put on loose jeans so she can enjoy the rides without her clothing cutting into her but they make her look even fatter. She's still wearing the pretend glasses and she's sick of it; they make her look geeky and old, but if she takes them off, someone might see who she was. Perhaps it's less likely with Ryan. Who would imagine Michelle Cameron could do something ordinary? Have a boyfriend who is tall and fit and holds her hand as if she's just another human being? With Ryan, she almost feels like she blends in, but she has to tell him tonight, get it over with. She's been building up to it for days. She needs to tell him now, before they get so close that it hurts too much when he leaves.

She wants to mess around with him the way she does with Zoe, not tell him the whole of it. His innocence means she could tell him almost anything and he would still believe her. But unless she tells him everything, what happened with Kerry will always lie between them. He will look shocked when she puts it into words. Horrified. She will repulse him. The word evil will pop into his head and he won't be able to shift it. She can't tell him. She wants to, but she can't. *Start small*, she tells herself. *Build up to it.*

Dusk begins to fall and the fair is coming to life. The rides that seemed shabby in daylight now start to shine as the lighting fires up their steel surfaces, flashing in time to the music. The space pulsates with sound.

She holds on to Ryan as they ride the Twister with its bouncing tentacles. She is thrown to the side and she fears she will fall, slip through the gaps, but the ride slows its pace and she stays in her seat. 'It's quite safe,' Ryan promises, and she wants to believe him but she's remembering the thing she has to say.

When the ride stops, they go to a rifle range where he shoots metal ducks that ping and drop out of sight at the back of the stall. In the smoky air she wills him to win her a bear but he is no crack shot. He puts down the gun, embarrassed. 'I'm

253

shit at this,' he says. She squeezes his arm to tell him that it doesn't matter.

They move away from the crowds and sit side by side on a bench. They share a bag of candyfloss. *Tell him*, she urges herself, even though it will ruin everything. *Start small, build up to it*. She takes a deep breath. 'What's the worst thing, the very worst thing you've ever done?' she asks.

'I don't know,' says Ryan, looking at the ground.

'You do,' she replies, with a giggle intended to conceal the gravity behind the question. She can hear the screams of adolescent girls as they dip and rise on XLR8, higher than the rooftops of the flats beyond the road.

He still doesn't look at her, but he says: 'I told my dad I hated him and I wished he'd never adopted me. I can't even remember what I was angry about. I didn't get the chance to take it back.'

'Because he died?'

'He died that night, driving home from work. His car was hit by a lorry.'

His voice is faltering. She thinks he's going to cry. 'But you were ten. At that age you say heaps of stuff you don't mean, everyone knows that. Your dad would have known it, too. You were just a child.'

'I still said it,' he says.

'And you still didn't mean it,' she replies.

There is silence. Then he says, 'What's your worst thing?'

It's meant to be her cue to tell him, but instead she says: 'When we were at school, me and Lucy used to be mean to this girl. She was younger than us. We made fun of her, pushed her around, shut her in a cupboard once. Made her life miserable.'

'How old were you?'

'About thirteen.'

'So you were young, too.'

She nods, grateful for absolution. She can't say anything more. The very worst thing he ever did was to shout at his dad, a stupid childish argument that anyone could have. He was just unlucky it was the day of the accident. How can this compare to the thing she did? It's the difference between a paddling pool and an ocean. 'Come on, let's go back. I want a ride on the dodgems,' she says.

They drive the bumper cars into one another recklessly, crashing so fiercely that they are made to leave. They move on to the Waltzer, clinging to the bar, hurtling round, paralyzed by centrifugal force; their grins are fixed. They see the streets of Neasden from the wheel and feel as if they're nesting in the trees. She should be happy. She wants to feel the fullness in her chest her greatest joys induce but instead there is only an emptiness she doesn't know how to fill.

'You've gone quiet,' says Ryan as they walk towards the doughnut stall. 'Aren't you having a good time?'

'Of course I am,' she replies with a little skip, the kind a four-year-old might give. 'I'm just a bit tired. I didn't sleep well last night.'

'One more ride?' he suggests.

They go on the Bounce, lurching up and down; she feels as if the nuts and bolts that hold the ride together will loosen from their sockets and she'll be flung into the centre of the crowd. She doesn't scream: the fear is far too real for that.

The fair winds down; the music stops. As they leave the park they feel as deflated as the lost balloons that sway slowly, wedged in the branches of the trees.

'You know what you said about bullying that girl?' asks Ryan as they cross the street.

'Yes,' she answers cautiously, pulling her jacket round her.

'I got bullied at school. We lived in the countryside, not far from Canterbury. Everyone in my class was white, except me and this other boy, George, my best mate. The others kicked the shit out of us most lunchtimes. The teachers never did a thing.'

She slows her pace, not sure what he needs her to say. 'I'm sorry,' is all she replies.

'Do you know why you did it, the bullying?'

'Not really. Boredom, maybe?' She hopes the answer is enough to end the questioning.

'Lucy had a mean streak,' says Ryan. 'She didn't bring out the best in people. She got Amber into all kinds of shit.'

'She told me once you fancied her.'

He is embarrassed. 'No, not really.'

'You did, though,' she continues, hoping he'll give her a reason to end it with him now, before she has to tell him what she did.

'Maybe I fancied her a bit.' There is a pause and then he adds, 'Not half as much as I fancy you.'

The words barely penetrate. 'Lucy was very pretty,' she tells him, trying not to sound jealous.

He takes her hand again and says: 'She wasn't a very nice person. Did you know she killed someone once, when she was about fourteen? Actually *killed* them?'

She remains silent, feeling herself go still.

'She told me herself or I wouldn't have believed it. She said it was some bloke who got rough with her. She stabbed him. It would have been self-defence, but still . . .'

'She made a mistake, I expect. There would have been a reason for it. One mistake doesn't make you a bad person, it shouldn't affect the way you're seen for ever.'

He considers this for a moment and then he says: 'She killed someone though. That's extreme. I can't imagine it.'

Perhaps she should say, '*I can imagine it,*' tell him the thing she's been hiding from him, but she can't say the words, they stay deep in her throat, impossible now to retrieve.

'Shall I come back to yours or do you want to come to mine?' he asks, unaware of her silence.

She hasn't seen the house he lives in with his uncle. She's been wanting to. It will give her an even stronger sense of who he is. But she shakes her head. 'Not tonight,' she says. 'Another time. I'm still really tired and I'm feeling a bit sick. I shouldn't have gone on any more rides after the doughnuts.'

He's disappointed, she can tell, but he only says, 'Okay then, see you tomorrow,' and he kisses her goodnight.

THIRTY-FOUR

Zoe thinks it's easy for someone to sit in her living room and talk about all the bad stuff. When it doesn't happen, she sighs or wriggles her foot, angry but not actually saying it. Sometimes she just looks bored. She is looking bored now. Then she says: 'It would be good if we could talk more about the past, but I know it's difficult, remembering. How would you feel about a visit to Whytefields Lodge? It might trigger memories, enable you to talk more easily.'

It isn't that she's forgotten. It's more that she doesn't want to remember. She's worked so hard at shutting the memories away. It isn't fair to make her get them back now. The thought of having to return to the places she's now left, literally and metaphorically, scares her too much. She starts to say this but she knows Zoe will never understand – she wants more stuff to put in her book. So instead she just says: 'I don't think Whytefields exists anymore. They closed it down.'

'It's still there, I checked. It's just uninhabited.'

She can tell by Zoe's tone – low and firm, passive-aggressive, insistent – that this is an offer she can't refuse. 'Okay,' she says, quietly. She's tired of being quiet. Quiet and invisible, as if she's barely there. Don't be seen, be careful what you say, hide yourself. She's sick of it.

Zoe says she can take a taxi all the way to Whytefields and gives her money for it – cash, in the usual envelope. It's a lot more than she usually gets. She calculates that if she catches a train and a bus, she can keep the money she saves, the way she usually does. But this is such a big amount. If she doesn't use at least some of it for travel, she could be sent back to prison and never see Otis – or Ryan – again. She doesn't know what to do.

In the end, she compromises, getting a train for part of the way and a taxi for the rest, deciding to enjoy the journey.

It's a dull day, but she still revels in the sense of space as she's driven past fields and pretty cottages with neatly cultivated gardens. But then Whytefields comes into view. Her stomach lurches even though it's smaller than she remembers it. She can't get out of the taxi. She stays inside for at least ten minutes, claiming to be waiting for someone, trying to summon the courage to walk through the grounds. The driver keeps checking the meter impatiently. The cost is mounting up. There's so much she could do with the money she's wasting here. She opens the taxi door and stumbles on to the footpath.

The gate to Whytefields has been left open for demolition vehicles. She starts to walk slowly up the drive alongside climbing weeds and shrubs that are growing into one another:

ivy throttles rhododendron bushes. The air smells damp. Much of the building has been boarded up and the tall, broken windows on the top floor remind her of the greenhouse where she used to play.

She is trembling, transported back into a past she needs to leave behind. The grounds are full of shadows, half-remembered things she doesn't want to see.

She pictures herself sitting on a bench by the back door surrounded by the fence that was far too high to climb. Her head is down. She can't look at anyone. She can't make this real. Slowly, she is starting to understand that Whytefields is where she will be staying until she is grown up: for ever, almost. She longs to go home – even seeing Fred would be better than the isolation she is feeling. She wants to be rummaging for bargains in the market with her mother or watching television late at night when everyone else is asleep. 'Can I go home now?' she says to every grown-up she sees. 'No, that isn't possible,' they tell her, gently at first, but after a while, their tone becomes sharper and eventually they stop replying to her.

For the first few months, she'd thought she would see her mother again. Every visiting day, she waited by the window thinking this time she would come. Each time, she was disappointed. The other children's mothers visited. Even Lucy's mum came a few times.

Zoe is walking up ahead. She has brought an expensive camera and she is taking photographs, capturing the decay of the place. The pictures will appear in the book, no doubt.

The main door has been left open. They go inside and Zoe takes more pictures.

She sits on a broken chair in the middle of an empty space with crumbling walls made worse by water trickling into brickwork. There is an old sleeping bag in the corner and several empty cans. 'Someone might come here, somebody's been sleeping rough,' she says, her voice tremulous.

'It's all been cleared and secured,' answers Zoe, 'I made arrangements with the security guards. Did you have any trouble getting here?'

Is she trying to find out if she spent the money on a taxi the way she's supposed to? Zoe is sly with her questions; you never know what she's really asking. She doesn't reply. Instead, she says, 'If you saw me in the street, would you think I was ordinary?' She is feeling conspicuous again, the taint of Whytefields, she supposes. It's like a badge she wears, one that says she's to be feared and avoided: put away.

'What do you mean by ordinary?'

The usual lack of a reasonable reply causes her to cry out, 'Just answer the question!'

Zoe looks angry for the briefest of moments but then she says, 'Words like ordinary and normal, they don't mean much to me. We're all ordinary and we're all special, I would say.'

Typical shrink speak. 'Crap answer,' she replies.

There is a moment or two of silence and then Zoe says: 'If I saw you on the street, I wouldn't think anything of it. I wouldn't particularly notice you.'

'I'd notice you.'

'Why?'

'You dress in a smart way, you wear unusual things, like your earrings and your coloured shoes. You stand out, like you want to be noticed.'

'Do you want to be noticed?'

'Only in a good way. Not because I'm her.'

'*Her?*'

'You know who I mean.'

'Can you not say your own name?'

'It isn't my name anymore.'

'What's it like having different names?'

'Confusing. I miss her, sometimes. I shouldn't, but I do.' She can hear her own voice echoing round the empty building.

'When you say "her", do you mean Michelle?'

She nods.

'What is it that you miss?'

'Memories, the ones that are hers, ones I can't have as Samantha or Carly.'

'I don't really understand why you can't keep your memories.'

'Because I'm not *her*.' She is tearful and frustrated. 'There's a story about myself that was made up for me by other people. I have a different date of birth. My mother isn't Sandra Cameron, my mother's surname is Robinson. We didn't live at my old house, we lived abroad. I'm not allowed in my old area. I didn't go to St Margaret's School. I was homeschooled. If I have to admit to having a criminal record, I have to say I did time for theft.'

'It sounds lonely.'

'Not lonely – weird. She can't exist, she was too bad to exist. The parts of her that are me are so terrible they can't even be talked about.'

'You can talk to me about them.'

'That's why I said I'd do the book, to be her for a while. But I'm not sure I want to.'

'Perhaps it would be a relief not to have to hide things.'

'And perhaps it wouldn't. What if the lid won't go back on?'

Zoe doesn't answer for a while. She seems to be deciding what to say. 'I can't promise it will be easy but you will be able to cope. It's my job to keep it safe for you and I intend to do that.'

She takes a can of drink from the pack that Zoe has provided. Most people would have used an old carrier bag, but Zoe has brought them in a cooler box. She likes soft drinks icy cold and Zoe has noticed. Another thing to bribe her with.

She looks at the staircase that winds up to the bedrooms. She'd quarrelled with Lucy once. She can't remember what about. A borrowed pen? A pack of sweets that had disappeared? Could have been anything. Lucy had tripped her up on purpose for arguing and she'd fallen headlong, cutting open the side of her head.

It's strange being back, like a bad dream. She wants to wake up.

'What was it like for you when you first came here?' Zoe says.

She doesn't reply. She is back. It's as if no time has passed at all. She doesn't want the memories.

Zoe has brought cake. She takes a piece and pushes a chunk of it into her mouth. It helps her to forget. She chews it thoroughly before she speaks: 'I don't remember anymore.'

'I don't believe that,' Zoe replies. She is looking cross again.

'I don't—'

She is interrupted by screeching and the flapping of wings. A crow bats its way through a chimney stack and falls a few feet from where they are sitting. Stunned at first, it remains still, but then it revives, fluttering round them, desperately trying to find a way out. Droppings land on Zoe's mustard-coloured coat. She tries to fend it off but the bird swoops again, its wings brushing her face. She hits out at it once more and it flies into the rafters and remains there, looking down on them, as if planning a further attack.

'Fuck,' says Zoe, swearing for the first time since she's known her. It makes her seem smaller, for a moment, not someone to be scared of. There is silence for a while. Then Zoe picks up her camera again and takes some carefully constructed shots of the bird for the book.

THIRTY-FIVE

Even without returning to the ruins of Whytefields, she would have remembered its long corridors, the locked cupboards in the corners and the cabbage-and-polish smell. She hadn't forgotten the isolation room, or the automatic doors that slid firmly shut, locking you in and the world out.

One of the things you need to do here at Whytefields is take responsibility for your own actions, said Dr Rowe. He was a pot-bellied man with a large nose and he spoke in a soft yet stern voice, a contradiction that always threw her.

She wasn't sure what he meant. She *had* taken responsibility. She wasn't telling him she hadn't done it anymore. She just didn't want to talk about it. Talking never changed anything.

Samantha?

Samantha: she'd chosen the name herself in the car on the journey to Whytefields. She'd been driven through London, across the river, on a bridge like a castle that went up and down to let ships pass. No ships that day; the bridge stayed flat. She saw the Tower of London, with its off-white turrets and heavy wooden doors, built in the days when people were hung just for stealing. The crown jewels were there, guarded by men who ate beef, liked ravens and wore uniforms with silly high hats. Beneath their coats were bayonets and hand-cuffs. There were railings with spikes, all round the buildings. Windows with bars. People gawping, taking pictures. Was that where they were putting her?

But they'd sped past and on to a dreary road that had a bingo hall and several chicken shops. In a small park with ramps and concrete blocks, boys careered up and down on skateboards; she watched them jump and spin, skidding to a halt and flipping the boards up with the heels of their trainers, catching them with one hand. Someday, she would learn to do that; they were street dancers on wheels, slick and cool. And then the woman, the social worker said: 'There's been a lot of publicity about you and you need a fresh start; Whytefields will help you to begin again. But you can't keep your old name. People will remember Michelle Cameron and the crime she committed and you've been in the news quite a bit, as you know, with a photo, so if you keep the name you have now, some of the older children especially might pick up on it. Do you think you could choose a new name for yourself, one you'd like?'

Michelle nodded. She imagined herself as Juliette. And Persephone. And Arabella. So why Samantha? It had just seemed to fit. She could never be Michelle again, they said. A good thing? She wasn't sure. But Michelle shouldn't exist anymore, she was all wrong. She had gone through the doors of Whytefields as Samantha, believing Samantha would do things right.

You are still in denial and you have to start to take responsibility for your own actions, repeated Dr Rowe, from the light brown armchair opposite.

But they weren't her own actions. They were the actions of Michelle Cameron, who didn't exist anymore.

'How did it go with Rowe?' asked Lucy when she returned to the recreation room. She was new to Whytefields and Samantha liked her and wanted to be friends.

'I'm in di Nile,' she answered.

'Help, help, I'm in di Nile and I can't swim,' said Lucy. It was the Whytefields joke, not even original - childish. But then they were children, weren't they? Albeit bad children, the kind no one wanted – scary little maimers, killers and arsonists – not what children were meant to be at all. 'Help, help I'm in di Nile and I can't swim,' the children would say to one another and then they would splutter with laughter. Each of them had been in di Nile at one time or another.

One day, Lucy was gone, just like that. No one seemed to know what had happened to her. Carly was still there, though. She had always liked Carly, she had just been a little afraid of her, not because she was scary or mean but because she wasn't. It would be so easy to damage her. And they had damaged her between them, her and Lucy, or at least she thought they had. But Carly was much tougher than she seemed as it turned out. Sometimes they would listen to the radio in the recreation room, or they would sit in the garden by the shed, sucking the sweets that Carly's parents had brought. She was good at sharing, not like her and the rest of the children, who guarded everything as if their lives depended on it.

Days and months went by, each more or less the same. She discovered she was good at English and maths and by the time she was transferred to young offenders', she had six GCSEs, all grades A or B, and two A levels, grade B. No chance of arsing about in class with only a dozen other children in it. Too visible by half. There were people to play with in the gardens in the evening, chucking balls. A swimming pool to work off all the excess energy. She learnt to swim slowly, determined to hang on to the float even when she'd got the hang of it. Occasionally there would be day trips to the sea or long country walks, and once, a few of them were taken to a theme park.

WHYTEFIELDS SECURE UNIT RUN LIKE A HOLIDAY CAMP, the headlines bawled one autumn. Not so many outings after that, but after a few months it had all died down and things returned to normal.

Whytefields. A sprawling low-rise building: windows with sheets of glass that never shattered. Gardens with vegetables. She could grow things if she wanted to, but it didn't appeal to her. There were no secret places here, not like the allotments.

Talking. Easing into memories. No, she didn't want to think about it.

You have to start taking responsibility for your actions and part of that is remembering.

She could remember being friends with Shannon. Shannon was skinny too and she had a pair of Rollerblades, gold with black flashes and bright red wheels. There was a swing in their back garden. Cold lemonade on sticky days. Biscuits and slices of cake when they were hungry. There was Baby Aaron, too, who often cried and stank the place out with his smelly Pampers.

'I need to change him,' Shannon's mother said.

'For a new one that isn't smelly and doesn't cry?' she suggested cheekily, and Shannon's mother laughed.

She was friends with Jessie, too. She and Jessie had a secret. *The allotments.* The glass house, with cracks in the windows and shrubs pushing in from the outside.

I don't want you staying in all the time, watching me every minute. Get yourself some chips, her mother said, pressing coins into her hand, *and don't come home until it's dark.*

She didn't want to be home, anyway. She wanted to be at the allotments with Jessie and now at least there would be chips. No one came to the glass house uninvited. Jessie had permission. And Kerry. Not Shannon, she would probably tell. There were cups in the glass house, and plates she'd smuggled out of high street shops. She was good at nicking things – she never got caught, even though there were cameras and security guards. Her mum knew and shrugged it off, *kids will be kids,* except when she wanted to make trouble. Her gran thought Shelley was a good girl. Not a thief and certainly not ... she couldn't form the words.

What would her gran think of her now, in Whytefields for

doing something they said was so bad she couldn't even have her own name? She remembered the cosiness of her grand-mother's house, the sound of soul music, the smell of ackee and saltfish as she ran through the door after school.

She didn't want to remember. It was over now, gone. It hurt to remember the good things even more than it hurt to remember the bad.

What happened, Samantha, down on the allotment? asked Dr Rowe.

She didn't want to talk about it.

Months of questions. Mostly she sat, arms folded, saying nothing.

Why did you take Kerry?

She didn't take her, not really. She and Jessie just wanted to play.

They were the same age, just one day between them. Jessie was more fun than Shannon because she didn't mind doing naughty things. They giggled together through lessons and shared lots of secrets. Jessie knew stuff about the world and its scariness, the same things Michelle knew. She never got into trouble; she was better at not getting caught than Michelle. She had long fair hair and green eyes.

Why did you take Kerry to the allotment?

'She was our pet.'

Your pet?

'Mine and Jessie's.'

It was a game the girls in the neighbourhood played. You befriended one of the little ones and you made a fuss of him or her. Like a dog, or a baby brother. You fed them sweets and pretended you were their mum.

It had been a warm autumn day and Michelle knew that the glass house would be snug from the heat. She and Jessie had gone to the Goslings' but there was no one in the garden except Kerry, who was putting a doll to sleep. They waited for Kerry's mum for a few minutes and then got bored. They would just take Kerry with them to the allotments without asking. No one would mind, they told themselves. They left the way they'd come in, through the back gate.

All this had been taken down by the policeman at the station. Michelle could recall his calm face. He'd given her ice cream and fizzy drinks. He had been kind to her before he'd worked out what had happened. After that he hadn't been calm anymore.

The story had been told again in court – some of it. She'd sat in the dock, thinking how strange it was that there wasn't any sea. Docks had boats in them, so she'd thought there would be water and a ship or two that you would be able to see through the windows.

The accused took Kerry Gosling through the back gate of the Gosling family home on Moorcroft Road and down to the allotments ...

It was hard to concentrate. Adam Kenyon really was a very boring man. Sometimes, she played games in her head; she imagined the judge in a much better wig than the curly grey one he had, one with dreadlocks, and a knitted hat. She gave him shades. He didn't look cool, he looked stupid and that made her giggle to herself.

Why the allotments, Samantha?

Why not the allotments? Why all the questions? She drew her fingers across her lips with a zipping movement and sat perfectly silent and still.

THIRTY-SIX

Zoe has had a haircut. It's just past her ears now. She has a small face, so it suits her, though it makes her look older and even more serious.

'What did you think of Whytefields, Zoe?' she says softly, deciding it's her turn to ask the questions for a change.

'It was difficult to get a real sense of it,' Zoe replies. 'There wasn't very much left. How did you feel afterwards? Was it hard to have returned there?'

'Not especially. It was nice to see it in ruins,' she answers drily.

Zoe laughs. 'But it must have stirred up memories?'

'Not really,' she says, deciding not to play.

'Do you have any happy memories of being there?'

'It was better than being at home, I suppose. In a way, I was lucky.'

'Lucky how?'

'It was better not to be at home.' Her tone shuts down further conversation.

JACQUELINE ROY

'Can you think of a time when you've been happy?' asks Zoe after a while.

She looks beyond Zoe into the space behind her. 'I'm happy with Otis,' she says, 'when he's sleeping on my lap or we're playing ball. And there's Ryan, of course. He's got a job now, in a café, as a chef. It's open long hours so we don't see each other as often as we did. He took me to the fair, though. I'm almost happy when we're together.'

'*Almost?*'

She looks down and doesn't answer.

'Almost happy but not quite?'

'I think we could be happy, but there's so much in the way.'

'Like what?'

'The past. My past. I haven't told him yet. I've tried to, but ... I will tell him. I know I'm going to do it, I just don't know when.' She lowers her voice, trying to steady it. 'Telling him could change everything, couldn't it? He might not want to know me anymore. But I have to tell him or it's not real, is it? If he doesn't know who I really am, he can't love *me*, it's someone else he loves, and what's the point of that?' She wills herself to be calm. Once Ryan knows, it will be easier, she thinks, even if he leaves her. She's so tired of hiding things.

'And then there's his past, too,' she continues. 'He did drugs, nothing hard, but they fucked his head and he ended up in hospital. He says he won't use anything ever again but there are so many ways it could all go wrong.'

'It must be hard,' says Zoe, 'never quite believing you can

be happy.' There is a long pause and then she says, 'Can you remember a time when you were happy as a child?'

She thinks and then replies, 'I was happy with my gran.'

'What was your gran like?'

'She was kind.' She smiles at the memory.

'What other words would you use to describe her?'

'Calm. She didn't panic about things. Huggy. She used to hug me a lot. She could cook. She did the best rice and peas. We used to have salt fish and yam and plantain. I wish I'd asked her to teach me how to cook them. I see them when I go round the market but I don't buy them because I don't know what to do with them. At the halfway house, as part of preparing me for outside, I got shown how to cook stuff but it was just boring things like rice pudding and beef stew. I hate rice pudding.'

'Did you see your gran often?'

'Most days, after school. I slept over sometimes. She had a room that was just for me. She let me choose the duvet cover. I got a purple one, with gold stars on it.'

'Your gran was your dad's mother?'

'Yes. She was from Jamaica. My dad went back there in the end. But Gran stayed here. She lived ten minutes away by bus, you could even walk it.'

'Your granddad wasn't around?'

'No, he died before I was born, it was just my gran. She used to get me clothes, sometimes, if I looked like I'd grown out of something. Once, my school shoes split across here—' she points to the side of her foot, '—and Gran said, "You can't keep

275

wearing those, they'll let water in," and she took me straight away to buy a new pair. She let me choose. They had to be black because they were for school. I'd have liked red ones.' She looks at Zoe's shoes. They are deep purple and pointed. 'I like your shoes. Where did you get them?'

Zoe doesn't reply. She says, 'Can you remember any other things you and your gran did?'

'I'll tell you something funny.' She leans forward. She is laughing. 'Gran liked football, I mean really liked it. Grans don't usually like football, do they? Especially not black grans. She used to say that the World Cup was just an excuse for nationalism with all the flag waving but she liked watching Millwall. We used to go to home games – not all the time, it's too expensive, even though they weren't even in the premiere league – just sometimes. I had a Millwall scarf and a blue and white shirt, the whole lot. Gran bought everything for me. They call the team The Lions. She could cheer, my gran, though she used to say that really, she should roar. Once we got told to fuck off back to our own country by a load of other Millwall supporters. You'd think it would have been the opposition that didn't like us, wouldn't you? I thought we were going to get the shit kicked out of us, but Gran stayed completely calm and just ignored them. They got bored in the end and went away.'

'She sounds like quite a character. Did she and your dad get on?'

She shook her head. 'I don't really know. She never talked about him much. I think they had some kind of falling out.

Once I overheard her saying to one of her friends that he was no son of hers. I asked her what she meant but she just said it wasn't anything important, just grown-up stuff, and I mustn't worry.'

'How old were you when your father left your mother?'

'Very little. I'm not sure I was even born.'

'But you saw him sometimes?'

'Oh yes, for a long time I saw him loads,' she lies.

'A while ago now, you told me your dad had promised to take you away with him but then you never saw him again. Do you know why he didn't come for you?'

She shakes her head. 'I might have got it wrong,' she says. 'He probably didn't say that. Or maybe something happened to him, like maybe he was really ill and lost his memory. You hear about that, don't you? People forgetting everything, even their families, and they can't help it. Sometimes they never recover their memories. I don't think he would have just not come. I worry a bit that he died. I sometimes think I should try to find him but I don't really know how to go about it. Do you know how to search for someone? I don't even think he lives in this country anymore. Or maybe it's not a good idea. If he just left me, I could find him and he could say he doesn't want to see me, or act like he does want to and then just leave me all over again. Sometimes I asked my mum about him but she was angry with him for buggering off and wouldn't even let me mention his name.'

'You must have asked your grandmother about it too. What did she say?'

277

'Nothing really.' Except that she had said things. She'd said he wasn't very reliable, because he had been ill and it would be better not to expect anything from him, though she hadn't said what kind of illness it was. 'He has always loved you, though,' she'd said, 'and he always will. That's why he asked me to take care of you.' But you don't just leave the people you love and he'd only come to see her about half a dozen times in her entire life. She knows now that what Gran said was a lie. She feels sad about that, but, she thinks to herself, Gran was the only person who ever tried to protect me, and a lie, when it's about sparing feelings, doesn't really count. 'I miss my gran,' she says, surprising herself by telling Zoe something that really matters. She knows it matters because saying it out loud really hurts.

'How long before Kerry did she die?'

'About six months before.' She takes a loud breath that sounds almost like a sob and adds: 'What if she'd died after? What if she'd known about the trial?'

'Was she ill for long?'

'No, it was sudden. She was a bit tired, you know? But I didn't think it was anything bad. Then Mum said she had a heart attack and died.'

'That must have been such a shock.'

'It was. I thought we'd go to the funeral but Mum said we couldn't. I don't know why. I never cried about it. I didn't cry about things back then. Well, not much.' She stands up. 'I want to go home now. I don't want to talk about this anymore.'

Zoe puts her hand out. 'Don't go yet. We don't have to talk

about this anymore if you don't want to, we can talk about other things.'

'No. I want to go home.' Her voice is rising. She is moving into panic. She rushes to the door and lets herself out. Panting, she runs down the street, barging through the crowds that throng the market. She doesn't stop until she gets to Notting Hill. But she isn't going home, she knows that now. Instead she gets a bus to Charing Cross. She knows where she is going, or at least she thinks she does. She catches a train to New Cross station and then she walks, just as she used to, through streets that are familiar but also strange – too many years have passed. Breathless now, she plods past rows and rows of houses, frightened she won't find it, but then she sees the football ground. It's different from the way she remembers it. She shouldn't have come, it's only emphasized the way that nothing stays the same. She sits on a wall by the side of the road and imagines it the way it used to be. She is sitting beside her gran. Millwall are winning three-nil, and they are eating hot dogs in the winter sun.

Thirty-seven

The portable TV is on in the bedroom. They are still in pyjamas even though it's almost midday. Otis is asleep at the bottom of the bed, snoring gently. She lies beside Ryan uneasily. He's changed the channel. It's ID: cops are investigating a murder in small-town America. They're about to interview a suspect; real footage of events has been spliced with actors playing the parts. 'Do you want to watch this?' she asks.

'It's interesting,' he replies.

It's like a sign. *Tell him now.* She waits for a moment. Then she says, 'I was on here once,' making her voice casual.

'What do you mean?'

'I was on this channel.'

He turns to face her. 'How come? Did you witness a true crime?'

She could back down now, lie to him, say she saw a real-life murder and had to be put into witness protection for her own safety. But instead she says, 'I wasn't a witness.'

'What then?' he asks. 'Are you being serious?'

'I had to change my name.'

'Why?'

'I was the Gosling Girl.'

He looks blank. 'What do you mean, the Gosling Girl? Who's she?'

There is a silence. She draws Otis to her and strokes his fur.

'Carly? What do you mean?'

'I used to be Michelle Cameron. They call her the Gosling Girl. I had to change my name.'

'I don't understand. Tell me who Michelle Cameron is.'

'*Was.* She was me. She did something very bad and her name had to be changed.'

'What did she do?'

'She killed somebody.'

The colour leaves his face. 'Did you stab that bloke with Lucy?'

'No, it wasn't that. I didn't know Lucy then.' She doesn't know how to continue.

Otis moves from her to Ryan and starts to lick his face. He nudges him aside. 'I don't understand,' he says again.

'I can't tell you,' she states, getting up to leave the room.

He stands up too. 'No, come on Carly, you can't leave it like that.'

'I have to. You'll hate me. You'll never want to see me again.'

'I won't hate you, I promise. If you killed somebody, it would have been because you had to, you were defending yourself. I know you wouldn't hurt anyone unless you had to.'

'You don't get it. I didn't have to. She was just a little girl.'

They are outside the living room. She opens the door and runs into the corner. She squats there, holding a cushion from one of the chairs against her face.

Ryan takes the cushion away and draws her round to face him. 'You killed a child?' he says, but he is speaking gently, as if giving her the chance to explain herself.

'Yes I killed a child, okay? Now do you see?' She starts to cry, breathless, heaving sobs.

He moves away from her and sits in a chair. 'What happened?'

'I don't know,' she says. Her voice is muffled. 'It was when I was young.'

'How young?'

'Ten.'

'How old was the little girl?'

'Four.'

There is silence again. Eventually he mutters, 'I don't know what to say.'

'There isn't anything to say.'

'Little kids don't kill other kids.'

The gap between them is so wide she'll never be able to close it. She clutches her head, determined to stop herself smashing it into the wall.

'Tell me what happened, why you did it.'

He thinks there are things she can say that will help him understand. He won't get it, she knows this, but she fumbles for the words. 'We used to play together, her and her big sister and my friend Jessie. We'd go to this allotment, at least me and Jessie would.' She's not sure she even remembers what happened properly now, it's been buried for so long and it's never seemed quite real. 'We'd have tea in the greenhouse. No one else was there. The gates had a padlock but my gran had a plot and when she got too stiff to grow stuff anymore I kept the key. I don't know why it stopped being used but no one came anymore so we played there. It was our secret place.'

She stands up. She can't control herself; the memories are like crackers thrown at her heels, causing her to move her feet up and down in agitation. It makes her look crazy, she thinks, and he will decide if she's mad or bad – she's lost him either way. She runs into the kitchen. Ryan follows her there. She stands in front of the cooker, still moving from one foot to the other, not daring to look at him. 'One day, we took Kerry with us – the little kid – and we played mums and dads. I was the dad. She got cross about something and wanted to go home and I was scared. I didn't want us to stop playing because then I'd have to go back to my house, so I smacked her and I told her how naughty she was and she died.'

Ryan folds his arms round his chest. 'So it was an accident, kind of?'

'I didn't mean to do it.'

'No,' he says, but she can hear a further question in his voice.

'Except I didn't just hit her. I put my hands round her throat.'

There is silence.

'I don't understand,' he says eventually.

'Stop saying you don't understand.'

'But I don't,' he says in a low voice.

'What don't you understand?'

'I don't understand any of it.'

She shouts at him, as if her raised voice will make it clearer. 'I didn't think she'd die.'

'What happened after that?'

'The police came and I was arrested. There was a trial. My name got changed. I got sent to Whytefields, a sort of secure children's unit.'

'How long for?'

'Until I was seventeen.'

'And then they let you out?'

'No, not then. After that, it was a young offenders' institution.'

'So nothing you've told me about yourself is actually true?'

'I'm not allowed to tell people,' she answers.

Otis jumps up at Ryan, demanding attention. 'But you've been lying all this time?' he says, putting the dog squarely on the floor.

'I had to. I'm not allowed to say who I really was. And you can't tell anyone, please, promise me you won't. If you do, I'll have to go away again, live somewhere else, *be* someone else. *Promise me.*'

He doesn't answer. After a while he says, 'I thought I knew you.'

She laughs. 'How could you know me? I don't even know who I am.'

'I can't stay here,' he says, hurrying into the hall.

She follows him. 'Don't go. You're the first person since

284

my gran who's really mattered, it's why I had to tell you.' She pushes past him and blocks his path to the door. He grabs her by the shoulders and positions her behind him.

'You won't tell anyone, will you? Please, Ryan.'

'Don't worry, I won't tell anyone,' he says abruptly. He yanks open the door and leaves the flat.

She closes the front door softly and picks up Otis. They go back into the bedroom. The television is still on. *Psychopath*, someone says. *Life for a life.*

What happened?

She remembers rage. She remembers fear. *Children don't die, only old people, like Gran.* She remembers her hands round Kerry's throat and Jessie hitting Kerry with a stone. She remembers thinking Kerry would wake up.

THIRTY-EIGHT

Everything has stopped, all the good things. She has Otis, but he's not enough, and there's nothing else. Before Ryan, she had managed with very little, but being with him has shown her what she's been missing: the hole that is left is too deep. She sits in the flat, willing herself to find something to distract her from the knowledge that he's gone, but there is nothing.

She can't get through this. The minutes are too long. She doesn't know what to do with herself. It isn't bearable. She starts to scream, a long, steady scream, followed by several more. She is baying now. Her own voice is too loud, but she can't shut it up, the noise won't stop coming. She starts to bang her head against the wall.

She is barely aware of the urgent knocking at the door. She stumbles to her feet, silent now, and stands in the hall. The letter box flips up. 'It's Natalie Tyler. Can you open the door?' She continues to stand, unable to move. Tyler is saying the door will have to be broken down if she doesn't open it soon. Otis is yapping frantically. How long has it been like this? She moves forward, unfastens the chain and lifts the latch.

Tyler steers her into the living room. 'Your neighbours reported a disturbance, a domestic. Are you okay?'

'They haven't worked out who I am, have they?'

'No, they haven't, it's all right. They heard sounds that suggested violence. They just wanted you to be safe. Is Ryan here? Was it him, or did someone break into the flat?'

She laughs. 'He hasn't been here for days.' Then she starts to cry.

'You're hurt, your head's bleeding. Did someone hit you?'

'No one hit me. I did it to myself,' she states.

'It wasn't Ryan?'

'No, it wasn't Ryan, I did it to myself.' She thinks of the neighbours imagining Ryan beating her up. She would have preferred that to him leaving her. Blows are familiar. She knows where she is with people's fists.

They go to sit down on the sofa in the living room, another charity shop find, but one that Ryan paid for. She wonders if he'll want it back. Tyler takes off a grey jacket, puts it beside her and picks some fluff from her rust-coloured trousers.

'I think you should see a doctor,' Tyler says.

'I'm okay,' she replies.

'The neighbours said there was a lot of noise.'

'It was probably me. And Otis might have been barking.'

'What's going on?' Tyler's tone is softer than usual.

'Ryan's gone.'

'Oh,' she replies, in a way that says, *Now I see what's happening*. 'And you're not coping?'

'I'm coping,' she answers. *I'm coping by banging my head and screaming a lot*. The absurdity of everything strikes her now and she laughs once more. There is silence for a while and then she says, 'Actions have consequences, don't they?'

'Yes, they do,' says Tyler.

'Well, you would believe that. You're police. Your whole job is based on consequences. You do something bad, you get locked up. Simples. No grey areas for you.'

Tyler looks at her. 'You would be surprised how grey I find most things,' she says.

'Wrong job then, I would think.'

Tyler doesn't reply.

'Ryan leaving is a consequence of me telling him what I did. So my whole life is going to be about what happened when I was ten no matter what I do. It will go round and round, no way out of it, not ever. Consequences: actions and consequences.' She is speaking quietly, at pains to seem in control of her voice, catching her breath each time it wobbles and feeling cross with herself for letting Tyler see how sad she feels.

'And you don't think that's fair?' she asks.

'I don't know if it's fair or not, I just know that's how it is. I know I did something bad, I've known that for a long time. Always, probably. If I could go back and change things I would, but I can't.'

'I think we all wish we could go back and change things sometimes.'

'What would you change?'

Tyler smiles wryly. 'Lots of things.'

'Like what?'

'That's for me to know,' she replies, but she continues to smile.

'So what do I do now?'

'Maybe it's time to come to terms with what you did. I know it's a cliché, but it might be time to accept yourself.'

'Do you think that's possible?'

'I don't know,' Tyler replies, 'you have no idea how much I wish I did.'

Tyler says she can stay for a while longer. They drink coffee. She thinks about the things she and Ryan had planned to do together. A holiday in Spain when they could afford it. Notting Hill Carnival on the August bank holiday weekend.

'Have you ever been to Carnival?' she asks Tyler, feeling calmer now.

'Yes, I've been,' Tyler replies.

'Why do they hold it in Notting Hill? South London would be better. I know someone who lives off Ladbroke Grove. It's full of rich people – you hardly ever see anyone black.'

'It wasn't always like that. Once it was full of run-down houses converted into bedsits. It was a deprived area so it was one of the few places that would rent out to immigrants. Carnival's so well established now that it's remained there, even though the area has changed.'

'What's it like? Is it as good as they say?'

'It's fine, I guess.'

She looks at Tyler questioningly and then she says: 'You weren't there for fun, were you? You were policing it.'

Tyler looks embarrassed. She plays with the little bowl of sugar resting on the table, spinning it round slowly with the tips of her fingers. 'They always draft in every black officer for carnival,' she says. 'Sometimes I think I'm on the wrong side.' She gets up hastily, aware, perhaps, that she's said more than she meant to. 'I'd better go. I hope things get easier soon,' she says, and sees herself out.

Once Tyler leaves, she goes to bed, even though it's only afternoon. She can't make any sound; the neighbours might hear. She stuffs the corner of the duvet inside her mouth.

THIRTY-NINE

Perhaps it's this loneliness that disturbs her most, the wanting deep inside that leaves her keening without sound in the middle of the night. Perhaps it's this that causes her to drag the razor blade across her skin until the wound shows globs of fat, and blood spreads down the sleeves of her shirt. She barely feels the pain; the wanting fades it out – *mission not accomplished*.

Tears rise up from the back of her throat. Or her chest. Or the heart of her. She doesn't know where they are from. She forces them back; she mustn't feel. She is dead inside (except for the longing). She can't feel, yet the yearning claws at her soul. What does she want? She doesn't know. If she knew, perhaps the longing would cease. With Ryan, sometimes, it had faded a little, but once it returned, it seemed love had fuelled its intensity. Love and loss intertwined. The hole there inside her is a circle of pain that stretches round her body, inside and out, searing the folds of her skin.

Cut it out.

She watches, mesmerized, as the skin splits and the blood starts to spurt. The wounds are deeper than usual: perhaps she will die.

She thinks of Ryan. Will he be sorry she's gone or will it be a relief?

She stands in the bathroom, letting her blood pump into the sink. She's hit an artery, she thinks. What to do now? She wasn't aiming to die but perhaps it's time. She's tired and the pain of everyday living is sharper by far than the blade of her knife.

But she didn't do this to end her life so she phones for an ambulance.

Paramedics arrive within minutes. She opens the door to a man and a woman, her arm dripping blood on the carpet. They speak to her calmly, in friendly tones. They don't behave as if she is a bother to them. She feels the unexpected kindness and it hurts.

At the hospital, when the paramedics leave, and she's questioned by people she doesn't know, and prodded and poked and attached to drips, she starts to panic. She shouldn't have let them bring her here. She wants to call Ryan but she knows she can't, so even though it's very late, she phones Zoe Laing.

Zoe sounds as if she's been woken from a heavy sleep. 'What is it?' she says, her voice deeper than usual.

'Can you come? I don't know what to do, I don't know, I just don't know ...'

'Try to calm down. Take some deep breaths. What's happened?'

'Nothing, I shouldn't have phoned.' She ends the call.

Zoe rings back almost at once. 'What's happening?' she asks, sounding kinder and more awake.

'I've cut myself,' she replies, in a whisper.

'Sorry, I didn't hear that. You've done what?'

'Cut myself.'

'How badly?'

'Pretty badly.'

'Are you at home?'

'No.' The same near-whisper.

'Where then?'

'Hospital. A&E. I couldn't stop the bleeding so I called an ambulance. Only I shouldn't have, it was stupid and I don't know what to do.'

'Have they finished treating you?'

'No, I think they're going to keep me in. I lost a lot of blood but no one's telling me what's happening. They're very busy. I've been here a couple of hours. I'm scared.'

'Scared of what?'

'Of being seen. Someone might realize who I was. There are notes for me somewhere as Samantha Robinson from when I cut before, ages ago, when I was at the halfway house. Should I tell them I was her? I don't know what to say about why I changed my name. I think they're going to keep me here. They're getting a psychiatrist to see me.'

'Just tell them you don't want to see one. They can't make you.'

'They were talking about having me sectioned. I got

upset – very upset – so they thought they'd better do something. I think they might know who I was.'

'How?'

'I nearly told them. I don't think I said enough for them to get it but I'm not sure.'

'Which hospital?'

'I forgot to ask. I think it might be in Acton?'

'Don't say anything more until I get there. I'll be about forty-five minutes . . . maybe slightly longer.'

'They said everything is confidential but I don't think I believe them.'

'Who said everything is confidential?'

'The nurse.'

'What exactly did you say to her? Can you remember?'

'I didn't say anything much to her, I just asked if it was confidential. I said more to the doctor, he's the one who might have worked it out.'

'Look, I'll be there as soon as I can. Stay put and try not to worry.'

In the cubicle, on her own, she goes over possibilities. Hospitalization. Endless questions from multiple Zoes determined to find out what makes her tick. Drugs that make her tired and sick. Anonymity at risk. The new flat empty and vandalized. Otis starving to death. Stupid to have called that ambulance – dying would have been better than this.

FORTY

Zoe ends the call and starts to round up the clothes she'd been wearing when she'd arrived home that evening. The areas of the flat that are exposed to visitors always seem tidy and clean but the rest of the space is a permanent mess – she'd be embarrassed if anyone saw it. In the bedroom, her jeans are on the floor and the T-shirt she was wearing is draped over a chair. She can't wear it; the front is splashed with drops of red wine. She meant to do a wash yesterday but she forgot – she forgot the day before and the day before that, too, so now she has no clean underwear. She looks at the clock on the wall: just after 4 a.m. *Fuck, fuck, fuck.* She turns a dirty pair of low-rise shorts inside out and puts them on reluctantly. She doesn't need a bra. At least she finds a clean top in a drawer where clothes are never folded.

She's hardly been home in the last couple of weeks; she's been doing extra hours at the clinic. Once she gets back, and has done some reading and writing, there is only time for five or six hours of sleep. She used to have a cleaner, but she went back to Poland a couple of months ago. She hasn't had time to replace her. The flat looks grubby – there is a ring of scum round the bathroom basin – and this early-morning call means that another day will pass with next to nothing done at home. Still, the Michelle Cameron book is worth it.

She runs her fingers through her hair in lieu of a comb and hurries to the kitchen. She needs black coffee, as much as she can drink. She lets the kettle boil while she finds her purse and car keys.

She drives slowly, knowing she still has alcohol in her system despite the coffee. Her evening routine tends to include several glasses of wine.

She finds a space in the hospital car park – much easier than usual at this time of night – and waits here for a few minutes, composing herself. She'll need to be calm when she sees her, patient and friendly.

As she walks to A&E, she remembers sitting with Michelle Cameron shortly after she'd been accused of Lucy's murder. She'd put her hand to her head in weariness and her sleeve had fallen back, revealing a series of scars. Zoe had asked about the damage, but she had withdrawn into herself and hadn't been willing to speak of it since.

'I couldn't help it,' she says, as Zoe reaches her cubicle, her tone more humble than defiant. 'I just wanted to feel less ... you know.'

'It's okay.'

'I'm sorry to be a nuisance.'

She knows that she is required to say that she isn't a nuisance at all, so she duly obliges. The agitation lessens.

'What would you like me to say to the hospital staff?' asks Zoe. 'I could tell them I'm your psychologist, which is more or less true. Or I could say I'm a friend if you'd prefer it.'

A look of pleasure crosses her face for a moment, then fades. 'Psychologist, I suppose. It might get me out of here more easily.'

Zoe wonders if a hospital stay might be warranted. Even before Ryan left, she'd been behaving erratically and her moods had veered from one extreme to another; she'd seemed low one minute and joyful the next. She could be suicidal, she's hinted at it. Her life has no meaning, she's said, stating that she doesn't belong in the world, there isn't a place for her in it. But if she's detained, it will be much harder to continue to see her and conduct the interviews. She's behind enough with the book as it is; better to keep her out of hospital if at all possible.

She sits upright and says, 'I'm never going to be forgiven, am I?'

'What is it you want forgiveness for?'

She shrugs.

Zoe repeats the question but she doesn't answer; she just says, 'Were you on a night out when I phoned?'

Zoe wonders if the question has been triggered by the smell of alcohol that's probably still lingering around her. She finds some gum in her pocket. 'Would you like some?' she asks.

She murmurs no.

She is quieter now, monosyllabic. Zoe wonders how to get her talking again but then she says: 'I've got a lot of scars.

They're so ugly. Ryan didn't know. He said I was beautiful. He said it more than once. Why do men lie so much?'

Zoe thinks about Oliver. Like her father, he'd had no compunction about an affair. He'd lied constantly.

A doctor arrives, looking heavy-eyed and sounding abrupt but he treats her matter-of-factly; he doesn't seem to have any idea who she is. Zoe watches as the wounds are examined. The sight of the criss-cross gashes on her arm makes her wince. It's the fact that the injuries are self-inflicted, she concludes. Impossible not to see the desperation behind them.

'The wounds are clean,' the doctor says, 'but we'll give you a tetanus jab just in case.'

As a nurse practitioner escorts her to another room for suturing, Zoe notices she is wearing cropped black trousers and green shoes. They don't look new; perhaps she's picked them up from one of the charity shops she seems to haunt. She is aware of being flattered by the imitation, though she wonders why it matters to her; perhaps Michelle Cameron is taking on a significance in her life that is disproportionate.

She follows her into the clinical room and watches as she sits on the couch, silent and expressionless. The nurse isn't gentle. He's tired and irritated at having to deal with some hysterical girl who's brought her injuries on herself, but she doesn't flinch. It's as if she is now inured to pain, past the point where anything can hurt her. Or maybe she thinks she deserves it.

By the time the psychiatrist arrives, she is calm enough to be downgraded to non-emergency status. Zoe assures him she'll get the support she needs. Beds are scarce; she can see he's pleased to avoid an admission.

The loss of blood means they will keep her under observation for several more hours. Zoe can't stay, she has patients to see at the clinic. She phones her that afternoon, hoping for a chance to talk about what happened, but the call goes straight to voicemail.

FORTY-ONE

She takes Otis for a walk. It's important to exercise him, whether she wants to or not. She does it early now, before there are too many people about.

She hasn't seen Zoe since the hospital. The wish to share how bad she feels has left her now that the acute phase of her anguish has subsided, but that could mean even more trouble. Zoe could threaten to report her to Dom, have her licence revoked, force her to attend their meetings again, the way she'd done that time she'd gone for her. There was probably a regulation somewhere that said ex-cons shouldn't gouge pieces out of themselves and end up in hospital. She'd given Zoe something else to hold over her. Even if it wasn't likely she would make good on her threats it was still a risk. She shouldn't have phoned her.

Otis sniffs the ground, hoping to find a stray snack, but she hurries him along – she needs to return to the safety of the flat. They climb the stairs, passing a woman on one of the landings. They see each other most days so they exchange a short greeting. Even that is too much. She lowers her head, hoping she won't encounter anyone else.

Her eyes are tracing the cracks in the floor so she doesn't see him at first.

'Carly,' he says.

Ryan is sitting on the landing, leaning against her door. She can't believe he's there. 'You came back, then,' she says, trying to keep her tone neutral.

'I wanted to call but I couldn't. Amber borrowed my phone. I don't have your number without my phone.'

She knows what he means by 'borrowed'. 'Do you want to come in?' she asks, wishing the flat was tidier. She picks up the towel on the floor in the hall and the tear-sodden tissues by the kitchen door. 'Go on in,' she says, gesturing to the living room. 'Do you want some tea?'

'Thanks,' he replies.

They are back to square one, awkward and formal.

Otis is pleased to see Ryan. He yaps, circling round him joyfully.

'Do you want to go for a walk?' he asks.

'We've only just come back. Anyway, it's raining.'

He looks disappointed.

'Okay then,' she says, 'I suppose we could. Otis doesn't mind how many walks he gets.'

They decide to take a bus. Otis sits between them on the front seat on the top deck, looking out of the window. She wants to ask if he's back for good but she can't risk it, so they remain silent throughout the journey.

They go right to the end of the route and end up at Hyde Park Corner. The rain is easing off. She pulls down her hood and moves on ahead, matching Otis's eager pace. Ryan remains slightly behind. They walk by the Serpentine, watching the geese, and buy hot chocolate in the café. Dogs aren't allowed so they have to sit outside. The seats are damp.

'I would have phoned,' he says, 'if Amber hadn't borrowed it.'

'*Taken* it,' she corrects him.

'I've been thinking about the things you said.'

She waits, her neck and shoulders tight. '*And?*' she asks.

'I knew you were hiding stuff from me. I thought it was just that you were a private sort of person. I don't blame you, it must have been hard to say it. I remembered something you said to me when I told you about the day my dad died. You said, "You were ten, you were just a child. You didn't mean it."'

She thinks of oceans and paddling pools. 'It's not the same,' she says to him.

'I know that. But I remember what it felt like to be ten because of my dad and I didn't understand anything then. I didn't know what the world was like. You didn't. At that age, you don't know what things mean.'

'I still did it.'

'I said exactly the same thing to you, remember? And you kept saying I was only young. We do stupid things when we're ten – terrible things – that we wouldn't do if we were grown-ups.' He takes her hand across the table.

She flinches; her cuts haven't healed and movement is still painful.

'You've hurt yourself,' he says, seeing the frayed edges of the bandage beneath her sleeve.

'Why do you think that?' she asks in fear.

'I know you do it. Did you think I never noticed the scars?'

She has always undressed away from him, been naked in the dark, and she never wears short sleeves. She thought she had concealed it from him. 'Why didn't you say you knew before?'

'I thought you'd tell me when you felt up to it. Do you know why you do it?'

'Some of it.'

'Is it because of Kerry?'

'Not all of it. A bit, maybe.'

'Were you trying to kill yourself?'

'I didn't do it to die. People don't understand. It isn't about dying, it's about staying alive.'

He thinks about this and then he says, 'Will you tell me next time it's bad and you feel like doing it?'

'Okay,' she answers, aware that she probably won't. It's not something she wants to share. It's her thing: no one else needs to be involved. And it helps, mostly. She isn't ready to give it up just yet and that's what he will want. 'It looks so ugly,' she says, rubbing the bandage. 'I must seem crazy to you.'

'They're just scars.'

She doesn't believe him but she likes him for saying it. She likes him for his quiet acceptance and the calm he is showing.

People aren't usually calm with her. 'There's something I haven't told you the truth about.'

'Go on,' he says, looking worried.

'I told you I was seeing a friend every other Tuesday, but I wasn't, it was Dom, my probation officer. I have to check in with him every couple of weeks. I'm out on licence, you see. I'll probably have to do it for the rest of my life.'

'What does it mean, out on licence?'

'It means I can be recalled to prison if I do anything wrong, anything at all.'

Ryan thinks about this. Then he says, 'But you won't be doing anything wrong again, will you?'

I'll try very hard not to, she thinks to herself. Then she sighs and says, 'You know when you said we do things when we're ten that we wouldn't do now we're grown-ups? Well, I don't know if that's true. I don't know what sort of person I am now I'm a grown-up. I might not have changed very much.' She doesn't want to look at him, so she looks at a lost ball that's bobbing on the water.

'You're funny, you make me laugh, you get me. I can talk to you. I feel like I can say anything to you. And you never call me stupid. You couldn't do all that if you were still the same as when you were ten.'

'Why would I call you stupid?' she asks.

'I'm not clever like you, I don't read books. You understand loads of stuff. You notice things. You could go to university if you wanted. My mum went, and my dad. Mum wanted me to go but I never got good enough grades. She said she didn't mind but I know she was disappointed. You're a bit like her – you don't get angry when I get things wrong.'

It's not the most flattering thing he could have said to her, that she reminds him of his mother. And she does get angry, inside. She's just learnt not to show it, most of the time. 'I'm not who you think I am. Don't go thinking I'm a good person, Ryan, because I'm not.' She is crying now, she can't help herself. Perhaps it would have been better if he hadn't come back. How will she stay good for him, live up to all his expectations?

'It's going to be all right,' he tells her, brushing a tear from her face with the tip of his finger. 'You're the only person I can really talk to. It's like we're the same. You get what it's like not to fit in, being left out of things. It's good that you told me what happened when you were young. You trusted me. That's good.'

'I haven't told you all of it. I can't, because I still don't know why I hurt Kerry, not really,' she says.

'It doesn't matter.'

'No, you don't understand. I think it probably does matter. I think I need to know why I did it, however bad it is. There's this woman called Zoe Laing. I'm writing a book with her about what happened. Well, I'm doing the talking, she's going to do the writing. She's a psychologist. She said it's something I have to talk about with her to understand it.'

She's been fighting Zoe for so long – fighting her memories – but maybe it's time to trust her properly, stop finding excuses for not seeing her and reasons not to remember. If she wants to have a real future with Ryan, perhaps she has to.

'It's no use thinking we're going to be rich because of the book,' she continues. 'I won't be getting any money for it, I'm not allowed. Zoe's going to get it all and the story isn't even about her, it's about me.'

Ryan looks at her anxiously. 'You wouldn't take any money, though, would you, even if you could?'

She knows her answer will be important for their future together, so she says, 'No, of course I wouldn't.'

It's obvious he thinks it would be wrong. Perhaps it would be. She remembers Shannon's mum and the birthday party she went to at their house when Shannon was eight. She'd never been to a party before – she wasn't popular. She'd pinch the other kids, punch them when she thought no one could see. But Shannon's mum was kind, so she got an invite.

There was a game. You had to run around the room and when the music stopped, you had to freeze. She was good at it, better than the other kids. She was still as still could be. She won a prize: a card game, Happy Families. Thinking of this causes her throat to tighten – the irony is obvious now.

Shannon had a cake. It was pink and green with fairies on and the sponge was melting light. Shannon's mother put an extra slice in her coat pocket, wrapped in Pooh bear serviettes. When she got home, she smoothed out the least sticky one and put it in the keepsake box she hid beneath her bed.

She's in hospital, Shannon's mum. She can't get past what happened. The papers called it blood money when they heard about the book. Is that what it would be? Perhaps she wouldn't be able to let herself take it, even if she was allowed to.

'I really missed you,' Ryan says.

'I missed you too,' she answers.

Ryan has come back. She is starting to take it in now, realize what it means. He isn't scared of her. He doesn't think she's bad to the core. He wants to be with her even though he knows what she did. He saw the scars and didn't think she was ugly or mad. He thinks they have a future together. They are sitting outside a café holding hands like any normal couple.

She can't imagine ever being happier.

FORTY-TWO

In Zoe's apartment, she's remembering the men at the house Fred would take her to, the knocks at the door that saw her scurrying to safety in the bathroom or beneath the bed. But there were no safe places in that house back then. She remembers pain, the soreness between her legs and lower belly and the sickly, sweaty smell the old men left behind, the smell she couldn't scrub away however much she tried. She'd slide under the water in the bath, holding her breath, longing to be clean again, wishing not to surface; but every time she'd rise up spluttering, still there, still visible. She remembers how her mother would lie with Fred, who snapped her arm because she cried. Why weren't the men ever punished for hurting her the way she was punished for hurting Kerry? He squeezed her throat: die, come back to life and die again. Don't tell. I'll find you if you tell, pop your eyeballs from their sockets and eat them for my breakfast. A fairy-tale ogre who was real.

'You were just a little girl,' says Zoe, 'nothing you could have done to stop it.' She should have stopped it, though. She should have kept herself clean, not allowed the dirty men to touch her. The memories are like tongues of fire that lick the surface of her skin and force their way inside.

She shouldn't have gone to the allotments that day. She shouldn't have got so cross. She should have controlled herself, forced the fury back inside her. She wishes she could take it back, she wishes it with every breath left in her. She remembers everything she did. Don't die. *Don't die. DON'T DIE.*

FORTY-THREE

It's her birthday – not her real birthday, that's next week – the made-up one, from the ID documents she received on her release from prison. Carly Wilson's birthday, not Michelle Cameron's. She doesn't tell Ryan this; everything's complicated enough without adding unnecessary detail. Besides, it's best to stick to the story, otherwise she might get confused and make mistakes.

If it wasn't for Ryan, there would be no presents and no card. Most years, she'd had nothing, though at Whytefields there had been a worthy gift – some soap, or some pairs of socks.

They are at the kitchen table. Ryan says her birthday surprise is in the living room. She has to close her eyes. He leads her in by the hand. When she is allowed to look, she sees a large, old-fashioned record player resting on a box in the centre of the room. It's not pretty: it's made of heavy cream and coffee plastic, and although it's obviously portable, it certainly isn't small. She approaches it excitedly. 'How do you work it?' she says. Ryan produces a record – a 45, he calls it – and shows her how to get the needle to drop on the edge of the vinyl as it spins around. It sounds scratchy and muffled but she loves it. Percy Sledge sings about warm and tender love. 'Let me try,' she says, when the song has finished. The mechanics of it fascinate her, the way the record goes round and round, its grooves and the scratches on its surface. The record, and the sound it produces, seem lived in somehow, more shared than a CD: a kind of secret few people even know about.

There is another record for her birthday, a second 45. It's called 'Young, Gifted and Black'. Only Ryan could have understood her well enough to have chosen this. It's the best present ever; she couldn't even have imagined getting anything more perfect. 'Where did you find it?' she asks. He tells her that the record player and the 45s were in a flea market near Brick Lane. She is impressed by his newly acquired shopping skills. She has been a good teacher. They play the records over and over, singing to them, slightly out of tune.

Ryan has the day off. He booked it specially. It's September and warm and it isn't raining so they are going on a picnic. They walk hand in hand, Otis following behind, nosing his way through the fresh-cut grass. Up ahead, two young black women are laughing together.

'I hate it when black people do that, don't you?'

'Do what?' she asks.

'Dye their hair blonde. It never looks right. It's like they want to be white.'

She had been admiring their hair, thinking she might want

to get hers done like that, but she says, 'I know.' Then she adds, 'But white people can do their hair any way they want and it's not a problem.'

'It's different for them. Their hair is just hair. Our hair has all kinds of different meanings.'

She doesn't think this is fair but she doesn't say it. *Why is everything so much more complicated if you're not white?* 'Did your dad tell you that?' she asks.

'No, I worked it out for myself,' he says, sounding cross. She's been clumsy and hurt his feelings. He thinks she believes he's not bright enough to have his own ideas.

'But he did teach you lots of things, didn't he?' she says, squeezing his hand to alleviate the crossness. 'Like my gran. I wish I'd had a dad like that.'

'You wouldn't if he suddenly died. Sometimes I think it would have been better if I'd never known him.'

She thinks about loss, the pain of it . . . she's been thinking about that a lot of late. She takes a risk and says: 'Sometimes I wish I was white. Or I used to wish it.'

'Why?'

'There's less trouble.' There is a pause while she thinks through what she wants to say and then she adds: 'No one thinks when a white person does something . . . something bad, they only did it because they were white. But they think that about us all the time.'

She recalls that once she called Tyler a black bitch. At least she hadn't heard. Ryan would be shocked, he would think she had no pride in herself. And perhaps she didn't have pride then. It's hard to feel proud when you don't think you have anything to be proud about.

They find a spot in the corner of a field. Ryan unpacks the food he's prepared. He's made a pork pie; a rich spicy smell fills the air. And he has baked her a birthday cake. She slices through the name spelt out in green icing: *Carly*. She giggles as apricot jam spurts down the front of her T-shirt. After they have eaten, they lie side by side, staring at the sky.

Otis lies on his stomach beside them, feet splayed out, eating the crust of the pie they haven't been able to finish. He is watching people at the same time and when they come too close, he gets up and charges at them, barking. They laugh at his protectiveness.

'Come on,' says Ryan, standing up, 'everybody's starting to look scared of the crazy dog. Let's walk.'

She gets up reluctantly. She was enjoying lying in the sun.

'Come on,' he repeats, 'I want to show you something.'

Curious now, she attaches Otis to his lead and catches up with him. All around them, children are rushing about on bikes or chasing balls.

Ryan looks at them wistfully. 'It would be good to have a family – children, one day, wouldn't it?'

Is he saying what she thinks he is? That he wants a family with her? She remembers a conversation she once had with Zoe. 'I shouldn't ever have kids, should I?' she'd said.

'Why shouldn't you?' Zoe had asked.

'You know why. She was just a baby, wasn't she?'

'Are you afraid you could do it again?'

'I don't think I could ... but I can't be sure of anything, can I? Me and Ryan, we'd be great parents, wouldn't we? An ex-drug user, fucked up by being dumped in care, and then losing his dad, and an ex ... what am I?' She doesn't want to say the words murderer, or killer, but she sees them in her head and she knows what she is. Funny how she's supposed to have such a good memory yet has managed to forget so much.

'What about you – do you want children?' asks Ryan, cutting into her thoughts. His tone suggests that her answer's a foregone conclusion.

'Maybe,' she says. 'I'm not sure.'

He looks disappointed, dejected even. Then he says, 'We've got plenty of time, we're still young.'

'I'm older than you. Do you mind that?'

'Why would I?' he asks, looking puzzled.

'No reason,' she replies.

'We could wait a while to have a family. In a few years we'll have a big house with a garden and I'll have my own café, probably a chain of them. Just think what I could get you for your birthday then.'

She should be elated that, in imagining his future, he sees *her*, but she feels wary. His optimism about what they'll be doing in a few years' time is too childlike. 'What was it you wanted to show me?' she asks, changing the subject.

Ryan steers her towards a tree. They have to fight their way through bracken and bramble bushes, so the area round it is deserted. 'This is *our* tree,' says Ryan. 'Look.'

He has chiselled their initials deep into the bark in letters that are more than a foot high. They are intertwined. There is a heart. He is watching her, waiting for the explosion of happiness he expects her to feel at this public declaration of love. And she does feel it. He is saying they belong to one another.

'This tree is ancient,' he tells her. 'I checked online. It's a thousand years old. It will be here for hundreds of years more. I had to get here at dawn to do it, before anyone else was up. Our initials, all linked up, will be here for ever – or as good as.'

She takes his hand. It's the most romantic thing she has ever heard. She repeats his words in her head over and over, savouring each of them. But the permanence of it disquiets her, too. She feels ungrateful, mean, because a small part of her wishes that he hadn't done it.

FORTY-FOUR

She loves the colour and the bustle of the market near Zoe's apartment but it doesn't have anything she can afford and, besides, it's Zoe's place, not hers, she doesn't fit in there. She prefers Brixton Market; it's a long way from her flat but she enjoys the journey on the bus and Tube and it's a lot like Deptford – full of ordinary people doing everyday things: pensioners whose home was once the Caribbean smoking on corners, teens leaning against railings with cans in their hands, mums greeting each other, toddlers in tow, catching up on the gossip. She goes to a stall with a stripy awning where raw fish are nestling on beds of crushed ice. There is a big, ugly monkfish with its mouth agape – it definitely needs braces. She sees octopus tentacles, ropey and gnarled, and dried and salted codfish hang from hooks. She gets a tub of shrimps, still with heads and tails, and hopes they're fresh. She'll do curry for Ryan tonight – it's not fair to expect him to cook all the time – so she also needs ginger, cumin and garlic. She finds them by smell – rich, peppery aromas that cause her nose to itch. Then she looks at shoes: ballet pumps and strappy sandals, plastic, cheap – affordable. She likes the pink and tries them on; they fit but she mustn't spend – she and Ryan are saving up for a holiday and they've only managed about fifty quid between them. When she gets a job, it will be easier. There's a man playing reggae from a stall up ahead; she hurries towards it. She looks at the rows of records in cardboard boxes. Her gran had lots of reggae 45s. They'd played them loud when she'd gone round. She forgets that she shouldn't be spending and buys several she remembers from her childhood. She can't wait to try them out on the record player back at home.

It's been weeks since Tyler did her hair and she's stopped wearing the comedy glasses, so she's looking more like her usual self. Getting her hair done would be expensive but she'd like to do it, get extensions. She used to have them before Tyler yanked them out. She'd have curls this time, or locks, maybe. Short hair would be cheaper, though. Maybe she could get the kind of cut that Tyler has, but her face is too fat; Tyler's face is long and narrow with high cheekbones that are accentuated by her cropped curls. She looks in the window of a salon, shielding her eyes to stop her reflection spoiling the view. Women are sitting in rows and chatting to each other, hair wrapped in towels. When she was working, she used to go to Miss Sarah's Afro Lounge. She'd liked the buzz of the place, and the chat.

She feels in her pocket for some change and finds she has enough for coffee and cake in the café on the corner but before she reaches the door, she sees Tyler walking towards her; the unexpectedness of it causes her stomach to flip.

Tyler sees her as well. Too late to run. Should she be there? How close is it to Deptford, the area she's excluded from? Perhaps she's in breach of the terms of her licence.

She mumbles hello, feeling caught out. She expects Tyler to walk on but she doesn't; she tells her that Brixton is her local market and she's going to a Caribbean café that serves the best jerk chicken. She points up the street and says the seasoning they use is a local speciality. 'Come if you want, it's worth a taste.'

The invitation surprises her. Why would Tyler want to spend time with her? 'Are you on duty?' she asks.

'Day off,' Tyler replies.

'So I'm not under surveillance then?'

Tyler laughs. 'Trust me, if you were, you wouldn't have seen me. Been shopping?'

She nods. 'I'm doing curry tonight. I got shrimps and spices. I like to come here. I came by Tube. It's a long way from Neasden but I like it. I like markets, the buzz of them.' She's rambling. She's not sure what Tyler's expecting from her. She glances at her, trying to pick up clues about how to handle this, but she is strolling along as if there's nothing unusual in it.

The chicken's amazing. She gets home-made ginger beer to wash it down. They are sitting at a long wooden table, painted orange.

'Brixton's changed over the years,' says Tyler. 'It used to

be a deprived area but it's been gentrified. At least there are remnants of the old Brixton in places like this.'

'Have you lived here long?' she asks politely.

'A few years now.'

'I wish I still lived in south London, but where I am now is close to Ryan. It was my birthday last week. He got me a record player, one of those old-fashioned ones that play vinyl. I got some records from a stall.' She pulls them out of the bag and shows them to Tyler.

'I love this,' says Tyler, looking at 'The Israelites' by Desmond Dekker. 'My parents had it. I used to listen all the time when I was a kid.'

'My gran used to have it.'

'My dad said it went to number one in the charts,' says Tyler. 'It was the days of skinheads, the 1960s.' She picks up another record. 'Oh and you've got this one. It's years since I heard Two-Tone. I remember dancing to it when I was really little. Skinheads again – different era. My mum spent her teens listening to this. She said the skinheads saw no contradiction in hating us as black people but loving our music.'

She absorbs the implicit inclusion in the words 'us' and 'our music' and is flushed with pleasure. 'What kinds of music do you listen to?' she asks.

'Grime, garage, hip hop, jazz – all kinds of black music,' Tyler replies.

It feels strange, sitting here with Tyler, being treated as if she matters. She wants to ask why things have changed but that might spoil the moment, so she focuses on the chicken, chewing slowly so they can stay in the café for longer.

'How's Otis?' asks Tyler.

'He's good, thanks.'

'And Ryan?'

'He's good, too. He wants us to get a place together.'

'Is that what you want?' asks Tyler.

There is a pause and then she says, 'Yes.'

'You don't sound very certain.'

'The thing is, we're not very grown up, either of us,' she says. 'Sometimes I worry it won't work out.'

'I suppose that's the reality of relationships, isn't it?' says Tyler, wiping seasoning from her fingers. 'They don't always work out. The trick is to recognize your own strengths, not rely on other people to get you through.'

Easier said than done, she thinks. 'Are you in a relationship?' she asks.

'Not at the moment.'

'Do you want to be?'

Tyler shakes her head. 'I need to be by myself right now, in my own head, not having to think about anybody else.'

She is surprised that Tyler is saying so much. She's normally so reticent, so private. She still doesn't get why they are sitting together.

Tyler looks even thinner than she usually does. She is wearing glasses. They suit her, give her gravitas. Perhaps she should have held on to the comedy glasses after all.

Tyler pays the bill. 'Call it a birthday treat,' she says. 'I hope things go the way you need them to,' she adds, as they part company.

Tyler used the word need, not want. The two things could be in conflict, she thinks. She wants to be with Ryan, but is being with him what she needs for the future? Can she trust him not to let her down? Can he trust her? She thinks about it all the way home. She thinks about it over the meal she cooks (disgusting, inedible, has to be chucked) and in bed with Ryan afterwards. She remembers the words that were used when she was talking to Zoe once: *almost happy, not quite.*

FORTY-FIVE

But happiness is relative, she decides, and she is more rooted – more hopeful – than she's ever been before. Soon she will be working: she's got a job in a call centre and she starts next week. She likes normal. Maybe she would like to have a family, children of her own. Maybe one day.

Sometimes, after she's been talking to Zoe and she's alone in her bed because Ryan is working in the café until morning, she thinks of all the possibilities. What if she hadn't gone to the allotments that day? If Kerry hadn't been on her own in the garden? What if she and Jessie had taken Kerry back home that evening, said sorry to her mum, promised never to take her off again and left her back in the house with the swing in the garden, eating her tea with Shannon and Aaron? What if Kerry hadn't wanted to stop playing and she hadn't tried to prevent her leaving? She hadn't wanted the game to end – once it ended, she knew she had to go home to Fred; she'd been so desperate about it. What if she hadn't been so scared? So *raging*? Would it have been different if her gran had stayed alive?

She wouldn't have gone to Whytefields or got exams or been inside. She would never have met Ryan (or Lucy). She wouldn't have spent hours talking to Zoe or sat in a café in Brixton with Tyler. What would have happened to her? Would she have been a version of Amber, strung out on crack and smack, shagging strangers to make ends meet? Or would she, somehow, have turned her life around, gone to university, become another Zoe? The only thing she knows for sure is that if she'd behaved differently, that day at the allotments, she wouldn't be the Gosling Girl, she'd still be Michelle Cameron.

When Ryan is home at night, it's easier. She shares secrets in the dark. And he shares with her. Her gran used to teach her things, history – how black people came to Britain, about Jamaica and the slave trade. Things that had made her angry. She'd put them to the back of her mind, not knowing what to do with them; she was angry enough already, she didn't need more stuff to be angry about. With Ryan, these things surface again, but they have somewhere to go, they can be shared. Sometimes, letting yourself see the things that hurt makes you stronger, less afraid. You can make more sense of the world. It becomes less strange, familiarized through conversations about who you are, what has formed you and the things that have isolated you. And Ryan has been isolated, too: raised in Kent without his dad, with no one who looked like him apart from his friend George, constantly stopped and searched by the police when he drove his mother's car. Seen as different, implicitly 'not like us'. She and Ryan have formed their own 'us'. In Ryan she sees a reflection of herself, a steadier, kinder version. With Ryan she can afford to be aware of cultural roots severed by dead and absent fathers. They share times when they've been hurt by n-words (the kind not used in hip hop songs), anti-immigration marches and speeches that tacitly reference rivers of blood.

And he's almost as scared as she is, afraid of being abandoned, terrified he can't be loved. Sometimes, he wakes up, his body so taut he's unable to move. She holds him then, not speaking, long into the night, until he falls asleep again. At first, these bouts had scared her, but as she came to understand how to calm him, she saw they drew them closer.

She would live her life differently if such a thing was possible, even if it meant never meeting Ryan. She wouldn't play with Jessie or Shannon or Kerry. She would run away from home, make something of herself. She says this to Zoe, who tells her it was never in her hands. Children don't get to leave their parents, raise themselves, become good people, unaffected by their pasts. Reality is different.

You can't change what happened, says Zoe.

She knows it's true. She remembers Kerry, alive and smiling, and it hurts.

PART FOUR

FORTY-SIX

She's been shopping, getting the things she needs for the job she's starting the day after tomorrow: a water bottle and a matching lunchbox with a cool bag. And a pen, even though the office is bound to have a few. And some smart black shoes.

As she walks from the shops on the high street, her phone starts to ring. She doesn't recognize the number but she answers anyway.

Fucking black cunt, the caller says. *Child killer.* She ends the call without speaking. It rings again, a different voice: *Bitch. I'll slit your throat, kill you like you killed little Kerry.* Then the texts arrive, flooding to her phone: MURDERER. WATCH YOUR BACK. They know who she is. They probably know where to find her. Tyler said she'd be safe, that the men who'd exposed her before wouldn't do it again. She ducks, as if this will shield her from the force of the words on the screen, and runs towards the flat. The main door is ajar. She stumbles up the stairs. Her front door's been kicked in. There's blood.

She finds Otis in the kitchen, lying still, his white fur matted red.

FORTY-SEVEN

The smell of human urine hits Tyler first. The TV is on the floor, the screen cracked across the centre. Over the mantelpiece, sprayed in red paint, is the word NIGGER. She is curled up on the floor. Tyler can only see the back of her and she doesn't move.

She touches her gently between the shoulder blades and speaks her name but there is no answer. She moves round to face her and sees that she is holding Otis to her chest. He is limp and his eyes are half closed; it may not be possible to save his sight. Tyler takes her phone out of her pocket. 'It's okay, I'm not going to move him, I'm calling a vet.'

She is rigid. Her low moans of pain echo the sounds Otis is making. Tyler crouches beside her trying to stem the bleeding from the dog's throat but there is nothing she can do and he stops breathing.

The forensic team arrives quickly to trawl through the mess. They work in silence, the sign of their repulsion. They are hardened to human corpses, but the torture of an animal has caught them off guard, leaving them without their usual defences.

Tyler watches as they photograph Otis and then the room, noting their thoroughness. Do they know they are in Michelle Cameron's flat? Probably not, unless they saw her being hurried to the car and put two and two together. Soon the rumour mill will start to grind, but for now, there is nothing to impede compassion.

She goes outside and lights a cigarette. She stands in the autumn sun, absorbing the warmth, her hands shaking slightly. Up ahead, Michelle Cameron is being attended to by a police doctor who is administering an injection of diazepam. Her details were leaked on social media again, though they were pulled very quickly; the tech team are tracing the source. A small crowd is gathering to find out what's going on. If they recognize Michelle Cameron, it will become a mob. 'I need to get her out of here,' says Tyler to herself.

The end of the day. Tyler goes to a pub by the river and buys herself a pint of beer. She is alone and prefers it that way. It's turning chilly but she remains outside – she likes the view, the sense of space as she looks across the Thames. It's hard to wind down; the chairs are chrome, designed more for effect than comfort, and Tyler can't get Michelle Cameron out of her head. She finishes her pint and gets a vodka and lime.

From her table on the south side of the river, she can see a small part of the wall of the Tate Modern, the bleak former power station that's now regarded as a landmark. She remembers going there with Maddie not long after it had opened. She remembers a steel spider that had filled the floor; a perfectly formed aberration of the kind that populate the edges of a bad dream or point to an apocalypse. In a corner of her mind it is linked to the barrel of a gun, metal upon metal, crawling stealthily towards her. She takes aim and shoots.

Until this moment, she had remembered the gallery only as a space of laughter and enjoyment. She hadn't returned since the break-up – it had been Maddie's thing, not hers. She had been there because Maddie had expected it. How many times has she stifled her sense of self to meet the requirements of somebody else? Her work with Michelle Cameron has exposed the extent to which she'd done so in the job. She is exhausted, angry with herself and angry too that, once again, Michelle Cameron's life has been upended.

Her phone rings: it's her boss. There mustn't be any suggestion that they've let Michelle Cameron slip through the net. If anything happens to her, the loony left, as he describes it, will be all over it, claiming they allowed racist hysteria to put her at risk. But at the same time, if they give her the protection she needs, the far right will be screaming that they put more into protecting the rights of immigrant perpetrators than the rights of their white victims. She terminates the call while he is still in mid-sentence. A reprimand will follow. She doesn't care.

Across the river, St Paul's Cathedral stands out in the floodlights. Tyler has never been religious, but as she looks at its imposing dome, she wonders what God, if he exists, makes of Michelle Cameron.

She finishes her vodka and gets another. The bar is quieter now, populated by a few young couples having pre-club drinks and plates of gravadlax with crusty brown bread. She feels like eating so she orders soup and chips.

The food arrives after too long a wait but the soup is good: chicken and vegetable, homemade. She hasn't eaten all day. She's surprised how hungry she is.

Michelle Cameron was ten when she killed Kerry Gosling but she will be punished for the rest of her life. Tyler remembers meeting her in Brixton Market. She'd taken a risk that day, treated her like a friend, eaten with her; she'd wanted to demonstrate that she saw her not as a monster but as a fellow human being. She remembers how grateful she had seemed for the acknowledgement. Tyler had been embarrassed. She hadn't wanted gratitude.

She sighs as she eats the last of her chips. She's tired of thinking about unfairness, dwindling resources, people slipping through the net and the way that prisons have become the new mental hospitals. It's not as if she can change it. She'd believed she could once: change things from within, she'd thought, as if that was possible – as if it didn't mean constantly being compromised.

She remembers the word emblazoned across the wall in red. She thinks of Dave Donaldson, who had called her one of us. You all stick together, he'd said. We don't, but perhaps we should, she thinks; she is tired of being on the wrong side. She remembers Otis, bleeding from the eyes and throat, and Michelle Cameron baying to the sky as he took his last breath.

She recalls Julie Gosling, holding cigarette butts to her arms. She doesn't want to go home just yet. She buys another drink, and then another.

The landlord calls time. As her taxi speeds towards home, Tyler finds herself crying. She puts it down to exhaustion – and to vodka and real ale.

FORTY-EIGHT

She is kept in hospital overnight. Tyler arrives the next morning to take her to stay with Ryan.

She is sitting in an armchair by her bed, rocking back and forth. The action grates. 'Can you stop doing that?' asks Tyler after a while, but she tries to keep her tone gentle. 'Ryan will be here soon,' she adds.

She nods. She'd refused to see him yesterday. She'd been too raw for any kind of comfort.

'Do you think you'll feel able to stay at his uncle's place?'

She nods again.

'Good. Would you like me to get you some water?'

She shakes her head. 'Do they know who did it yet?' she asks.

'Not as far as I know,' Tyler replies. 'It's too soon.' There was a lot of forensic evidence: urine that will be tested for DNA. Fingerprints, too, in all probability. The perpetrators should be easy to find.

'You probably don't get much of a sentence for killing a dog,' she says flatly.

'It was breaking and entering, too. And it was a hate crime, racially motivated – the writing on the wall and the texts prove that.'

She shrugs. 'When will I get my phone back?' she asks.

'Soon, I expect,' Tyler replies.

Despite the diazepam, which was topped up earlier, she is still in a state of agitation. She leaves the chair and starts pacing up and down the length of the ward.

Ryan arrives. He takes her in his arms but she remains unresponsive. 'I'm sorry,' he says to her.

'It wasn't your fault,' she replies.

She is still unsteady so he helps her on with her coat. 'The thing is,' says Ryan, leaning against the edge of the bed, 'I think it could have been my fault.'

She stares at him. 'What do you mean?'

He glances at Tyler who pretends not to be listening; she is gathering up the few things Michelle Cameron brought to the hospital and putting them in a plastic bag.

'You know when Amber took my phone? I thought she would have sold it, but she didn't.'

'She kept it? Have you got it back?'

He looks away from her. 'She accessed stuff I'd been looking at online, stuff about Kerry – you know, after you told me. She put two and two together. I said it was true.'

'You told her it was true?'

Tyler looks at Michelle Cameron. Her face is contorted with pain and fear.

'Amber already guessed; I just told her it was true. I never expected her to do what she did.'

'Why not? She's always wanted you to herself. Why *wouldn't* she do something like that? You promised you wouldn't tell. You *promised*. She told everyone, didn't she? Otis was killed because of Amber.'

Ryan stands there, helplessly. She starts to pummel him with her fists. He takes her by the wrists and holds her at arm's length.

'How could you tell her?' she asks, breathlessly. 'How could you do that?' She pulls away from him. She looks at Tyler. 'I have to go home now,' she says.

'I didn't mean it, Carly,' he tells her, but she doesn't hear. She heads towards the double doors that form the entrance to the ward, her feet still bare.

Tyler follows. 'He didn't mean it,' she says, echoing his words, feeling protective of Ryan. 'He couldn't know what it would lead to.'

There is no reply. She carries on walking. Ryan follows her. 'Stay away from me,' she shouts. The other patients are staring, hoping the entertainment will continue. The ward is usually dull.

'Don't go yet,' says Tyler, but she is ignored. She grabs the plastic bag and follows them down the hospital's bustling corridors, staying back a little, hoping that, somehow, they will be able to resolve this.

Ryan catches up with her. 'Please, Carly,' he says.

She pushes him away with all her might.

He stumbles into the wall. 'Carly, I'm so sorry,' he says, trying to steady himself. 'I love you, I never wanted to hurt you.'

'You betrayed me,' she says, rage in her voice. She starts to run. He hesitates, then follows her.

Tyler isn't sure what to do. Three of them, running at speed down a hospital corridor, will attract an audience so she continues to keep her distance, walking briskly behind. She can see them up ahead, Michelle Cameron waving her arms and shouting, Ryan in silent pursuit. She hopes she can catch them up. They are outside now, in the hospital grounds. She quickens her pace. 'Leave me alone!' she hears her cry. 'I never want to see you again! Leave me alone, do you hear?'

Tyler stands beside Ryan. She sees Michelle Cameron's despair as she starts to bang her head repeatedly against an outside wall. 'You'd better go,' she says to him in a low voice. 'I'll deal with this.'

He walks away slowly, turning to look at Michelle Cameron every now and then, his arms crossed against his chest.

They sit in Tyler's car. Her head is bleeding. She is crying without sound. 'We should go back to the ward and get your head checked. You may need stitches,' says Tyler.

'No,' she answers flatly.

They sit without speaking for a while. Then Tyler says, 'What do you want to do?'

She doesn't answer.

'You can't stay here and you can't go back to your flat. What do you want to do?'

'I'm not moving again,' she says in a voice that has determination in it.

'Listen to me, you have to move, it's not safe to stay at that address anymore, too many people know where you live.' It's the conversation they had in the police cell some months back. Cycles repeating themselves, Tyler thinks.

'I have to go back. Otis is there.'

'You know he isn't there, don't you?'

'His presence is there. I'll be able to smell him. Fur, from when I combed him, will still be on the floor.'

They continue to talk, but she is resolute.

On the way back to Neasden, Tyler's mobile rings. It's Zoe Laing. She's heard what's happened. Tyler wonders how she got her number. Her father's connections, no doubt. They speak for a while. Tyler ends the call and says: 'Zoe has suggested you go and stay with her. Do you think you could? It will be much safer than the flat and I don't think you should be on your own right now.'

She nods.

Relieved, Tyler reverses the car. They speed towards Ladbroke Grove.

FORTY-NINE

It's strange, being in Zoe's apartment as a house guest. She stands in the hall, wondering what she's supposed to do. The cat sidles up to her and she welcomes the distraction. She strokes her for a moment but the feel of her fur reminds her too much of Otis, so she backs away. Tyler and Zoe introduce themselves to one another and make superficial conversation. She wishes she still had her phone. She could be playing music now, shutting them out.

Once Tyler has gone, Zoe shows her round the apartment and tells her to make herself at home. She puts the few possessions she has left on the bed in the guest bedroom and then goes to find the television. She expects to see a sixty-inch version, but there is only a small one, tucked away in the corner of the kitchen-diner as if it is insignificant.

Soon Zoe will expect her to talk in lieu of rent. She will be obliged now. No more prevarication, she supposes, when it comes to her mother or her absent father.

Why did Ryan have to tell Amber who she was? If only

he'd kept quiet, she would still be in her flat waiting for him to come over, feeding Otis, checking his water bowl or taking him for a walk round Neasden's streets. She would still be looking forward to starting the new job. She would still be saving for their holiday.

She picks at the pasta Zoe has made. It's okay, but she has no appetite. Things must be bad, she thinks to herself.

And they are bad. Otis is gone and it's over with Ryan. She will never be happy.

She won't cry. She is tired of crying and tired from the Valium she's been taking. She looks across at Zoe who is staring at her, trying to work out how to handle this. She is tired of being handled.

They go into Zoe's living room. The recorder is switched on. She talks but she barely knows what she is saying. Stuff about Ryan, stuff about Otis, her memories of Fred, her mother, her sense of defeat. Everything is over, she repeats. Zoe squats beside her. She cries, even though she told herself she wouldn't. Zoe holds her tight; in the warmth of her arms, she cries even more.

When she awakens next morning, she feels less agitated. She doesn't take the Valium on the bedside table. Most of her clothes were destroyed in the attack so she's brought very little with her. The T-shirt she was wearing yesterday has splatters of blood from Otis, so Zoe has laid out a clean one. She's seen her wearing it: it's purple with fine grey stripes. She puts it on and looks in the mirror. She is different – new, and not in a good way – but it scarcely matters: she hasn't been anyone she recognizes for the whole of her adult life. She goes to the kitchen carefully, as if she might shatter into pieces if she moves too fast.

Zoe greets her. There is avocado on toast for breakfast. She doesn't like it much. She's never eaten avocado before, it has a strange eggy taste – and Zoe's gone and put an actual egg on top.

Zoe asks if she feels up to talking.

She nods, though she doesn't. There's nothing left to say.

In Zoe's office, she tries to make conversation but it's hard. She talks more about Ryan. She can't forgive him, she says, over and over again. Amber was more important to him than she was. Why does she never matter enough? Why does everyone betray her? The people who should have kept her safe – her mother, her father, even her gran – had all failed her. And now there is Ryan, too. She is giddy with disappointment in Ryan. It squeezes her tight and she finds it hard to breathe.

Zoe tells her that the break-up's for the best. She needs to work out who she is before she can have a healthy relationship with another person. That's something I can help you with, she says. She seems to think it's a good thing the relationship is over.

Zoe wants to carry on talking – and talking and talking and talking – but she can't talk anymore, she's all talked out.

That evening, Zoe tells her she has a meeting she has to attend. She is relieved. No more talking then, not tonight. She will relish the silence.

She'd thought she'd feel better once Zoe had gone and she

had the apartment to herself, but instead she feels afraid. She goes from room to room, trying to make it seem familiar. Zoe's bedroom door is locked. She is insulted. Does Zoe think she will steal? Or pry, perhaps? If she did pry it would only be tit for tat.

She sits on a short flight of stairs facing the front door. The landing is in darkness; she couldn't find the switch that puts on Zoe's lights. She waits for her to come home. She doesn't want to be alone.

But she is alone. She has always been alone. In the room Fred decked out for her in nursery colours – primrose, pink and pale pistachio – she had been alone, the teddy bear nightlight her only company. She was at her most alone when the men were with her, and now their faces grimace at her in the dark.

FIFTY

Zoe should have known the work with Michelle Cameron would stall after the flat had been vandalized, even though having her as a house guest meant they could talk for hours at a stretch. For the most part, she's silent, unwilling or unable to discuss the things that need to be said. It's clear that she's been traumatized by the loss of Ryan, and even more, perhaps, by the death of the dog, and she understands that, naturally. Her distress is so marked, it's impossible not to want to alleviate it.

She's arranged time off from the clinic in order to be at home more consistently while she is there but that's difficult financially, and it's infuriated the clinical director, who thinks she's left her colleagues (and her patients) in the lurch. She's starting to realize that this arrangement could continue for weeks rather than days; she should have made it clear that it was time-limited. Too late now. She is doing the work that the police should have done, providing another safe house, and at no additional cost to the state. No wonder Natalie Tyler had looked pleased with herself as she had dropped her off. It had seemed like the best solution at the time; the Home Office could have had her moved to another part of the country and she would have struggled to maintain contact – if Michelle Cameron had allowed the interviews to continue at all. But still, caution would have been wise.

She likes having the apartment to herself. She is pleased when friends come to stay but she's even more pleased when they leave. Having to consider another person every hour of the day, particularly one that needs a lot of nurturing, is something she'd thought she'd left behind with her divorce. And having to cook as well . . . she does it with the capability she brings to most aspects of her life but she doesn't enjoy it, she'd rather eat out. She has to shop, too, and keep the apartment clean. She feels drained.

She has asked to borrow a radio and is in the guest room, playing music too loudly. If she'd thought, she would have said no; with nothing to do, Michelle Cameron might have needed conversation. And the noise is irritating: it's not the kind of music she would choose to listen to. There is constant sound. If it's not the radio, it's the television. She longs for silence.

She is surprisingly tidy, though, and far more self-effacing than she was previously – a consequence of the losses she's suffered, no doubt. It's as if she thinks relative invisibility will protect her from further harm.

As she considers all this, Zoe realizes that this behaviour can be included in the book more extensively than she had originally planned. It will make an interesting chapter that addresses Michelle Cameron's neediness, her childlike retreat into loud music when she is upset or afraid, and her lack of friends and other kinds of support. While the book is mainly about the past, Michelle Cameron's present is important too, in as far as it can be revealed without compromising her identity.

Zoe's phone rings. It's her father. She doesn't really want to speak to him but he could be useful.

He hasn't heard that Michelle Cameron has come to stay. He is surprised and concerned. 'Dad, I know what I'm doing,' she says. 'It's such a huge opportunity to do the work that's needed to get the book finished. Her being here means I can observe the way she is day to day when she's less defended; she's already said some things she's never said before . . . Well, yes, of course . . . It's been hard to get to the real her. It helps that the boyfriend's out of the picture; that's worked out well. Now she can't depend on him, she'll need to share more with me . . . I know that . . . Well, that's a risk of course, but it's one worth taking . . . We need to understand why kids do the kind of thing she did. It's really important. The book's important, I wouldn't do this otherwise . . . I know . . . It's obvious that she has a personality disorder . . . Look, can you find out if the Home Office will finance another safe house not too far away? Otherwise, she could be here for weeks and that's going to be far too long. She's very needy, difficult, and there's a limit to how much . . . Thanks, Dad . . . Look, I'd better go, I have to start sorting out dinner . . . okay, speak soon.'

Zoe ends the call. She looks up. She is standing in the door-way. She has obviously been listening. She tries to remember exactly what she said, assessing how it will have come across, and how damaging it might have been. 'Look, I don't know how much you heard but it's not what you think ...'

She is staring, looking angry – *hurt*. There is another expression on her face that Zoe can't quite read. Betrayal? No doubt she will add her to the long list of people who have let her down. She really hopes this is salvageable. 'Come in. Come and sit down,' she says.

She remains where she is.

Zoe hovers, not sure whether to take a seat herself or to remain standing. 'Please understand, I needed to talk to someone about all this, make sure it's safe for both of us.'

'Safe? What do you mean, *safe*?'

'I suppose I mean ... *appropriate*.'

'Appropriate?'

Zoe starts walking towards her.

She backs away. 'You were talking to Adam Kenyon,' she says.

'To my dad. Yes.'

'You said I'm very needy and difficult and there's a limit. You said it was good that Ryan is out of the picture.'

'I didn't put it quite like that, and I meant it's better for you. You were too reliant on him. It wasn't a healthy relationship.'

'That's not what you meant.'

'You heard what I said out of context.'

'And you said I had a personality disorder. What's wrong with my personality? I thought you liked me.'

'It's a clinical term, that's all, it doesn't really mean anything. It doesn't reflect the way I see you.'

They are facing one another. They are both full of

345

adrenaline; it's causing them each to tremble. Zoe holds out her hand, hoping it will be taken and they will sit together and talk about this rationally, but the hand is ignored. There is silence. Zoe tries to think how to break it. 'I'll make us some coffee,' she suggests eventually. 'I got some of those cakes you like. We'll eat those.'

'You think I'm that stupid you can put a plate of cakes in front of me and everything will be all right. You think all I care about is food.'

'Of course I don't think that.'

'All you've done, right from the start, is bribe me, with food, with perfume – even with being your friend.'

'That really isn't true—'

'I want to go,' she says. 'I've had enough.'

'Please don't go. Let me make it right. I can see this is my fault, it's a boundary issue.'

'What do you mean, a boundary issue?'

'It's been hard for you to know what's been going on because I haven't been clear enough about whether I'm your therapist or the person you're writing a book with or your friend – or all three, perhaps. That's made everything a bit messy and I'm sorry, it's been confusing for you.'

'There you go again, treating me like I'm stupid. I'm not confused, I'm just sick to death of the way you treat me, the things you think about me!' She pulls the purple and grey striped T-shirt over her head and hurls it at Zoe. She is standing in the hall now, in her underwear. She runs up the stairs.

Zoe follows her. She is putting on the T-shirt she arrived in.

It's been washed and dried but the bloodstains are still visible. She shoves her remaining possessions into a plastic bag.

'I'd really like you to stay. It's safe here.'

'You think?' she says coldly.

'I haven't handled this well, I know that, but I've been feeling stressed, I've had a lot on at work. I really want to continue helping you. Will you let me?'

'*Helping* me?'

'I can get you through this, help you to be strong enough to deal with it. You've had a terrible shock. You're grieving for Otis. You need support. I can give you that.'

She heads towards the front door.

'Where will you go?' says Zoe. 'Your flat isn't safe. I don't want you to come to any harm, people know where you live. You would be much safer here.'

'That word again, *safe*, like it means anything. You're trying to scare me just to make me stay.'

'Can't we try to sort this out? I don't want you to leave like this, you're in no fit state.'

'The only thing you don't want is to be left with an unfinished book.'

'You're much more important than any book,' says Zoe.

She laughs.

'I mean it.'

'Sure you do,' she says. 'You lock your bedroom door when you go out. That's how much you think of me. You don't even trust me.'

Zoe sighs. 'Well, you've obviously tried to get in there,

haven't you, or how else would you know the door was locked?'

'You said, "make yourself at home".'

'I'm entitled to my privacy just as you are entitled to yours.'

'What privacy do I get? You want to know everything about me, every little thing. It's like you want to dig around inside my fucking soul. You don't have the right, no one does. I'm not doing the book anymore. I don't want you to write it. You're a liar, you tell lies.'

'You need to calm down. You're not well. Of course you're angry – who wouldn't be after what happened to the flat and to Otis? But taking it out on me won't help – quite the opposite, in fact.'

They are standing on the doorstep. Both are still trembling. 'Do you ever *listen*?' she says. 'I'm going to Natalie Tyler, to stay with her for a while.' She pushes her way past Zoe and runs from the apartment.

FIFTY-ONE

In the office that afternoon, Tyler receives a call from Zoe Laing. It seems there was a confrontation; Michelle Cameron has gone.

'I thought she'd be with you,' says Zoe. 'She said she was going to stay with you before she ran off.'

'And you thought her coming to stay with me was an actual possibility?' Tyler doodles circles in the notebook that rests on the corner of her desk.

'She must still be on her way. Can you persuade her to come back? There's still a lot of work we need to do. She likes you, she might listen to you.' There is a pause and then Zoe adds, 'Have you noticed she's started dressing like you now?'

Tyler had assumed that the grey jacket and the rust-coloured trousers she'd seen Michelle Cameron wearing when they'd met in Brixton were just coincidence but there was disappointment and frustration in Zoe's tone; it seemed that, unwittingly, Tyler had become Zoe's rival for Michelle Cameron's respect and admiration.

They talk for a while longer about the attack at the flat, whether or not it will be possible for her to get back with Ryan, and of course Zoe's book, and her limited progress with it.

'It's a mess,' Zoe concludes.

Tyler doesn't contradict her. She promises to update her when there's further news.

As she wonders what to tell her boss, she gets a message: there is a young woman waiting for her in reception.

Tyler hurries down, hoping no one has recognized Michelle Cameron. She is sitting quietly, her anxiety only evident in the rapid movements of her feet.

'I've left Zoe's,' she says softly, as she looks up and sees her approaching.

'Come on, let's get out of here,' Natalie replies.

They walk silently until they reach a square surrounded by shrubs and piles of fallen leaves. It's almost dusk. Starlings are circling; the beat of their wings creates an eerie sound. They sit on a bench, aware of a homeless woman pushing a supermarket trolley of old clothes entangled with rusty pots and pans. A few yards away, two men sway and clink their bottles together, raising a toast.

'What happened?' asks Natalie, observing that her eyes are red.

Her agitation grows as she talks about the tension she'd felt throughout her time in Zoe's apartment, feeling wanted and not wanted at the same time – confused – and then finally finding out, through an overheard phone call, that she was nothing more to Zoe than fodder for her book. 'She said I had a personality disorder. Zoe's personality isn't all that great either, in my opinion. She was pleased I'd broken up with Ryan because it meant I'd be forced to talk to her instead.'

Natalie isn't sure what to say in response to her palpable despair.

'I should never have agreed to do the book. I tried to tell her I wasn't going to do it ages ago. I'd been upset and I'd gone for her and she said she'd report me to Dom if I didn't keep on talking to her. I'd have been sent back to prison for it. She was so two-faced.'

'Are you sure that was what she meant? That it wasn't some kind of misunderstanding?'

'It was what she meant, but she'd say it was a misunderstanding, I'd got it wrong, I was confused. Either that or she'd make out I was just lying to get attention and she wouldn't dream of forcing me to do anything. I bet the book will say I loved talking to her, couldn't get enough of it, thought she was brilliant. I thought I could trust her. Shows how stupid I am, doesn't it?'

She pulls up the hood of her jacket so Natalie can no longer see her face.

'I thought she meant the things she said to me,' she continues, 'that I wasn't a bad person, that I was worth something.'

'I don't really know Zoe but I think she's probably quite complicated. She might have been desperate to do the book with you but I think she wanted to help you, too, make things easier for you, so she probably did mean the good things she told you,' says Natalie, hoping this is true.

'I was wondering, can I come and stay with you?' she says suddenly, as if she is afraid she'll lose the courage to ask if she doesn't get the words out quickly enough.

Natalie doesn't speak for a moment. Eventually she replies, 'That's just not possible.'

She looks so hurt that she wishes she'd phrased the rejection less starkly.

'Then I'll have to go back to the flat,' she says, in a voice that's dull with disappointment. 'Otis isn't there anymore, or Ryan, it will be just me. I realized in Zoe's apartment, it's always been just me anyway.'

Natalie wants to take away the pain of all the loss, but she knows she can't.

The starlings take flight simultaneously. Their piercing cries reverberate and Natalie can barely hear her own voice as she says, 'I'm sorry.' The sound of the birds begins to fade. Now she can hear the breathless sobs that Michelle Cameron is trying to suppress, her face disturbingly still.

'We went to that café in Brixton,' she says, pushing out the words. 'I thought you liked me.'

'I do like you,' says Natalie warmly, wishing she had a solution.

There is silence for a while and then she says, 'Otis died because of me, because of what I did to Kerry.'

Natalie tries to light a cigarette but the lighter's low on fuel and it fails to spark. She puts it back in her pocket. 'No, Michelle, he didn't. Otis died because a bunch of racists decided to vent their hatred on somebody. They took Otis away from you, and that's a really horrible thing, but it wasn't your fault. It wasn't Ryan's fault, either. Try to patch things up with him. Don't let them take Ryan away from you as well or there will just be what happened with Kerry and nothing else for the rest of your life.'

There is another uncomfortable silence that Natalie is the first to break. 'Let me talk to my boss. We'll try to set up another safe house for you.'

'I'm not moving, I've done it too many times.' Michelle looks towards the homeless woman with the trolley and she adds: 'I keep making a life for myself and then it gets taken away again. It's the hope that's hard, thinking that maybe this time it will all be different. I don't want to keep hoping. I don't want to keep starting again. I'm too tired of doing that. It's too ... it makes me too sad.'

'Don't rule out starting again. You have done it before, it's something you're good at. You've dealt with so much and you still managed to make a life for yourself.'

Michelle says nothing.

Natalie fingers the shrivelled leaves that are resting on the bench beside her. 'I'll make some calls then, have the flat made as secure as it can be.'

'Any more secure and it will look like a dealer's flat. I'll be accused of selling crack cocaine to school kids next.' She starts to laugh hopelessly and, as she walks away, the hollow sound fills the autumn air.

PART FIVE

FIFTY-TWO

A notification lights up Zoe's MacBook: GOSLING GIRL FOUND DEAD AT HER HOME IN NEASDEN. THERE ARE NO SUSPICIOUS CIRCUMSTANCES.

It must be a hoax. She goes to the BBC news site. The death is confirmed: Michelle Cameron has died suddenly, with heart failure as the likely cause. There is an article that describes her as deeply troubled and it regurgitates the circumstances of Kerry Gosling's death. Zoe skims it, still unable to take in the news. Where does this leave the book? she wonders.

She phones her editor, sounding agitated, aware only of all the work that still needs to be done. They speak at length. It is as Zoe feared: there will be a spate of books and articles, all re-examining the Kerry Gosling killing in the immediate aftermath of Michelle Cameron's death, then interest will start to wane. The publication date will need to be brought forward. When can she submit?

Zoe doesn't know. She'd thought she would be able to persuade her to return to complete their conversations. There are still so many questions. She has plenty of notes and recorded interviews, but no actual book as yet, and the bulk of the research focuses on life after her release. The editor suggests a new timeframe. Zoe agrees – it's that or miss the peak of public interest.

She ends the call and thinks back to the day she left the apartment. Were there signs of physical illness? She certainly hadn't looked well, but that wasn't surprising given the loss of the dog and the end of her relationship with Ryan. But *dead*? It's hard to believe.

#GoslingGirlDead is trending on Twitter. Zoe reads some of the tweets: *The Goslings must be celebrating at last their ordeal is over* (@DaveDonaldson). And another: *send them all back one less now.* Not all are vitriolic. Someone has written: *Tragic short life where's the compassion? just a kid herself when she killed Kerry.*

A statement has been issued by the Goslings and it is broadcast on the evening news. It is read by Dave Donaldson, a family friend, who looks full of himself in the gaze of the media: 'The Gosling family would like to say that the death of a young person should never be cause for celebration. However, they hope that from now on, they will be allowed to remember Kerry in their own way and without the attach-ment to Michelle Cameron, that has plagued their thoughts of their daughter for so long.'

Zoe pulls the blinds and sits at her desk. She hasn't known what to think or feel all day. She liked her, of course she did: it's impossible to sit with someone and hear them talk about their life without gaining empathy and a sense of what makes them tick. But she's aware of wishing that she'd pushed her more, asked more direct questions. Too many gaps and very little time now to fill them. She looks at the Notes folder on her MacBook. The biggest holes relate to her early life so it would make sense to track down some of the people who knew her back then. Her mother is the obvious place to start – she's been wanting to see her from the outset – but would she be willing to be interviewed? Zoe remembers various newspaper articles and concludes she's unlikely to object – she's always had plenty to say on the subject, with false reluctance that should have made her daughter far more angry than she was.

Midge scratches at the door and Zoe recalls how nervous the cat had made Michelle Cameron at their first meeting; she'd thought there was someone else in the apartment. She lets the cat into the room, draws her on to her lap and strokes her rhythmically, finding it calming. She'd been nervous the first time Michelle Cameron had come to see her, though it probably hadn't shown; she'd been far too anxious herself to have noticed. She'd sat in the chair, frowning, curt to the point of rudeness. Zoe had fed her doughnuts and coffee, an obvious bribe, treated her a bit like a greedy child, and it had paid off, eased their relationship. That first meeting will need to go into the book. She thinks about ways of describing Michelle Cameron: childlike, disarming. More than pretty – beautiful, really, but not in a conventional sense. Large eyes, dimples when she laughed, which wasn't as seldom as people might have imagined. Always pleading to be noticed – *liked*. And she was likeable, in her way – funny – and thoughtful too at times. Her years living with Fred, in Whytefields and in the young offenders' institution had taught her to be observant. Misjudge people or events in those contexts and it can cost you everything. She thinks of what else she will say. Her own nervousness was to do with an awareness of the fragility of the situation. From the outset it was clear she could clam up. She could have withdrawn her co-operation with regard to the book at any time. There were a number of occasions when it seemed as if she had. So she'd had to woo her, get her on side. She doesn't know how much of that part she will reveal.

She puts the cat on the floor, feeling more optimistic. She's done the groundwork. She's spent hours speaking to Michelle Cameron and no one else has done that, so she's already way ahead of the game. She knows how she wants to approach this; she's been thinking about it for months. Again, ahead of the game. She can put everything else to one side and work day and night on this book if need be – she's worked like that plenty of times before. She doesn't need to worry, it will work out, she'll make sure of it.

FIFTY-THREE

Zoe can't get hold of any records concerning Michelle Cameron's death, including the coroner's report. It's not in the public interest, she is told. Even her father is blocked from accessing them. So much about Michelle Cameron has been shrouded in secrecy that in some respects, she isn't surprised, but it does fuel her suspicions. She no longer believes she died from natural causes. There are things she needs to confirm. She phones Natalie Tyler in the hope that she'll co-operate.

She isn't in the office, they say. No one seems to know when she'll be back. Her colleagues are guarded about her absence so Zoe decides to phone her directly. She hopes the call won't go to voicemail; her hostility towards the book has been clear, so she probably won't respond to a message. When she answers, Zoe is relieved. 'I'm sorry to ring you like this but I couldn't get hold of you at your work, they said you weren't available.'

There is a long pause. Then Tyler says, 'This is about Michelle Cameron.'

'I was hoping we could talk, completely off the record.'

'I don't know ...'

'Just a few questions. Please, it would really help.'

There is another lengthy pause. 'We could meet somewhere, I suppose. There's a café I sometimes go to. Can you come there?'

They meet at the café the following morning. It's quiet, off the beaten track. They order tea and toast and sit at a corner table. Natalie looks tired and unwell, and Zoe wonders if illness accounts for her absence from work. 'I wanted to talk to you about the circumstances surrounding her death,' she says. 'I've been trying to get information and it isn't adding up. I was wondering what your take on it is.'

Natalie stirs her tea slowly and says: 'I don't think it's adding up, either. I was her liaison officer. When she died, I should have been involved but I didn't hear about it until it was on the news. Something isn't right. Do you think it could have been suicide?'

Zoe still hasn't ruled this out, so she says, 'It isn't out of the question.' She remembers how Michelle Cameron had been as she'd left her apartment; her despair was palpable. One last angry gesture. Take pills or put a rope around the neck, two fingers to the world. It would explain a cover-up; death by natural causes and no one is culpable. A suicide, on the other hand, could be seen as the result of police bungling with regard to the Lucy Fields murder and the exposure Michelle Cameron had been subjected to in consequence. The whole mess could lead to unpleasant enquiries; they could even invoke the Home Office. She could see why such a thing would need to be kept quiet. 'You know there's no public access to any of the usual documentation?' she says. 'And her body hasn't been released yet – that's strange, too.'

Natalie nods. 'As you know, just three or four weeks before she died, Michelle Cameron was the victim of a serious, racially motivated attack. There would have been so much DNA at the flat but no one was even interviewed about what happened, let alone charged. Then she's found dead and there doesn't seem to have been any kind of official inquiry.'

'So you think this could be a racially motivated murder that's being covered up?'

A man enters the café. Natalie looks up and lowers her voice. 'It's a real possibility. They said it was natural causes so it didn't need to be investigated but the decision was taken too soon. With someone as young and vulnerable as Michelle Cameron, you'd expect the death to be treated as suspicious until it can be proven otherwise, but it seems to have been treated as natural causes from the outset.' She pulls at the strap of her watch with short, sharp movements. 'I tried to find out why and I talked to my boss but he just said it's out of our hands, nothing to do with me anymore and to leave it alone. When I tried to push it, they said I was obviously under a lot of strain and needed to take some sick leave.'

'You think they're trying to keep you quiet?'

'They definitely don't want me to investigate. I'm being gaslighted.'

A waitress comes over and asks if she can get them more tea. They order another pot. Natalie is looking anxiously at the only other customer, as if he might overhear, but he is listening to music; Zoe can hear the tinny beat leaking through his head-phones. Despite this, Natalie lowers her voice even further. 'The CCTV footage for the night of her death and the days immediately after isn't available – or not to me, anyway,' she says.

Zoe thinks this is confirmation that the truth is being concealed. 'I've been hoping to speak to Ryan, Michelle's boy-friend,' she says, 'but I haven't been able to find him. Any idea where he is?'

'That's another thing, no one knows where he's got to, he's disappeared. He hasn't returned to his mother's house in Kent, I checked.' Natalie stops looking at Zoe and stares at one of the pictures on the wall. Zoe sees how much it's costing her to make these disclosures; they compromise a professionalism she values.

The waitress brings fresh tea to the table. As Natalie pours, her hand begins to tremble. She stops, puts down the pot and visibly steadies herself before picking it up once more. She glances at Zoe as if she's trying to see if she's noticed.

'How have you been?' Zoe asks.

'All right,' she says.

'Is it difficult for you, not being able to be at work at the moment?'

Natalie takes a sip from her cup. 'No, not really. I haven't felt good about work for some time. My parents are very active in the local community. They've never approved of the job, though they've tried to hide it.. They thought I'd joined Babylon, and now I see what they meant; the treatment of Michelle Cameron has brought all the racism into sharp relief.'

'It's understandable that you're extra sensitive about it but I don't think Michelle Cameron's treatment was to do with racism.'

'*Extra sensitive?*' Natalie says. 'So your book on Michelle Cameron will be another whitewash, will it?'

'I really resent that. You need to step back for a minute and think about what you're implying here, it's insulting.' Zoe speaks calmly, not wanting a drama in the café. If Natalie didn't seem so fragile right now, she'd be far more angry about her outburst. 'I don't see colour,' she adds, 'everyone's the same to me.'

Natalie looks angry. 'If you pretend you don't see colour, then you don't have to see unfairness or discrimination. They never brought a case against the other girl, did they, the white girl who was with Michelle Cameron when Kerry Gosling was killed? She must have been equally involved but it was decided that she couldn't have been responsible, she was mentally ill – unfit to plead – and easily led. Her parents took her abroad eventually. She was allowed to keep her anonymity. And Freya Fields. You heard about her? She'll get the most lenient sentence it's possible to hand down, you wait and see. Even Lucy didn't serve her original sentence because the family had enough money to buy her out of trouble. All these white women got away with murder – literally. And yet you're saying Michelle Cameron's treatment had nothing to do with race.'

An awkward silence follows. Then Zoe says: 'Are you okay? You don't seem yourself.'

'I am very much myself, thank you – more myself than I've been in a long while.'

'I heard you were involved in a firearms incident.'

'Was that something your father ferreted out for you?'

'It wasn't hard to get the information. The point is, with PTSD—'

'Zoe, I'm not Michelle Cameron. Don't try your therapy on me.'

Zoe changes the subject. 'If Michelle Cameron was murdered, who do think was responsible?'

'I really don't know. I can't believe it was Ryan, even if he'd started using again, but why would he have disappeared? Perhaps he was angry with Michelle for rejecting him, and he lashed out – I don't know.'

'Look, Natalie, I don't want to stick my nose in where it's not wanted but if you ever need some help—'

'I'm fine, thank you. I shouldn't have agreed to meet you. I just wanted to know what had happened and, ironically, you seem better placed to find out than I am. I wanted to check something with you, too. Michelle came to see me the day she left your apartment. She said you threatened to report her to Dom, her probation officer, when she said she wasn't going to do your book. Is that true?'

Zoe is annoyed. 'No, of course it isn't true, I would never do anything like that. As you know, she was very troubled emotionally. I never tried to coerce her into anything, I didn't need to. She was desperate to tell people her side of the story, set the record straight.'

Natalie smiles slightly and says, 'Yes, she told me you'd say that.'

Zoe minds that Michelle Cameron still has the capacity to wrong-foot her, even from the grave. She says, 'She was very important to me, you know.'

'She was important,' Natalie replies, 'though most people thought her life wasn't worth anything.' Then she adds, as if speaking her thoughts aloud: 'She was distraught the last time I saw her. Perhaps if I'd let her stay with me she'd still be here now.'

'I've been thinking much the same thing,' says Zoe. 'If she hadn't overheard that conversation . . . but it doesn't help anyone to go down that road. We each knew her pretty well, we're bound to have been affected by her death. I've barely been able to sleep since it happened. My work has been suffering because of it.'

Natalie laughs. Zoe isn't sure what's amusing her until she says: 'Whatever will we do without Michelle Cameron to pin our failings on? We're all going to be so lost without her.'

There is a long silence. Natalie fingers a teaspoon and pushes it up the table.

Zoe sees a traffic warden through the window of the café and hurries outside to move her car from the yellow line she'd risked parking on. It takes longer than expected. By the time she gets back, Natalie is no longer at the table. She thinks she's gone, just walked out, and she is angry for a moment, but then she sees her returning from the toilet in the basement. As she comes closer, it becomes clear that she's been crying.

They sit down again and Zoe says, 'If you're thinking in terms of revenge for Kerry Gosling's murder, you can't rule out her family.'

Natalie shakes her head. 'I've met them, I can't imagine any of them being capable of something like that.'

'But it's a possibility, isn't it? No one would want to see one of the Goslings accused of murder, there would be a media frenzy. If she was killed, and there's been a deliberate failure to investigate, it's likely to relate to the Goslings.'

'What do you intend to do about all this?' she asks.

'Talk to people, see what I can find out. And I'll see what I can dig up on the suicide aspect. I'll also keep trying to get hold of a coroner's report. If it's possible to do this while you're on sick leave, see if you can find out about the video recordings. There was so much security around Michelle Cameron's flat, there must be something somewhere we can look at.'

'So you don't think it was natural causes either?'

'No, I don't believe so,' Zoe replies.

Natalie gets up. 'You said on the phone that this would be off the record. I really don't want this conversation ending up in your book,' she says.

'You don't need to worry about that,' Zoe replies. 'I really am concerned about you, Natalie. When I couldn't get hold of you, I asked around because I thought something must be wrong. I'd like to help you, if I can.' They go to the till; Zoe pays the bill. 'I know a therapist who's done a lot of very good work with PTSD sufferers,' she says as they leave. 'Give me a call. I'd be happy to put you in touch.'

Natalie doesn't reply.

FIFTY-FOUR

Zoe had always intended to seek out Sandra Cameron but her daughter had continued to oppose it with such vehemence that she had kept postponing it, hoping that eventually she would talk her round. Now that there is no longer any obstacle to a meeting, Zoe drives towards west London.

Throughout their conversations, Michelle Cameron had said as little as possible about her mother, deflecting questions or responding with 'I don't know', her usual way of dealing with discomfort. Zoe had deduced that memories of her mother were too painful to be dredged up; in some ways, they seemed more threatening to her stability than her recollections of Fred. What had been clear was that once, Michelle Cameron had loved her mother, and the pain of rejection had been so great that it had been easier to shut out the memory of her.

Zoe has done some further digging with regard to Sandra Cameron. A few years after the trial, she had married a much older man who had left her a house in Chiswick and enough

369

to live on when he died. She is now Alexandra Neale and Zoe wonders if the lengthening of her name has been done for effect or in order to aid anonymity and distance herself further from her daughter.

She is early for their meeting. She's not familiar with this part of London and she always enjoys being by the river, so she parks the car and walks beside the Thames, taking in the view. Chiswick Bridge, low and built of stone, stretches out ahead. A rowing boat glides past, coxed by a girl in a tracksuit who chants rhythmically as a women's team moves in unison. Willow trees brush the surface of the water and gulls swoop for bread being thrown to ducks by a mother and her toddler.

Caught off guard by maternal feelings she believed she had muted, Zoe thinks how different her life would have been if she'd had a child. During her marriage to Oliver, she had put off getting pregnant, thinking she had time and that a baby would obstruct her career, but in her mid-thirties, maternal longings had unexpectedly come to the fore and she'd decided that the time was right for a family. It was then that Oliver had shocked her by saying he no longer believed they should bring a child into a world that was so hostile, both environmentally and socially. She had started to work on him to change his mind, but then he'd got another woman pregnant, the woman he'd gone on to marry. They had two children now. She would never forgive him for that. She had found herself the best solicitor and had got as much as possible from him in settlement. If she could have squeezed more money out of

370

him she would have done, but at least he had been forced to pay for her flat, and the car. And she has to keep remembering it's not too late. The next part of the advance for the book will pay for a pregnancy, even if she has to go to the States to set up sperm donation. She's thought of starting a long-term relationship – it would certainly be cheaper – but time is running out; she can't afford to wait. A one-night stand is chancy in every way, including genetically. And it's easier if the father is completely out of the picture; there are no legal constraints, you have sole say on how the child is raised. She watches as more young mothers, slim in designer jeans and tops, drop the older kids at school, then gather to exchange exasperated tales of clueless, inept husbands.

She approaches a Victorian semi that has custom-made wooden shutters at the windows and a newly built garage to the side. There is a small front garden and a stone lion guards the entrance to the porch.

Sandra Cameron is slender in a figure-skimming dress, with well-cut shoulder-length hair, subtle make-up and shiny, manicured fingernails. She isn't what Zoe was expecting; nothing about her, including her modulated voice, conveys a deprived childhood in Bermondsey. It's possible, Zoe thinks, that she made up being raised in care to elicit sympathy after her daughter's conviction. She'll need to check.

The interior of the house is open-plan and the furniture is contemporary. Zoe is seated in a spacious kitchen that is spotlessly clean and offered coffee. She tries to work out how old Sandra is, remembering she was just eighteen when she gave birth. That would make her about forty-three; like her daughter, she looks a lot younger, and she is similarly attractive, with the same nervous gestures: the clenching of the fingers and fidgety movements of the feet.

Zoe thanks Sandra for taking the time to see her and offers words of condolence.

'No one should die so young,' Sandra replies. 'I never thought I'd end up mourning my own daughter. Even though I haven't been able to see her for a long time, I miss her, miss knowing she's around.'

'It must have been a big shock.'

'Heart failure? It's hard to believe, not at that age.'

'Is there any word about when the body will be released?' asks Zoe.

Sandra shakes her head. 'I can't get any information out of them. Do you know anything? Why's everything been delayed? I'd like to have a funeral, be able to scatter her ashes but they just keep saying there's a delay and they'll let me know as soon as possible.'

She places the coffee in front of Zoe and offers her some biscuits, which she declines. She tells Sandra it's important to get her side of the story for the book she is writing about her daughter.

'I hope it will be accurate,' says Sandra, pushing aside the Yorkshire terrier that is prancing at her knee, demanding attention.

'That's why I'm here – I want to make sure I present you as accurately as possible.' Zoe checks the details that she already has and Sandra insists that she was indeed brought up in care from the age of three.

'I was taken away from my mother. I don't have a lot of information. I think it was to do with neglect. It wasn't the best of starts but I promised I'd make something of myself, and I have, haven't I?' She opens her hands in a way that encompasses the house and its furnishings and waits for Zoe's approval.

She gives it with enthusiasm.

'I've started a bit of a sideline locally as an interior designer,' she says. 'It's word of mouth but it's going well. I've done a couple of houses in the area.' She starts to look anxious. 'I've made a new life for myself here. If I give an interview about the past, I always say no photos, and keep my new name out of it. Can I rely on you to do that?'

Zoe confirms that she can.

'And you said there'd be a fee?'

Zoe confirms this too.

Sandra nods, seeming satisfied.

They talk more about her life in care and the way she used to make ends meet as an escort, as Sandra describes it. 'You might not believe this now but I could have been a model back then, I had the looks, it's just hard to get the breaks.'

Zoe nods.

'Of course, having a baby didn't help, it's not like you can model swimwear anymore, is it, once you've got the stretch marks? I could have got rid of her, but I didn't. I wanted her. And I did love her, you know, whatever anyone thinks. She was my daughter. I thought the world of her.'

'It must have been hard, having a child so young, and the father not being around.'

'People haven't a clue what it was like for me back then. Would you like another cup of coffee?'

'No, I'm fine, thanks.'

'I'll get myself another one then, if you don't mind.' As she refills the cafetière, she says, 'I'm not saying Michelle didn't have her good points, of course she did. She could be quite loving at times, kind, you know? Quite soft. Everyone thinks what she did must have been my fault, but it wasn't. She was a difficult baby and she grew into a very difficult child. You couldn't say no to her, she just didn't understand the word, and she wanted attention every minute. Even at school she was a nightmare, but you'd think the teachers would be able to cope after all that training, wouldn't you? She was excluded, you know, before Kerry and the trial. She picked up a chair and threw it at another child, cut the side of her head. They had me up at the school but I said she's ten years old, what does it say about this school if you can't sort out a child of that age? They said they had to think about the other children. They didn't think about me, having to have her around all day, bored with nothing to do. They were meant to sort out something else for her but they dragged their feet and then of course it was too late, she ended up at Whytefields.'

'Why do you think she was so difficult at home?' asks Zoe.

'You tell me, I just couldn't understand it, still can't.' The dog jumps on to Sandra's lap. 'This is another one that wants attention all the time,' she says, petting him fondly.

'What about her grandmother? She spent quite a lot of time with her, didn't she?'

'I didn't really want her involved, to be fair, but Estelle was one of those people ... pushy, you know? And she was all right, I suppose, in her way. Trouble is, they weren't a good family. They came over in the sixties like a lot of them did, and they didn't really take to our ways.'

'How do you mean?'

'It's going to sound ... but I'm the last person you could call racist, or I wouldn't have gone out with Curtis or kept Michelle, would I? But they weren't a good influence. They didn't even try to fit in when they came over here. No one made them come, they chose to do it, but they kept on complaining. You've got to make an effort, haven't you? They make a big song and dance about this country treating them unfairly but life is unfair, isn't it? I should know, taken off my alcoholic mother, shoved into care and pregnant at seventeen.'

Zoe considers this. Sandra Cameron's life would have been almost as hard as her daughter's. Small wonder then that she hadn't had the capacity to give her what she'd needed.

Sandra continues to speak in a slightly agitated voice: 'I went round there for a meal once and they had all this spicy food, rice and peas but without any actual peas in it, and this fish that smelled a bit off. I tried to be polite but I really couldn't eat it. Estelle, Curtis's mother, wanted Michelle to be like them, eat their food, have her hair in little plaits. She wasn't black – well, what I mean is, she was half white – but Estelle was filling her head with all sorts of bad ideas about herself. Don't get me wrong, Estelle had her when I was busy or Fred and me wanted to spend some time alone together, she was good like that, but Michelle was easily led. I was her mother, she needed to take after me, not Curtis and his family. I've often thought her behaviour was something to do with her genes, it's the only explanation, and those genes didn't come from me.'

'Can you tell me more about Curtis?' It's one of the blanks Zoe needs to fill.

'Usual story. Quite a bit older than me. Good-looking bloke, had a bit of money, a car, all that. Took me out for meals, got me into the best clubs in London, so naturally I fell for him. Got me into another kind of club too, of course. By the time I realized what he was like, it was too late. Men like him, they don't want to earn an honest living, they just want to make quick money; he dealt drugs, hard stuff. He didn't stick around once he knew I was pregnant. I was so naïve, just another notch on his bedpost. He saw Michelle once or twice when he visited his mother and he promised her the world. Next thing you know, he's inside and after that, he was deported back to Jamaica. Good riddance if you ask me. Even his mother was embarrassed by him. That's why she gave Michelle so much attention. I think she was trying to make up for it.'

'When did you meet Fred?'

'Michelle would have been about eighteen months old? Under two, anyway. We were together over thirteen years. It ended not long after she was sent away to Whytefields. What people don't get is that I lost everything because of what she did, I had to give up my house and move out of the area, change my name ... Fred went in the end and I lost my daughter, too.'

'Sandra, why did you never visit your daughter after the trial?'

'I went to see her,' she says indignantly. 'Fred and I both went, he drove me there, he knew how much it meant to me to see her. Why, did she tell you I didn't go? Of course I went. I wasn't going to leave her on her own, was I? But the bottom line was, seeing her dragged me down too much, I could hardly get out of bed the next morning, so Fred said it was best not to go back, my own health was suffering too much.'

'So you lost touch with your daughter?'

'You have to understand, there's only so much you can take. During the trial the papers went crazy for it, Gosling Girl this and Gosling Girl that, everywhere you looked. And it didn't stop when the trial ended, either. Don't get me wrong, I loved her, I always will, but it drained the life out of me. In the end, I couldn't take it anymore. It's not like I was going to be in her life that much anyway, she was going to be inside that Whytefields place for years. I said to her on the phone, don't contact me, it's better if you don't for both our sakes. Besides, it wasn't safe. Reporters and all that, tracking me down for a story. Not to mention all the threats. I got death threats, like it was me who'd done it. Once I met John, it seemed better, kinder in a way, just to make a clean break of it and start again.'

Zoe thinks about how to broach the next topic. 'What kind of stepfather was Fred to Michelle?' she asks.

'He treated her like his own; he loved the bones of her.'

'And did Michelle like him?'

'Yes, of course she did. She knew she couldn't give him any lip but that was a good thing – she needed discipline from somebody. He used to give me a break from her some weekends, take her away to places. If I'd had her opportunities as a child – days out, boat trips, holidays, I would have considered myself lucky, but Michelle just couldn't be grateful.'

Zoe watches Sandra keenly, trying to gauge whether or not she genuinely believes what she is saying, but her blank face gives nothing away. 'Michelle said some things to me about the times she was with Fred,' she says.

'Did she?' replies Sandra, mopping up a spill of coffee from the tabletop.

'She didn't experience them as happy.'

'Well that's what I mean. She couldn't be grateful for anything. She was jealous of me and Fred, that was the trouble, she wanted me all to herself. Or maybe it was Fred she wanted, I was never sure.'

'I don't think it was jealousy, or a lack of gratitude . . .' Zoe pauses, continuing to study Sandra's face, but she still reveals nothing. 'Michelle said Fred abused her, sexually, when they were away. There were other men, too.'

Sandra slams down her empty coffee cup, causing Zoe to start. 'I knew she'd make up something like that, she always was a liar.' She is close to tears. 'Fred was a good man, how could she say he wasn't? You don't believe it, do you?'

Zoe remains silent.

'I can't believe you swallowed all that. Michelle needed to find an excuse for what she'd done and that was the best she could come up with. She was always cunning. And you, you're no better. You'd love it to be true, wouldn't you? Sell more copies of your book. I'd like you to leave now. Go on, get out!'

She shows Zoe to the door, fury evident in her rapid movements.

Zoe remembers what Michelle Cameron had said to her not long before she died. There had been such sadness in her voice as, sitting in the consulting room, she had described the sense of betrayal she'd felt when she'd told her mother about Fred and the other men and had been smacked around the head for it. *Lies*, her mother had said, *ugly, dirty, lies.*

FIFTY-FIVE

They are no closer to learning what happened to Michelle Cameron. Natalie is disappointed. She'd hoped Zoe's nose for a story would produce an explanation but all enquiries have proved fruitless. She has confided in her for nothing and now she will be exposed. Natalie knows she will make an appearance in the book, whatever Zoe has promised, and it won't be flattering. She envisages the way she will be represented: the cop who failed to keep Michelle Cameron safe and bungled the investigation into her death. Her name will be changed, but her colleagues will recognize her as a closed, unstable detective (far too close to Michelle Cameron) who was traumatized by a firearms incident in the line of duty.

Perhaps it doesn't matter anymore. Michelle's death has strengthened her resolve to leave the job; she's been on the wrong side for the very last time. She doesn't know what she will do but the lack of a firm plan no longer scares her. She'll find a different career, one that's more suited to the way she sees the world, one that won't require the suppression of her racial and cultural identity – the things that make her who she is. She might go home to her parents for a while. When they hear she's left the *force*, as they insist on calling it, with all the emphasis they can bring to the word, they will pretend to sympathize, but secretly they will be elated: no more embarrassing conversations with family friends about their daughter's shameful occupation. You'd be quick enough to phone the police if you were burgled or attacked she'd reasoned, when she'd told them she was applying to the service, but they had refused to see her point. Too many of us have died at their hands, they'd replied, referring to deaths in custody. She's never told them about the man she killed. She doesn't know if she ever will.

She is still sad about the death of Michelle Cameron and the loss of all the good things she might have become. She thinks of everything they'd had in common. In spite of her surface intellect, Zoe Laing will never see the complexity of their connection, forged through a shared identity and an inability to fit. In the book the link between them will be presented as little more than a symptom of post-traumatic stress disorder.

FIFTY-SIX

The Michelle Cameron book is almost finished. A few loose ends still have to be tied up and further verification of one or two facts is needed but at last Zoe can see it coming to a close. She is still looking into the circumstances surrounding Michelle Cameron's death. Everything about the investigation has been fraught but one or two leads have come her way in the last few days and, with luck, they will confirm her belief that it was not from natural causes. She is exhausted. Everything about Michelle Cameron has always been exhausting.

When she'd first heard that she had died, Zoe had thought it would be a catastrophe for the book but, if anything, it's been the opposite. She has been freed up to write about Michelle Cameron's life following her prison release in ways she never could have done if she'd still been alive; no concerns about providing information that could expose her further now. And no possibility that Michelle Cameron could insist on reading the manuscript and then decide to withdraw her support – not that this would have changed anything, but still, it would have been unpleasant. Zoe could imagine her camping on her doorstep, refusing to go away unless she promised to make changes. At least she doesn't have to deal with that. And, unexpectedly, Michelle Cameron is still very much alive in the public imagination, and speculation about suicide – and even murder – remains rife. A new BBC documentary is being filmed and Zoe is its main contributor. The advance publicity is promising that the book will expose the truth about Michelle Cameron; sales are expected to be even bigger than first predicted.

Sometimes Zoe wonders what Michelle Cameron's life would have been like if she had lived. She was very dependent. Her mental health was fragile and her borderline personality disorder had left her with complex identity issues. Without Zoe's continuing support, she would have floundered, and most of the things that had been achieved through their work together would have been lost. It was unlikely she would have worked again or sustained an intimate, healthy relationship. Her future would have been bleak. She would never say so, of course – it could be misinterpreted – but Michelle Cameron's death was probably the best outcome.

PART SIX

FIFTY-SEVEN

In a studio flat that's never cool enough, she sits on her bed and looks at the package, still unable to open it. The grey-green walls are dull and there is a single window with bars. Sometimes, on waking, she forgets where she is and thinks she's in a prison cell.

The package has been sent from London and she remembers how much she misses being there. She would end this exile if she could, but she knows she can never go home.

She takes a jug from the fridge and pours herself some water. The coldness helps her to focus. She draws in air, willing herself to be calm, and tears off the thick brown paper. The book she ordered has arrived at last. In the semi-darkness of the room she has to squint to read the title: it's called *The Gosling Girl*.

There is an image of a crow on the cover, wings spread, hovering over a child as she covers her eyes with her hands. She recognizes the backdrop – it's the crumbling interior of Whytefields from one of the pictures Zoe took. She will have been pleased with the mock Gothic setting and artful use of photography to symbolize Michelle Cameron's distorted inner world. No doubt she will see her book as more than a psychological examination of the killing of a child by another child. It will be a work of creativity, significant and bold, its dramatic cover evidence of this.

On the back, there are lines from the reviews:

> An important book, full of compassion and humanity, that will aid understanding of the reasons children kill.

And:

> Zoe Laing's account of Michelle Cameron's life demonstrates the flaws in a criminal justice system that facilitated the demonization of a child. It is courageous and moving.

She starts to read, but she can't take in the words, they are devoid of meaning; she doesn't recognize herself. She leaves the book on the bed and goes to the window: there is no view, only another stark white building with a heavy, reinforced door. She returns to the bed and opens the book again. She needs to know what's being said.

Zoe states she is committed to the truth and then proceeds to present an account of Michelle Cameron's troubled childhood, Sandra's role in this – and Fred's.

Michelle Cameron emerges from the pages of the book better than she'd feared: a confused and frightened child-like figure; insecure, needy and sad – desperate at times – but not evil, and no psychopath.

She is bemused by Zoe's theory that Michelle Cameron was murdered and the police failed to investigate – or, worse, they actively covered it up. Perhaps it was a group of far-right activists, the ones who broke into the flat in Neasden, killing the dog. Or maybe someone decided to avenge Kerry Gosling's death: a life for a life. Or could it have been the boyfriend? Immediately after her death, he disappeared without a trace. No police interest in finding out the truth. They would prefer to forget about Michelle Cameron, Zoe states indignantly, her eyes on the commercial prospects of the book.

She wonders how to tell Ryan he is now a murder suspect, even though reports of her death have been greatly exaggerated. He'll be scared and agitated; she'll need to calm him down. He'll wonder what his mum will think, even though she knows where he is and will be coming out to visit in the spring.

At least she isn't on her own with the terrifying newness of the world she now inhabits. In the evenings they comfort themselves, watching feel-good films with popcorn from the supermarket. She wonders how she would have borne the isolation if he hadn't come to join her. She hadn't intended to take him back but he'd worn her down with his persistence, the notes of regret he'd posted through her door and his insistence that if she gave him a second chance, he'd do the very best he could to be there for her. She'd liked the limitations of his promises: no declarations of undying love, just a will to try. She'd remembered what Natalie had said: *It wasn't his fault; don't let them take Ryan away from you too.* And she'd called her Michelle, saying it kindly, as if her name was ordinary, as if it could be spoken out loud in ordinary conversation. She *is* Michelle. She will always be Michelle Cameron, however many times she has to reinvent herself.

When she and Ryan had met again, she'd still been full of rage, barely able to contain it, but she hadn't wanted to destroy him as she'd feared she would. She knew he would be safe with her, and maybe she'd be safe with him. She knows he's not equipped for new beginnings but he's drawn on all the courage that he has just so he can be with her.

Leaving, the impossibility of it, and the necessity.

We can't protect you anymore, the resources just aren't there, they'd told her, two stern, suited men from the Home Office, accompanied by Dom. They'd put out a press release announcing her death from a defective heart. She wonders if the choice of illness was symbolic. It's the only way you can stay in London, they said; if you no longer exist, the public's need to seek you out will end.

It might have worked, if Zoe had let it lie, but her insistence on finding out the truth had put her at risk of exposure again. She'd laughed when they'd told her they were sending her abroad. In time-honoured British tradition she was to be transported overseas, out of sight and mind. She'd put up a fight at first but then she'd seen the possibilities. She wouldn't have to hide. She'd no longer be the Gosling Girl.

She lives in Johannesburg now, a city more troubled than London, but there is beauty in the sun as it sets upon the Klip and the colours of the early-morning sky. She has a job. It doesn't pay much, but she manages. She misses the buses and the Tube, but not the weather, and she has a new city to explore; she intends to make it her own. Will she and Ryan be able to hold on to the life they've started together? Perhaps, but it's all so fragile and she's never believed in happy endings. Maybe he will stay, and she will feel stifled, desperate to find a different way of being. Or perhaps one day he will disappear – get up and leave – too fearful to tell her that he doesn't love her anymore. Whatever happens, she will remake herself; she thinks she might be good at that.

ACKNOWLEDGEMENTS

The following books were particularly helpful with regard to the research undertaken for this book: Blake Morrison: *As If* (1997); Gitta Sereny: *Cries Unheard* (1998); David James Smith: *The Sleep of Reason* (1994).

I would like to thank my friends for their generous support, especially Ann Sarge, Kate McGowan and Ann Germanacos.

Thanks are also due to my editor Clare Hey at Simon & Schuster, for providing some very helpful insights.

I would particularly like to thank my brilliant agent Milly Reilly at the Jo Unwin Literary Agency, who has given invaluable advice with patience, kindness and humour.

READING GROUP GUIDE

1. What was your first impression of Michelle?

2. Which ideas did you start to form in your mind about Michelle's life and upbringing?

3. Did you find yourself caring whether Michelle was guilty or not?

4. Did you resonate with any of the characters and their reactions towards Michelle? If so, which characters and why?

5. Which of the characters do you believe cared about Michelle the most and how did this impact her?

6. Why do you think Natalie Tyler began to care so deeply for Michelle? Do you think there was more she could have done for her?

7. Which passages did you find yourself returning to or underlining?

8. In your opinion, should Michelle be continually punished for her mistake? Did her being a child at the time of the crime make any difference to your view?

9. Did the book end how you expected it to?

10. How might this story have been different if Michelle had come from a white family?

AUTHOR'S NOTE

As a writer of fiction, I'm particularly interested in questions of guilt and responsibility and how identities are formed. What has made us the people we are? It seemed to me that a story about a child who kills another child would throw such questions into sharp relief, so this was the foundation of the novel that eventually became *The Gosling Girl*.

Although it is rare, there are some well-known cases of children in the UK killing other children: Robert Thompson and Jon Venables were convicted of such a crime in the 1990s and there was also Mary Bell, in the 1960s. These children were all ten years old but they were tried as adults in adult courts.

These cases fascinated me, and I knew as I read about them that I wanted to explore some of the issues they raised. I found myself wondering what it must be like to have committed such a serious crime at such a young age, before you really have a sense of who you are, and to carry the consequences of this for the rest of your life.

The children in the cases cited were named by court judges, so on their release they had to be given new names for their own protection – new identities – and this was of great interest to me as a writer. It meant that once the children were grown up, they would carry this huge secret around with them, the secret of their crime, and their old names would embody this. The fear of discovery must have been immense. I decided that this would be at the heart of the novel: Michelle Cameron has a huge secret, and she has to conceal her past or face exposure and vilification in the media. Potentially, her life could be at risk. Some of the questions I wanted to ask were: Is it possible for someone to remake their life after committing such a crime? Should they be allowed to do so? Should the sentence for taking a life, whatever the circumstances, be life in prison, or can an offender, particularly a child, be reformed in some way?

I called the novel *The Gosling Girl* because Michelle Cameron's identity is inextricably bound up with that of the child she killed – Kerry Gosling – and in calling Michelle The Gosling Girl, the media remove not only Michelle's identity but also Kerry's, which devastates Kerry's family. It seemed very important not to ignore the effects of such a crime on the family of the victim in telling the story.

The role of the media in sensationalising crime was something I also wanted to explore. The character of Zoe, the psychologist who is writing a book about Michelle Cameron, was created, at least in part, to address this aspect of the novel. She is someone who purports to be helping

Michelle but ends up exploiting her for her own ends. She deliberately keeps her in the public eye in order to further her own career.

As a writer of colour, I'm interested in racial identities and how these develop, so the central character, Michelle Cameron, is of dual heritage. She has to come to terms with her very troubled past, and the trauma she undergoes in her early life is compounded by the racism she experiences. There is also a black police officer in the story, Natalie Tyler, who, through the treatment of Michelle Cameron has to think about institutional and systemic racism and the role she may have in upholding and perpetuating this.

The writing I enjoy most is the kind that generates questions for the reader, and that was my aim with *The Gosling Girl*. I wanted to raise questions about the way that we, as a society, often neglect children, and the potential consequences of this. I also wanted to generate questions about the way that power works, whether it operates through race, class, gender or sexual orientation. I wasn't aiming to provide answers – the questions were the most important thing.

But I also wanted to tell an engaging story, so I aimed to make Michelle Cameron someone readers could relate to, despite her crime. This meant trying to make her as believable as possible. As a writer, I like developing flawed characters as they offer the opportunity to explore areas that are challenging and sometimes unsettling. I didn't want to let Michelle off the hook – she killed a child – but I did want to make the reasons for her crime understandable. Once a character's motives are understood, it's easier for a reader to feel some empathy for them, even if their crime is a terrible one, opening up debates about justice and criminality.

THE LIKELY SUSPECTS

A **CRIMINALLY GOOD** LINE-UP OF BOOKS FROM **SIMON & SCHUSTER**

LIKELYSUSPECTS.CO.UK

@LIKELY_SUSPECTS

JOIN THE LIKELY SUSPECTS CRIME COMMUNITY TO GET YOUR HANDS ON THE HOTTEST PROOFS BEFORE ANYONE ELSE